DOCTOR WHO™

SHORT TRIPS:
REPERCUSSIONS

A SHORT-STORY COLLECTION
EDITED BY
GARY RUSSELL

BIG
FINISH

Published by Big Finish Productions Ltd.
PO Box 1127
Maidenhead SL6 3LW

www.bigfinish.com

Range Editor: Ian Farrington
Managing Editor: Jason Haigh-Ellery
Consultant for BBC Worldwide: Jacqueline Rayner

Doctor Who and TARDIS are trademarks of the British Broadcasting Corporation and are used under licence. Doctor Who logo © BBC 1996. Licensed by BBC Worldwide Limited.

ISBN 1-84435-048-7

Cover art by Stuart Manning 2004
Sleeve design by Clayton Hickman

First published July 2004

Reprinted February 2005

CONTENTS

Repercussions...

Charley woke with a start. Golly, how uncomfortable TARDIS armchairs could be, she considered. After all what was the point of having a huge armchair one could curl up and fall asleep in, if, upon awakening, one found one's joints and bones aching so.

Charley decided that she would point this out to the Doctor at the first available juncture. Oh, yes. And another thing, fabulous as this TARDIS thing was, it was currently being very noisy and seemed to be shaking a bit.

Hang on, she was positive that the TARDIS didn't make noises. Certainly she had only been travelling with the Doctor for a matter of days now, but she distinctly remembered him saying that as the – now, could she remember this correctly? – external and internal dimensions operated on different planes of reality – yes, that was it! – therefore outside influences shouldn't affect the interior. Which had sounded grand and clever, she recalled, until they had been thrown to the polished wooden floor by an outside influence. The Doctor, having moved them out of something called 'the vortex' assured her it wouldn't happen again. And whilst she certainly wasn't being thrown around the room, there was still a definite vibration. And what's more, it was one that seemed familiar. Almost akin to...

No!

No, it couldn't be. She wouldn't accept that.

Charley opened her eyes and took in her surroundings.

It wasn't the TARDIS. However, with a slight sense of relief, albeit it tinged with apprehension, she noted that she could not be where she had feared – this was not the *R101* airship, despite the similarity in its movements, vibrations and sounds.

But, without a doubt, this was not the TARDIS and was a similar craft to the huge airbarge from which the Doctor had initially rescued her. The furnishings were grander, the decor less militaristic and the air smelled... sweeter. Less, well, fuelly, she decided. But an airship none the less.

When Charley had fallen asleep, she had been in the TARDIS library. She had said goodnight to the Doctor, fed Ramsay the Vortisaur and headed off to the library to do a spot of research before bed. The Doctor had recently taken her to the space year 26-something or other and shown her bizarre bazaars, scary Cybermen and galactic gangsters. Which had been, quite frankly, terrifying, and afterwards the Doctor had suggested that she read up a bit on 'history'. History! To Charley, history was Agincourt or the Restoration or the Roman occupation of Britain.

The twenty-seventh century was the future. But the Doctor said he had encyclopaedias that could give her all the answers she needed (she doubted this – the Doctor frequently exaggerated) and so that's what she had done.

'It's important, Miss Pollard,' he had said, 'for you to know what you are getting yourself into by travelling with me.'

She thought this might well be true and so had settled down in a marvellous Louis XIV's chair, a big Bartholomew's Gazetteer of the Stars on her lap and begun reading. Naturally, the dull prose and never-ending minutiae had started her eyelids fluttering and she guessed she'd fallen asleep.

So, why, and how, was she here now and not aboard the TARDIS?

Unless this *was* the TARDIS – of course! It was a vast machine, this could just be an area she had yet to explore.

And yet that didn't explain the room full of people before her. No, something told Charley this was not the TARDIS at all. This really was an airship, full of passengers, most of whom seemed to be chatting animatedly to one another and completely ignoring her.

Time to get up, Charley decided.

She pushed herself out of the armchair and realised that in fact it wasn't the same one she had dozed off in but was a much smaller, less fancy one. With a harder cushion, which explained the aches she felt.

No one acknowledged her very much as she made her way into the mass of people, although one young man smiled at her. He was maybe a year or so older, with dark red hair, spectacles and a cheerful looking face. He was wearing a shortsleeved buttonless top with the words 'I went to Agora and all I got was this lousy shirt' emblazoned across it.

'Can I get you a drink?' he asked in a soft English voice. Charley smiled back and said she was fine by herself, but thanked him. He nodded and turned to speak to a tall, blue-skinned woman beside him, who just stared imperiously across at Charley.

Charley tried smiling at her, but she just turned away so Charley wandered further into the mêlée of people. She guessed there were about fifty, maybe sixty people in the room. They were not all human by any means, but the majority were. They came in different ages and sizes – there was a woman with two young children sat by a table, and a couple of scaly reptile-men tapping the side of what looked like a rather plain cupboard situated by a green-baize card table. Sat at the table were a dishevelled looking man who was clearly losing whatever game he was playing with the centaur opposite.

Wait a minute! Centaur? Yes, definitely the traditional half-man, half-horse look, a dapple-grey body that reminded her of her sister's horse back home.

How odd – thinking of home and yet not feeling the slightest pang of remorse or sorrow for being away.

Just goes to show, she thought, that I must be doing the right thing.

Charley made her away across the room, still aware of the steady throbbing beneath her feet from the airship's engines. When she had been aboard the *R101*, she had thought nothing of it. Now she found herself constantly aware of it. How quickly she had become accustomed to the TARDIS, then. How quickly she thought of it, and the Doctor, its strange, curious, engaging, enigmatic occupant, as comfortable. Home, even.

'Good morning, Miss Pollard,' said a slightly accented voice to her right.

She looked across – she was now stood next to a bar, laden with drinks, dishes of nuts and a finger bowl of water. Dotted occasionally along the bar were small vases with a couple of flowers in them. Different colours, shades even that Charley had never seen before. Some were full, stemmed flowers, others little more than shrubs or posies. The speaker was the bartender, his bright eyes welcoming her and she instantly liked him. His skin was a dark olive, and he had a small beard on his chin, but no moustache to accompany it. He was dressed in what she recognised as a steward's uniform – after all, she'd been wearing something similar when she had met the Doctor – but this gentleman's was a crisp white that almost reflected the artificial light above him.

He tapped the peak of his white cap as she smiled at him.

'I'm the Steward, Miss Pollard. The Doctor said you'd be joining us on today's trip.'

'Where is he?' asked Charley.

The Steward just smiled. 'Occupied, Miss. But you'll see him shortly, I'm sure. In the meantime, can I get you a drink?'

Charley sat upon a velvet-cushioned barstool and was about to ask for a long port and lemon when she became aware of a slight musty smell. She glanced sideways and sat on a stool beside her, nursing a glass of water (or neat gin perhaps?) on the bar was a tramp. He was ignoring everything and everyone around him, just gently turning his straw around his drink.

Charley shrugged and looked back at the Steward. 'Where are we?'

The Steward smiled again. 'On a journey,' he said. 'They're all on a journey. You and me, Miss? We're just here for the ride. My job is to make sure they're all happy and comfortable for the duration. Excuse me.' He turned away as a rather haughty young woman stood beside the tramp, casting a disdainful look at the little man before asking the Steward for a glass of some blue liquid Charley had never heard of. The Steward obliged but Charley noted that no money changed hands. The

Steward said something to the woman that Charley couldn't hear, but the woman nodded and glanced over at her. And smiled. It was a smile that transformed her whole demeanour. Charley's first impression had been that this woman was cold and aloof but now she seemed to radiate warmth and manners. Breeding, Charley's mother would have said.

The Steward returned to Charley. 'This is the Lady Tianna,' he said. 'I told her you knew the Doctor and she is also acquainted with him. She wonders if you would care to join her?'

Charley was concerned that she still didn't know where she was, or why she was no longer in the TARDIS, or where the Doctor had gone or how the Steward knew her but she also guessed that those answers weren't forthcoming.

And she had little else to do.

The tramp looked up at Charley, then at the Lady Tianna, snatched his drink from the bar and hobbled away.

'Frightful man,' the Lady Tianna said, settling on the stool next to Charley's. 'But I'm sure there's a reason he's here. There's a reason for everything you see,' she said.

Charley nodded slowly. Maybe this was going to be a philosophical conversation. She wasn't very good at those, but it would be rude to walk away now. 'How do you do,' she said. 'Charlotte Pollard. My friends call me Charley.'

Lady Tianna took the offered hand and shook it. Her skin had a cold, almost icy touch and Charley nearly snatched her own away in surprise.

'Why are you here, Charley?' asked Tianna.

'I don't know,' Charley answered truthfully. 'I just woke up here. Yourself?'

'Ah,' Lady Tianna laughed lightly. 'Now that is a story. I gather you know the Doctor.'

'I do.'

'Do you know he's a Time Lord?'

Charley nodded. 'But I've never been to Gallifrey,' she added.

'Lovely place.' Tianna sighed. 'Well, it was.'

'You've been there? Did he take you? The Doctor, I mean.'

Tianna shook her head. 'No. No, I met him there. You see, I too am a Time Lord. Let me explain.'

The Time Lord's Story
Iain McLaughlin & Claire Bartlett

The Lady Eltiannachrisanik hurried through the ancient corridors of Gallifrey's Capitol just a little quicker than was seemly. A few old Time Lords grunted and grumbled at the thought of someone rushing in these hallowed halls but couldn't muster the energy to be really offended.

With less than a microspan to spare, Eltiannachrisanik – Tianna by choice – arrived at her office in the Department of Administrative Records. She shucked off her robes and collar and dropped them carelessly over the back of a chair in the corner of her outstandingly bland little office before settling down at her console for another day's mind-numbing tedium. Of all the jobs she could have landed after graduating from the Academy, this was undeniably the worst. Twice a day, she checked to see if any new records had been sent through channels to her office and twice a day she was disappointed. In all the interminable time she had been in the job, she had received three messages. One which was intended for the Department of Time and two from members of her family, eager to let Tianna know how disappointed they were with her new position.

The truth was that Tianna didn't need to be there at all. The records that passed through her department were all computerised and she was there purely in case of an emergency. Of course, with this being Gallifrey, nothing as exciting as an emergency ever happened. In fact, nothing ever happened at all as far as Tianna could make out.

Tianna flipped her long, unruly, red hair back over her shoulders and checked her controls. No messages. That meant no work, and so Tianna turned her attention to her pet project. She called up a file from her computer's database.

'File Tianna 03a. Renegades,' she said. Information scrawled across her screen verifying her voice print, giving details of the file and finally opening before her.

'Request instruction,' the computer said in a monotone. 'Which renegade's data do you wish to access?'

Tianna punched a button and a woman with long dark hair surrounding a strong intelligent face full of a cat-like superiority stared at Tianna from the screen.

The computer acknowledged this. 'Resuming the Rani...'

'No,' Tianna interrupted. 'Open the Master's file. Start at the time he left Gallifrey.'

'Order accepted,' the computer droned.

More information scrolled across the screen, text mixing with diagrams, reproductions of documents and images of a man sporting a neatly trimmed goatee beard. His dark, sinister eyes seemed to follow Tianna around the room. She felt a slight frisson of a thrill. He wasn't her favourite renegade but there was something enticing about the Master. Even though his actions were reprehensible, his lack of care for the rules appealed to Tianna and she had to admit that he'd had a certain style and charm before his unfortunate visit to Tersurus.

As she always did when accessing the renegade files, Tianna checked her console to ensure that her actions weren't being monitored. While not strictly illegal, her superiors would certainly frown on her reading these files, especially when she should be working. The fact that she didn't actually have any work to do would be neither here nor there. Halfway through running her checks, Tianna stopped dead still. Someone had accessed the old records. Someone with high-level security clearance, and someone intelligent enough to cover their tracks against the regular security measures. Tianna had only discovered the intrusion because of the extra safety protocols she had added to hide her own unauthorised computer use. She scrolled through the accessed files, a nervous sweat appearing on her face. The list was filled with the most secret and restricted files in the database. Most of them required clearances she had never even heard of. Whoever had accessed the files had been smart to cover their tracks. Unauthorised access to the files was likely to land the offender three or four lifetimes in a penal colony.

Tianna's hand was automatically reaching for the communications controls when she caught herself. She had been going to contact the Chancellery Guard but the level of clearance the intruder possessed worried her. Could she trust the communications on an open channel? Could she trust the Guard itself? In fact, short of the President herself, who could she trust? And the President wasn't even on Gallifrey. Rumour had it that she and that rusting robotic pet of hers were off on an adventure to Earth with...

'Computer,' Tianna instructed urgently. 'Call up the file for the Doctor.'

The TARDIS materialised with its usual distressed grating sound and a few moments later the Doctor bounded through the open TARDIS doors, the tails of his greenish black velvet coat billowing behind him. 'Here we are, Romana. Right in the middle of the...' He stopped, the smile dying on his narrow face as he saw the small office the TARDIS had landed in, and the slim, attractive, red-haired young woman watching him intently. 'Not the TARDIS bay in the Capitol?'

The red-haired woman shook her head. 'No.'

'Oh.' The Doctor's face fell. 'You're sure? You haven't redecorated?

Moved things a little? Put poky little offices where the TARDIS bay used to be?' He smiled hopefully.

'Sorry,' the woman answered. 'My poky little office is just a poky little office.' She smiled at him. 'My name is Eltiannachrisanik. My friends call me Tianna.'

'Oh, very good, Doctor,' Romana chuckled, emerging from the TARDIS. 'The TARDIS bay?' She smiled affectionately at her friend. 'That dear old TARDIS of yours is as unpredictable as ever.'

'Well,' the Doctor cut in, quick to defend his ship. 'Given that we've travelled several hundred light years and a considerable distance through time, I think missing the target by just a few yards...' he looked to Tianna. 'Hundred yards?' he asked. She shook her head. 'Anyway,' the Doctor continued. 'Missing by such a tiny fraction of a percentage shouldn't really count as missing at all.'

Romana was clearly unconvinced. 'A miss is still a miss, Doctor, whether it's by a metre or a million miles.'

'Excuse me, Madame President,' Tianna interrupted nervously. 'The Doctor's TARDIS didn't actually miss its landing coordinates. I altered the landing coordinates you were sent.' She wafted a hand around the office. 'So that you would land here.'

The Doctor beamed. 'Inch perfect. I think you owe the TARDIS an apology, Romana.'

'I think this young woman owes us an explanation,' Romana countered sharply. 'Redirecting a TARDIS inside of the Transduction Barrier is a very serious offence.'

'I know that,' Tianna answered uneasily. 'But so is accessing classified data from the time of Rassilon.'

'What?' Romana suddenly seemed very serious. Both she and the Doctor knew better than almost anyone on Gallifrey how dangerous the classified data from the dark times could be. In fact, they were probably the only people who fully understood the dangers they presented.

'What data has been accessed?' the Doctor demanded.

Tianna's nimble fingers skipped across the control panels and information scrolled across the screen. 'There,' she said. 'Restricted data time-coded from the Rassilon era.'

The Doctor leaned across the console panel and tweaked a control. 'Ooh, very nasty,' he murmured. 'There's some very arcane knowledge in these files. I can see why you wouldn't want them to be public knowledge, Romana. Very nasty indeed.' A small section of the display grew larger and he brushed his finger lightly across a sensor pad. Codes ran across the screen. 'And whoever accessed these files didn't want anyone knowing they'd been sticking their noses where they shouldn't,' he added thoughtfully. 'That's some very clever cryptography.'

Romana turned to Tianna. 'Why in Rassilon's name didn't you report this to the Chancellery Guard?' she demanded. 'Or to your superior, at least?'

The Doctor answered before Tianna could open her mouth. 'Look at the level of the security clearances used here, Romana.' He called up the relevant information. 'She had no idea who she could trust, did you?' He turned to Tianna and gave her his widest, most boyish grin. In spite of herself, Tianna couldn't help smiling back. 'I'm the Doctor, by the way,' he said cheerfully. 'But I imagine you already know that. This is my good friend, Romana.'

'Doctor,' Romana interrupted. 'I'd hardly be doing a very good job as President if people in my own Capitol didn't recognise me.'

The Doctor continued, ignoring the intrusion. 'As I was saying, Tianna, this is Romana, but you can call her Fred. Or President Grumpy.'

'She most certainly may not,' Romana protested. She turned to Tianna. 'If you even think of calling me either of those I'll see to it that you get posted to the waste reclamation plant.'

'And that,' the Doctor pointed down towards the floor. 'Is K9.'

The dog dipped its head slightly in a bow and wagged its tail. 'Mistress Tianna.'

The Doctor popped his hand on top of Tianna's head and spun her back to the controls. 'So, you spotted this little indiscretion in the records and decided to contact the President.'

'Very sensible,' Romana nodded her approval.

Tianna squirmed. 'Not quite,' she admitted. 'I saw the unauthorised access and, well... I sort of decided to, well...' she hauled in a deep breath and charged on. '... I decided to contact you, Doctor.'

'You'd contact the Doctor ahead of the President?' Romana sniffed.

'Not really,' Tianna cut in hurriedly. 'I knew you'd be with him, Madame President. It's all over the Capitol that you went off on an adventure with the Doctor.'

'Is it?' Romana answered. 'I'm not sure I like my comings and goings being all over the Capitol.'

'Then you shouldn't have become a politician,' the Doctor answered. 'Whatever the reason Tianna had for diverting us as she did, she's got us both now and she's got us both interested in this little mystery of hers.'

'I suppose you're right,' Romana conceded with a sigh. 'This is serious, Doctor. It will have to be investigated thoroughly.'

'That could take an age,' the Doctor protested. 'You know how things are here. Layer upon layer of bureaucracy. You'll have to organise a committee to arrange a meeting to discuss who should head up the task-force to decide which minion should give the order for the investigation to start.'

'Things have changed a little here, Doctor,' Romana argued. 'But you might be right. We need someone to begin investigating now, while I get the wheels of officialdom moving.' She smiled at him. 'And I can't think of anyone more suited to the job.'

'Oh.' The Doctor's face fell.

'Oh, come off it,' Romana scolded. 'You know you were going to do it anyway. You could never resist a mystery like that.'

'I know,' the Doctor answered sullenly. 'But you making it official takes all the fun out of it.'

'Get to work, Doctor,' Romana said firmly, turning towards the door. 'I need answers and I need them quickly.' She pressed the door control and the door slid open to show a familiar, if not entirely welcome face. Romana made no effort to put any hint of false warmth in her voice. 'Hello, Vansell.'

'Madame President,' Vansell smiled falsely. 'I'm delighted that you are safe,' he continued, still failing dismally to produce any sincerity. 'We were worried when your transport was...' he trailed off as he saw the Doctor standing by the solid blue shape of the TARDIS. 'Oh, it's *you*. I might have known you'd be responsible for almost losing our President.'

The Doctor only smiled in return.

'Vansell,' Romana called. 'We have work to do.'

'Indeed,' Vansell agreed. 'What work?' But Romana was already out of the office and halfway along the corridor, the Chancellery Guards Vansell had brought scampering after her. 'Madame President,' he was calling. 'Madame President!' It was more of a snarl that time. He ran after the guards, trying hard to make it look as if he was walking fast rather than actually running.

Tianna watched the door slide shut behind Vansell. 'I don't think he likes you very much.'

'You could say that,' the Doctor agreed cheerfully. 'But then, as coordinator of the CIA, he doesn't like many people, does he, K9?'

'Negative, master,' the dog agreed.

The Doctor clapped his hands together, a decision apparently made. 'So, we'd better get started,' he said briskly. 'First things first, let's see if we can find which terminal was used to access those files.'

Tianna watched the Doctor's finger flitting across her control panel. 'Sorry to disappoint you, Doctor,' she said. 'But that's not possible. The terminals don't log an identity...' She stopped. A diagram of the Capitol had appeared on screen with a little red dot marking the guilty computer terminal. 'How did you do that?'

The Doctor leaned close and whispered in a conspiratorial manner. 'I've been president twice. I've left a few little back doors about the place for myself.'

'Oh. Is that legal?'

'No, but it's very useful. Anyway, it's been very nice meeting you, Tianna.' He headed for the door. 'Come on, K9. Walkies.'

'What?' Tianna grabbed her robes and hurried out of the door after the Doctor. K9 trundled along behind them as fast as he could manage. 'Now wait a minute,' Tianna called. 'You don't think you're leaving me back there, do you?'

The Doctor stopped at an intersection of corridors to get his bearings. 'Well, it is where you work.'

'But something strange is happening here,' Tianna protested. 'By the way, you need to go this way.' She pointed in exactly the opposite direction the Doctor was looking.

'Right, thank you.' He turned and walked off. 'This is Gallifrey, Tianna,' he called back. 'Something strange is always happening here.'

Tianna ran to catch up. 'Not to me,' she objected. 'I sit in that dismal little office day after day, feeling the will to live abandon me a little more each and every microspan.' She sighed. 'You of all people should understand that. Isn't that the reason you left?'

'I suppose,' the Doctor conceded. 'So you've been reading up on me, have you?'

'There's not a lot else to do in my job,' Tianna confirmed. 'And you're my favourite of the renegades.'

'The renegades? You make us sound like a rock band,' the Doctor laughed. 'Tonight, for one night only,' he said loudly, making the elderly Time Lord they passed jump. 'Playing their biggest hits before saving the universe, it's Doctor and the Renegades.' He beamed at Tianna. 'Sounds very sixties. Talking of which, I must remember to get that velvet jacket back from Jimi Hendrix some time.'

'Doctor,' Tianna said carefully. 'I haven't the slightest clue what you're talking about.'

That only made the Doctor beam even more broadly. 'I know. Fun, isn't it?' He scrutinised her for a moment. He recognised the same ennui in her that he had felt himself in the days he had walked these corridors, the same feeling of being stifled. 'All right,' he said finally. 'You can come with us, but be careful. It'll probably be dangerous.'

'So is being so bored you wonder about regenerating just to relieve the tedium.'

'I'm serious,' the Doctor answered darkly. 'This will be dangerous. Do as I say, or failing that, do as K9 says. He's probably the most sensible one of the lot of us.'

'Affirmative, master,' the dog agreed readily.

'Right,' the Doctor said to Tianna. 'They've redecorated since I was here last. I don't like it. Earn your supper and lead the way to that terminal.'

As Tianna led the way along the corridor, the Doctor could have sworn that she actually skipped a couple of times and he wondered how long it was since anybody had skipped in these corridors.

'Madame President, this is highly irregular.'

Romana wasn't sure if the disdain in Vansell's voice was for the cramped surroundings of the small antechamber she had led them to, or simply because he loathed the idea of her being President. She didn't particularly care which. 'Of course it's irregular, Vansell,' she snapped. 'Normally we would meet in the Council Chamber with the full council and spend several months discussing what to do about these breaches in security by which time whoever was responsible would have had the chance to cover their tracks. That is not going to happen this time.'

'I assume there's a reason you aren't informing the High Council?' Vansell asked.

Romana touched controls on a computer panel and a screen filled with information from Tianna's terminal. 'The security clearance required to access this data is of a level that might implicate a member of the High Council.'

'Interesting.' Vansell scrutinised the data. 'It could also implicate me,' he offered.

'True,' Romana agreed. 'But I think you're more than devious enough to have ways of accessing this information without being caught.'

Vansell bowed, as though taking a compliment.

'You don't seem particularly surprised that someone is hunting for this data,' Romana said thoughtfully, watching Vansell carefully. 'It's almost as if you knew what they would be looking for.' She waited for a denial. None came. 'You do know what's happening,' she stated.

Vansell thought for a moment, weighing his words carefully. 'For some small time we have been aware of a small group's interest in gaining access to ancient knowledge,' he admitted. 'We would have told you when we had all the details to hand.'

'I'll bet,' Romana snorted. 'Well, I know now and I am not prepared to wait until you have all the facts before doing something. Tell me everything you know about this little "group", Coordinator.'

The computer terminal on which the restricted data had been accessed was just about as far out of the way as it was possible to be while staying inside of the Capitol. It was located on a level that had been disused for centuries while planning for redevelopment went through various committee stages. Tianna watched as the Doctor ran a finger through the dust on the console. Apparently even the cleaning 'bots had abandoned the area.

'The ideal place for out-of-the-way skulduggery,' he muttered, before turning to Tianna, who was accessing the guilty control panel. 'Anything?' he asked.

'Nothing yet,' Tianna answered. 'There are an awful lot of encryption layers to go through here.'

'Get K9 to do that,' the Doctor suggested. 'He's good at that, aren't you?'

'Affirmative, master,' the dog replied.

Tianna motioned at K9. 'I've read all the reports about you and the President's adventures but it never occurred to me that her pet here would be the same robot that travelled with you in your TARDIS.'

'How much have you read about me?' the Doctor asked.

'Oh, lots. All of it, really. Well, apart from your very early days. That's classified for some reason. I shouldn't really say so,' Tianna said conspiratorially. 'But you're one of my favourite regenerations of you.'

'Am I?'

'Oh, yes. I quite like your fifth, too. The one with the fair hair. But your second regeneration was my favourite,' Tianna carried on, ignoring the Doctor's slightly bemused expression. 'You always seemed to be enjoying yourself so much when you were him.'

'I suppose I did have a lot of fun,' the Doctor agreed. 'Jamie, Zoe, Victoria... good friends.'

'That's something that makes you different from the other renegades I've read about,' Tianna said. 'They nearly always travel alone but you like to have friends with you.'

'It's a big universe,' the Doctor replied. 'Lots to see, lots to do and it's much more fun when you have someone to enjoy it with you.'

'I doubt if I'll ever set foot off Gallifrey,' lamented Tianna. 'Maybe I should stow away in your TARDIS when you leave.' She was positively bouncing at the thought.

'Then we'd both be in trouble.' The Doctor answered.

'Nothing new for you there,' Tianna countered.

'You know, I think you may have read too much about me.' He hunkered down beside the robot dog. 'And this isn't getting us any closer to our mystery file-reader. You can't pick up any DNA traces, can you, K9? Say, less than a few days old?'

The dog's ears swivelled for a moment. 'Negative, master,' it said sadly.

'Some sniffer dog you are,' the Doctor said sourly. 'See if you have more luck with those encryptions.'

'Master.' K9 wagged his tail and extended the probe from his head towards the console, 'Now, Tianna, while K9's busy with the encryption, let's see if our mystery guest has left us any clues.'

'What kind of clues?'

'Haven't you ever read Agatha Christie?' the Doctor tutted. 'Clues! Torn pieces of material, droplets of blood, a button snagged on a door, a carelessly discarded book of matches from a shady, smoke-filled nightclub. *Clues*.' He looked expectantly at Tianna. No reaction. 'When we're finished with this lot I'm lending you my full set of Miss Marples. Just lending, mind. Agatha signed them all for me. I didn't actually ask her to. I just couldn't stop her. And you haven't got a clue what I'm talking about.'

'No.'

'Fair enough,' the Doctor conceded. 'Look around. See if they left anything behind.'

'Apart from scuff-marks in the dust?'

'Yes,' the Doctor nodded. 'That sort of thing.'

'Oh.' Tianna sounded deflated. 'I thought they might be useful.'

The Doctor placed his boot beside a tread in the dust. 'Well, it narrows down the culprit to someone with roughly size 11 feet. It's a start I suppose.'

'Not those.' Tianna pointed to the control panel where the dust showed signs of having been disturbed. 'There.'

'So,' the Doctor peered at the dust. 'We have a left-handed member of the Chancellery Guard who's at least six foot three and above the rank of Commander.'

'You're making it up,' Tianna snorted. 'You can't tell all that from those marks in the dust.'

'Look again, Tianna.' The Doctor indicated the larger disruptions in the dust. 'The marks are predominantly made by the left hand, even though some of the controls are closer to the right hand.'

'Left handed!'

'Obviously.' The Doctor rummaged in his pocket for a moment. He piled various knickknacks from the pocket in his free hand – a yo-yo, a broken circuit from the TARDIS's navigation unit, the heating element from an electric kettle and a dozen other articles made an unsteady pile. A paper bag was next out of his pocket. 'Jelly babies! I didn't know I still carried them.' He thrust the bag into Tianna's hands. 'Help yourself. You eat them. They're very good.'

'They look like deformed children.' Tianna examined a red sweet from the bag. 'Am I really supposed to eat it?' The idea of eating something that looked like a person made her a little queasy.

'Of course you are,' The Doctor replied absently. He had fished a magnifying glass from his pocket and held it over the dust. 'This indentation in the dust shows where the wrist was resting. The design left an imprint. He homed in on a slightly deeper indentation. 'Undeniably that's the cuff of a Chancellery Guard uniform and he has to be above a certain rank to have been able to access all of this, wouldn't you say?'

'Probably,' Tianna agreed, biting the head off of a jelly baby. She was surprised to find the taste wasn't at all unpleasant. She popped the rest of the sweet in her mouth. 'But what about his height? You can't tell that from the way sat at the controls.' She paused uncertainly. 'Can you?'

'If I can be Good King Wenceslas for a moment.' The Doctor planted his foot a little to the side of a footprint and took long, lurching strides to keep his own footprints on a level with the set left by whoever had accessed the computer earlier. 'The length of stride indicates someone at least six foot three, possibly taller. Much taller than me, certainly.'

Tianna looked surprised. 'So you weren't making that up?' She pulled another sweet from the bag and munched it, feet first this time.

'What on Gallifrey would I do that for?' The Doctor seemed taken aback by the idea. 'No, that's who we want all right. K9, how are you doing with the codes?'

'Complete, Master,' K9 said smugly.

'Good boy,' the Doctor patted the dog's head warmly. 'You've earned a Scooby Snack.'

'Master?'

'Never mind. What did you find out?'

K9's tail wagged as he settled into his subject. 'The codes were quite complex, Master, with over four thousand variables in each line of encryption, each of which was phased through a random...'

'Yes, yes, yes,' the Doctor interrupted. 'I know how very clever you are, and that nobody else on the planet could have done that half as quickly as you, but I need to see the results without the working.'

'Very well, master.' The dog definitely sounded miffed at being cut off in mid-stream. 'The codes were all variations on names associated with the Arcalian Chapter, Master.'

'So, it's an Arcalian. If you add that to everything else we know about our sneaky little villain and run it through the computers, can you muster a name, K9?'

The dog's ears swivelled as he communicated with the Capitol's central computers. 'Commander Handrel,' he said.

'Handrel?' the Doctor muttered. 'Never heard of him.'

'I have,' said Tianna, chewing on another jelly baby. 'A traditionalist. Probably up for a seat on the High Council in a century or two.'

'It sounds as if he got tired of waiting,' the Doctor stated. 'By the way, don't eat all the black jelly babies. And try to leave a green one. They have a bit of a tang.'

'Sorry.' Tianna scrunched the empty paper bag into a ball. 'I got a bit carried away.'

'Oh, well. Can't be helped, I suppose,' the Doctor sighed. 'I might have some gobstoppers stashed away somewhere.' He turned to K9. 'Where are Handrel's rooms?'

'Level Six-Alpha, Master,' the dog answered.

'And where's Handrel?'

'Unknown, Master.'

'I think we should have a look in old Handrel's rooms. Come on.'

Tianna ran to catch the Doctor as he strode from the room. 'We're not going to break in, are we?'

'We broke in!' Tianna yelped. 'I don't believe you did that, Doctor. Breaking into a senior Time Lord's quarters is a serious offence.'

The Doctor held up a finger to Tianna's lips. 'Technically, I didn't break in. K9 did. And if anyone has a problem with that they can take it up with Romana – the President.' He grinned. 'But now that we're in here, it would be a shame not to have a look around.'

'You're arguing semantics,' Tianna accused.

'If you've read my file you'll know I'm always up to some antics. Oh, hello… hello…' The Doctor stopped at a computer terminal. He touched a control and text scrolled across the screen. 'Take a look at this.'

Tianna peered at the screen but didn't recognise the language. 'Some of it's vaguely familiar but…'

'It's Old High Gallifreyan,' the Doctor interrupted. 'And Handrel is reading copies of some very secret old files about races that are best forgotten.'

Tianna wracked her brain for any vestige she may once have learned of Gallifrey's ancient language. Nothing came. 'I don't suppose you'd care to translate this.'

'I don't suppose I would,' the Doctor answered quickly. 'You're too young to be reading this.'

Tianna's jaw dropped in protest. 'I'm almost a hundred and twenty.'

'Come to think of it,' the Doctor continued, ignoring the interruption. '*I'm* too young to be reading this.' He switched the monitor off and turned his attention to the rest of the room.

To Tianna's eyes, the room was as dull as she would have expected from a senior politician on Gallifrey. Books, scrolls, ancient ornaments, old robes – old, old, old. 'Is this what's waiting for me in a few centuries?' she wondered aloud. 'Respectability and tedium?'

'This is interesting.' Apparently, the Doctor hadn't heard Tianna's questions. He was lying face down on the floor, peering at small spatters of mud through his magnifying glass.

'Mud?'

'Not mud exactly,' the Doctor answered thoughtfully. 'More claylike. Or is it artificial? K9, what do you make of it?'

The dog trundled forward and extended its probe towards the mud. 'Sample contains stagnant water, rovie faeces, hefzi moss and large traces of a building compound used several millennia ago on Gallifrey.'

'We might not know where Handrel is,' the Doctor exclaimed, bounding to his feet, making Tianna take a startled step backwards. 'But we know where he's been going.'

'We do?' Tianna sounded surprised, then caught herself. 'Oh, of course. We do.'

'And that is?' the Doctor coaxed. 'Stagnant water, old Gallifreyan masonry, moss and mouse poo?'

'Well…' Tianna ummed.

The Doctor extended a long finger and pointed directly downwards.

'The old city,' Tianna exclaimed. 'Of course. The Capitol was built on top of the old city from back in Rassilon's time.'

The Doctor smiled broadly, like a teacher whose star pupil had just solved a particularly difficult problem. 'And that was built on the city that was there before it – and so on. We'd better get moving.'

'Shouldn't we wait for the President to bring guards?' Tianna asked hopefully. 'Guards with big guns?'

'We'll meet them down there,' the Doctor said briskly. 'After seeing what Handrel was reading, I don't think we have long to waste.'

'That's heartening,' Tianna grumbled.

'You can always stay here,' the Doctor offered. 'You'll be safer.'

'And miss the only interesting thing to happen here in a century?' Tianna exclaimed. 'You must be joking. I know the way to the old city.' She strode off towards the end of the corridor. 'This way.'

'Keep an eye on her, would you, K9?' she could hear the Doctor ask. 'And send a message to Romana. Let her know where we're going.'

'Master.'

'Idiot!'

'Madame President?' Vansell asked.

'Not you,' Romana snapped. 'Well, that's open to debate. I mean the Doctor.' She swivelled the display panel so that Vansell could read it.

'He'll be killed if he runs into this group by himself.' Vansell didn't sound at all unhappy at the prospect.

'Get together as many men as you can muster,' Romana instructed. 'Reliable ones you can trust. No,' she corrected quickly. 'Reliable ones *I* can trust. Quickly!'

'Madame President.'

'What a miserable dump,' Tianna grumbled, looking at the damp, crumbling old streets around them. 'I'd heard you went to some pretty unsavoury places, Doctor, but I didn't expect to find one quite so close to home.'

'Oh, this is nothing,' the Doctor answered airily. 'It's positively spacious compared to some of the dungeons I've been locked in over the years.' He led the way along the passageway, their feet making hollow sloshing sounds as they walked through unhealthy-looking green-tinged puddles.

'And this water stinks,' Tianna continued.

'I'm not surprised. It's older than either of us. How are you doing with these puddles, K9?'

'This unit has been equipped with a water-tight inner seal, master,' the dog answered smugly.

'You're waterproof, you lucky dog,' the Doctor chuckled softly.

Tianna shook her sodden foot and water splashed the wall. 'I wish these shoes were. You know, you might have warned me that I'd need to dress properly for one of your adventures, Doctor. Not that most of your companions seem to have bothered over the years. I suppose I should have worked it out for myself, really...'

'Tianna...'

'Yes?'

'Quiet. I imagine we're getting closer to Handrel and his merry band.' The Doctor's eyebrows arched, questioning. 'Do you really want to tell them we're coming?'

Tianna cursed herself for getting carried away. She had read the files on the Doctor's escapades. She should have known better than to babble. 'No, Doctor,' she said quietly.

'Good.'

They continued in silence for a few minutes. Tianna noted that once they passed through a large chamber, the passageway sloped downwards more steeply and the phosphorescent moss that illuminated their way became less prevalent. The passage took on an altogether gloomier and more sinister feel and Tianna made a point of staying closer to the Doctor. He offered a thin smile that didn't reassure Tianna nearly as much as she was sure it should. After a few more minutes, the Doctor stopped again.

'Listen.'

Tianna tilted her head and strained to hear whatever the Doctor had heard. 'I don't hear...' She stopped. The *was* something. Something dull and low, almost below the range of her hearing. 'Machinery?'

'Affirmative,' K9 confirmed. 'Machinery and I also detect breathing.'

'Handrel and his friends?' Tianna asked.

'Negative,' K9 replied. 'Breathing is of various races of non-Gallifreyan origin.'

'Aliens?' Tianna squeaked. 'Here? In the Capitol? That's...' she tailed off, shocked.

'Isn't it just?' the Doctor agreed. 'How far ahead, K9?'

'Approximately twenty-eight metres, Master.'

Tianna shivered. This had all become very real, very quickly and for all the time she had spent dreaming of leaving Gallifrey and heading off on an adventure, Tianna had a slight hankering for the safety of her dull little office. She pushed the thought aside. This was what she had dreamed of. Now she would have to deal with it – and she was determined to relish it.

The hum of power led them to a row of old chambers, their rotten, buckled doors now replaced by throbbing blue-hued force-fields – the source of the humming sound. Inside each of the cells – for they could be called nothing else – an alien was kept as a solitary inmate. Tianna recognised some of the races. The Doctor recognised them all, and with each race he recognised, he looked a little more worried.

'Not a bunch you'd want to meet on a dark night,' he murmured.

Inside the nearest cell, a creature roughly shaped like a man but covered with green, pulsing vegetable tendrils swung at the sound of the Doctor's voice. Its arm shot out and spat a tendril towards the small group in the corridor. The Doctor didn't flinch as the tendril crashed into the force-field.

Tianna peered round his shoulder into the cell. 'You know what that is?'

The Doctor nodded sadly. 'And I know what it used to be. Look at what's left of his clothes. He was an Outsider.'

Sure enough, through the force-field's blue haze, Tianna could make out the skins and roughly woven material hanging from the creature's lower limbs. The style and markings were undeniably from Gallifrey's other inhabitants – those who had refused the benefits of life among the Time Lords. Despite their differences, Time Lords generally talked – albeit with disdain – of the Outsiders as being of their own kind. 'They did this to one of our own?'

The Doctor was sombre, his face half hidden in shadow as he tried to see through the gloom beyond the cells. 'They clearly have no morals. No sense of the worth of life.' He swung his face to Tianna, his face grave, and for the first time she saw something hidden behind the enigmatic, adventurer's façade she had come to know from his files. A sense of outraged moral righteousness radiated from him. After so many years in the sterile atmosphere of the Capitol, Tianna found the open emotion exhilarating – and just a little unsettling. 'They have to be stopped,' he said with conviction. 'No ifs or buts. They have to be stopped now before they do something far worse – and far more stupid – than they've done to this unfortunate.' Without looking back, the Doctor led them into the gloom.

From further ahead, the sound of more machinery became clear. A low hum so deep that the vibrations could be felt through the stone in the passage, and quiet voices, their voices distant enough that none of the actual words were distinct.

'How many of them are there?' Tianna asked nervously. She could

18

discern three separate voices, perhaps four at a stretch. She was sure that with K9's help – and that blaster weapon in his nose everybody talked about – they could deal with Handrel and two or three of his cronies.

'Eight,' the Doctor answered, deflating Tianna instantly. 'At least. K9?'

'There are thirteen separate voice patterns emanating from the chamber ahead,' the robot replied.

'I hope that's not unlucky for us,' the Doctor muttered.

The end of the passage opened into a wide, circular, domed chamber around twenty metres in diameter and perhaps fifteen metres high at the apex of the ceiling. Arched doorways led into the chamber at regular intervals around the curved walls and alcoves were cut into the walls a few metres above ground level. Stone statues of Gallifrey's long-gone and forgotten nobles watched the activity in the chamber impassively from the alcoves. Arranged against the wall furthest from the entrance where the Doctor and Tianna kept to the shadows, a large and complex group of machines fed tubes of red liquid into a huge, transparent tank three metres high and double that in length. Inside the tank, something moved. Something bulky and powerful, though its movements were jerky and uncoordinated.

'Idiots,' the Doctor breathed. 'How could anyone be so stupid?'

'What is it?' Tianna asked.

'Let's get a closer look.' Staying in the shadows, the Doctor skirted the edge of the chamber, keeping Tianna tight behind him and taking cover behind fallen columns and broken statues. Long metal tables, akin to operating tables, and banks of computerised equipment also threw shadows long and dark enough to hide in. Moving carefully, they circled around the chamber until the liquid-filled tank was close enough for them to better see the creature inside. Huge limbs leading to a muscular body floated in the middle of the thick red liquid.

'Doctor,' Tianna said nervously. 'That red liquid… it looks rather like…'

'Doesn't it just?' The Doctor agreed. 'I wonder which species gave their blood for this experiment?'

'What kind of creature would need blood to live like that?' Tianna knew the answer before she asked the question. 'A vampire.'

'Indeed,' the Doctor breathed. 'Though not a very big one.'

Tianna gawped at the massive figure in the tank. It twitched, more of a nervous reaction than a voluntary action. As the limbs moved, the enormous, bonded chains holding the creature in place swung and thudded against the side of the tank. 'That's a small one?' she asked, her voice suddenly very tight.

'Oh, yes,' the Doctor agreed. 'It's not fully grown.' He squinted, peering through the bloody murk. 'Barely more than an infant, I'd imagine.'

'That's something, then?' Tianna offered hopefully. 'If it's not fully grown…'

'It's still the most dangerous creature on this planet,' the Doctor said bluntly. 'It has the appetites and needs of a full-grown vampire but not the maturity to control them.' He paused ominously. 'It's probably ten times more dangerous than an adult.'

Tianna opened her mouth to speak and then promptly shut it again. Tight. In her dreams of adventure, she had always managed to come up with a witty remark, a sparkling one-liner to sum up the situation. Now that it was real, she couldn't think of anything to say. In fact, she was sure that if she hadn't clamped her mouth so tightly shut her sole contribution would have been her teeth chattering. She forced herself to concentrate and found the Doctor looking at her expectantly. 'What?'

'I want you to do something for me,' the Doctor said.

'Right,' Tianna gave herself a shake and pulled herself together with effort. 'Like I was saying, what do want me to do?'

The Doctor nodded towards the arched doorway they had entered through. 'I want you to go back there and tell K9 to contact the President and tell her exactly where we are. Can you do that?'

'Of course I can,' Tianna forced indignation into her voice. She had a sneaking suspicion the Doctor was just getting her safely out of the way, but she wasn't complaining about that. 'What will you be doing?' She was pleased with how calm her voice sounded.

'Well,' the Doctor puffed out his cheeks and shrugged. 'I'll be winging it, I suppose. It's a talent of mine.' The Doctor waved his hand towards the doorway. 'Now on your way. No, wait.' He fished in his pocket and produced a crumpled paper bag.

'Jelly babies? You had another bag?'

'You've earned them.' He handed the paper bag across. 'Now go.'

Tianna slipped away through the shadows, expecting who-knew-what to leap at her from the darkness. After what seemed like an eternity, she reached the doorway. She slipped through and hurried into the alcove where K9 waited. Looking around nervously, Tianna talked to the robot. 'K9, the Doctor wants you to tell the President where we are.'

'Affirmative, Mistress.' Somehow, the dog managed to make the reply sound sarcastic. Or was he just huffing at being told what to do by someone as lowly as Tianna? Either way, she didn't care as long as he did as he was told. 'Message sent,' he said after a moment.

Inside the chamber, the machinery's hum grew louder and changed pitch. Something was happening. 'K9?' Tianna asked.

'Machinery being brought to full power,' K9 answered.

'So whatever they're doing with that vampire, they're going to do it now?'

'That would be a logical assumption,' K9 agreed.

'So should we do something?' Tianna didn't sound keen.

K9's head lifted. 'Doctor Master is already taking action.'

That spun Tianna's head around sharply. Sure enough, the Doctor was nimbly climbing over a fallen stone column. He caught sight of Tianna in the corner of his eye and made a small gesture for her to stay back.

'Hello?' The Doctor waved a hand at the cloaked Time Lords who were busy working at their equipment. The Time Lords turned *en masse* to the Doctor. Two produced stasers while another drew a weapon the Doctor didn't recognise. All the guns were aimed squarely at him, but he ignored them and continued across the rubble towards the shocked Time Lords. 'Hello,' he called again, quite cheerfully. 'I represent sanity and good sense. I was wondering if I could interest you in some. You see I can't help noticing that you're about to do something incredibly stupid and dangerous.' He glanced briefly at the vampire in the tank. 'I thought as much. An infant.'

One of the Time Lords, taller than the rest and wearing a slightly more ornately decorated cloak, stepped forward. The Doctor noted that he had a nose curved like the beak of an eagle – certainly a predatory man.

'You shouldn't interfere here,' the man said.

'Well,' the Doctor raised a finger in protest. 'Technically I haven't interfered. Well, not yet anyway.' The cheerful grin froze on his face and his eyes became colder, harsher. 'But if you know who I am, you'll know that I always interfere when there's good cause.' He nodded at the tank, 'And I'd say bringing a vampire onto Gallifrey merits a little interference, wouldn't you, Handrel?' He let the name hang in the air for a moment. 'And now that the introductions are out of the way, would you mind explaining all of this?'

Handrel pulled the cowl from around his head and glared suspiciously at the Doctor. 'Why would I do that?'

The Doctor shrugged. 'Let's just say I'm insanely curious.'

'Insane certainly,' Handrel agreed, his grey eyes flicking around the chamber, searching for more intruders but finding none. 'Coming here alone is quite an insane thing to do.'

Out of the corner of his eye, the Doctor saw Tianna in the doorway, shrinking back into the shadows and hopefully holding her breath.

'Like seeks like,' the Doctor countered. 'If I'm mad, I'll be at home here. Why do you have a vampire here? I assume it's not as a pet. They're not always house-trained.' He pushed and prodded at the instruments beside the medical tray. 'Something to do with those experiments you have caged out there, undoubtedly.' He grimaced. 'An interesting selection of races. All of them have an unusual ability to use genetics to survive. And it looked like there'd been a little genetic experimentation on each of those creatures out there, sometimes mixing the genes of more than one species. That's very dangerous if you don't know what you're doing.' He paused a moment before adding, 'And utterly despicable if you do.'

'A moral lecture, Doctor? I would have expected better.'

'I like to surprise people.' The Doctor took in the machinery in the chamber, able to see all of its functions for the first time. 'A timescoop – an early one but obviously still working.' He sniffed. 'Unfortunately. So you used the Timescoop to bring these creatures here and experiment with their genetic code, am I right? I assume it's not for the benefit of science?'

'How old are you, Doctor?' Handrel asked.

'That's a personal question to ask someone you just met.'

Handrel snorted. 'You are barely over a thousand years old and yet you have regenerated seven times already. With rejuvenation and care, Time Lords can live ten times as long as you have lived before their first regeneration.'

'Actually, it just seems like that long,' the Doctor answered glibly but his face remained impassive.

'You are more than halfway through your lives,' Handrel continued. 'Time is running out for you, Doctor.'

'Time catches up with us all, even Time Lords.'

Handrel shook his head. 'Not any more, Doctor.'

'Wait…' the Doctor ran the pieces of information he'd assembled round in his mind again. They came together into the very unpleasant picture that confirmed his suspicions. 'Immortality.' He sounded disappointed.

Handrel's face quirked a little. 'In a manner of speaking, Doctor. Perpetual regeneration. Think of it,' his voice took on an appealing, coaxing tone. 'You have done more with your life than any other Time Lord since the ancient times of Rassilon when we were a true power in the cosmos. Think of all you could achieve if you had unlimited time.'

The Doctor sighed and looked at the cloaked Time Lords, clearly confused. 'What is it about Time Lords and immortality?' he asked. 'You lot, Borusa, even the Matrix is a way to cheat death.'

'Borusa was a fool,' Handrel snapped. 'He had the opportunity to join our number but chose to proceed alone. His failure set us back centuries.'

'I'm glad he didn't completely waste his time,' the Doctor answered quickly. 'Immortality?' he sneered. 'Time Lords already live for thousands upon thousands of years and never do anything with the time they've got.' He was fairly spitting the words out. 'Races, like humans, with short life-spans take more from a single day than we take from a lifetime. They know their lives are limited so they relish the time they have. Whether it's the smell of a flower or holding a newborn baby or walking through a field on a warm spring morning and feeling dew between their toes or creating something that would have been impossible a century before. That's what matters in life. The colour, the flavour, the joy. That's what makes life worth living. What do you want with immortality? Longer to

22

complain about having nothing to do? Rassilon was right about immortality. It's a curse, not a blessing.'

'Rassilon?' Handrel barked. 'You know nothing about Rassilon. Not the real Rassilon.'

'And you do?'

'Our order dates back to the great days of Rassilon, to the days when Gallifrey was a power.'

'To the days when we were conquerors,' the Doctor countered.

'To the days when we were more than the impotent observers we are now,' Handrel snapped. 'We can shape and change the universe for the better.'

'Better in whose eyes?' the Doctor asked. 'Yours obviously. But who gave you the right to choose?'

'Rassilon did not give us these great powers to waste.'

'He didn't give us them so that we could conquer either.' The Doctor waved a hand at a nearby console. 'He outlawed that Timescoop. Do you think he would have approved of you using it to capture these creatures?' He shook his head. 'You're nothing more than a secret boy's club dreaming of the golden old days that weren't all that golden in the first place.'

Handrel took a step forward. 'We are so much more than that,' he said menacingly.

'Ooh, is that meant to be scary?' The Doctor asked, sarcasm thick in his voice. 'You have to tell me these things. I do miss them from time to time.' He clapped his hands together. 'Anyway, it's been lovely visiting, a pleasure to see you all but I think I'll be going now.'

Handrel laughed. 'You think we're going to let you walk away?'

The Doctor pondered for a moment. 'All things considered,' he said thoughtfully. 'I don't think you have much choice.' Behind him, armed Chancellery Guards spilled through the doorway into the chamber, taking positions, their stasers aimed at the rebel group. Behind them, the Doctor could see Romana and Tianna in the doorway. He turned back to Handrel and shrugged. 'Did I forget to mention that I'd asked some friends along?'

Vansell barged his way past Romana rather less politely than might have been expected and marched towards the Doctor and Handrel. 'You are all under arrest,' he announced. 'Apart from you, Doctor,' he added, more than a hint of disappointment in his voice. 'Put your weapons down and there needn't be any trouble.'

And then the shooting started.

At the sound of the first staser blasts, Romana leaped back into the cover of the doorway, hauling Tianna after her. 'Oh, very good, Vansell,' she muttered. 'Very subtle.'

'He said they wouldn't resist arrest,' Tianna protested, poking her head round the corner of the doorway, eager to see what was happening in the chamber. If she had spent any time studying Earth history, she would have recognised it as something akin to a scene from the Wild West. The Chancellery Guard were taking cover behind statues and fallen columns while Handrel's sect used their computer consoles for protection. Bolts of staser fire flew back and forth, filling the chamber and blasting chunks of stone from the walls, melting metal consoles and blowing limbs from the stone nobles in their alcoves.

'Madness,' Romana hissed. 'Look out.' She and Tianna ducked as a stone hand blasted loose from a statue, flew over their heads and punched a crater in the wall.

'Where's the Doctor?' Tianna risked raising her head again. She saw the Doctor heading towards the blood-filled tank, darting from one hint of cover to another ducking stray staser bolts as he went. 'He's going for the vampire's tank.'

'Idiot,' Romana hissed. 'He'll get himself killed... again. He'll never change.' A brief, rueful smile flitted across her lips. 'Thank goodness.'

Tianna yanked her head back sharply as a staser bolt fizzed past her nose and melted a statue's leg. The statue lurched and toppled against the wall of its alcove. 'What's he going to do when he gets to the tank? Don't tell me – he'll wing it.'

Romana shrugged. 'The same as he always does.'

The Doctor skipped over a toppled statue and ducked into cover behind a column for a second, before hurrying to the tank's controls. He was glancing warily into the tank. The staser fire had caught the vampire's eye and made it more agitated. Heavy chains clunked against the sides of the tank as the creature began to pull against its restraints.

'Don't worry, old lad,' the Doctor murmured. 'Soon have you back where you belong.' He grimaced a little. 'Of course, I don't know whether that's good or bad – for you or anyone else – but that's the way it's got to be.' His hands flitted across the controls. 'Now, if we just reverse the Timescoop...'

The panel in front of the Doctor erupted in an explosion of sparks. Handrel's pistol was aimed at the Doctor. Ducking low, he hurried towards the Doctor. 'You've ruined everything, Doctor.'

'You're not the first person to say that,' the Doctor answered, 'and technically, *they* ruined everything.' He indicated the Chancellery Guard. 'I only delayed you a little.'

'Do you know what will happen to us?' Handrel raged. 'Do you know how we'll be punished?' He looked towards Vansell, fear clear on his face.

'There's an old saying on Earth,' the Doctor answered, his voice measured. 'If you can't do the time, don't do the crime.'

'I'll have some measure of satisfaction before I'm done.' Handrel raised his gun and aimed it at the Doctor. He squeezed the firing mechanism – and yelped as a laser bolt hit him squarely on the wrist. His arm jerked to the side and his shot flew wide of the Doctor. He turned sharply towards the source of the laser fire and saw K9 trundling towards him, with Tianna close behind. 'That…' Whatever curse Handrel was about to utter died in his throat as staser fire hit him between the hearts. A second burst of staser fire slammed into his head, melting his brain. He crumpled to the floor, beyond any hope of regeneration. As he fell, his hand spasmed around the alien pistol in his hand and he fired one last, wild shot.

Instinctively, the Doctor dropped behind a fallen column. He raised his head warily. The shooting seemed to have stopped.

'Doctor, are you all right?' Tianna was picking her way through the debris towards him, with K9 now a little behind her while Romana seemed to be arguing with Vansell about the captive remains of Handrel's group.

The Doctor ran a hand through his hair, dislodging a cloud of dust. 'I'm all right, I suppose,' he said sadly, looking at Handrel's body. 'Such a terrible waste.'

'Doctor!' Tianna's eyes widened in horror.

For a moment the Doctor thought the sight of Handrel's body had caused Tianna's cry but then it became clear that her eyes were staring past him towards the blood-filled tank. He turned, just in time to see the tank bulge outwards, the pressure inside pushing at a scorched area weakened by the wayward hit from Handrel's energy weapon. He barely had time to yell 'Get down!' before the tank ruptured, sharp splinters of the transparent casing exploding outwards, followed by a deluge of sickeningly warm blood.

Tianna gagged and choked as she felt the blood rush into her open mouth. She staggered back, stumbling and falling as the wave of blood engulfed her. As the blood passed, she coughed violently, certain she was going to vomit. She saw that the Doctor, too, was on the ground, drenched in blood. 'Doctor?' Tianna choked. 'If this is what happens on your escapades then I'm not sure I…' The sentence died in her throat. Broken chains dangling from its arms, the vampire was pushing itself free of the broken tank. Tianna opened her mouth to yell but nothing came. The creature's yellow eyes burrowed into her, holding her rigid. She wanted to scream, to run, but she could do nothing except watch the vampire pounce towards her and see the razor-sharp teeth swoop towards her neck and she felt the screaming pain as her throat was torn out.

* * *

'Shoot it! K9, shoot it!'

K9 reacted to the Doctor's command, instantly firing a full-powered laser blast. Vansell and the Chancellery Guard added their firepower to K9's. The concentrated assault forced the vampire to back away from Tianna, confused and stung but unharmed. Romana watched as the Doctor bolted to the control systems. His hands hit buttons and pulled dials, and a few moments later, a triangular black obelisk materialised at the roof of the chamber. It swooped towards the vampire and engulfed it before spinning away towards the ceiling again. By the time the obelisk and the vampire inside had disappeared, the Doctor was kneeling by Tianna's side. Blood poured from the gaping wound where her neck had been, spilling across the floor and mixing with the blood from the tank, giving her splayed hair an almost black hue.

'No,' the Doctor was muttering. He felt desperately for a pulse, for any indication of hearts beating, any hint at all of life. 'No, it can't happen like this.' His voice sounded brittle. 'She can't die like this.'

Romana placed a consoling hand on her old friend's shoulder. 'I'm sorry, Doctor,' she said gently. 'She can't have survived that attack. The damage was too severe for her to regenerate.'

'No!' The Doctor shook off Romana's hand. 'There must be something you can do. You're President of Gallifrey. If you can't even save this one life, what's the point of your titles and powers?'

Romana ignored the anger in her friend's voice. She knew he was just lashing out. She knew him well enough to know that he would only ever really blame himself. 'We'll take good care of her, Doctor,' Romana said gently. 'She'll be treated with respect.'

The Doctor shook his head. 'I...' He stopped abruptly. 'Wait.'

A glow had begun to appear around Tianna's body, growing more intense until it obscured her battered form, and then it began to fade, revealing Tianna's familiar face and a perfect, unblemished neck.

Romana shook her head is surprise. 'I...'

A huge grin spread across the Doctor's face. 'Never underestimate the will to survive. She's coming round.'

Tianna's eyes flickered and opened. Blood-red pupils stared up at the Doctor and pale, bloodless, lips pulled back into an animalistic snarl, showing sharply pointed teeth. She sat bolt upright, grasping for the Doctor with clawing fingers. A staser bolt slammed into Tianna's chest, directly between her hearts and she slumped back into the crimson mud.

The Doctor scrambled to his feet, helped by Romana.

'She's regenerating again,' Romana said.

Already the glow was fading from Tianna's body. It faded and her red eyes flickered. Again, Vansell blasted her between the hearts. 'I'll do this for all of her regenerations if need be.'

'You can't.' The Doctor's voice sounded hollow.

'Spare me your weak-hearted idealism, Doctor,' Vansell snorted. 'She's no better than an animal now.'

'Perhaps, perhaps not,' the Doctor said. 'It's just that you can't kill her.'

'We'll see.'

'Don't you understand anything, you stupid man?' The rage in the Doctor's voice even took Romana by surprise. 'Don't you understand what Handrel was doing here?' he continued. 'He was trying to combine Gallifreyan and vampire DNA to give perpetual bodily regeneration.'

Vansell blasted Tianna again. 'So no matter what I do...'

'You can't kill her,' the Doctor finished for him. 'You could probably cut her head off and she'd grow a new one – and if you're thinking of trying it, don't. I won't allow it.'

'You won't allow it?'

'No. I won't.' He turned his gaze to Romana. 'And neither will the President.'

'You're asking a lot, Doctor,' Romana said softly.

'I know,' the Doctor answered. 'But I have to find a way of helping her.' Their eyes remained locked. 'Please.'

Romana thought hard for a moment, weighing her options. Ultimately, she did what she had known she would do. 'All right,' she conceded. 'Place her in a stasis box.' Vansell opened his mouth to protest but Romana cut across him. 'For once, don't argue, Vansell. Just do it.'

'As you wish, Madame President,' Vansell huffed. He called for one of his guards to have a stasis box despatched and a few moments later a rectangular box slightly larger than a coffin materialised in the chamber.

Another concentrated blast from Vansell's staser thundered into Tianna's chest and she began another regeneration.

'Quickly,' Vansell ordered. 'Put the restraints on her.'

'Is that really necessary?' the Doctor started towards Vansell but Romana caught his arm.

'Yes, Doctor, it is necessary,' she answered. 'I've already broken more laws than I care to count here but I won't endanger any more lives.' She paused. 'Not even for you.' She waited for the Doctor to argue but he turned sharply away and strode towards Vansell, who was overseeing his men as they manhandled Tianna into the stasis box.

'Gently!' the Doctor called.

The Guards settled Tianna into the box and operated a control on the side panel. A pale glow appeared over the top of the box, leaving only a small space free over the face. Moments later there was an animal scream of frustration from the stasis box and it began to shake.

'You would be better advising your friend to calm down, Doctor,' Vansell said sourly.

27

'She's hungry.' The Doctor ran to the shattered tank that had held the captive vampire and dipped a handkerchief in what remained of the blood inside. He brought the sodden handkerchief back to the stasis box and squeezed it above the gap in the box's protective field so that the blood dropped into Tianna's mouth. Slowly, the red glow faded from Tianna's eyes and the needle sharp teeth drew back into her gums until she looked as she had when she had first met the Doctor, only a few hours before.

'Doctor?' Her eyes locked desperately on the Doctor. 'What's happened to me?'

'You know what happened, Tianna,' the Doctor answered softly. 'The vampire bit you.'

'Did I regenerate?' her voice was pleading.

'Not exactly.' The Doctor forced himself to continue. 'The bite changed you, Tianna. You must know that. You can't deny your hunger for blood.'

Tianna squeezed her eyes shut. 'Kill me.'

'What?'

'Kill me, Doctor,' she implored. 'I can't live like this. I won't. You know how to kill vampires. I know you've fought them before. Destroy me before I kill someone here. Please.'

The Doctor shook his head bleakly. 'I can't. We can't kill you. You can't die. Not like an ordinary vampire.' He tried to smile but couldn't make it look real. 'And I don't kill my friends.'

'I don't want an eternal life.' Tianna tried to smile but it was as false as the Doctor's had been. 'I just wanted some excitement.'

'I know,' the Doctor answered. 'You got the immortality and Handrel got the excitement. It's not fair, is it?'

'Please, Doctor,' Tianna begged, but already the red glow was returning to her eyes. 'Find a way to destroy me. I can feel the hunger already. I won't be able to control it.'

'I'll find a way to help. I promise, I'll do everything I can.'

'Doctor, I...'

Tianna's sentence was cut short as the Doctor hit the control to operate the stasis field. He allowed himself one final look at Tianna's impassive face, frozen in time inside her small prison and then he straightened and turned away. 'I'll find a way.'

Romana set a hand on the Doctor's arm. 'You know there's nowhere in the universe she can go where she won't feel that same hunger.'

'I know.'

Charley sat back, involuntarily moving as far from Tianna's mouth as she could.

Tianna just smiled. 'I can sense the heat in your body rising, Charley.

28

I can see the hairs on the back of your hand rise and I can hear your heart rate increasing.' She suddenly looked forlorn. 'Be careful what you wish for in your life. Your heroes often have feet of clay.'

'But why are you here? Now?'

Tianna stood up from the table and bowed slightly. 'That's not my story to tell you. But you will find many others aboard our vessel with similar stories. The outcomes may not always be as... violent as mine was, but all are interesting.' She held up her glass of blue liquid. 'I can vaguely remember what it tasted like.'

Charley frowned. 'Is it... human blood? Coloured blood?'

Tianna almost smiled. 'No. No, Gallifreyan vampires rarely touch human blood. And this? This is a rather splendid Martian spirit. T'rss, I believe they call it. I used to like it. Now... now I just have the memories.'

And she moved away, melding with the crowd of nameless people. Charley tried to keep her eye on her, see who she spoke to next but within seconds, Tianna was out of sight.

The Steward placed a fresh drink before her. 'I have another story, if you want one,' he said.

'More cheerful than hers, I hope,' Charley said, sipping.

The Steward shook his head. 'I doubt it.' He moved one of the smaller vases of flowers in front on Charley. 'It stays in bloom forever,' he said. 'They all do. None of them wilt, lose petals or decay in any way.'

'Where are they from?'

The Steward pointed at the blossom of the flower. 'Who knows? Look. What do you see?'

'I see a flower. A pretty, bright orange flower.'

'Look closer.'

Charley frowned and then gasped. 'A face... I can see a face...' She looked again but it was gone. She frowned. 'But I was sure...'

'Ghost flowers they call them,' said the Steward. 'I once asked the Doctor why he has them aboard the airship.' He wasn't smiling now. 'I wished I hadn't. He said they were commemorative as well as decorative. I wondered what they commemorated so he told me.' The Steward shrugged. 'Drink up, Miss Pollard, and I'll fill you in.'

The Ghost's Story

Trevor Baxendale

The TARDIS had landed on a broad shelf of rock at the top of a wide valley. Further down the hillside, clumps of scrubby violet grass dotted the ground, interspersed with long razor-sharp blades of indigo and black, which swayed in a dusty breeze. A shallow, cracked canal led down through the vegetation for as far as the eye could see. The end of the valley was lost in a mist-heavy haze, but a series of strangely shaped, yellow-grey rocks were visible, jutting out of the ground near the dry river bed.

Ace took in the view while the Doctor locked the TARDIS doors and gave the space-time machine an affectionate pat. The soft light of a blue sun made the police box's old paintwork look like new. 'Is this where we're supposed to be, then?' she asked.

'Well, no,' admitted the Doctor, scanning the purple horizon with his careful eyes. The concerned expression broke into an impish smile. 'But it's as good a place as any.'

'What for?' Ace wondered as the Doctor set off down the hillside.

'Exploring!'

She caught up with him, her boots churning up clouds of dust, and he held out an elbow for her. Together they trudged down the slope, arm-in-arm, while he pointed out interestingly shaped rocks and unusual planets with his umbrella.

At one point they found a great swathe of tiny mauve flowers, growing close to the dry soil like miniature mesembryanthemums, and each with a glowing amethyst at its centre.

'Oh,' said the Doctor wistfully, 'look: bioluminescent gemstones. They must be very beautiful at night…'

'We could stay until it gets dark,' suggested Ace. She shielded her eyes and gazed into the cerulean sunset. 'It must be evening now.'

The Doctor agreed. 'And while we're waiting for night to fall, we can have a look at those old ruins.' He drew his companion's attention to a series of tall, rocky outcrops a little further down the valley. Only now, when she looked at them properly, Ace could see that there was a definite purpose to their arrangement, a symmetry or functionality, which could only mean one thing: intelligent life!

'Wicked!' she shouted, and started forward. 'Come on, Professor!'

They were buildings, deserted and half buried, with strange globular chambers scooped out of the porous stone. Ace thought it was like walking around inside a giant honeycomb.

Whoever – or whatever – had once lived here was long gone. There were no signs of habitation, only the empty shells of places that might once have been homes.

The Doctor was poking around at some yellow-green lichen which had formed on the rocks. It was thick and fibrous, but with a dry consistency. It turned to dust under the attention of his umbrella's ferule.

'Hey, Professor,' Ace's voice echoed from within one of the rock chambers. 'Come and look at this!'

Ace had found some markings on a curved wall. They reminded her of cave paintings, although the marks were spiky and uneven, like letters. If it was writing of some kind, then Ace couldn't read it and certainly didn't recognise the language.

'Pictograms,' said the Doctor, studying them with great interest. 'They tell a story in pictures and symbols.' He pointed to a four-limbed figure. 'Humanoid,' he interpreted. 'And here's some kind of animal, a beast of burden, perhaps. And here – numbers. These smaller runes may be children. Representations of a human colony, certainly. Long extinct.'

Ace shivered. She felt like an intruder now, poking around in someone else's home. 'What did them in, then?' she asked.

'Who knows?' the Doctor replied sadly. 'Natural disaster? Old age? Invasion? Plague? There is any number of fates in this universe…'

'Let's go,' said Ace.

On the way back to the TARDIS they stopped by the jewel-flowers, which were glowing brightly in the gathering dusk. It was, as the Doctor had suspected, a beautiful sight. When he tapped Ace on the shoulder and pointed up at the darkening sky, she gasped with delight. High above were two perfect moons, each glittering in the light from the setting sun.

'It's fantastic,' Ace yelled, and her voice echoed up and down the valley, while the Doctor simply smiled and nodded. As the last rays of the blue sun faded into night, the stars brightened visibly and the twin moons sparkled as though a child had decorated them with glitter.

'There must be jewel-flowers growing on the moons as well,' observed the Doctor. 'Inter-satellite pollination – fascinating.'

Ace had been tempted to take one of the glowing flowers back to the TARDIS, but was too scared that its light would fade at the moment of picking. That wasn't a memory she wanted.

They walked through the shining field arm-in-arm, marvelling at the colours and frosty petals. When they turned back to look at the ruins, they saw odd patches of green glowing all over the distant stonework.

'It's the lichen,' the Doctor pointed out. 'It must be luminous in the moonflower light.'

Ace thought it looked a bit creepy, like a spreading disease or patches of decay. As she watched, a faint, milky vapour seemed to rise around the base of the ruins. The Doctor said it was lichen spores, lifted on the warm air as it evaporated from the ground into the cold night sky. They watched as it swirled and drifted through the ruins, silent but purposeful in the darkness.

'Come on,' said the Doctor, taking Ace's hand. 'Time to go.'

'What's wrong?' Ace asked, sensing the Doctor's increased pace.

'Some places are just too beautiful,' was his only reply.

When they made it back to the old police box, Ace was breathing a little harder. The Doctor unlocked the door and then, pausing on the TARDIS threshold, looked back down the valley once more. His eyes narrowed and Ace followed his gaze.

She couldn't see anything, but she guessed what he was looking for. She, too, had felt the presence of someone – or something – following them up the valley. She hadn't liked to say anything, fearing that it was only her imagination. The eerie mist slithering around the old ruins was fresh in her mind.

The Doctor watched for a few seconds longer and then disappeared inside the TARDIS. Without another word Ace followed him.

The Doctor dematerialised his ship and made them both a mug of hot cocoa. Ace watched him check the TARDIS instruments for the second and third time since taking off before broaching the subject.

'You felt it, too, didn't you, Professor?'

He didn't look up. 'Felt what?'

'That someone was watching us when we left that planet.'

'It's your imagination,' he replied dismissively.

Sullen-faced, Ace folded her arms. She felt cold, although it was usually warm in the TARDIS, and that wasn't her imagination: she had the goosebumps to prove it.

The Doctor appeared to have lost interest in her: his attention was now fully absorbed by the flashing readouts on the big, hexagonal console.

Suddenly the main lights dimmed and the room was wreathed in shadow. The Doctor looked up, his face illuminated only by the soft glow of the transparent column in the centre of the console.

'What's happened?' Ace asked, unable to hide her anxiety.

'I don't know.' The Doctor flicked some switches and the roundels which covered the control room walls began to glow. 'Emergency lighting,' he explained.

Ace shivered. 'It's cold,' she said, and this time she could see her breath in the air.

The Doctor moved around the console, checking the instruments carefully. He took off his straw hat and scratched his head in puzzlement.

'What is it?' Ace asked. 'Some sort of power drain?'

He shook his head. 'No, nothing like that… I don't know what it is.'

'I still feel like someone's watching us.'

'Don't be silly,' said the Doctor. 'I told you, it's your imagination.'

It was then that Ace first heard it: the soft, quiet laughter from nowhere. Absurdly she felt herself glance around the sterile white room, but there was no one there - except her and the Doctor. 'Did you hear that?' she asked him.

'Hear what?'

'Someone laughing.'

The Doctor looked at her for a moment. 'No.'

She heard it again, then - and so did the Doctor, she could tell by the flicker in his eyes. It was a distant sound, a gentle but mischievous chuckling… and it made her skin crawl.

The Doctor had turned his attention back to the controls. 'How very odd,' he mused. 'I thought I heard something then myself.'

Ace stepped closer to him, her breath steaming in the cold, gloomy air. 'I don't like it, Professor. Something's in here with us.'

'Nonsense. Nothing can get in the TARDIS while it's travelling in the vortex.'

Another quiet laugh.

'Who's there?' Ace asked aloud, but her voice simply echoed back without reply. For quite a while they heard nothing more, as if Ace's direct question had frightened their unseen companion into silence.

The Doctor concentrated on the TARDIS controls, trying to return the light and heating to normal levels but without much success. 'I don't understand it,' he confessed eventually, 'there's nothing intrinsically wrong with the control systems. It's almost as if the TARDIS is refusing to cooperate!'

They heard the laughter again this time - distinct, but distant, as if the amusement had been overheard from another room. But there was no question in Ace's mind that it came from inside the console chamber, seemingly from the very air itself. From something that now shared the TARDIS with them.

'Get rid of it!' she pleaded.

'Don't be scared,' chided the Doctor gently.

Ace bridled. 'I am not scared. I just don't like it.'

'Of course not,' agreed the Doctor gently. 'It's never very nice when someone laughs at you.'

'Is that what it's doing?' Laughing at us?'

'Something seems to find us very amusing.' The Doctor pressed some switches on the console and the roundel-lights dimmed. 'Let's try something…'

Soon the only light in the room came from the console. The pastel glow of the central column cast strange, crystalline sparkles over the walls and ceiling. All Ace could see of the Doctor now was his face, pale and ghost-like in the darkness.

And behind him, another face: faint, transparent, laughing.

It vanished the moment she saw it. 'There!' Ace pointed. 'I saw it! A face in the darkness, behind you!'

The Doctor turned and stared intently into the shadows, but there was no one there. 'What did it look like?'

'A child. A little girl, I think – very young, smiling.'

The Doctor pursed his lips, deep in thought. 'Some sort of temporal relapse, perhaps?' he postulated, largely to himself. He cocked his head and regarded Ace balefully. 'An image of yourself, from long ago?'

Ace shook her head empathically. 'This has nothing to do with me, Doctor.'

There was the laughter again: a light, girlish titter from the darkness. Ace felt the hairs on the back of her neck stand up.

'Come out, come out, wherever you are,' sang the Doctor. 'We know you're there. You might as well let us take a look at you.'

No response.

'Oh, don't be shy. We don't mean you any harm.'

Silence, except for the soft hum of the TARDIS.

'How did it get in here?' Ace wanted to know.

'Questions, questions,' the Doctor complained. 'How did she get in? What is she? Who is she?'

A chuckle in the shadows, and the merest hint of a small, human face – and this time the Doctor saw it too. He quickly circled the console. 'Hello?'

'It was a child,' Ace said. 'Only about seven or eight years old, I'd say.'

'Perhaps she's trying to make contact…'

'She doesn't seem very worried, not when she's laughing like that.'

'No…'

'And what's she laughing at any way? It's not very funny.'

The Doctor's face suddenly brightened, his eyebrows jiggling. 'But what if we give her something to laugh at? Maybe that'll help!' And before she could stop him, the Doctor had produced a pair of dessert spoons from his jacket pocket. He started to play a tune – Ace thought she recognised a mangled version of *My Old Man's a Dustman* – clapping the spoons together on his hand, knuckles, elbow, knees and finally the back of his head.

The child visitor found it most amusing. She appeared on the other side of the room, her soft young face bright with laughter, captured in the glow of the central column.

Encouraged, the Doctor launched straight into a metallic variation on

Rock Around the Clock. The little girl laughed and even Ace felt herself smiling. Eventually the Doctor finished with a flourish and a bow, rolling his hat back up his arm and onto his head with a goofy grin.

The girl stayed where was she was, clapping her hands with delight.

'Who are you?' asked Ace.

The girl stopped laughing, started to fade away. Ace ran quickly over to her. 'No – don't go! It's all right. What do you want?'

The girl started to speak, but no sound emerged. She grew more and more transparent, until they could barely see her any more. 'She's fading away,' said Ace. 'Stop her, Professor!'

A series of lights flashed brightly on the console by the Doctor's elbow, catching his attention. The readout panels blinked and a series of warning bleeps erupted from the controls. Instantly he began flicking switches and twisting dials, his hands moving in a blur, a look of intense concentration on his face.

'What's happening? What's wrong?'

'Anomalous chronicity!' he blurted, in the same way a lorry driver might say, 'Brake failure!' while barrelling down the fast lane of a crowded motorway.

Instinctively, Ace grabbed the edge of the console as the TARDIS began to shake. Leaning over the instruments, the Doctor continued to wrestle with his ship. The TARDIS whirled and pitched, as though it was careering down the time vortex, impossibly ricocheting between the then and the now. Eventually the ship settled, with a few loud bangs and flashes from the electronics.

And the little girl laughed.

'I'm glad you think it's funny,' remarked the Doctor peevishly, and she giggled again, reappearing fleetingly on the other side of the console, to run around the shadowy walls, becoming visible only when passing through the dim light of the roundels.

The TARDIS moaned, long and deep, like a vast injured whale communicating its distress across the ocean. The Doctor stared anxiously at the console. 'I wish she'd stop doing that.'

'Doing what?'

'Annoying the TARDIS!' snapped the Doctor, and the girl's distant laughter echoed around them. '*Hurting* it.' He reached out to touch the console, but his fingers stopped shy of the edge just for a moment, as if he had been struck by a tiny premonition of danger. And then, because he didn't believe it, he *did* touch the console, in a deliberate challenge; and then it happened. A horrible spasm of energy threw him backwards, lifting him clear off his feet. When he hit the floor, strange black sparks flashed and crackled around his fingers.

'Professor! Are you all right?'

He struggled to sit up, looking crumpled and old. 'The TARDIS rejected me,' he gasped, sounding hurt in more ways than one, and the phantom girl laughed. 'No, wait,' said the Doctor. 'It's not me. It's *her*. The TARDIS is rejecting *her*.'

He scrambled back to the controls, searching the instruments for a particular readout. All the while, the girl kept up her soft chuckling, but the Doctor's face was as grim as Ace had ever seen it. 'The TARDIS has detected something inside itself that is anomalous to the Web of Time,' he explained, eyes darkening. 'Something that shouldn't be here, Ace. Something that shouldn't be anywhere – or anywhen.' He turned and stalked around the shadowy chamber, and the thin, intangible girl floated mischievously away from him.

'What's she doing?' Ace asked, moving to cut her off.

'Existing!'

The girl glanced between the Doctor and Ace, and then rushed toward Ace. With a merry laugh, she passed straight through Ace like a chill. Her laughter tinkled inside Ace as she emerged behind her and disappeared into the darkness. Ace clutched her chest, feeling as though the blood in her heart had been painfully frozen.

She could still hear the laughter as she fell.

'Ace! Wake up!'

The voice was calling to her, calling, calling... She turned over and buried her head in her arms. She was lying on something cold and hard like rock or marble. When she opened her eyes, it was as dark as night. A face appeared in the gloom, close up, one she recognised.

'Professor...!'

He was shaking her by the shoulder, gently but urgently. 'Ace! Come on, wake up...'

When she heard the little girl's laughter, Ace shut her eyes tight. When she didn't hear the Doctor's voice again, she opened them.

He was kneeling on the floor, arms loose at his sides, head back. The skin of his face looked sunken and grey, and for a terrible moment she thought he was dead. She could see the veins standing out like wires under his skin. 'Doctor?'

'Ace!' the word hissed explosively from between clenched jaws. 'Open the doors!'

Ace looked at the control console. The central column was motionless, indicating that the TARDIS had landed. Without waiting for an explanation, Ace crawled over and pulled the door lever.

The big grey portals groaned open. There was a shrill cry and a blast of wind seemed to whip out of the TARDIS, carrying the Doctor's straw hat with it into the deep blackness outside.

Something snapped the Doctor free of whatever force had held him, and, pausing only to grab Ace's hand, he charged out after his hat.

They were back on the same planet, possibly even the same night they had left. The flowers twinkled in the moonlight. Further down the valley, the lichen-covered ruins glowed softly green. The Doctor was already heading for them, clambering down the dusty slope. Ace followed him, kicking up sparks from the flowers in her rush.

She caught up with him at the edge of the ruins, where he stood for a while contemplating the strange, hive-like edifice. The lichen had coated his shoes in a film of luminescent dust. He tapped his chin with the handle of his umbrella, his eyes steady and full of thought.

Ace checked behind them, looking back up the valley to the rocks where the TARDIS stood. There was no sign of the little girl, and nor had they heard her laughing since leaving the ship.

The Doctor walked into the ruins, silent and contemplative. Ace watched him carefully as he again examined the pictograms on the internal walls. He was tense, distant, but she could see the concentration on his face as he strove to decipher the glyphs. There might have been a laser beam connecting his eyes to the pictures.

'What is it?' she prompted him. 'What've you found?'

'I misread the pictograms,' he replied tersely, tapping his umbrella against the wall. It sounded hard and gritty, like an old gravestone.

'All the people here died,' he continued. 'But their extinction wasn't caused by some natural disaster or space plague.' He turned grimly to Ace and said, 'They were murdered, while they slept, by an indigenous life form.'

Ace felt her pulse beating faster. She automatically glanced around, looking for homicidal green blobs or monsters. But there was nothing else here, just her and the Doctor. When she looked back at him, he pointed at the ground.

She looked down and saw the soft, velvety lichen covering the sand and rocks beneath her feet. Glowing spores clung to her boots.

She blinked as the realisation hit. But it was impossible. She looked back up at the Doctor. 'The lichen?'

He nodded solemnly.

'How?' Ace instinctively tried to step away from it, but the lichen covered everything here, like mould on a rotten fruit.

The Doctor prised a flat piece of rock from the ground with his brolly, and then used the rock to scrape away the lichen. The sand beneath shifted as he began to scoop out a shallow hole.

As Ace watched, the Doctor quickly uncovered something buried in the sand, dry and white. He delicately brushed away a last skein of dust to reveal a piece of bone, shining in the moonlight.

A few more minutes work revealed a skull, perfectly preserved, ribcage, spine and arms. The position of the skeleton made it look pathetic rather than frightening. The Doctor cleared the sand and lichen away from one arm, which appeared to be thrown, outstretched, holding something in its bony fingers. It proved to be another hand, connected to a second skeleton.

'They died holding hands,' realised Ace sickly. The two skulls, once revealed, were looking directly at each other, empty eye sockets seeing only each other.

'How sad...' said the Doctor, a little coldly. He straightened up and brushed the dust from his hands.

Ace wandered out of the dome, feeling cold in the silvery-blue light. Looking down, she could now see shapes in the sand beneath her feet, shapes that had been there all along, but somehow unrecognisable. With the toe of her Doc Marten, she scraped away the grey dust until she glimpsed bone.

There were bodies everywhere, huddled together beneath the thin blanket of sand, as if seeking warmth or comfort at the moment of death.

'It's around here somewhere,' she heard the Doctor say. He sounded grim, as he cast about the lichen-covered rocks and dirt, his eyes burning into the ground, deciphering the shapes beneath, interpreting the faded language of the dead. 'It must be!'

'What are you looking for?' Ace asked.

He had wandered some distance from the ruins before he finally stopped and knelt, pushing aside dusty clumps of lichen, digging with his bare hands in the soil beneath. It was loose and dry, parting easily beneath his fingers.

He uncovered it soon enough: a small, perfectly human skeleton. Smooth, delicate white bones lay in a fetal curl, hands tucked beneath the skull as if sleeping.

'This one's quite a way from all the others,' Ace noted. She was over the shock and nausea now; she could start to analyse the position of the graves.

'She died alone, I should think,' said the Doctor.

'She?'

The Doctor pointed with his umbrella, a look of distaste on his old, crumpled face. 'Look.'

Something stirred in the sand around the shallow grave. The lichen was moving, the yellow-grey fungus beginning to spread out over the ground, silently, slowly, curling over the edge and then creeping towards the tiny skeleton. Spores appeared on the bones, speckling the surface like mould in a speeded-up film, until the fibrous growth seemed to crawl like flesh all around the body.

Lichen bulged inside the ribcage like lungs, and then a heart formed, sprouting arteries and veins and ligaments. Tissue surged up around the spine and into the skull, fleshing out the throat and mouth from the inside. A dusty film of skin settled over the features as they formed.

It was the girl.

She stood up and looked at the Doctor and Ace, her eyes glinting strangely in the alien moonlight.

'Who are you?' asked the Doctor.

She laughed, and it seemed exactly the same as it had in the TARDIS. But coming from this weird, lichen-made simulacrum, the laughter sounded strange and sinister. She had walked a little way towards the old ruins and when she stopped, she turned to look back at the Doctor and Ace with a more somber expression. 'I'm an evil little witch,' she told them quietly.

The Doctor followed her, stepping softly through the remaining patches of lichen. 'I don't understand,' he said.

'Course you don't,' she sniffed.

'Then explain!'

'I'm the one who did all this,' she said. 'I'm responsible.'

Ace looked at the ground, and saw the shapes of the bones beneath the sand. 'You killed them?' she asked, feeling the anger mounting inside her chest.

The girl laughed. 'I told you I was evil.'

'But what did you do?' asked the Doctor.

'Didn't *do* anything.' She scuffed her shoe against the rock. 'I just found it, that's all.'

'Found what?'

'All this.' She gestured toward the ground, the rocks, the ruined dome, and suddenly Ace realised what she meant.

'The lichen?'

'It wasn't always here, was it?' said the Doctor. 'Where did it come from? Where did you find it?'

'Where the flowers used to be,' answered the girl.

'Which flowers?'

'The ones that light up at night, the pretty little fairy-flowers that sparkle in the dark.'

The Doctor and Ace exchanged glances. 'When?'

'Long time ago. Long, long, time ago.'

'Tell us.'

'Why do you want to know?'

'I'm interested.'

'No one else was interested! No one else cared – except when they started dying.' The girl looked down. 'Couldn't help that, could I? I didn't know it was going to do that, not to everybody. How could I?'

'You found the lichen by the flowers...' the Doctor prompted. 'And brought it back here.'

'Only wanted to show people, that's all...' She looked up. 'The sparkle-flowers had gone out. They never lit up at night anymore. I went back there every single night but it was always dark. I wanted to see another one light up, just one, but they never did.'

'And the lichen?'

'I didn't know what it was. The flowers all died and they got covered in this stuff.'

'It killed the flowers, didn't it?' Ace asked the Doctor. 'Then she brought it back to the settlement.'

'Where it killed everyone here.'

'They called me names and were nasty to me!' blurted the girl. 'Evil little witch, they called me!'

'They were frightened,' said the Doctor.

'Well, I didn't know that. They just looked angry to me. Angry and mean. They made me go away, take the lichen with me. It was all over my hands and I couldn't get it off, no matter how hard I scrubbed. I tried wiping it off on the rocks, and I wiped and wiped till my fingers bled, but it *wouldn't* come off. It was all over me, suffocating me.'

'And the grown-ups?'

'It was all over them too. Choking them and making them dead.' She was crying now. 'I never wanted that! But they threw rocks and things at me and said I'd ruined everything!'

Ace watched her carefully, not knowing what to say. The girl looked lost and utterly dejected. 'But – how come you're still here? Still alive?'

The girl smiled then, little yellow-grey teeth visible behind the yellow-grey lips. 'I'm not alive, silly.'

'It's the lichen,' said the Doctor. 'Or some alien property of it. The spores we carried back into the TARDIS, on our shoes... Allowed the memory of the lichen, or the child it had absorbed, to live on.'

'That's horrible.'

The Doctor nodded grimly. 'It should never have been allowed to happen.'

'Does it matter?' asked the little girl – or rather, Ace now thought, the lichen. 'Does it matter how I came back? I'm alive! I can live again, and dance and laugh and play!'

'No,' said the Doctor forcefully. 'That must never happen.'

'But it already has!'

'What happened here was a terrible tragedy,' the Doctor said. 'But it *happened*. Nothing can change that now.'

'*You've* changed it...'

The Doctor shook his head. 'You're not the little girl who died here.'

'Am too!'

'No. You're an echo, a phantom, a *ghost*.'

'Am not!'

'Ace,' said the Doctor in a commanding tone. 'We're leaving.' He turned on his heel without another word and stalked away.

Ace hurried after him, glancing back at the lichen. 'Can't we help?'

'No, Ace,' the Doctor replied emphatically. 'No! I will not stop here to bandy words with a... a...'

'Ghost, you said.'

'A trans-temporal memory,' he snarled, 'given form by a semi-sentient lichen predator.'

Ace looked back at the ruins, but there was no sign of the girl. 'Why hasn't it attacked us?'

'Perhaps it will, given time.' The Doctor pushed on, his little legs eating up the yards at a great rate. 'Perhaps it only attacks during a particular season.'

They had reached the glow-flowers, and Ace thought that their bioluminescence was on the wane. They didn't seem to be as spectacularly pretty any more. They glinted in the earth like a hundred tiny cat's eyes, watching her, waiting for her to hesitate. But the Doctor had paused to prod at the ground around the flowers with his umbrella. 'The lichen is starting to form already,' he remarked, 'possibly as a natural by-product. Best not to linger.'

'I'm with you there,' Ace said, hurrying along with him, up the slope that led to the TARDIS. She was beginning to puff, but there was, thankfully, no sign of pursuit.

The Doctor already had his key out when they reached the police box. 'Wipe your feet,' he advised, and Ace quickly made sure her boots were free of lichen spores.

'I want to go too,' said a voice close by. Ace whirled around in shock, but the girl was nowhere to be seen.

The Doctor was frozen halfway into the TARDIS. 'You can't,' he said coldly. 'I'm sorry.'

'You can't leave me here,' pleaded the little girl's voice.

'I *must*,' said the Doctor.

'But I'll be all alone.'

'I'm sorry.'

'Let me in!' A swirl of grey-yellow dust blew up around the TARDIS, born on a breeze that didn't exist. Ace could faintly see the girl in the midst of the spores.

'You heard the Doctor,' Ace told the image. 'You can't come in!'

The girl floated closer, clearer now but still translucent in the starlight. Her eyes were blazing darkly. 'You must let me come with you!'

Ace stepped in front of the police box doors. 'Get lost!'

'I can't stay here! I can't!'

'All right,' said the Doctor. 'All right. I'm sure we can reach an agreement on this.' He thought hard for a moment or two. 'But you must understand – you've already been inside my TARDIS, and you very nearly caused it to crash! It maintains a very precise and delicate relationship with the Web of Time, and *you* are a dangerous temporal anomaly. You've got to give me time to work things out with the TARDIS first – or it will just reject you again.'

'I must be free!' insisted the girl. 'I want to go home!'

'I understand,' he said, not unkindly. 'But you'll have to give me a minute or two.'

Ace said, 'Are you sure about this, Professor?'

'You heard her,' replied the Doctor stonily. 'She wants to go home.' And with that, he disappeared into the TARDIS. With a last, nervous look at the girl, Ace turned to follow him.

'Wait!' said the girl. 'It's a trick. You'll leave me here!'

'No. The Doctor wouldn't do that,' Ace said. 'Wait here.'

She went inside to find the Doctor frowning over the controls. Immediately she was in, he slapped down the door lever and started pressing buttons and flicking switches.

'What are you doing?' Ace was wide eyed, as the central column started to move and the ship began to grind and roar.

The Doctor's hands flew over the take-off controls. 'Dematerialising!' he shouted. 'It's our only chance!'

The TARDIS hummed and rattled, straining against time and space. The Doctor's brow was deeply furrowed, and, as the ship began to slip away from its landing site, he looked suddenly stricken.

A terrible wail echoed around the console room, a scream of torment that ended in an infantile sob of terror – and then nothing, except for a distant echo that might have been Ace's imagination.

The TARDIS stopped shaking and the central column rose smoothly up and down.

'What did you do?' asked Ace again in the deep silence that followed. 'You said – '

'I know what I said,' the Doctor replied. 'But it was *impossible*. She couldn't come with us. She couldn't come into the TARDIS. *She should never have existed.*'

'That's terrible.'

'I know.' He sounded old and weary, and leant on the console for support. His face was dark and heavily lined. 'I know…'

Ace felt the anger boiling inside her. 'Wasn't there *anything* you could do?'

'I think I've done enough already.'

Ace frowned. 'I don't understand!'

'It's possible – just possible – that bringing the lichen into the special relative environment of the TARDIS caused the... ghost... to exist in the first place.' He wouldn't meet her eyes as he spoke, fumbling with the brim of his old straw hat. He blew imaginary dust from the crown. 'If she... *it*... had come with us – been allowed into the rest of time and space, instead of remaining here, isolated and unreal... Well, the result could have been catastrophic. I couldn't allow it.'

'She only wanted to go home, Doctor...'

'She can't go home, Ace. She isn't alive. She's *dead*. And the TARDIS can't take her where she needs to go now.'

'But that's awful,' said Ace, with feeling.

'Yes,' said the Doctor. 'It is.'

Charley eased the vase away from her, back towards the Steward. He just nodded understandingly and without speaking, turned to serve a couple of of men who were standing at the bar.

Charley looked them up and down. The nearest was blond, clearly well-built with a good tan and powerful hands that gripped tightly on the green bottle of beer the Steward passed him. He wore a chunky jacket, red with off-white sleeves and an image of a lion sewn over the breast. He glanced at Charley, nodded reassuringly at her and then tapped the other newcomer on the shoulder.

'Fancy a round of poker, Joe?' He was an American, Charley realised. His companion was also drinking straight from a bottle, his brown, the word 'Ale' written in huge letters across it. Before he replied, Charley guessed he'd be a Londoner and she wasn't proved wrong.

'Nah, mate, not right now.' He took his trilby off and brushed something off his herringbone checked suit. It's had clearly seen better days. As his American friend wandered away, the Londoner spotted Charley. He winked at her and Charley found she was smiling. 'Hello,' she said simply.

'Been aboard long?'

Charley shook her head. 'I don't think so.'

'What did you do, then, Miss...?'

'Charley,' she replied. 'Just Charley, please.' She frowned at his question. 'Do? What do you mean?'

'How d'you break it then?'

'Break what?'

He smiled. 'You *are* new, ain'tcha? The "Web of Time", Charley. You must've done something bad to be here. Listen, I'll tell y'what I mean...'

Charley sipped her drink and listened...

The Rag & Bone Man's Story

Colin Brake

It all started in a junkyard.

The best stories always do, don't they?

Most people think that they are dirty, dangerous places, full of rubbish. But they're not. One man's junk is another man's jewel. Everything's got value for someone.

Back then we still used to do the rounds with the horse and cart. The wagon had been my old man's, but he didn't go out much by then. This was the early sixties and the cough that carried him off was already keeping him in his bed most days. So me and the General did the rounds on our own.

It wasn't always a barrel of laughs, ambling slowly round the streets of the East End, wearing my throat hoarse with the traditional street cry – 'any old iron.' The trick was to run the words into each other, so it just became a strange guttural howl. It was murder on the vocal chords, but it did the job, carrying into the houses so folk would know we were there.

We took everything: old clothes, furniture, crockery; anything and everything. Metal was best of course, easily and swiftly converted into hard cash, but a smart man could make money out of anything that was chucked out and my dad hadn't raised any idiots.

Some said my old man was a skinflint. They'd say it was easier to get a drink in the Sahara than get one out of old man Galloway down the Fox and Hounds. It wasn't true. He could be generous in his own way. He lived by a simple motto: watch the pennies and the pounds will look after themselves. And he did. He was never in debt. Not even when the old horse had to go to the knackers yard and he had to stump up to buy the General.

So there I was. A Rag and Bone Man in East London. Christmas of '62. Not as snowbound as the winter the following year but cold enough. The last weeks of the year hadn't been good, they never were. Everything was being hoarded, made good and fixed up ready for the festive season. January's a better time. All those unwanted gifts!

I must have been doing the rounds on my own for a couple of years by then. Dad joined me sometimes, on the odd summer's day, insisting on taking the reins and making the cries as long as his lungs held out, which wasn't long, but never in winter. If there was a hint of frost it was just me, the General and my hip flask on the cold streets, looking to scrape a living. I was only just an adult really, but already it looked like my life was mapped out. I wasn't much of a looker, I guess, and the job didn't really get me very far with the ladies. I didn't reckon much for my chances of getting married any time soon.

And then my luck changed.

As well as the rounds, and the shop where we sold what we could, we also did house clearances and the like. They were a bit of a risk; you could spend a backbreaking day carting every last thing out of a house and have nothing but total junk or you could strike it lucky and walk away with a small fortune. A couple of house clearances at the right time of the year meant the difference between getting down to Margate for a week in the summer and no holiday at all.

It was a few days before Christmas, and I'd not had a customer all day in the shop. Then, just as I was closing up, this bloke came in and said he had something needing clearing. An entire junkyard. I thought at first that he was pulling my leg. He was a short man, softly spoken, well dressed. I don't think he was local. He said his name was Hawkins. He smiled. 'No, no Mr Galloway, I can assure you that I am genuine about this.' His voice had the trace of an accent, but I couldn't place it. 'You see I rented this yard to a man called Smith, who seems to have disappeared.'

'There's a lot of it about, eh? Like them teachers that went missing last month.'

It had been in the local paper. A pair of teachers and a girl, from the same school that they'd taught at, had all disappeared. It was all a bit queer from what I heard. Hawkins knew more than the papers. He told me that the girl's guardian – one Doctor John Smith – had been his tenant. What was a doctor doing in a junkyard? Hawkins hadn't been able to answer that. All he cared about was the land, not what was on it. Hawkins wanted to build on it but needed it cleared first. Was I interested or not? He offered a fair fee to clear the lot and said I could make use of anything I took off the site. How could I have refused?

I thought it was my lucky day.

I didn't know how right I was.

Or how wrong.

'Susan my child, do be careful with that!'

'But Grandfather, it's such a beautiful thing. I've never seen anything bend light like this.'

The Doctor tutted again and hurried across the Console Room to where his granddaughter was examining the delicate crystal structure resting on her palm. Carefully he plucked it from her.

'This is not just a pretty trinket, you know.'

An annoyed frown appeared on Susan's forehead. Why did he have to keep treating her like a child all the time?

'So what is it?' she asked haughtily.

The Doctor was now placing the crystal into a receptacle on one of the panels of the console; a strangely shaped slot that Susan was sure hadn't been there before.

'Hmm... I don't think it has a name as such...'

'What did the Tacunda People call it? The Blessing Star?'

The Doctor smiled at this and turned to look at Susan, his hands tugging at the lapels of his jacket.

'The Tacunda are a simple people, cave-dwellers, a pre-industrial society, you don't think they made this do you?'

'I don't know, I didn't really think about it.'

'Then you should. You can't always trust your eyes and ears Susan, you need to think about what you see and hear. That's why I want to stop our travels for a short while.'

Susan bit her lip, upset at the Doctor bringing this subject up again.

'Now don't try and get me to change my mind. You know I won't. I think it will be good for you, just for a while, to be in one place, one time.'

'But you can't always control where the Ship goes, Grandfather...'

'Exactly. Which is why I couldn't resist picking up this little chap when I saw it on that primitive altar...'

Susan could see that the Doctor was initialising the dematerialisation process. The familiar groaning and moaning of the Ship's engines began to fill the room. On the console panel the alien crystal lit up with a myriad of colours.

'I still don't understand. What is it? How can it help you guide the Ship?'

'It won't but the tiny creature that lives inside it will.'

'It's alive?'

'After a fashion. The creature is microscopic but is a powerful empath. It responds to desires, and generates a field of positivity.'

The engines were really loud now. Outside in the real world the ever-adaptable outer plasmic shell of the Ship, currently looking like a large native tree, would begin to fade from existence.

'You mean it makes good luck?' Susan couldn't believe it possible. Surely Grandfather was always telling her that magic didn't exist. 'But that would be like magic.'

'No, no, no my dear. As I told that young Mr Clarke, what the primitive mind perceives as magic is always the result of a science it cannot understand. This creature uses a sophisticated technology, advanced even by our standards, to manipulate multi-dimensional mathematics and alter reality. And it's just what I need to help the Ship's computers direct us to where I want us to be...'

However, even as the Doctor was speaking, smoke was beginning to billow from the console panel containing the alien crystal.

'Grandfather!'

The alarm in Susan's voice was enough to get the Doctor's attention but it was too late. A torrent of sparks exploded from the panel, glass shattering from readouts and sprinkling the floor with shards. The central column came to a shuddering halt and the overhead lights flickered and then went out. The engines protested and then shut down with an ominous deep thud. For a moment there was silence and then, from somewhere deep within the bowels of the space-time craft, a bell could be heard tolling a dire warning.

'Grandfather?'

This time Susan's tone was more tentative. There was the sound of a match striking and then a glow of light as the Doctor lit one of his everlasting matches. He quickly found a candle from a cabinet set into one of the wall decorations. He held the candle horizontally over a flat surface on one of the panels and then set it down in the pool of melted wax he had created.

'It would appear that it wasn't compatible with our systems, hmm?'

'Is it… damaged?'

'The Ship? Nothing too serious, I imagine. But it may take some time to repair.'

'No, Grandfather the creature. Have you harmed it?'

'No, no, it's perfectly safe as long as the crystal remains unharmed. But I don't think I'll be using it again somehow… Far too dangerous… Would you like to have it?'

'Do you think I need good luck, Grandfather?'

The Doctor smiled. 'We all need that, my child.'

He operated the doors and together they looked out into the world that would be their home over the weeks and months while the Doctor repaired the Ship.

Through the doors they could see piles of rubbish and bric-a-brac, old twin-tubs, bed-frames, shop-window dummies, wardrobes, all manner of bits and pieces in various states of disrepair.

'A junkyard.' *The Doctor declared with a hint of smugness.* 'Perfect.'

'But where are we Grandfather? What planet?'

'Earth, of course. Late twentieth-century England. Exactly where I wanted to be.'

The name on the wooden gates was IM Foreman but whoever Mr Foreman was he wasn't here now. Nor was the mysterious Doctor Smith who'd been paying Hawkins rent for the last nine months. When I got the gates opened and guided the General into a small clearing it was instantly clear that it was going to be a big job. The yard wasn't large but it was crammed with stuff.

Whilst the General had a feed, I began to sort through the piles of junk, selecting the most obvious pieces that I could easily make some money on. Within an hour the cartwheels were groaning under the weight of the things I'd piled on it. It certainly was my lucky day.

And then I found it.

There was an area of the yard that was emptier than the rest. There was, of course, a semi-circle of space in front of the gates currently occupied by the General and the overloaded cart but there was also another area to the right linked by a corridor lined either side with junk. In this section of the yard there was a circular area in which it was clear something with a square base had stood for a while. From the dimensions of its footprint, clearly visible in the dust and muck that caked the floor like a carpet, it must have been some kind of small shed or hut. But how it had been removed was a mystery. There was no sign of anything heavy having been dragged from the area. It was as if some gigantic hand had reached in and plucked it into the sky. I was distracted from thinking about this puzzle any further by the glitter of something shiny peeking out from the junk that would have been behind the now absent shed. Carefully I reached toward the sparkling object and my hand closed around some kind of crystal. It was the strangest thing I ever saw. It was like a crystallised representation of a snowflake, delicate and beautiful, but at the same time it had warmth like a stone that had been lying in the sun.

I looked at it, nestled in my big clumsy hands and felt a peculiar sensation wash over me. Even in the cold of that winter's day I felt a sudden inner warmth and a feeling of immense good fortune. I just knew this was going to be my good luck charm, my rabbit's foot. I clutched it to my chest and made ready to leave. My first load of material from the junkyard would not be my last by a long road, but I had already found my treasure.

Taking the crystal into school had been a mistake, Susan realised now. She'd found it hard enough to settle into the routine of a normal life with time plodding on in such a dull linear fashion. She wasn't used to Tuesdays following Mondays, Wednesdays following Tuesdays, and so on with such relentless predictability. She missed the freedom of stepping in and out of the timelines, of playing hopscotch with chronology. Not to mention the thrill of seeing New Worlds. Having enjoyed travelling the length and breadth of all known Time and Space with her grandfather, being stuck in one small part of one stale planet in one segment of consecutive time was a nightmare. And school was just the icing on a very bad cake.

She'd tried hard to fit in, she really had. But she was an alien to her classmates in so many, many ways. She was smart, and articulate and opinionated; qualities Grandfather had always encouraged her to have but in Coal Hill School they were attributes that just accentuated her otherness both to the other school children and the staff.

She knew too much about some things, too little about others and the net result was to mark her out as a strange and unearthly child. Taking the Blessing Star into school had been an act of desperation.

The problem was that it was too successful. How it worked she didn't know; she knew it wasn't magic, so she had to assume that it was a higher science as Grandfather had suggested. She was no slouch at maths, as the Maths teacher Mr Cooper could vouch, but she had never realised that mathematics could actually affect reality in such a direct way. She had asked her Grandfather about the subject and he muttered something about some place called Logopolis before being distracted by another failed systems repair.

Day by day the Ship was getting back to its previous condition but it was taking forever. Susan was beginning to think that Grandfather was deliberately taking longer than necessary to complete the task, as if he wanted to stay here in this backwater for some time. But then she'd caught him flicking through star charts and other memorabilia from their travels and she was reassured. The wanderlust was still strong in him. They would resume their travels soon. But until then she needed to find a way to get along with her new contemporaries; so she'd taken the Star into school.

It had been an immediate success; the girls in particular were amazed at its delicate beauty but even the boys were interested, especially when she demonstrated its weird warmth. A lad called Christopher thought he felt it throbbing, as if it were alive. And then the luck started. First she won a game of cards without really thinking about it, then she came top in an unexpected History test (not always her best subject, as she tended to have different ideas from the text books about certain historical events.) Some of the other children had started joking about her then, saying she had the luck of the Irish today and calling her Paddy. And then at lunchtime she'd been sitting near a group playing a game of football in the playground. Susan had never shown any interest in sports, and had certainly never been known to kick a football but when the ball had rolled out of play and landed at her feet she'd made an effort to kick it back into the game. The ball had curved through the air, between the goalposts and was caught in the back of the net. The boys were stunned – it had been a fantastic kick, an astonishing fluke. The girls were horrified – now the weird new girl was showing off to the boys at their own game. All the progress she had been making was lost in a moment. Now Susan was standing out more than ever.

After school, Susan had hesitated as she reached out to put her key in the police box door, still thinking over the events of the day. However it worked, she was now convinced that the Blessing Star did have a way to influence events but wasn't sure what to do with it. Something that powerful inside the Ship might be a danger to them. When the repairs were complete she wanted to go back to having travels throughout Time and Space again but with the Blessing Star on board she would be constantly worrying that it would interfere again. And the next time they might get stranded somewhere even more primitive than late twentieth century Earth. Susan decided that it would be best for everyone if she left the crystal outside the TARDIS.

Behind the Ship she bent down and pushed the crystal into a small hole in a mound of junk and then rearranged some other items to mask its hiding place. Grandfather need never know, she thought to herself, with a sense of relief.

As soon as I got the thing home it started working for me. I didn't realise the connection at first but then as my luck changed so consistently I couldn't ignore it. I really did have a lucky charm: it was changing my life.

It started with a little pools win. That started the ball rolling. It wasn't anything too much, just a nice little windfall but it was the beginning. I was able to retire the General and get a van. I started getting more house clearances. And the stuff I was picking up started getting better in value. An antique chair here, a Chinese vase there, before I really knew what was happening the junk shop had turned into an antiques shop. I took on staff, got Mum and Dad a place down near Margate as a retirement home; everything was looking up. I even got engaged, to a wonderful woman called Margaret. We were married in April 1965, and had a two-week honeymoon. I was on a roll and no mistake.

And then in 1966 there was the big one. The World Cup. With the way my luck was running how could I resist? And I had the money to put up a hefty stake. If Bobby and the boys could pull it off, I was going to be made. I mean we were the host nation and all that, but that's no guarantee is it? But I went for broke. England to win it in extra time. And then I polished my little crystal just to be sure.

The Doctor was feeling happy. Something about this planet always cheered him up. Maybe it was the humans themselves: such complicated creatures, so contradictory, so much potential for good and evil. Or maybe it was the planet itself: the unique combination of atmosphere and gravity that so reminded him of his own birthplace so far away. Perhaps that was it – Earth was a home from home for him and every exile needed a place like that.

It had been a while since he'd been here, both subjectively and in real time. The London he and Susan had lived in for a while had still been crawling from the monotone fifties but this present era was full of youth and colour and, at the moment at least, football fans from around the world. The Doctor recalled that when he and Susan had begun their time here that the locals were still bemoaning the failure of their national team in the 1962 competition in Chile. Brazil had beaten them in the Quarter Final. Now it was time for the next competition for the Jules Rimet Trophey and the pressure was on the home team to lift the trophy. The streets of London, so recently threatened by WOTAN's War Machines were now host to fans of the beautiful game from every continent. The city felt alive and vigorous.

The Doctor was satisfied that his young companion Dodo would find happiness here if she chose to stay, as he knew she would. The prospect of travelling alone again had raised ghosts in his memory, of those who had travelled with him before. Steven, the space pilot, now helping the Elders and the Savages, young Vicki, tragic Katarina, Chesterton and Barbara and, of course, the first to leave him, Susan. His own granddaughter, now once again living a mortal's existence in the Dalek-ravaged Earth of the future… He would never admit it to his companions but he often thought of Susan. Should he really have let her go like that? Was it wise or fair? Hours he spent in silent contemplation in the Zero Room deep within the Ship, his heart heavy with such thoughts. Finally he convinced himself that she would be all right, come what may. After all she had that alien device, the Blessing Star, didn't she? That would see her right.

The thought nagged at him. Something about that crystal. The more he thought about it the more he was sure that he had been mistaken and that Susan hadn't had it with her when she left the Ship for the last time. In fact he couldn't recall when he had last seen it. Finally the nagging thought had to be dealt with. After Steven's departure the Doctor had waited until Dodo was sleeping and had then gone to the room that had remained locked and untouched since Susan had left. When Ian and Barbara had travelled with them she'd slept in one of the communal rooms, for the sake of sociability, but this was her private room, her own sanctuary. As soon as he opened the long-locked doors he knew the truth; it wasn't here, and hadn't been for a long time. Where had it gone? The truth became obvious as the Doctor worked his way back through his memories of the past few years – it must still be on Earth. Susan must have left it there in the junkyard in Totter's Lane. Another loose end to be sorted out when he next landed on Earth in the right period. Perhaps the Ship's telepathic circuits had responded to his needs, for the next dematerialisation had brought Dodo and the Doctor here, to London in the summer of 1966.

As soon as he had dealt with WOTAN the Doctor had slipped off to attend to his unfinished business. First he'd visited a certain graveyard but he found the Hand long gone. For a moment he felt something akin to panic but then he calmed as the obvious explanation came to him. He was, after all, a traveller in time. At some point in his future he would clearly land on Earth between 1963 and 1966 and deal with the Hand. The Doctor smiled, taking comfort that he had a future to look forward to.

His next priority was to locate the Blessing Star. The site of the junkyard that had been their home for a while was now a building site. The Doctor had made some enquiries and tracked down the name of a rag and bone man that had been paid to clear the site. A man called Joseph Galloway. A man who, according to local gossip, had been enjoying the most amazing run of luck these last couple of years. The Doctor was sure now who had the Blessing Star, now all he had to do was find it.

So there I was: July 1966. Things were going well; Margaret had just fallen pregnant, business was good and we had money in the bank. And if England pulled it off, we'd soon have a good deal more. But I still couldn't get tickets for the final. I thought about crossing town, to see if I could flash some cash and pick up a ticket on the black market but then I had a better idea.

I must have had twenty-odd people crammed into our living room. The television was the biggest set money could buy but still a tiny screen set in a massive wooden box. Even through the tiny television speaker the noise was incredible. The cheers of thousands of men, women and children, accompanied by the unmistakable clatter of hundreds of wooden rattles, filled the stadium.

I can remember the match in perfect detail. They took the lead, then Geoff Hurst equalised. Then Martin Peters put us on top. And then finally just before time the Germans scored again. It was going to extra time.

Play had barely restarted when there was a knock at the door. Margaret popped her head into the lounge to tell me I had a visitor. Who could be calling at a time like this?

The man at the door was old but sprightly. His eyes shone with a great intelligence.

'Young man, I think you have something that, er, belongs to me,' he began without any preamble.

I knew immediately, instinctively, what he was talking about. I'd always known that one day someone would come looking for my little miracle. That day had finally come. But I didn't have to make it easy for the old codger.

'Don't know what you're on about Granddad,' I told him firmly.

'But I think you do,' the old man was equally firm; his expression seemed to have hardened at the suggestion that he was a grandfather. 'The Crystal doesn't belong to you.'

The oldster wasn't a big man, he looked physically frail but somehow he had an authority that allowed no argument. In spite of myself I reached inside my jacket for the Crystal.

'What is it? Really?' I asked as I looked at the thing for what I knew would be the last time.'

'Something beyond your comprehension. Something that should never have found its way to this planet,' the old man answered, 'Now if you'll please…'

He reached out for the crystal but I held it to my chest for one last wish.

At that moment, in Wembley, Geoff Hurst struck the ball at the German goal, hit the underside of the crossbar and it deflected downwards.

The mass desire of thousands of England fans flooded the crystal, which suddenly felt red-hot in my hand.

In the stadium the linesman signalled that the ball had crossed the line – it was a goal!

In my garden I let go of my talisman, which flared and shone with an intense light before exploding into a cloud of golden dust.

The old man, cleared his throat, in an annoyed fashion.

'Well, that seems to have taken care of that,' he commented then turned to go. 'Good day.'

And with that the old man left.

That last twenty-odd minutes were a nightmare. Every time the Germans got the ball and threatened Banks in the England goal my heart was in my mouth. But then Geoff Hurst – who else – got his hat trick. This time the ball firmly and unarguably hit the back of the net. Fans poured onto the pitch. 'They think it's all over…' exclaimed the TV commentator. And I knew that it was.

'And that's my story, Miss. After that I had no more luck than the next man. I made the best of what I had gained though – I cleaned out the local bookies and got a life ban for my troubles, but I didn't care. I wasn't planning on making any more bets, not without my little helper. So I got on with raising my family. I thought I'd done okay with my life but…'

Charley leaned forward, interested. 'What happened?'

'One day I woke up and I was here, on this strange airship. The Steward tells me something's gone wrong with the big story, that somehow I've mucked up history.'

'You've broken this "Web of Time" thing?'

'So they say Apparently, my son developed a weapon, something hideous. Steward told me what but I can't say I understand. Some kind of man-made disease? Anyway, my son was able to do this because of the capital he inherited from me. Or would have inherited if I'd died leaving a will. But now I won't, will I? No body, no will, no inheritance. And no weapon! That's the price I've paid, see, for taking advantage of that lucky charm. I should have left it where it was.'

'It wasn't really your fault, though.'

The Rag and Bone Man shrugged. 'Maybe. What about you? How'd you meet the Doctor?'

Charley sighed. 'That's complicated. But it sounds as if I might've done something similar to you.' Charley paused. 'But…'

The Rag and Bone Man interrupted her. 'So tell me something if you can. Did we ever do it again… did England ever win the World Cup again?'

Charley smiled at him.

'Who knows…?'

He returned her smile and went back to the crowd.

Charley sighed. Things hardly seemed very fair for these people and she wasn't entirely convinced that the 'Doctor' that the Rag and Bone Man or the Steward had described were 'her' Doctor at all. Could this be mistaken identity? Was she here because someone thought her Doctor was responsible for these poor people's predicaments?

'The same man,' said a harsh voice beside her suddenly.

She turned to be faced by a slightly alarming-looking, middle-aged man, with a slight tick to his left eye. He was nodding as if hearing an internal monologue with himself, but then he touched Charley's shoulder. 'The same man,' he repeated. 'I never realised it then, but I do now. Different faces, different clothes, but all the same man.'

Charley said nothing and with a final, almost aggressive shake of his head, he wandered away.

As he moved out of Charley's vision, his departing body revealed the tramp sat once more at the bar. He was finishing his drink and then, slowly, as if aware he was being looked at, he lowered the glass back to the bar and remained staring at the empty vessel.

The Steward silently leant forward and poured more clear liquid into it but the tramp didn't drink. Instead he turned and looked straight at Charley, making her feel almost uncomfortable with the intensity of his look. Charley took a deep breath and eased herself off the barstool and decided to circulate a bit.

Glass in hand, she eased her way through the crowds, some standing and talking or laughing, others seated in groups at small tables. Around the edges of the room were other tables, all of which had games being played. The Centaur was still winning at cards, a couple of non-humanoids were using what looked like octopoid tentacles to play dominoes, and two small human boys were playing an electronic game on the screen, similar to the computer screens she had seen in the future, in the Garazone system.

Charley was determined not to let anything she saw faze her, and instead made her way to the outer edges, where windows leaned back at almost forty-five-degree angles all along one wall. Well, if nothing else, she might be able to see what was outside.

Moments later, she was staring out but all she could see was endless bright blue sky above and below. No sign of land or structures of any kind. They could be underwater for all she could tell.

'Beautiful, isn't it?' said a man beside her. He was tall, commanding and straight-backed, dressed in a long, flowing grey robe, with ornate tapestry around the hems, cuffs and neckline. Charley guessed he was an official of some sort. Perhaps he was in charge?

He sighed. 'I wish I could go home again.'

'Can't you?'

He shook his head. 'I did a bad thing, ma'am. This is my penance.' He gestured back towards the room. 'All of us. Penance. From the darkest soul to the brightest gem. One thing in common: we all crossed him.'

'Who?'

'The Doctor.' The robed man pointed at the Centaur. 'He used a time machine to cheat at the games.' Next he indicated an elderly lady with bright red skin and horns. 'She tried to patent atomic energy years before her people should have discovered it.'

Charley pointed at the tramp, still sat at the bar, alone.

'Him?'

The robed man shrugged. 'Not sure about him.' He pointed at a man in a cream linen suit, sat at a table alone, writing in a notebook. 'Now him. His story is interesting, they say. I've not been here long enough myself to hear it.'

'You're new, too?'

The robed man nodded. 'I awoke about two hours ago. Been hearing stories ever since. Shall we?'

Together they approached the note-writing man. He looked up and smiled. 'Hello.'

'You seem very calm,' said Charley. 'Amid all this hustle and bustle I mean. Mr...?'

'Katsoudas,' he replied. 'Professor Katsoudas. I may look calm outwardly, Miss. But I must tell you that I'm still shaking inside.'

The Seismologist's Story

Peter Anghelides

Jo Grant saw the TARDIS light bounce and jolt, until it vanished into the depths of the chasm. Even when it was no longer visible, she could still hear the police box bang and scrape its way further into the pitch dark. She tried not to panic, to sound calm instead. 'Doctor! This is getting to be a bit of a habit.'

Beside her, in the dark, the Doctor huffed with indignation. 'No, the whole point of those repairs was to prevent this sort of thing. I thought I'd reprogrammed the TARDIS so that it wouldn't happen again. Oh, dear. Now let me see...'

There was a muffled rattling sound, a flaring light that made Jo blink, and the distinctive sulphur tang of a match. The Doctor's nose loomed large in the sudden illumination. He peered carefully over the rock precipice, as though he might see the TARDIS parked safely a hundred metres below.

'You're a bit hopeful,' she told him.

'Everlasting matches,' he replied.

'You'll need them,' retorted Jo. 'We'll be looking forever.'

The Doctor struck a second match and gave it to her. He climbed carefully down onto a stony shelf a metre beneath them, and then onto another below that.

Jo followed reluctantly. 'Perhaps there'll be some helpful miners to drag it back up again. Though with my luck, these caves will be full of ravenous horned beasts instead.'

The Doctor growled. 'We're not on Peladon, the readings made that clear. This is 1950s Earth. We're slightly off course.'

'Slightly?' She resisted the urge to tease him further. Even in the guttering match light, she could see his eyes had that strange look again.

She recognised it from when they had first landed. He had started to admonish her for stepping from the TARDIS onto the dark, rocky ledge. But then he'd stopped, halfway out himself, framed in the illumination that spilled from the open TARDIS doorway, his hair a halo around his head.

They had both heard the ominous creak as he had transferred his weight to the ground. At this, he had half-turned to stare back into the TARDIS, and Jo had thought he was ready to bound back in, leaving her, going off alone in the ship. Had that glance in her direction been to confirm that she was safe before he abandoned her?

The decision had been made for him. The ground had seemed to ripple and slip sideways. With a mighty groan and a spray of displaced shingle,

57

the TARDIS had toppled over backwards and begun its noisy descent into the abyss. As suddenly as it had started, the ground tremor had ceased, and Jo stopped –

'Jo! Stop!' The Doctor's barked command snapped her back to their immediate predicament. 'It's like a cliff face in front of us now, with no way down.'

The second of the ledges was a sheer drop. They both pondered this for a moment. The only sound now was the continuing trickle of loose pebbles from above them. Until that abruptly stopped.

Just as unexpected was the sudden brilliance above them, flashing so fiercely that it illuminated the whole area. At almost the same time, Jo felt the ground undulate beneath her feet. The flashing light plunged past them, and clattered down into the chasm in a series of sickening crunches. They were soon engulfed in darkness again, and behind her own calm breathing she could hear the renewed sound of dislodged stones.

'That's impossible,' she said. 'That was…'

'… a police box, yes.' She could hear the Doctor scratching his chin.

He spent a couple of minutes studying the little cascade of sand and small stones from above them, briefly interrupted when he dropped his everlasting match and had to strike another.

The sound of falling pebbles stopped again. The Doctor dropped his freshly lit match, and in the dark Jo felt his hands pressing on her shoulders so that she was dumped down on the rough ground. She barely had time to complain before the rock face shuddered violently again, and brilliant flashes of light surrounded them. A fresh cacophony of jolts, bangs and scrapes confirmed what she had already half suspected. The crashing noises faded into the distance far below them, and gloom enveloped them once more.

They had both dropped their matches. In the gloom, she could just make out the Doctor fumbling for the box in his pocket. 'I never thought I'd run out of these,' he grumbled.

Jo stared at him. 'Doctor… who's throwing TARDISes at us?'

'It's the same TARDIS, Jo.'

'And those tremors?'

'The same tremor,' said the Doctor. 'It's too close together to be the same earthquake, or aftershocks.'

'Earthquake?' wailed Jo. 'And what are you smiling at? I don't want to be stuck down here in the pitch black dodging police boxes! What are we going to do?'

'Well, it's obviously time for a glass of ouzo,' grinned the Doctor.

'Time for…?' She felt like hitting him. 'Wait a minute, how come I can see you?'

'Your eyes have become accustomed to the dark. And that faint light high above us is our way out. Come on, we'll have to make our move after the next police box. Honestly, you wait for centuries and then four arrive at the same time.'

Jo stretched up her arms in a languorous gesture, and savoured the view across the open-air taverna. A good-looking Greek guy was chatting with the staff at the bar. He was wearing jeans and a khaki vest, and his dark tan was unexpectedly offset by his bleached hair. Perhaps she could catch his eye and get him to join them – he was bound to be better company than the Doctor today.

Either the noon sun or her second ouzo had warmed her nicely. She was just about forgetting their half-mile trek down a dusty road, but not quite ready to forgive the Doctor for his infuriating reluctance to explain what was happening. Unless she counted some incomprehensible nonsense about causality spirals that made her dizzy just to think about.

The palm umbrella over their table offered cool relief from the sun. Jo looked into her empty glass. 'I'm glad you think we've got time to sit around drinking, Doctor.'

'Time,' chuckled the Doctor. 'Ah yes, time. Well, there's always time for a glass of ouzo and some interesting conversation.' He was treating their predicament with apparent equanimity. In fact, he seemed more perturbed by some scorch marks in the velvet of his sleeve. 'I'm afraid those everlasting matches have left their indelible mark.'

'I suppose it is a smoking jacket,' giggled Jo. 'Are you warm enough?'

'Filthy habit,' he said, oblivious to her sarcasm. 'I blame myself for not persuading Sir Walter that potatoes were a more profitable crop.'

Jo caught the waiter's eye. 'Σερβιτορε? Θα ηθεδα ενα κιαο ροδακινα.' His reply baffled her, and the Doctor laughed aloud. 'What's the problem?' Jo asked him. 'Don't they have fruit juice in the Greek islands?'

'Well, you asked him for a kilo of peaches,' said the Doctor. 'Δενπειραζει,' he told the waiter. 'Besides, we haven't got time to eat.'

'We seem to have time to sit around boozing. How can you be so calm at a time like this?'

'Like what? The TARDIS is going nowhere. Or rather, it's going to the same place repeatedly. We need a little time to think things through. Better to do that out here than in those cramped caves.' He steepled his fingers and leaned his elbows on the rickety table. 'Think it through, Jo. What do we need to get the TARDIS back?'

'Heavy lifting gear, at the least. Or a large net, perhaps? Catch it on the way past.'

'Getting it out of a time loop is the tricky bit. Didn't you understand what I told you about causality spirals?'

59

'I heard you talking,' muttered Jo, 'but you didn't seem to be saying anything. Oh, I know! We could ask the Brig!'

'We're in 1950s Greece,' the Doctor reminded her, 'that much was clear from the instruments before I got out. So no UNIT, no Brigadier.' He wasn't looking at Jo now; his attention seemed to have wandered to the table on their right, where a balding, middle-aged man in a crumpled linen suit wafted himself with his straw hat. 'The Brig was a Second Lieutenant around these parts about seven or eight years ago, so by now he'll be earning his promotion back on active service in Palestine. So instead...' And at this point he leapt to his full and rather daunting height, sprang across the taverna, and plonked himself down rudely at the adjacent table. '...perhaps we should ask this gentleman, hmm?'

'Doc-tor!' hissed Jo. She followed him to the table, and smiled sheepishly at the solitary man who sat there toying with the remains of a fruit salad. 'I'm sorry about my uncle.' Jo tapped her forehead. 'Touch of the sun. Come along, uncle...'

'Δενμενοιαζει,' said the man, and then in unaccented English: 'My name is Professor Katsoudas. You should have joined me sooner; I could have offered you some of my peaches.'

'Very funny,' said Jo. Then she dropped into a spare seat, furious. 'Hang on... you must be *spying* on us!'

'Yes, yes,' snapped the Doctor, 'never mind all that, old man. I want to know why you brought us here.'

'Brought us...?' began Jo. 'Wait a minute, do you two know each other?'

'Not exactly, Jo,' said the Doctor. 'But I recognise a Time Lord when I see one – even one who is trying to shield his mind from friendly inquiry by a fellow Time Lord.'

Professor Katsoudas heaved a deep sigh. 'Oh, all right,' he conceded. He reached out to twist the top off what Jo had assumed was a table decoration. Instead, it seemed to be stuffed full of electronic equipment. A hexagonal aerial popped up, and started to spin in an uncertain circle accompanied by a warbling whistle. Jo felt her ears go pop and had to swallow to hear properly again.

Yet no one else in the taverna seemed to notice this weird commotion from their table. Her good-looking Greek at the bar was now wending his way across the taverna with a tray of drinks, unconcerned by the racket. She wished fleetingly that he might come over to their table and talk to her. He raised his tray high, laughing and apologising to a couple at a nearby table as he tried to negotiate a way past without spilling over them –

– and then he suddenly wasn't there any more. Jo spotted him back at the bar, where he was loading the same drinks onto his tray and paying the waiter for them. She watched his progress across the taverna – hoisting the tray on one hand, laughing and apologising to the couple at another table, squeezing past… and vanishing. He was back at the bar again.

'Do you make a habit of this?' inquired the Doctor tartly. 'It's amusing enough as a parlour trick, but the time loop back in the tunnels is much bigger.'

'Yes,' said Katsoudas smugly. 'That's why we've brought you here.'

'We?'

'Well… yes. I've agreed to help Them out for a change. It's a little tricky back on the old Home World at the moment.'

Jo thought that the Doctor's previous sunny disposition had vanished as fast as an English afternoon. 'What's gone wrong this time?'

Katsoudas coughed apologetically. 'They put a group of their renegades into a time loop, as they do, and then… erm… cast them off on random coordinates.'

Jo thought that the Doctor looked angry enough to slap the unfortunate Professor. With what seemed like a huge effort he appeared to control his temper. 'Renegades indeed!'

'Unfortunately,' said Katsoudas, 'the renegade ship ended up stuck and time-looped deep under the Aegean Sea.'

'Along with my TARDIS!' spluttered the Doctor.

'Yes, and you see,' continued Katsoudas, his enthusiasm building, and clearly oblivious to the Doctor's growing annoyance, 'if you manage to untangle the time loop, then you can have your TARDIS back!'

'It was *you* that dragged the TARDIS here!'

'Well, They provided some assistance.' Katsoudas studied his nails modestly.

'Wait a minute!' said Jo. 'If the Doctor untangles this time loop, won't the renegades be able to escape?'

The Professor smiled at her as though she might be one of his more slow-witted students. 'If he frees the renegades, then They can't be blamed, can They? Couldn't be seen to do it for Themselves.' He pouted at the Doctor. 'Tricky for Them. Small problem with an unsound conviction, you know how it is.'

'Why should I trust you?'

'You shouldn't, of course. But if you don't, you'll never get your TARDIS back.' The Professor made a desultory effort to finish his fruit salad.

The Doctor seemed to be considering things carefully. While he did so, Jo watched her good-looking Greek thread his way across the taverna again. He must be about her age, but his hair made him look older. Was it actually bleached? His eyebrows were also quite white, startling against his warmly-tanned skin. He raised his arm, and she could see his bicep flex as it took the weight of the tray. A laugh, an apology, and he'd vanished abruptly – already, impossibly, back at the bar.

'All right,' the Doctor was saying. 'How do you propose to get down to these trapped renegades? We could be snatched up by that wretched temporal loop and trapped in it forever. Is there a way to drill down the rocks to either side?'

'I have a better idea. As far as these locals are concerned, I'm a seismologist. And I have a drill site on the next island with which we can get a borehole down to the renegades' trapped ship!'

'How convenient.'

'So, if we're ready, we can go to the drill site,' concluded Katsoudas. He flicked one long finger at the table-top device, and the aerial folded back into the machine.

Jo had forgotten about the horrible warbling whistle until it stopped. She felt her ears go pop again, so she closed her eyes and gave a big gulp. When she reopened them, she was mortified to see the bleach-blond guy standing over their table, smiling his heart-melting smile at her. 'Do you think I might… ?' he asked. His English was slightly accented.

'Er…? Um…?' she flustered.

The newcomer gestured with his tray. Jo finally understood, and leaned back to allow him to place the tray on the table. As he reached past her, she could see that the tuft of hair in his armpit was white, too. Only after noticing this did she spot that he had brought four drinks to the table, even though she and the Doctor had not been sat there when they were ordered. 'You were expecting us?'

'Yes,' said the newcomer. 'But I fell into conversation with my friend Christos, the barman, or I'd have returned sooner. Sorry.'

'I should hope so, Nikos,' said Katsoudas. 'I was beginning to think you'd never get back here.'

The saltwater spray drenched the powerboat, threatening to soak them even as they huddled at the rear. Jo wasn't sorry to sit close to Nikos Spiridakis at the rear of the boat. She put her ear close to his mouth to hear him better, and felt his warm breath against her cheek. Jo only half-listened to him explain about their drill site, the Deep Geodynamic Laboratory here in the Gulf of Corinth predicting earthquakes in the Alpide belt.

Meanwhile, more predictable than any earthquake, the Doctor had insisted on steering the vessel, delighted in his ability to throw the thirty-five-foot Chris-Craft Constellation across the bobbing waves. Katsoudas watched over him with a mixture of amusement and faint concern.

The boat crested another tall wave, and Jo snuggled closer to Spiridakis. She became preoccupied with the way his hands formed shapes in the air to describe how oceanic and continental plates collided. 'Strong interpolate coupling,' he explained, 'means a fault that can accumulate stress.'

'Tell me about it!' she laughed.

'OK.' His hands created new shapes. 'By inserting an array of seismometers, we've create a moving net of geological sensors which can detect microquakes.' Not quite what she'd meant, but she loved the sound of his voice. 'So now we should be able to predict larger quakes in future. And this is detecting them directly, not through miles of rock that obscure and distort signals. We've drilled down a kilometre, so we can see it up close! We'll learn so much more about the structure and the evolution and the... *dynamics* of the area. Maybe also the physical processes controlling earthquakes, volcanic eruptions...'

'Speaking of physical processes...' she said. 'How is it your hair is so white? You can't be albino, your eyes and skin are so brown.'

At first she thought she'd offended him, but then she saw that he was just surprised by the change of subject. He was so earnest, and so good looking, she thought. So passionate about his field of expertise. Spiridakis laughed for the first time since the taverna. 'I think it must be stress. He works us so hard!' he shouted, so that Katsoudas would hear. 'I had very dark hair when I started on the project three years ago. Perhaps it's just sympathy for the old guys I'm working with!' And with this, he was off again on his favourite subject – fault-zones and rock deformation and accretionary wedges. But while he wanted to talk about the role of fluids in earthquake recurrence, she found herself just staring into his fluid brown eyes, alive with enthusiasm.

'Nikos, I could listen to you talk about persistent minor seismicity all day!'

The Doctor had reluctantly relinquished the wheel to Katsoudas, who steered the Chris-Craft to its mooring. At an adjacent berth, a small crowd of American GIs packed empty crates onto a small transport vessel, ready to sail out to their ship anchored further offshore. Katsoudas acknowledged them with a nod as he led his own small party into the main building – a squat, flat-roofed building that reminded the Doctor of a prefab house.

He drew Jo aside before they went in, and pointed to a tall framework of ironwork and wheels that clearly indicated a lift mechanism. Spiridakis was walking towards it. 'Jo, you should accompany your young friend. It's obvious that he's close to this whole thing.'

'From what he was saying on the boat? About the Laboratory?'

'No, just from looking at him. All the dead cells in his body have been affected by temporal acceleration. A mid-term effect of time distortion.'

Jo frowned.

'His hair – it's too old for him. And did you notice his nails are cracked and distorted, too? Because he's sweating in this heat, the effect is less obvious in the dead skin on the outer layer of his epidermis.'

'Eww!' said Jo, scrunching up her nose.

'See if he will show you this deep dig.'

'How?'

'Oh, I don't know,' said the Doctor innocently. 'Tell him you want to investigate strong interpolate coupling, perhaps?' He grinned at her stuck-out tongue.

Jo caught up with the young Greek, and took his arm. A couple of grey-haired men, late middle-aged, stepped from the lift. From their brief conversation with Spiridakis, the Doctor knew they must be colleagues completing their underground shift and now returning to the surface.

The Doctor hurried into the squat building to look for Professor Katsoudas. The main room was a chaotic mix of electronic gadgetry and paperwork. Crumpled, discarded scraps bore witness to calculations of shear modulus, and faded wall charts showed isoseismic maps. An accelerograph was half buried beneath sheaves of paper containing temporal correlations of earthquake focal mechanisms.

The two grey-haired men entered the room briefly, collected their jackets, and shouted 'Ζαιπετε' to Katsoudas before leaving.

'Temporal correlations,' mused the Doctor, and then more loudly: 'A lot of this equipment is very advanced for the 1950s, Professor.'

Katsoudas looked up from where he was adjusting a broad bank of equipment. 'Couldn't you have guessed that from my temporal table-top toy earlier?'

'I'm more concerned,' admonished the Doctor, 'that this is all so freely displayed and available to your research team.' He gestured after the two who had just left. 'How many all together... half a dozen?'

'Five,' said Katsoudas. 'Six, if you include Szef. I developed this equipment myself, and Senator Szef is the head of the US Senate subcommittee who funded it.'

'I suppose Szef and the others think you're researching earthquake prediction, not rescuing falsely-imprisoned aliens. Poor Spiridakis, everything he was telling Jo on the boat is just a sham.'

'Not exactly,' said Katsoudas.

The Doctor raised his eyebrows to suggest he couldn't believe this.

'Really,' protested Katsoudas. 'In fact, I can predict earthquakes more accurately than they yet realise. Let me demonstrate.'

Around them, as though issuing from the rocks of the island, a bass note began to vibrate the building around them. Paper piles scattered and smeared over the equipment. The naked bulb in the centre of the room swung like a mad pendulum.

The Doctor sprang over to the seismogram. 'How could you possibly have predicted that from these readings?'

Katsoudas laughed. 'Of course I could predict it. I started it!' He swivelled one of the controls back, and almost immediately the rumbling that had engulfed the room began to die away, until only the wild swinging of the light bulb bore evidence of any disturbance.

The Doctor confronted Katsoudas, arms akimbo, face like stone. 'That's incredibly dangerous.'

'Nonsense. You saw how easily I started it. Just like conducting an orchestra –'

'– and you were lucky to stop it. You're messing with the basic forces of nature, man! A soprano could start an avalanche by singing one pure note, but could she then stop it?' He broke off as a dreadful thought struck him. 'The lift mechanism! They could be trapped underground!'

'There's no one down there,' replied Katsoudas. 'We saw Costas and Manolis come up after they finished the final shift of the day.'

The Doctor was already hurrying from the room. 'You fool! Jo asked Spiridakis to take her down in the lift.'

As soon as the quake started, Spiridakis had thrown himself over Jo to protect her. The drop had been short-lived but frightening, and had ended abruptly in an emergency stop. Jo squeezed out from his embrace carefully to check the phone on the cage wall of the lift. 'The landline's dead,' she called across to Spiridakis, and then immediately panicked that he might be, too. Her hurried examination revealed that he was unconscious. His breathing was a little ragged, and his left arm was twisted, possibly dislocated.

Jo could see they had stopped only a couple of metres above their destination. The lift gates were ajar, and the internal light threw a patch of light into the rocky corridor beyond. Maybe she could find help for Spiridakis. She dangled herself over the edge of the cage by her fingertips, and dropped the remaining metre.

No sooner had she reached the rocky platform and dusted herself down than the lift behind her suddenly crackled back into life, and started its ascent back to the surface.

Jo didn't even have time to shout after it. Light seemed to flare up behind her. She turned to face the monstrous silhouette of a huge creature just as it opened its jaws. The rancorous stench of decaying meat almost overpowered Jo. She finally found her voice in time to scream.

When the buckled lift reached the surface, the Doctor was dismayed to find only Spiridakis struggling groggily to his feet. The Doctor loped back to the main building to accost Katsoudas, and found the Professor apparently still fiddling with the lift's emergency override controls. 'Come on!' insisted the Doctor. 'You have an injured man in that cage, and there's no sign of my friend. Can you send me back down in the lift?'

'I've reset it,' said Katsoudas, 'we can all go down to the drill head.'

The Doctor almost dragged him from the room.

As they descended in the lift cage, Katsoudas loudly berated Spiridakis for allowing Jo to accompany him to the drill head. His disoriented junior allowed this torrent of invective to wash over him or, the Doctor considered, perhaps he was in no fit state to properly understand it. Spiridakis couldn't even explain where Jo was – the last he remembered was when the lift gears had slipped during the earthquake.

And on that very subject... There was a powerful vibration, a throbbing bass note again that was more than just the lift mechanism working. The Doctor confronted Katsoudas: 'What have you done?'

Katsoudas smiled, unconcerned. He was even humming a little aria.

Around them, the lift groaned. Small stones began to cascade down the walls and rattle against the ironwork.

'You've started another local earthquake, haven't you? And we're travelling down into it. Are you quite insane?'

'Let me show you, Doctor,' said Katsoudas, 'how I can conduct this particular avalanche like an orchestra.'

Jo sat on a rocky spur and calmly waited for the monster approach her for a fourth time.

Unlike the previous occasions, Jo noticed, the whole area around her seemed to be vibrating. And yet when the concealed door slid quietly open again, the same powerful tungsten-bright radiance overwhelmed the flickering lights of the lift behind Jo, just as before. She was ready for this, of course, and shaded her eyes to watch the alien stalk its way over the polished floor of its spacecraft and then across to her.

The creature was the ugliest thing Jo had seen outside of the UNIT fancy dress ball. She decided this time that its drooping fangs and broad flat face meant it was more like a walrus than a warthog. And a bipedal walrus in a spacesuit, at that. With appalling breath.

It loomed beside her, and its jaw gaped.

'Hello again,' she grinned. 'I believe we've met before.'

Right on cue, the spaceship door snapped shut, extinguishing the light. Simultaneously, the creature flipped out of existence.

'See you again soon,' said Jo. 'This is getting predictable.'

Only this time, it wasn't. 'Miss Grant,' a familiar voice said. 'What a pleasant surprise.'

'Jo? Jo!' The Doctor's voice was muffled in the rocky enclosure beside the lift. Around him, the penetrating vibration of a minor earthquake continued. It had built slowly during their long descent.

Spiridakis stepped from the lift cage behind him. 'All our sensors are on the next level. I didn't know we could descend to this further level.'

'There's nothing down here,' said the Doctor. Even his keen eyes could make out only a small blank enclosure of rock.

'Oh, I wouldn't say that,' smiled Katsoudas. A door opened from nowhere, and they were bathed in a harsh radiance.

The Doctor stepped back, instinctively adopting a defensive posture as the squat bulk of a huge creature loomed at them. From the sight of its hairless grey forehead and powerful curved mandible, not to mention its powerful odour, the Doctor recognised it as an Odobenidan. Its tiny eyes were located high and toward the sides of its head. They swivelled to look glassily in the Doctor's direction.

Before he could decide whether to greet it or fight it, the Doctor was astonished when it simply vanished and all the lights seemed to go out. His eyes adjusted to the weaker illumination from the lift. He could feel the earth tremor still rippling beneath his feet.

Spiridakis cowered in the lift cage. Katsoudas was unfazed by the creature's appearance and, indeed, its disappearance.

'Another of your time loops?'

'No, Doctor. We're close to the imprisoned renegades.'

The Doctor barked a laugh. 'Renegades? I don't think so, Professor. What's really going on? Or do I have to ask that Odobenidan sentry?'

Katsoudas moved forward to join him, bringing a reluctant Spiridakis with him. 'We could certainly do that. He'll be back in a minute.'

And so he was, in a fresh blaze of light. Katsoudas pushed the Doctor towards the alien, and dragged Spiridakis with him. And this time, the Odobenidan did not vanish before their eyes, but neither did it show any signs of seeing them.

'You idiot, Katsoudas!' groaned the Doctor. 'You've brought us into the time loop ourselves.'

'No matter,' said Katsoudas, already stepping through the door into the alien spacecraft. 'I'm going to convert the kinetic energy of the earthquake into temporal energy and release us all.'

The Doctor followed him through into the Odobenidan ship. Several of the thickset aliens wandered past, apparently indifferent to their presence. 'You're remarkably well informed about transitional temporal mechanics, Professor.'

'Well, I must admit that I had a bit of help. Ah, here we are in the control room. Yes, I can say that I couldn't have managed it without the assistance of Senator Szef.'

'I mean the theory and the technology, not the funding from your generous US sponsor,' said the Doctor. 'Though I'd very much like to meet him.'

'You already have, Doctor,' said Senator Szef, who was sat at a suite of controls on the far side of the room.

With hindsight, the Doctor reflected, he shouldn't have been quite so surprised to discover that Senator Szef was the Master.

The Master was childishly pleased to see how surprised the Doctor was. And he relished the way his old rival tried to conceal his relief when reunited with Miss Grant.

He had no need to conceal his own surprise. That had already occurred when the Odobenidans had brought the police box into their ship. How long ago had that been? Less than a day for the Doctor, perhaps, but it felt like a month for the Master. He studied the Doctor. 'It's surely no coincidence that you have found me here in mid-twentieth century Earth?'

'You flatter yourself,' said the Doctor, who was meandering around the room and trying not to look as though he was studying all the controls. 'What brought you here?'

'I offered to help the Odobenidans with a business transaction – a spot of temporal mechanics, on a consultancy basis.'

He wasn't pleased when the Doctor laughed out loud. 'So this time trap is of your making? You really should have paid more attention in the Academy, old fellow.' He jabbed the nearest Odobenidan with his elbow. 'And you're still letting him take charge?'

'Spare me your sarcasm, Doctor. And there's little point trying to talk our hosts around, they're currently almost exactly repeating their actions on a thirty-minute cycle – less at the periphery of the looped area, of course. They'll have forgotten what you said in about five more minutes. They barely acknowledge my presence any more.'

Miss Grant piped up in her over-earnest way: 'I suppose that being a Time Lord you can move around within the time loop.'

'But not beyond it. That's how I was able to drag you in, Miss Grant. And why I must make best use of Professor Katsoudas now that he is here... No, don't!' he snapped suddenly. He slammed his gloved hand down sharply, and trapped the fingers of the timid young Greek who had been examining the equipment on a nearby counter. 'Touch nothing, young Nikos, or I will dislocate your other arm, too. And then as the time loop embraces you fully, you'll suffer that fresh pain every thirty minutes, forever.'

Knowing that the new arrivals were now helpless and cowed, the Master began to brief Katsoudas before the time loop had a chance to affect the Professor.

The Doctor drew Jo aside, and explained urgently to her. 'I'll distract the Master, but you and Spiridakis must talk with Professor Katsoudas. Even if you end up trapped in the time loop together, you must spend that time persuading him to prevent this earthquake!'

Jo pointed to the blue shape in the corner of the room. 'Could we kidnap him in your magic blue box?'

'In dangerous situations like these, the TARDIS is programmed to take off as soon as the pilot steps on board. That would be disastrous.'

'So why not just let the Master and these creatures escape and leave the planet?'

'Jo,' said the Doctor earnestly, 'the Odobenidans may decide to *stay* on Earth. But worse, releasing this ship would exaggerate the effects of the earthquake. You can feel it building around us now, can't you? Now, imagine a tsunami wiping clear every beach in the Mediterranean. It wouldn't stop until it had washed right over Gibraltar. Allowing this criminal gang of alien miscreants loose would be the least of Earth's immediate worries!'

'All right, Doctor, I'll do my best to persuade the Professor.'

While Jo explained to Spiridakis what she was planning, the Doctor stepped around the nearest couple of burly Odobenidans and drew the Master to one side.

'You know what you're doing, of course?'

'I'm suffering your prattling distractions, as usual Doctor.' The Master continued his work without looking up.

'I didn't plan to get stuck down this deep bore hole, y'know. Though it's probably fortuitous that I did.'

'Doctor,' said the Master, 'I didn't plan to get stuck talking to a deep bore like you. Luck had nothing to do with that.'

'You're unleashing uncontrollable forces…'

'Oh Doctor, you're not going to go on about sopranos and avalanches again, are you?'

The Doctor stared at him pensively. 'How could you know I said that to Professor Katsoudas? He hasn't had the opportunity to…'

The Doctor's train of thought was interrupted by the return of Katsoudas. He was gripping Jo's hand fiercely, dragging her with him. Spiridakis followed them both, dazed and bemused, protesting that the Professor should stop hurting Jo.

Despite himself, the Doctor was impressed. 'I must concede your mental prowess is remarkable,' he told the Master. 'When I first met Katsoudas, I recognised a Time Lord mind. I had no idea it was yours.'

'I'll accept that as a compliment, Doctor. It was a happy accident that brought the Professor's investigative dig so close to this ship in the first place. And although I couldn't step beyond the edge of the time loop, I was able to get close enough to hypnotise him without drawing him into the trap himself. He's been my eyes and ears for months now. Though in practical terms, for me that's been decades down here.' He rolled his eyes theatrically. 'When your TARDIS literally fell into my hands, I had

Katsoudas involve you because I thought you might help him. But then dear foolish Miss Grant went missing. And so here we are, having to make do without your unwitting assistance.'

The rumbling, grinding noise of rock crushing against rock grew abruptly louder. A couple of the Odobenidans looked around incuriously.

'In any event,' concluded the Master, 'the US military installed an extra generator today, so Katsoudas was able to kick off a seismic reaction that will generate enough power to break this temporal loop.' He waved in the direction of a tall plain cupboard nearby. 'I couldn't use the equipment in my TARDIS, of course, because that's trapped within the loop already.'

'Please don't do this,' said the Doctor. Behind him, Spiridakis was growing increasingly frustrated with Katsoudas, whose grip on Jo had tightened. 'Now that I *am* here, we could try to combine our TARDISes to escape. Leave the Odobenidans. Stop this infernal earthquake.'

'No, Doctor,' the Master admonished him. 'I can hardly leave my clients behind. Besides, I have an agreement with them about my new role on Earth once they've recalled their mothership. It's a simple choice.'

'Choice?' raged the Doctor. The whole ship was quivering and rattling now as the vibrations grew. 'The real choice is whether or not you allow this huge earthquake to devastate the Mediterranean.'

The Master laughed at this. During this momentary distraction, Katsoudas relinquished his grip on Jo's arm, and took an uncertain step forward towards his controller. The Master snapped an immediate look straight at him, and suddenly Katsoudas was also laughing. Too hard.

'Stop it,' said the Doctor coldly. 'Don't force him, you're hurting him.'

The tumult of noise from the earthquake shook and shuddered everything around them. The Odobenidans continued to sleepwalk their way around the ship.

The Master laughed still harder at the Doctor's anger, until Katsoudas's laughter finally coughed to a halt. The Professor's eyes brimmed with tears. The Doctor couldn't decide whether they were caused by exertion or by shame.

'I think that really is enough,' said the Doctor.

Jo tried to decipher the look in the Doctor's eyes. It was as though the Master's treatment of Katsoudas has brought him to a difficult decision. He turned away from her and faced the Master, his hands clasped behind his back like a minor royal. In the clamour and confusion all around them, Jo almost didn't notice that he was waggling the TARDIS key at her behind his back. Of course – the Doctor couldn't open the box, but *she* could!

'Katsoudas is already breaking free of your control,' he shouted to the Master over the tumult. 'If he was in the neutral time of a TARDIS, he'd be completely free of you.'

Jo looked around for the Professor. He had gripped Nikos by the shoulders, and was staring closely into his face. The grip didn't seem to hurt Nikos, despite his dislocated arm. 'Come on guys,' Jo urged them both, 'we're getting out of here!' She checked whether the Master was watching her before she hurried to the Doctor's TARDIS and opened the door. An Odobenidan soldier shuffled past, looking right through her as though she wasn't there.

She bundled Katsoudas through the doors, and looked back to see what had happened to Nikos. He had moved in the opposite direction, and was adjusting controls on a panel.

The Master spotted Jo in the TARDIS doorway. 'A nice try, Miss Grant,' he smiled.

'Nikos!' she yelled across the room. 'Come on!'

The Master's smile evaporated instantly when he saw what Nikos was doing. 'Stop that!'

Before she could see what happened next, Jo was dragged back into the TARDIS by Katsoudas, and the doors closed.

'Professor, what are you doing?'

Katsoudas was at the TARDIS console. 'We can ride out the temporal distortion here. This vessel will be spat out like a champagne cork from a shaken bottle.' The monitor screen jumped into life above their heads. The growing earthquake made the image jump and wobble.

'But the Doctor and Nikos!' cried Jo.

On the monitor, she could see the Doctor wresting the Master away from the panel where the young Greek worked feverishly at the controls. Nikos seemed oblivious to the pain in his dislocated arm.

With a heave, the Doctor threw the Master head over heels across the room. The Master stumbled to his feet between a couple of indifferent Odobenidans. 'You're too late, Doctor!' he snarled. He turned smartly on his heel, and stepped into his own TARDIS.

The relayed image swam before Jo's eyes. 'We must rescue them!'

'That room is full of time eddies,' said Katsoudas. He slumped on the TARDIS console, suddenly exhausted. 'We'd not survive.'

Jo stared frantically at the monitor. In one corner of the room, an Odobenidan slumped to the floor, its skin atrophying in seconds until it was reduced to bones. Just beside it, another melted into its uniform, the tusks withdrawing up into its shrinking face, and Jo realised it was ageing backwards.

The Doctor seemed unaffected, and was pulling Nikos away from the controls. The young Greek twisted around, and Jo saw that his hair was now dark brown. Another step away from the controls, though, and he was white-haired again, his back stooped, his face suddenly like an old man's. The Doctor clutched at him desperately, seizing his thin, withered

71

body, urging him to the safety of the TARDIS. But the time eddy washed relentlessly over them, and the Doctor was left clasping the brittle bones of a human skeleton in the shredded remains of a khaki vest.

Jo wailed in despair, and opened the TARDIS doors, ready to rush out to Nikos.

Before she could leave, the Doctor was at the doors. 'Too late. Stay inside. He's turned the seismic energies into a localised timequake.' Now he was at the TARDIS controls, adjusting the scanner image. 'Multiple chronostrophic planes shifting against each other, distorting local time.'

'What's happening?' moaned Jo.

'Your brave young friend seems to have confined the effects to the immediate area. This whole area is being twisted out of existence, with surgical precision.'

The monitor image flared, distorted, and vanished. The TARDIS bucked and lurched sideways, throwing Jo to the floor. A giddy wave of confusion overwhelmed her, and Jo swooned in a sick faint.

After the cacophony of the timequake, the quiet hum of the TARDIS controls was a blessed relief. It smelled a lot better than the foetid atmosphere of the Odobenidan ship, too, Jo realised. The monitor now showed an expanse of empty sea, with a bobbing motion that suggested the TARDIS was floating, though she could feel no movement inside the ship.

Katsoudas was a forlorn heap of crumpled linen on the floor. 'You weren't a Time Lord after all,' Jo told him bitterly. 'I can't even blame you for killing Nikos, because you were controlled by the Master all the time. Even the Doctor was fooled by you. But none of that time stuff was your work, was it?'

Katsoudas bridled at this. 'I was his willing assistant. He was... my academic supervisor, guiding me – advising, not controlling. Teaching. You must have known, when I hypnotised Spiridakis – that was easier than I had anticipated, because he so much wanted to rescue you, Miss Grant. More than he wanted to save the project, I finally realised.'

Jo gasped. 'You mean you were free of the Master before you entered the TARDIS?'

'Yes. I knew that I no longer wanted him in my mind, no longer needed him there. He wanted to control, I will create. I can remember quite enough to reconstruct my equipment.' It was as though her harsh pity had galvanised him. His mind was obviously racing now, alive with possibilities. 'I could put together another of my table-top temporal toys as a demo to get more funding!'

'Oh dear,' said the Doctor, quietly. Jo had almost forgotten he was listening from the far side of the room, where he was making a pot of rose pouchong. 'I was rather hoping to persuade you not to do that. I wondered why my TARDIS ended up here. We weren't really drawn here by the Master, how could he have reached out to us? No, we were sent here by the Time Lords. Which means that I was supposed to sort out the mess for them after all.' He rubbed his cheeks pensively between both hands. 'I'm sorry to say that I finally know what that mess was... or rather, is.'

'You can be on your way, then,' Katsoudas said. 'Leave me to my experiments in peace.'

'I don't think so,' replied the Doctor slowly.

Jo stared at him. 'Doctor, what do you mean?' She could see he was looking at the Professor oddly. 'Surely you can just explain to the Professor how reckless it would be to continue his research?' The Doctor's expression remained unchanged, so she said: 'Come on, let's have that cup of tea and talk about it.'

'No time!' snapped Katsoudas, and leapt to his feet. 'I must get back to work.'

'Time,' smiled the Doctor. 'Ah yes, time. Well, there's always time for a cup of tea and some interesting conversation.' But his smile didn't reach his eyes, Jo noticed. They were full of hesitancy, the same look he'd had in the TARDIS doorway when it had first tottered on the brink of the precipice.

The Doctor began to pour the tea, and Jo wondered: What will he decide?

The seismologist looked up at Charley and her robed friend.

'So there it is. I thought I'd survived the timequake, only to fall victim to the aftershock.' He chuckled mirthlessly. 'I suppose I should feel ashamed.'

The robed man nodded. 'We all have things from our past we are ashamed of, isn't that so?'

Charley realised he was looking straight at her.

'Yes. Yes, probably.'

The robed man cocked his head slightly. 'Why are you here, then?'

Charley thought about this for a moment. 'I... I'm not really sure. I haven't known the Doctor very long.'

The seismologist shrugged and flicked a couple of pages in his notebook. 'None of us did. Long enough I suppose to wind up here though.'

Charley frowned. 'But I can't think of anything I've done to bring me here. I mean, I'm not perfect. I ran away from my school to be... to be where the Doctor met me. But nothing that affected... well, this Web of Time thing.'

'Are you sure?' That was the robed man again.

Charley suddenly felt very cold. Of course, there was one very obvious thing. Something she had tried to put right out of her mind, and yet she knew that it was probably the reason. She had always hoped she could ignore it.

'I'm dead,' she said simply.

The seismologist smiled at her, not unkindly. 'My dear young lady, evidently that's not true. No matter what we have done in the eyes of whoever is judging us, none of us are dead.'

'That's not true,' said Charley. 'The flowers on the bar. The story of the Ghost...'

The robed man shrugged. 'That's different. The Ghost should never really have existed in the first place.'

'Is that an excuse to deny it life?' asked Charley. 'Who are we to make moral judgements like that?'

'We're not,' said a new voice. 'But the Doctor evidently is.'

The seismologist shook his head at the newcomer, a young Englishman in a black leather jacket and denim trousers.

'That's not fair, Jake,' the seismologist said.

Jake scratched at his close-cropped hair. 'Seems that way to me. Thinks he's God.'

The robed man frowned. 'And you are?'

The seismologist stood. 'My apologies. Jake Morgan, this is an Inquisitor from Braspral and... I'm awfully sorry...'

'Charley Pollard. From Hampshire.'

Jake Morgan shrugged. 'You're wrong about something else, Prof.'

'What's that?'

'About no one being dead.'

Professor Katsoudas frowned and looked into the crowd. 'I'm sorry, I wasn't aware of anyone there who is –'

'No,' said Jake. 'Not them. Me. I'm dead.'

Charley gasped. 'How? When? Who?'

'Who d'you think,' spat Jake Morgan. 'The Doctor. The Doctor killed me.'

The Dead Man's Story

Andrew Frankham

Jake Morgan looked up from the television upon hearing the front door opening. A big smile spread across his face, and he switched the TV to mute. He leant his neck back so that he could see the hallway through the open door.

'Hi, Fables!' he called.

There was no answer. Jake just smiled more. His girlfriend was up to something, or else she would have replied. He listened as she pottered about in the kitchen. He closed his eyes, imagining her emptying the shopping bags and putting things away. In his mind he could see her reaching the top shelves, her jumper climbing up her back to reveal a tantalising glimpse of the tattoo on her lower spine. He sighed. He was a very lucky man.

'Get your mind out of that gutter, you.'

Jake opened his eyes. Fay was standing before him, having managed to enter the room without him noticing. Despite having been at work all day she looked radiant, unlike most days when she usually looked very drawn. As usual she had her long chestnut hair pulled back in a ponytail, and she was wearing her woolly jumper and faded black jeans.

'It's a nice gutter to be in,' Jake said.

At this Fay screwed up her face. 'Oh my god, I can't believe you just said that! *You* are so corny.'

'Well, you know me, I'm a hopeless romantic. It's why you love me,' Jake said, making a silly face at his girlfriend.

'Yeah.' Suddenly Fay looked a little embarrassed. She placed one hand in her jeans' pocket and looked at the silent TV. 'You know it's a leap year?' She turned back to him and he nodded in reply. 'Know what that means?'

Jake pursed his lips together and shrugged.

'It means I get to do this.' She removed her hand from her pocket and lowered herself to one knee. It was only then that Jake noticed that she was holding a little box, from which she removed a ring. She placed the box on the floor, took Jake's hand in hers, and looked him directly in the eyes. 'Will you marry me?'

Jake's reaction was instant. 'Yes, oh, yes.'

Fay's face fell, and she released his hand. 'Oh. You were supposed to say no.'

'I was?' He could not hide the confusion in his voice.

'Yeah, it's tradition. The woman proposes on a leap year, the man refuses and then he has to buy her a silk dress to make up for it. I wanted a lovely silk dress.' It was only then that Fay smiled, her eyes glinting, and poked him playfully in the stomach.

Jake laughed and hugged her. 'You nutter,' he said, and helped her put the ring on his finger; he then reached forward and kissed her. 'You'll have the best silk dress ever,' he promised.

Jake Morgan was buoyantly crossing the road when, through the driving rain, he saw a most unusual sight.

A blue box was standing next to the entrance of the petrol station. Above the doors, one of which was open, were the words 'Police Public Call Box'. Jake had only seen such a box in one place before, although he had no idea what it was for, really. He knew that it had not been standing there the previous night when he had popped over to the garage for some Pepsi, which left him wondering why anyone would place it there during the small hours of the morning.

His natural curiosity taking over, he approached the police box to take a peek inside. As he drew nearer he heard a voice from within. It was a man's voice, sounding old and drawn. Jake stopped, caution superseding his curiosity.

'Yes, Jeremy, that one. No, not that one! *That* one there!' the man said, sounding rather peeved.

There was a bang and a flash of light. Jake's hands instinctively rose to cover his eyes, but they could not protect him from the jet of cold air that shot out of the police box. Blasted back, he hit the ground with a crack as his spine collided with the stone paving slabs. Despite the pain that was coursing through his body, part of Jake's mind could still make out a younger male voice coming from nearby.

'Oh, I say!' it said.

Jake lay there for a moment, while the pain subsided to a manageable level. He flexed his fingers and placed his palms on the ground. Slowly he pushed down, attempting to lift his back and expecting much pain for his troubles. He was surprised by the lack of feeling, pain or otherwise, and got to his feet very slowly, just in case.

He looked up and stepped back in surprise. There was a man emerging from the police box, looking at him uncertainly. Jake narrowed his eyes at the man's choice of clothing. Despite the frilly shirt, the way he dressed gave the man an elegant air, enhanced by the fine mane of white hair on top of his lined face.

The man smiled broadly and held a hand out. 'Sorry about that, old chap, Jeremy is a bit clumsy, but he means well.'

Jake smiled. 'I'm fine, mate, probably end up with a sore...'

No sooner had Jake started speaking than the man's expression changed from happy and helpful to confused. He ran a finger across his lips and his eyebrows crossed together. Shaking his head, the man stepped back inside the police box.

'Oh, well don't mind me,' Jake muttered, annoyed by the man's reaction. He marched over to the police box, but before he could set foot inside the door slammed shut.

'Hey!' He shouted and went to slam a fist on the door. His hand passed right through its surface and a strange wheezing and groaning filled the air around him. He stood back, stunned, and cast about for the source of the noise. The sound died down and Jake returned his attention to the blue box, only to find that it was no longer there.

'Bloody hell.' He stretched his arms out before him, half expecting to feel the solid mass against his palms, but there was nothing. 'What was all that about?' he wondered, unsure whether he had imagined the whole episode or not.

Jake Morgan stepped up to the front door a couple of hours later, still a little baffled by the strangeness of the evening so far. It had started off wonderfully enough, but after his possible daydream by the garage and the strange non-reaction from Robert in town, he was beginning to wonder what more could happen before he went to bed.

He reached into his pocket, pulled out his key and moved to insert it into the lock. His hand continued into the door and out the other side. Jake pulled back quickly, only to find that there was no key in his hand after all. He glanced down at his trousers and noticed the shape of the key still inside his tight pocket.

His brow knitted tightly and he looked at the door before him.

With the police box he was almost certain he had made the whole thing up. That there had never been a police box, which is why his hand has passed through it, but this time…

There was no denying what had just happened.

Taking a deep breath, he pushed, and watched his hand sink into the door. He whistled out a breath of amazement.

'Damn,' he said, closing his eyes, and walked forward.

Despite everything Jake still expected to have his nose squashed by the solid door, and was only half surprised when this did not happen. Instead he passed through the wooden door and came out in the small hallway beyond.

'Fay!' he called out, but no reply was forthcoming. All he could hear was the soft sounds of music drifting from the living room. He was about to go check it out when he remembered his shoes. Both he and Fay had agreed at the beginning that shoes were not to be worn indoors.

He knelt down to remove his trainers only to discover that he could not get a grip on them. As with the door his hand passed through the leather *and* his foot, into the floor below. His lifted his hand out of the floor and stood up again, his heart rate increasing.

The first hint of a suspicion was forming in his mind, and he did not like it.

He took a tentative step onto the carpet then raised his foot. Where there should have been a muddy shoeprint there was nothing. He inspected the sole of his shoe, and was unsurprised to discover that there was no mud there, despite the stormy weather outside and the fact that he had cut across the grass to get home and out of the rain.

'Just a sec,' he said and rushed down the hallway to the mirror on the far wall. If it was raining then surely he should have been wet.

He looked into the mirror, and caught his breath at the sight that greeted him. Despite his fears he could see himself in the mirror, but only just. What he saw was a shadow of himself. He still looked like him, but he could see the reflection of the hallway through his semi-transparent body. He ran his hand through his, very dry, blonde hair and his reflection mimicked the action. No contact was made, and he watched with a strange mixture of horror and amazement as his hand went below his hair and into his skull. He twiddled his fingers and was relieved to discover that he could not feel the insides of his head. It was a small consolation.

He thought back to his trip into town, and how Robert had ignored him. At the time Jake had just assumed that his best mate was in a huff about something, maybe simply stressed out because of the long hours he was working, but now, looking at himself in the mirror, Jake was beginning to suspect otherwise. Could it be that Robert had not seen Jake because he was…

Jake shivered. He could not complete that thought.

For a moment he closed his eyes. When he opened them again he almost jumped in shock. Fay stood before the mirror. She was brushing her hair, whistling along with the tune playing in the living room. Seeing her eyes smile, Jake's heart melted as the love he felt for her overtook his reasoning. The deep feeling was soon replaced when he noticed that both of them were occupying the same space.

Jake staggered back a few paces.

Fay still remained before the mirror, completely oblivious to that fact that she had, only a second earlier, been standing *inside* Jake.

'Fay…' he began, but could not find any other words to say. Even if he could, he doubted that she would be able to hear him. He opened his mouth to try again. He had to say something. If anyone would be able to hear him and see him it should be her. They had been through so much together in the previous two years, and he had to believe that their love counted for something. As it turned out he did not need to speak for it was then that Fay turned around. Their eyes met. For several seconds they lingered, and Jake stopped breathing.

The moment passed and Fay continued into the living room. Jake remained where he was standing, his mind awash with the thought that she had seen him. There had been an unmistakable recognition in her eyes.

He followed her into the room and watched as she switched CDs. 'Fay, I know you saw me then. Even if it was just for a second. Come on, babe, look at me again.'

She did not.

He stood there, thinking, and an idea came to him. He walked up behind Fay and leant forward until his mouth was just behind her ear. Slowly, and gently, he blew. Nothing happened. Not a single strand of Fay's hair moved. She stood up and walked over to the sofa, passing through Jake as she did so. He straightened up and turned to watch her.

Jake was not sure how much time passed while he stood there. She listened to her classical music while reading several chapters of Marcel Theroux's latest novel, and then turned the TV on to watch the news. In all that time not once did she look at Jake. Several times he tried to speak to her, but she gave no sign of hearing him. As time passed by Jake's heart sunk further and further. He could not help but think that she was ignoring him on purpose, like Robert had been doing.

He walked across the room, passing through her line of vision, and stood by the window. Outside, the world continued to turn. He stood there for a time, lost in his thoughts. Things would not have seemed so bad if only Fay would acknowledge him, as it was…

'Yes, he went straight there to tell you. You really haven't seen him?'

The words drifted into his thoughts. He turned to see Fay on the phone, a look of concern on her face. He moved forward and knelt before her. She looked right through him, but nonetheless Jake reached out a hand to comfort her. For a split second he had forgotten about his condition and was, as a result, taken aback when his hand passed through her leg. Jake pulled away as if stung.

'Come off it, you're pulling my leg, right? He's been gone for four hours, Rob.' Fay paused while Robert said something. She smiled. 'Yes, we've got engaged! And we've set a date for the wedding.'

Jake sighed, as the tears built up in his eyes. Seeing the smile on Fay's face was too much. He thought back to the moment they had agreed to get married. After he had promised to buy her a silk dress they had hugged. In that moment he felt like he was one with her, more so than he ever did when they made love. He sighed again. How could the wedding ever happen now?

'Yes, a date,' Fay was saying, the happiness in her voice slowly diminishing. 'He'd better bloody get back soon, though, otherwise we'll seriously have to rethink the whole thing.'

His heart aching, he turned to leave his home.

Jake Morgan stood at the edge of the pavement, waiting for the lights to change. People were shuffling into position behind him. Some of them, the more impatient ones, were barging forward, intent on being the first ones across the road, as if there was some kind of prize for getting there first. He hated the way people in London pushed each other aside, as if no one else existed but them. He took a glance behind him, just in time to notice a very large man shove forward. Jake braced himself, not wanting to be pushed onto the road and as a consequence into the oncoming traffic. Once more he had forgotten his new condition, and was reminded when the large man stepped inside him.

Without any further thought Jake crossed the road, elated with the knowledge that nothing could hurt him. Not even the double decker that was racing towards him.

Once he was across the road his mind went back to Fay. Being around her and not being able touch her was more than he could stomach, which was why he was now on the streets of Hammersmith, hoping the distance from Fay would relieve a little of that pain. Darkness had fallen since he had returned home, which provided Jake with the illusion that it was later than it really was.

He turned onto King Street, and was happy to see that there were few people about. It was a Friday, which meant that soon the road would be bustling with people; some heading to and from the Lyric Theatre, others coming out to have a pizza. He liked to come here on a weekend evening, it was one of the rare occasions that he felt that Londoners became aware of each other. As it was the few people presently on King Street were so caught up in their own lives that they barely had time to notice the people around them. Jake remembered many mornings' walks to work, feeling like he was invisible.

Now he really was, and that made Jake smile.

Part of him knew that he could have some fun with his new status. Being really invisible in a city of people who might as well be invisible could be fun. He could do so much and get away with so many things. He could help himself to whatever he wanted, never having to worry about being caught. He could become Fay's guardian angel, protecting her from anyone who tried to hurt her.

He came to a stop outside of a burger bar, and watched through the windows at the people eating. It had been hours since he had last eaten, yet he did not feel the slightest bit hungry. That did not come as much of a surprise to him. The dead did not need to eat, after all.

He had to accept that small but important fact. He was dead; it was the only explanation for what had happened when he visited Robert, and for when he had returned home. As he thought back he realised that only one event could account for his present state of being. The incident at the police box. Whatever happened had happened then, and he was sure now that he had not imagined it.

That blast of air, that flash of light, somehow it must have killed him.

His heart dropped at that thought. In his mind he could see Fay talking to Robert on the phone, smiling as she told him about the wedding. *Well, it ain't gonna happen now, is it?* He took a deep breath as his eyes began to well up.

He turned away from the burger bar and blinked away the tears, and his eyes made contact with a familiar face. It was the man from the police box. Still dressed in frilly shirt and green velvet jacket, the man was standing outside the chemist looking directly at Jake. If there was any doubt, the fact that he could see Jake was confirmed when the man smiled at him.

'Oi, pal!' Jake called out.

The man's smile faded quickly, and he raised a hand to his left ear. He frowned as he fiddled with his ear, then shook his head. Looking extremely annoyed the man turned and began to walk away.

'Oh no you don't,' Jake said and set off after the man.

Despite his attempts to attract the man's attention, Jake was ignored. It was as if he were not there, which, Jake realised, was true; although he could not ignore that fact that just like the last time he had seen the man, the man had, at first, shown signs of seeing Jake.

Side by side they walked down King's Street. Jake had no intention of leaving the man's side; whoever this man was, he knew something about what was going on and Jake wanted to know as well.

They turned the corner into Macbeth Street, and once they had neared the school that stood there, Jake noticed the police box in an alley alongside a block of flats.

Jake smiled. At last they were getting somewhere.

The man crossed the road and entered the police box. As he stepped inside a voice greeted him. 'Any luck, Doctor?'

'I'm afraid not, Jeremy. Almost, though.' The man sighed. 'And I was nearly…'

However he ended that sentence was lost to Jake, as the man closed the door behind him. With a grin Jake stepped forward, knowing full well he could step straight into the box, and find out what the man who Jeremy called 'Doctor' was up to. Step through he did, and came out of the other side.

He span around in surprise. 'What's going on?'

Just as he was about to try again, the light on top of the box started flashing and the curious wheezing noise began to rise again.

'No, wait!' Jake called out, but the police box faded from sight before his eyes.

While he was walking with the Doctor the possibility that he was not alone had become real, and with it came the hope that maybe he could still marry Fay. If the Doctor had been able to see him, if only for a few moments, then maybe he could cure Jake, too. But along with the disappearance of the police box went his hopes.

He looked up to the dark sky above and shouted out.

'Oh, god! Please don't let me be alone!'

Jake Morgan spent another hour sitting on the wet grass in Ravenscourt Park, not that the dampness below him was a problem. *The joy of being dead*, he thought bitterly.

For a while, after the police box had gone, he had considered wandering around Hammersmith, but he could not stomach the thought of being among so many people yet being so alone. So he decided to take some time out in the park, closed as it was, in the hope that the isolation would not seem so obvious. For the most part it worked.

Every now and then he would notice a group of people walking down the street next to the park, laughing and joking as they started their night out. Memories of such nights out with Fay, Robert (and his latest fling) would rush unwanted into Jake's mind.

Ahead of him, above the arches, the occasional train would hurry past, through Ravenscourt Park Station (closed at weekends) and on to Hammersmith. Silhouettes of people in the train could be seen from where Jake sat. All those people together, ignoring each other, not realising the wonderful gift they had. The gift of sharing their lives with other people.

In the moments when there were no people and no trains he would consider some deep philosophical thoughts, which was most unlike him. When he had been alive he had never been a religious man, quite content to be his own boss, and unwilling to contemplate that there was a plan for his life other than the one he created himself. Now he was dead he found himself thinking about such things.

Was there really more to this life? Considering his current predicament he would hope so. But if that was so then why was he still here, walking the earth as a ghost? Jake did not know. He knew very little about ghosts, beyond what he saw in horror films. He refused to accept that for the rest of his time (eternity?) he would have to haunt people. If he was a ghost, Jake rationalised, then what about all the others who died? Was he really the only ghost in Hammersmith? He did not think so, after all there must have been loads of people who had died in the area. Muggings that had

82

gone wrong, old folk in their beds, and as for the people who must have died in Charing Cross Hospital...

This led him to consider something he had once heard. Something about how ghosts were dead spirits who had to make peace with their former lives so they could move on to the next life. Jake did not know the specifics, he did not need to know, but it made sense to him right now, sitting alone in the park.

He stood up. There were scores left unsettled in his life, between him and his father. Jake had not seen him in many years, not since they had moved the old man into the nursing home. They had never really been close, but in hindsight, Jake realised, that was no excuse to not go and visit.

Jake stood up and started for the way out. Before the night was over he was determined to resolve some things so that he could move on to whatever was next.

As he walked one other thing came to his mind. Somehow he would have to sort things out with Fay, let her know what he felt...

Jake Morgan looked down at his father, lying in the bed, looking frailer than Jake had ever seen him. His dad was asleep, his breathing shallow and irregular.

'I just wanted to drop by and say I'm sorry, Dad. I should have visited you before now, so we could both make our peace. Well, my peace, since it was me who shut you out of my life. So much has happened since I last saw you.' Jake smiled. 'Got engaged today. You'd like her. Fay's lovely, and she's got a wicked sense of humour. We're gonna get married in...' Jake stopped himself. 'We *were* going to get married, but... well, bit difficult since I'm dead.' He shook his head. 'I should have visited you sooner, Dad, I really should have. But I was such a prick back then. It's my fault, isn't it, this trouble with your heart? I broke it when I betrayed you...' He reached up to wipe away the tear that fell, but could not. Jake wanted to be strong about everything, but he felt so exhausted. What he wanted most of all was to be held, to be comforted by his dad. He looked closer at his father. 'You don't look long for this world, either. Guess I'll be seeing you soon, then,' he added, trying his best to make light of the situation.

He abruptly turned to leave, but then looked back. 'We can sort things out after, we'll have the rest of time to do so.' This time there was no flippancy in his tone. Seeing his dad looking so close to death hit Jake more than he would have expected. 'Bye, Dad, see you soon.'

He walked to door and as he was about to pass through it he heard a sharp guttural sound from behind. Jake span around quickly. His dad was convulsing, clutching at the blankets. With a dawning sense of dread Jake realised that his dad was trying to clutch his heart.

The old man was having a heart attack.

Jake rushed over to the side of the bed. 'I didn't mean it! You're a fighter, come on!' He ran out of the room, and once in the hallway he shouted out. 'Somebody come! He's having a heart attack. He's…' Jake stopped and looked back at the door to his dad's room. 'He's dying,' he finished limply, and, giving in to the exhaustion, he collapsed onto the floor.

It was almost fifteen minutes before he felt strong enough to go back into the room. Jake swallowed and waited for his dad's ghost to sit up, but nothing happened. His dad's dead body remained inactive, forgotten about. Jake shook his head. 'I really am alone,' he said.

Jake Morgan stopped by the police box, which now stood outside his house. He tried to place his palm on the box, but, as he expected, it passed right through.

'See me yet?' Jake asked, hoping the Doctor could hear him. 'If you can, then I just need to sort out one more thing.' He turned to his house and walked up to the door.

Jake Morgan found Fay in their bed, but she was not sleeping. She lay there on her side, one arm wrapped around herself, the other holding a tissue up to her nose to prevent it from running, while she tried to hold back her tears.

He looked at the clock on the bedside table. It was almost one thirty in the morning. He had left to see Robert almost eight hours earlier, and as far as Fay was concerned he had not come back since.

He walked across the room and knelt beside the bed. 'I'm so very sorry; I would give anything to hold you, but…' He reached out to touch her hair, and let his hand hover less than an inch above her head. 'We would've been so good together, just you and me against the world.' He smiled sadly. 'I love you, more than anything in my whole life, but I've got to go now. Be strong. I'll never forget you.'

Jake stood up and walked to the bedroom door. He stopped there for a moment, eyes closed tightly, his lower lip quivering with emotion. Deep within he felt so hollow, as if his soul had been ripped out. He looked back at Fay, and whispered; 'I love you. Goodbye, babe.'

Jake Morgan stepped through the front door. He had come to think of the police box as his carriage into the next life, wherever it was that ghosts went. The man who was called 'Doctor' was his guide, waiting for Jake to let go of the mortal realm first. Saying goodbye to this life had been the hardest thing he had ever done, and staying around longer would have torn him apart. It was time to go.

He stopped, looking at where the police box had stood. The pavement was empty.

'No,' he said softly, and quickly walked over to the spot where the box had been. He looked around, down the street, from one end to the other. All of a sudden it seemed like the street was never ending.

'I was ready,' he said.

Jake Morgan was his name, but it had been over two weeks since anyone had addressed him. As a ghost destined to roam Hammersmith forever he wondered why he would need a name. No one ever spoke to him. They did not even know he was here.

For the first few days he had kept himself busy by accompanying either Fay or Robert to work, but that had soon bored him. There was only so much he could say without a reaction, and listening to Fay on the phone all day, or watching Robert unpack boxes of books, soon became more than a little tedious.

From time to time he would return to the nursing home, hoping that his father might turn up. Despite how he had let his dad down in life, in death he hoped they would be able to make up for wasted time. His father never did appear.

Soon it all became pointless. All the fun things he had thought about held no interest for him now; there was little joy to be had when you could not touch anything.

In the end he spent all his time at his house, doing his best to stay close to Fay. He had had to sit there and watch her mourn him. For a few days she tried to be hopeful, going to work and carrying on with her life, but as the days passed he could tell her hope was starting to break. Robert came over often to check up on her, as did her parents and brother, but Jake was the only one still around to know that Fay put on an act when they were there.

No one had visited for a couple of days, and Fay decided to book time off work. Jake was glad in a way, because that meant more time alone with her.

That had not worked out as he had planned.

Instead she had used that time to visit some friends living in Scotland, unknowingly leaving Jake all alone.

Three days with no one for company left a lot of time for thinking, but two weeks being a ghost with no one to talk to had given him enough time to think of everything he needed to think about. For those three days he resolved to sit in the corner of the living room doing nothing at all.

He was still sitting there, in complete silence, when he heard a familiar sound. It was a sound he had given up hope of hearing. It was that strange wheezing sound. He slowly rose to his feet and walked over to the window. Outside, gradually coming into being, was the police box.

He ran outside quicker than he had ever moved before.

Moments after the police box had become solid the narrow door opened and a man Jake did not know stepped outside. He jumped when he noticed Jake, and poked his head back through the door.

'Doctor, he's here!'

'Excellent,' came the old voice from inside the box.

The young man was not much taller than Jake, with a lot of dark hair and dressed like he had just come out of the seventies. This must have been Jeremy.

'I knew you could see me,' Jake said with a lot more emotion than he would have expected.

Jeremy nodded. 'Oh yah, the Doctor's a wiz at creating these sorts of gadgets,' he said, pointing to a small silver device attached to his left ear. The apparatus seemed to go inside the ear, while a small protrusion pointed out parallel to the man's eye. 'Helps me see you. He's jolly clever.'

'Yes, thank you, Jeremy,' the Doctor said, as he stepped out of the police box. 'Maybe you should go and wait inside the TARDIS?'

Jeremy looked crestfallen, but nonetheless did as he was told and entered the police box. Once Jeremy was inside, the Doctor turned to look at Jake. He, too, was wearing one of the silver devices.

'I'm terribly sorry, old chap,' the Doctor said.

Jake had so much to ask, but for now he pointed at the silver device. 'Is that a ghost spotter?'

The Doctor fingered the device. 'Good grief no, it just enables the wearer to see into the reality bubble.' He frowned, and scratched his nose, and Jake almost smiled at the amount of movement the Doctor managed to put into one simple expression. 'Oh dear, you haven't spent the past two weeks thinking you were dead, have you?'

Jake nodded. 'Well, I am. That beam of light killed me.'

'Oh no, that just created a dimensional bubble around you. My dear chap, you're not dead. No one can see you, and you can't make contact with anything, but you're not dead. I'm not a killer you know, well,' and at this the Doctor rubbed his upper lip, 'never intentionally.'

Jake was trying his best to take it all in. 'If you knew this, you got a reason why you've waited two weeks to tell me? Got any idea what I've been going through?'

'I can only imagine. I've been trying to find a way to, ah, burst the bubble, so to speak. You see that light that "attacked" you was temporal energy, released by Jeremy's attempts at being helpful. It created a bubble of reality around you, a reality different from the one you should be in. Fortunately, though, your quantum signature is strong enough to act as an anchor, holding you in this reality. Unfortunately I can't seem to burst the bubble, so you're stuck as you are.' There was a deep sadness in the Doctor's eyes, and Jake knew then that what the Doctor said was true.

'I suppose to all intents and purposes as long as you're anchored to this reality you *are* dead.'

Jake's hopes vanished, blinked out by the Doctor's words. He looked to the ground and slowly shook his head.

'I can take you somewhere in the TARDIS,' the Doctor said hopefully, and indicated the police box, 'where you can live with people who will be able to see you. It's another reality, the same as the bubble that you're in. It will mean a new life, but at least you will have company and not be alone. I've already arranged it with... erm... with a friend. I'll take you to him and he will take you the rest of the way.'

'But...' Jake began and looked over at his house. 'You reckon anyone wearing that ear device can see me?'

'Well, of course, I designed it,' the Doctor said, with just a hint of smugness.

'What about her?' Jake pointed at Fay, who was just getting out of her car. The Doctor looked over, then back at Jake, his features uncertain. 'She's my fiancée, and I have to say goodbye to her. She thinks I'm dead.'

'It might be better if you left it like that.'

'What?' Jake walked past the Doctor and pointed at Fay. 'Better? I love her. She's spent two weeks destroyed because she thinks I'm dead. If she knew the truth maybe it would help her heal.' He looked over at his fiancée as she started walking towards the house. 'Do you have any idea what it's like to be in love?' he asked the Doctor. 'To feel so incredibly happy just because someone smiles at you?' When Jake turned back to the Doctor he found the old man smiling.

'Yes, I do remember such a time,' the Doctor said with fondness at his private memory.

Jake Morgan's heart felt lighter than it had in two weeks. Fay was sitting on the porch of their house, still looking up at Jake with disbelief.

It had taken the Doctor mere moments to convince Fay to put the silver device in her ear, and when she had she had almost fallen over with the shock of seeing Jake before her. He had made a move to steady her, and realised painfully that he still could not hold her. Instead he had to settle on simply talking.

He explained everything as best as he could, and the more he spoke the more he could see that Fay was beginning to understand. He knew it would take her a while to fully get to grips with everything, but at least this final talk would give her closure. It was all that Jake had left to give her.

'It's time we both moved on,' he said finally.

Fay took a juddering breath. 'But I don't want to move on. I can see you with this thing,' she said and pointed to the device sticking out of her ear.

'I can wear it all the time, then we can still be together. You can be...'

Jake shook his head sadly. 'It'd never work. Both of us being around each other; you being the only person who can see me.'

'I could let others borrow this. Like Robert, he'd love to see you again.'

Jake chewed his lip, feeling terrible because he had to crush all of Fay's hopes. 'It would just hurt you more, and me. Never being able to hold each other again. You deserve to be happy, not left hanging on for something that's never gonna happen. We can't live like that. You need to find someone you can be with. For real.'

'I'll never love them the same.'

Jake inhaled deeply. 'Promise me you'll find someone to make you happy.'

Fay attempted a smile. 'I'll try.'

'That's all we can do,' Jake said. 'Listen, Robert is still around. He's so much like me sometimes, at least being around him will feel like a part of me is still here.'

At that Fay really did smile. 'Yeah, and he's nuts, too.'

Jake laughed softly. 'Maybe he will get you that silk dress?'

Fay stood up. 'Jake,' she said, not even trying to hold back her tears. Jake just nodded at her, doing what he could to hold back his own feelings. The moment was made all the more precious for him since it was the first time someone had called him by his name in two weeks. After several moments of silence Fay managed to mouth the word 'bye'. Jake smiled and walked away.

Once he reached the TARDIS he glanced back. 'I love you,' he said to Fay's back as she entered the house.

Jake Morgan took one last look at his former home, then turned and stepped into the time machine. He closed the door firmly on his previous life.

Charley looked from the Professor to Jake and then to the Baspral Inquisitor. 'Is the Doctor who you met the same one that the Professor and Jake encountered, or is there yet another version of the Doctor?'

The Inquisitor shrugged. 'My memory of the Doctor doesn't match theirs, no. But in many ways, they are similar. See if you agree.'

And so he began his tale...

The Inquisitor's Story

J. Shaun Lyon

There is no such thing as perfect darkness. It is that most fragile of creatures; anything can defeat it - light, colour, shape, form. But the absence of light, of something tangible and visible, breeds the onslaught of nothingness, of void... and sometimes, it can be something filled with fear, revulsion, misunderstanding. The mind becomes the enemy in the blackness, for it cannot fathom the idea of something so truly empty of meaning.

For the man in the cell, emptiness, darkness, absence - that was his world.

It was such a terrifying nemesis that his mind nearly couldn't tolerate the sudden flash of light, peering under the corner of a door that only moments ago hadn't been there. The phantom light shone upon him; his weary eyelids beat in rapid succession, reflections from his multicoloured coat cast upon the walls, and for several moments he allowed himself to believe it was real until logic got the better of him, and he chalked up the notion to his mind playing tricks upon him. But there were sounds as well, like footsteps upon steel plates echoing in all directions, and he began to pull himself into the reality of the tangible.

'The sensation will pass,' said a voice from the doorway. The visitor entered the room, the door shut, and a warm orange glow began seeping into the room from all corners. The prisoner stayed motionless, seated as he was on a small grey cot, his eyes undulating, his body shivering in the coolness of his surroundings. He could barely see the man who had arrived, walking toward him. It was only at the touch of the man's hand on his shoulder that the flood of his memories began to return.

'Your eyesight will return shortly,' added the visitor, who made a motion to a small device on his belt. A soft white light in the far corner slowly began to rise to comfortable levels. 'Your system wasn't designed to cope with the drugs we gave you during interrogation. I believe you went into some advanced form of shock. I've never seen it happen before, but then again, you're not from around here, are you?'

Drugs, thought the prisoner. Interrogation. Prison. *Incarceration...*

And then it hit him.

'How... dare you...' The Doctor looked up at his visitor. 'Why am I... here...?'

'You were taken into custody, Doctor,' said his keeper. 'To pay for the crime of which you have been convicted.'

'Crime -'

'All will be explained.' The man removed his hand from the Doctor's shoulder. 'How is your head?'

The Doctor paused. He held his palm against his forehead. 'Like Bourbon Street after Mardi Gras,' he said. 'What did you hit me with?'

'Low-level stun blast,' the man replied, moving away from the Doctor toward a small table in the corner. 'Standard issue to security patrols. It too will pass momentarily. I assume.' The man, who was dressed in a grey gown, lined with silver etching that ran in swirls down the parting, swept his hand across the table, the folds from the gown flowing effortlessly in the air. From out of nowhere, a flicker of light developed about six inches above the table, floating in the air, which grew quickly into a plane of light decorated with patterns – obviously an advanced computer readout, projected holographically. The man studied it. 'I see you were taken into custody rather publicly.' He shook his head. 'I'd hoped to avoid that.'

'And why is that?'

'Because,' the man said, 'it complicates matters. Justice is far easier to dispense in the darkness.'

A beat, then the Doctor spoke. 'How true that is. Sadly.'

'You see, Doctor, someone is going to die today.'

The Doctor looked down at his coat. 'And yet I failed to dress for the occasion.'

A slight chuckle formed in the man's throat. 'You jest, Doctor, and yet you clearly underestimate the importance of our meeting.'

'As a matter of fact, I believe I've underestimated how *ludicrous* it is.' He paused. 'How do you know my name?'

'Because you have visited our planet before. Do you remember what happened to you this morning?'

'Very clearly,' said the Doctor. His curiosity piqued considerably, he started feeling closer to his usual self. 'I was sitting on my own in a café – *minding my own business*, I should add – when two of your very brusque security guards walked up and fired their crude laser weapons at me without so much as a "good morning". Now, despite Baspral's rather lacklustre accomplishments in the pursuit of jurisprudence, what I know of your planet's unwavering hospitality doesn't mesh with that sort of treatment. Care to enlighten me?'

The man's eyes shot up, though his head stayed motionless. 'You do admit you've been to Baspral before.' It wasn't a question, but a statement... almost as if an unspoken fact that suddenly grew to consequential importance as he said it. The man's hand moved toward the flickering light display hovering over the table; he motioned with his fingers, and the display changed.

'Of course I have. Twice, in fact.' The man at the table sat back slightly as the Doctor continued. 'I was here once to see the famous Gardens of

90

Baspral, but there were riots and my friend and I were unable to visit them. Horrible time, mass executions, terrible war.' His voice trailed a bit, as if sadness crept upon him. 'Almost as if the planet had erupted into some giant nightmare.' He nodded, clearing his mind.

'It had. Please continue.'

'I returned a few years ago, on my own, to find the planet had changed quite dramatically... the gardens were lush again, the architecture strong and proud. Like the morning after. Are you taking this down?'

'Should I be?'

The Doctor frowned. 'This is a post-trial interview, isn't it? The last part of business before the axe falls.' The man sat at the table, motionless, saying nothing. 'Oh yes, I know who, or rather what, you are. You're an Inquisitor, aren't you?'

The Inquisitor smiled. It wasn't a proud or terribly inviting smile; it was the sad smile of a man obviously weighted down with a terrible burden, as if life had passed him by and he'd been far too busy to notice.

'As I said,' the Doctor continued, 'I know a little of Basprali justice. The Inquisitor: judge and jury all rolled up in a neat little package, dispensing the law without a moment's notice or a passing thought. Utterly barbaric... and yet perfectly forgivable, in light of your planet's recent past.'

'Please continue with your story, Doctor,' the Inquisitor said. 'What happened to you on that last visit?'

A pause. 'As I said, I was delighted to see things had returned to normal, and the gardens were in full bloom. It didn't take me long to realise I was wrong. I'd arrived too early; the wars hadn't started yet. None of this seems to bother you, I've noticed. Travel in time and all that.'

'Nothing on Baspral surprises me anymore,' the Inquisitor replied.

'I took a stroll up the hill overlooking the city. I wanted to see the view. But...' The Doctor's eyes widened a bit, and he sat back into his chair. His multicoloured coat had obviously felt the shock of his assault, he thought, because somehow it seemed a little less bright, a bit more faded, more subdued. 'That's what this is about, isn't it? About that boy.'

The Inquisitor's eyes lit up a bit, as if he'd made an important connection. 'Which boy would that be?'

'You know perfectly well,' the Doctor said, matter-of-factly. 'The boy whose life I saved that day. What happened, Inquisitor, did someone report him missing? Is this some sort of colossal misunderstanding?'

'Hardly, Doctor, though we're on the right track. Tell me about him.'

The Doctor sighed, thinking back several years. 'The boy, and the old woman trying to drown him. In the stream, next to the old mill on the hill overlooking the city. You must know it.'

'I do.'

'It was complete coincidence – not that I believe in coincidence, mind you. I've seen far too many things in my time to believe that the universe doesn't work in its own pattern,' and as he glanced momentarily down at his colourful patchwork coat, the Doctor's voice started to drift slightly away. 'He was screaming. He couldn't have been more than six or seven years old... young and innocent. And the old crone, she kept holding his head beneath the water, pulling it out again. He had barely enough time to catch his breath before she pushed him back into the water. By the time I reached them, the boy had stopped breathing. If I hadn't got there in time –'

'And what did you do, Doctor?'

'I stopped her. Of course I stopped her. And when she wouldn't let go, I tore her hands from his throat. What would you have done?'

The Inquisitor squinted slightly. 'What I would do is irrelevant. You saved his life. You admit it.'

'And that is my crime?' asked the Doctor. 'Why would saving the life of a boy be considered a crime? I thought this planet had left its madness buried in the past, where it belongs.'

'Indeed.' The Inquisitor glanced at the floating screen. 'Oh, we've had our bad spells. Terrible, monstrous times of unspeakable evil, as you recall. The Great Cleansing, Doctor. War and chaos, fifteen million people ready to leap over the cliff on the sole command of a brutal dictator, waging bloodshed on countless innocent lives. So much waste. A brutal, regrettable incident in our history. Anyone who lived through those times...' His voice trailed a bit. 'They would be changed, dramatically.'

The Doctor felt something peculiar awash over him, almost as if the Inquisitor were trying to tell him something by *not* telling him. 'Any rational person would be changed by events spiralling out of control like that.' He leaned forward in his chair. 'So why would you condemn the illogic of fascism and yet condemn me for saving the life of a young boy. Unless...' And then it suddenly hit him. 'No. No, it couldn't be.'

'Yes, Doctor.' The Inquisitor moved his hand over the table, and the ethereal display console vanished. He sat back in his chair. 'Yes indeed. Do you know whose hands you pulled away from that boy's neck? Her name was Galena. She was a senior member of the Seers' Union. Have you heard of them?'

He shook his head. 'Not especially, no, but I've heard that some Basprali women possess the gift of future insight. Real or imagined, I've no idea. I've never checked their references. But every planet has its fortune tellers, male or female.'

'The Seers here are revered, Doctor. Their time-honoured ways have guided us through many difficulties in our history.'

'Difficulties.' There was disdain in the Doctor's voice.

'Perhaps you are not as familiar with Basprali history as you might care to believe. Until the Great Cleansing, there had never been as ruthless and brutal a dictator. Unlike countless worlds I could name, we avoided centuries of bloodshed and pain. The Basprali were an artistic culture, famed throughout the cosmos for our unique insight into emotion and sensation. Our works still hang in the galaxy's most treasured museums and libraries, long after we abandoned the more aesthetic parts of our culture for... less civilised pursuits.'

'Yes,' the Doctor replied, 'during war, art is usually the first thing to go. So the Seers of Baspral have guided you through the years –'

'Ensuring our survival. We give them free reign, and we don't usually intercede when one stakes a claim. And that boy –'

'– grew up, didn't he,' the Doctor answered, 'to wage the very war you mentioned? The Great Cleansing.' He was incredulous; he immediately stood up, looking down at the Inquisitor before him. 'That's it. That's why you've condemned me... because you think I'm responsible for letting that boy live to grow up to be a power-mad dictator? Why don't you bring the boy's parents in here and throw them on the chopping block as well? Or his schoolteachers, perhaps? Anyone who has ever come into contact with him.'

The Inquisitor sat there, in front of him, motionless.

'I saved the life of a child, and now I'm condemned because I simply *should have known better?* What right do you have convicting me of nothing more than an act of kindness? Where is the nobility in your oft-quoted Basprali justice, Inquisitor?'

The room was silent for several seconds, before the Inquisitor spoke again. 'You don't understand, do you? I was there, Doctor. I saw you help him. You see, I was an adjunct in the Basprali militia, assigned to the Seers' Union. I witnessed your "act of kindness". And ten years later, I saw him drown Galena in the very same stream. Yes, Doctor, as she ran away, as you cared for the boy and brought him back to health, all the while he remembered who she was, and why she had tried to kill him.' He paused, ever so slightly. 'I remembered exactly what you had done, too. I heard what she said to you. Do you remember?'

The Doctor scratched his head. 'It has been a while...'

'She said she'd known you would be there, that you would try to stop her.' The Inquisitor seemed more agitated, quickly losing patience, his speech hastened. 'She said you couldn't help it.' He looked into the Doctor's eyes. 'Surely, you remember now. What was it she called you, Doctor?'

A brief pause, then: 'A meddler.'

'A meddler, yes. A busybody. Interfering in events you have no business being involved in. What was it she said after that, about fate...?'

The Doctor shook his head. 'That I walked hand in hand with Fate herself.'

'Indeed. You couldn't help yourself, could you? You couldn't leave well enough alone.' He scratched his chin. 'I too walk with Fate, you see. It wasn't enough that I'd merely watched that moment. When conscription came to call at my door, I was forced to serve that boy who had grown up to terrorise us. A soldier in an army of madmen, fighting a war purely out of my own cowardice for being too afraid to speak any differently. No, you never thought about the consequences, did you? You interfered on a whim, never mindful of what the result might be.'

'If I had known...' the Doctor started, then he stopped himself, perhaps knowing full well that any sort of repentance might not necessarily be the truth.

'You as much as anyone shaped me into the man I am today, Doctor. I have lived with my personal demons every night since that terrible war began. I've had to live with the faces of those whose lives were shattered for the greater good. And so, when he was dead and his armies overthrown, I hid away. Wiped the slate clean. Started over.' A pause, and then: 'Today, instead of condemning innocent people to death, I make certain proper justice is done. Until finally, we come to this moment.'

The Doctor stared at him. Suddenly the darkness around them didn't seem like so much dark any longer. 'Proper justice. By arresting me, instead of turning the eye of scrutiny upon yourself. Tell me, Inquisitor – where were you when I left the boy alone, after I'd saved him?'

Nothing.

'If you're so convinced that by my own action I'm guilty as charged, surely you are guilty of the same crime by your own *inaction*...'

The Inquisitor did not move.

The Doctor looked up at him, the faintest hint of a smile striking the left side of his mouth. 'And now we've come to the crux of the problem here. Haven't we, Inquisitor? You think I'm guilty. But more importantly... you believe you're as guilty as I am.'

The Inquisitor turned away from him, looking back at the empty table, now sullen and dark without his elaborate technology to illuminate it. 'I –' he began, and then stopped himself.

'You must realise,' the Doctor said after a moment, 'how senseless this is. If I hadn't intervened, if I'd allowed that small boy to be killed, then I'd have been faced with being an accessory to murder. And, how the guilt would have eaten away at me.' Another pause. 'There are worlds out there, billions of them, that face the same *fait accompli* every day. Move to the left for one path, move to the right for another. Centuries of bloodshed to be avoided simply by going back and changing the course of one brief moment in time. Think of it, Inquisitor.' He placed his hand on the other

94

man's shoulder. 'To go back and simply remove the problem at its foundation? Ah, how easy that would be... stop an assassin's bullet, or the collision of a freight train. But why stop there? Murder a small boy in Austria, knowing well that you'd stopped his rampage across Europe... but all the while without the knowledge of what would happen in its stead.' He shook his head. 'The watcher faces the choice, but then, who watches the watcher?'

'Perhaps it's not enough to watch, Doctor. Perhaps it's our responsibility to make order from chaos. You could have walked away and let what would happen, happen. Instead, you chose to interfere.'

The Doctor laughed. 'Ah, but to actually change things, hmm? Is that what she meant by walking with Fate? Condemned to meddle, to rewrite history endlessly until all trace of evil and harm are erased? Believe me, I've faced that decision before.' He thought back to Skaro, to two pieces of fragile wire, waiting to connect them, waiting to end the madness... 'No, Inquisitor. It's not enough to will all of our pain and suffering out of existence. Without darkness, after all, there would be no light. A wise man once said, life is a contrast, a study in twilight, in shades of grey.'

'But we are responsible,' the Inquisitor replied, turning back to face the Doctor again. 'We could have ended the suffering of this planet by changing one action, by ending his life –'

'And what would have happened then?' the Doctor interrupted. 'Who's to say that the result would have been better than what had gone before? There's no way to know. Actions have consequences. Evil almost instinctively begets good, bringing allies together, forcing people to bury their differences, drawing the line in the sand. Remove that from the equation, and the world loses balance.' He paused again. 'Yes, I remember that day. And I remember what she told me... she said she knew I would come. So why did she choose to bring the boy there, to the old mill on the hillside? She could have simply gone elsewhere. Down the street, into a field, anywhere. She knew I would be there at that moment. Yet she let me find her.'

'What are you saying?'

'That maybe, just maybe, she knew something neither of us did that day. You see, I know a little more of this planet's history than you give me credit for. Ten years ago, after the wars were over, Baspral joined with the Earth Alliance in facing a Dalek advance. Countless worlds had fallen, but Baspral had a massive war machine ripe for the picking. If you hadn't faced that Great Cleansing, would you have been strong enough to help them? Would you have been able to face a Dalek slaughter on your own?'

'I... don't know.'

'More importantly, if your Seers had foretold that, what could you have done without that army? The Daleks would have overrun the Earth

Alliance, and then would have turned their sights on you. I guarantee you, Inquisitor, your planet would have fallen in less than one night.' He stopped. 'The end doesn't justify the means, necessarily, but it does tend to explain it. Dare I say it, but Baspral today is a better world than it would have been. Or should be. Where does that leave you?'

The Inquisitor sat back in his chair, dropping his head into his hands.

'I did what I did,' the Doctor continued, 'because it was the right thing to do. Because at that moment, that child wasn't a killer, or a murdering mass dictator foisting terrible war and ethnic cleansing upon your people. He was only a boy.'

There was silence for several moments. The room seemed slightly darker, as the light in the corner seemed to lose a bit of its brilliance.

'Yes, he was,' the Inquisitor finally replied. 'Just a boy. So was I, for that matter. And that moment has haunted me the rest of my life. I'm sorry.'

'Sorry? For what?'

The Inquisitor, suddenly looking frail and disillusioned, rose his head from his hands and looked into the Doctor's face. 'The executioners are due soon. Very soon,' he said at long last, pain in his voice. 'And there's nothing I can do. You had already been convicted in absentia.'

'Ah. Basprali justice, swift and sure. That will change, too, eventually, for the better.' He shook his head, demonstrating a bit of his knowledge that he dare not share. 'But for now...'

The Doctor sat back on the cot, his back straight, his head held high. He folded his hands.

'I... don't understand,' the Inquisitor said. He rose again from the chair, moving slightly toward the Doctor with one step, then a second. 'They know you're here, what crimes you have been convicted of. You're going to die within the hour.'

The Doctor looked deep into his gaoler's eyes. 'Yes.'

'And you're not afraid?'

A slight hint of smile crossed the Time Lord's lips, again. 'Terrified. Hoping rather foolishly that someone will come to the rescue. Perhaps not today. But I would hope that from my death, perhaps a greater good will some day come.'

And there was silence once again.

After what seemed like an eternity, the Inquisitor stepped forward and turned, then sat down beside the Doctor on the small cot. 'You must leave. I realise that now. What you did was indeed not a crime, Doctor. It was the only human thing to do. Perhaps I just needed to hear *why*.'

The Doctor turned his head to look at him. 'We can only do what is in our nature, Inquisitor. When you come down to it, we don't change the soul within.'

'But as I said, someone will die today. The executioners will be here

96

soon.' The Inquisitor reached into his pocket, removing something that he then placed into the Doctor's hands. It was a small disc-shaped object, which the Doctor immediately recognised as a standard Basprali door key. 'Take this, Doctor. Leave at once.'

The Doctor looked immediately confused, looking over the Inquisitor's face for evidence of trickery or foolishness. But there was none of that. Only sincerity. 'What are you suggesting, Inquisitor? That I leave you here to die in my stead?'

The Inquisitor touched the Doctor's hand. 'I died years ago, Doctor. As I watched my planet erupt in madness, I knew what I'd done... what I had failed to do, to stop the slaughter. A part of me died with every falling bomb, with every child killed. You are not of this planet; you are not responsible for our failings. But I was here, Doctor. I was a part of it. You are not responsible, but I am.'

At last... the truth. 'When you came in here, you said someone was going to die today.' The Doctor shook his head. 'You weren't talking about me, though, were you? You never intended to leave this place alive.'

'As I said, I needed to hear it from you, Doctor. Why you saved his life. And now I know... *because it was the right thing to do.* Yes, Basprali justice is swift and sure, but that does not equal just and proper. We could all stand some scrutiny.' He shoved the key into the Doctor's hand. 'Take it, Doctor. Take it and leave this planet. The executioners live in seclusion, away from the populace; they know me no more than they would know you.'

'Absolution, is that it? A lifetime of guilt exorcised by your death? It solves nothing.'

'It solves everything!' the Inquisitor retorted. 'You have the power to change what happens. I have the power to change nothing, and yet I yearn for the day I could but try. Stalemate, Doctor. One of us here will die.' His eyes moved to the ground. 'Don't you see? It mustn't be you. Because on that terrible morning, so many years ago, I would have let her kill him. I would have *helped* her kill him. And then spent a lifetime revisiting that moment, his lifeless eyes staring up at me. I would have remembered them as the Daleks or whoever came here tore my world apart, or something else even more terrifying.' A tear formed in his eye. 'You were not there, years later, when I met Galena again, before she was murdered.'

'The Seer,' replied the Doctor.

'She had only these words for me: "You will know pain, and you then will know death, and then you will know peace." I never knew what that meant, Doctor, until I saw you come back to us. I have known pain, and I will know death. And I long for peace.' He was shivering slightly. 'Perhaps, as you say, a greater good will one day come... perhaps you could one day come back and tell them what happened here. Make them know that not everyone has forgotten the past, or forgiven it. Make them realise that justice must not be so blind. But you must leave now, before they come for you.'

The Doctor looked into the sad man's face. 'I don't want to leave you here.'

'I have to face this, Doctor. I am an Inquisitor, an extension of Basprali justice, yet justice has always been blind to me. I've always taken the easy way out. Perhaps today I can find what's eluded me for so long.' He reached out and closed the Doctor's fist around the key. 'Go now.'

'I won't forget this,' the Doctor said. 'Or you. Remember that.' The Doctor turned and moved toward the door, disappearing within moments until the Inquisitor was all alone.

The Inquisitor was left in the cell, sitting on the small cot, the only light from the small, fading lamp in the far corner. He watched as the light appeared to dim, perhaps reflective of the fading darkness of his planet's rare history. He thought of Galena, and how she had given him a glimpse into his own destiny. He thought of that terrible dictator, and then of the boy he saw the Doctor rescue. He thought of the Doctor himself...

And he smiled. Perhaps justice would be done today, after all.

There is no such thing as perfect darkness. But today, in a cell on Baspral, as a man sat awaiting his fate, the darkness had been lightened, ever so slightly.

'So you see, my friends,' the Inquisitor said to the assembled group, 'my fate was sealed. And I had accepted it.'

Jake Morgan shook his head. 'I don't understand. Why – '

' – am I here? I was led off, under guard, to the execution chamber. None of them recognised me, and I never said a word. They strapped me to the chair, covered my eyes with a blindfold, delivered the slightest hint of a prayer, and left, sealing it up as they went. And I sat in that chair for what seemed like an eternity, contemplating what I had done... what I had failed to do.' He sighed. 'And then... it all came so suddenly. I was released from the chair, dragged somewhere else. And when my eyes were uncovered, there was the Doctor, standing over me.'

'He came back for you?' asked Charley.

'Indeed. I was prepared for death. I felt guilt over what I had failed to do, and how I had convicted him without hearing what the Doctor had to say. But I realise I wasn't prepared for life thereafter. And so the Doctor returned and told me that he could not bear the idea that I was left to die while he had escaped.' He sighed heavily. 'Perhaps that is what makes him the man he is.'

Charley was incredulous. 'But why could you not go back home? Tell them it wasn't the Doctor, but you instead? I'm sure you could have convinced them of that.'

'Ah, I think I can answer that,' said Professor Katsoudas. 'I believe that actions have consequences,' he said. 'For every path taken, events spiral out of control. You see, the Doctor then shared part of this gentleman's planet's future history.'

The Inquisitor agreed. 'My discussions with the Doctor were not spoken in solitude. Someone else had been listening... one of the prison guards. And he went on to become Inquisitor himself, one day, armed with new sensibilities; he fought the system from within, and changed Baspral's laws. Within a decade, my planet was born anew. Light from darkness.'

'And new hope for your world,' Charley said.

'I cannot go back. There's simply too much at stake, a world of endless uncertainty where even the actions of one man can make all the difference. As the Doctor did, by meddling yet again.' He smiled faintly. 'Perhaps the wrong choice, but for the right reasons. As are all of his decisions, I believe. There are always choices to be made, by him, by you, by me. In the end, I know that I finally made the right one.'

Charley stumbled for the right thing to say. 'I'm... sorry.'

'Don't be. You see, I have known pain, and I have met death. And now, I will know peace.' He smiled. 'I hope one day you do as well. Good night, Miss Pollard,' said the Inquisitor, reaching out with his hand and touching her shoulder. Then he turned away.

And Charley could only watch, silently, as the Inquisitor walked back into the main group gathered at the centre of the room.

With a sad smile, the Professor returned to his notebooks and Jake Morgan headed towards the bar, head lowered.

Charley took a deep breath. These people were being brought by the Doctor onto this airship because something had gone wrong with the Web of Time. Their lives had had impacts that they should not have. Which was all well and good, except that it wasn't always their fault! It wasn't fair.

'No, Miss Pollard, it rarely is.' The Steward was beside her, clearing the glasses from around the Professor, who ignored them both. 'Would you care to see more of the airship?'

'Not really,' snapped Charley. 'To be honest, I'd rather like to find the Doctor and ask him to explain his actions. Is he here yet?'

The Steward smiled. 'Oh, the Doctor won't be joining us, I'm afraid.'

Charley was taken aback. 'But I thought... I assumed that was the point. That he was going to explain all this to these people!'

The Steward shook his head. 'No explanations necessary, Miss Pollard. Despite what they might say themselves, deep, deep down, they all know why they are here. They all know, even if they don't accept it, that they are here for the greater good.'

'And me?'

The Steward just smiled again. And started back towards the bar.

With a last look at the all-consuming blue outside, Charley followed him, politely easing her way through the people. As she walked, she saw more people she'd not noticed before.

A man in a silver spacesuit, the American flag on his sleeve. A translucent woman carrying a bag, which she hugged protectively, ensuring no one else could touch it as they milled around her.

The Centaur had a new card partner – a man in what she knew from history lessons were seventeenth-century clothes. Beside him, a young girl of about eight, carrying a tiny glass tube with a stopper in one end. Charley couldn't see exactly what was in the tube, but it seemed to be a pile of different coloured sweets. The Centaur laughed out loud at a joke the seventeenth-century man had just made, and one or two bystanders joined in.

The tramp pushed past Charley, but she ignored him and instead caught up with the Steward.

'Excuse me, but is there anyone aboard who actually justifies being here?'

'Define "justifies",' said a quiet female voice. The speaker was leaning against the bar, facing outwards, staring at the ground, determinedly avoiding eye contact with anyone, Charley thought. Least of all her. Either side of her were two children, although one certainly wasn't human. More dog than anything else. 'I don't think it's "justified" that he brought us three here,' she continued in what Charley placed as an Australian accent. 'Now, them… They deserve all they get.'

Charley followed the woman's pointed finger but couldn't work out who she was pointing at. Indeed, it seemed to be a group of about ten people from different cultures and planets even, gathered next to the wooden cupboard she'd seen when she first woke up.

'Oh, yes, indeed,' the Steward piped up from behind the bar. 'Let me tell you about them.'

'But who?' asked Charley. 'I'm not sure which of that lot you mean.'

'You will, Miss Pollard. But it's quite an involved story. Listen carefully.' And the Steward started to explain what the Australian woman had meant.

The Gangster's Story

Jon de Burgh Miller

Jack Green was one of the tough guys, a man you could always depend on in times of need. If someone owed you money and you needed it paid back sharpish, if someone had betrayed you and needed to be taught a lesson, Jack was the guy who would sort it out for you. A shop would burn down, a shadowy figure would appear out of nowhere and beat someone to a pulp, or a simple, threatening letter might arrive in the post, demanding money in exchange for the recipient's right to remain alive. But Jack wasn't the one pulling the strings in these matters. That was Jack's boss, Charlie Shutter, one of the most notorious gangsters in the East End of London.

Jack had never wanted a life like this. He'd been thrown from one care home to another as a child, had been forced to find his own way in the world. Falling under Charlie Shutter's wing and growing into his right-hand man had provided an easy solution to his troubles. But he was older now, less willing to take his chances with the law. He wanted a normal life like everyone else had. A safe life, an easy life. A life where he didn't live in fear of the regular torture ritual Charlie relished dishing out to those in his employ in order to ensure they remained loyal.

Jack had tried to escape from his life once. He'd failed, and had been hospitalised for weeks. He had come to terms with the realisation that he could never escape Charlie's grip. Not while Charlie had the punishment method known as the Lightning.

And so, standing in the empty warehouse in Leyton that Charlie used as an office, trying to explain why the day's bank robbery had failed to come off, Jack saw the glove on Charlie's right hand and felt his heart race and the pit in his stomach become a cavern as he prepared to endure the familiar brutality. The glove meant Charlie was seconds away from dishing out a dose of the Lightning, and Jack was seconds away from pain.

And then, before Charlie could act, something unexpected happened, something that would change Jack's life forever. Three strangers, a man and two girls, came marching into the room.

One was a tall blond man dressed in a pale cream jacket and hideously coloured trousers that looked like they'd escaped from the bad end of the seventies. His accomplices were two young girls, one with pale skin and the other dark.

Charlie stood up from his desk and pulled a gun on the strangers. 'Who the hell are you?' He scowled at Jack. 'What's going on here, who are these people?'

'I'm the Doctor,' the man said, introducing himself, seemingly oblivious to the gun that was trained on him. 'This is Peri and Erimem, and we believe you have something that doesn't belong to you.'

Jack couldn't believe this man's audacity. 'How did you get past Barry?'

'Am I right in thinking you have a specific interest in weather patterns,' the Doctor continued. 'More specifically, an interest in lightning?'

Charlie's eyes widened. 'What do you know about that?'

'I've been watching you and your friend Jack here for a while now,' the Doctor explained. 'I know what you've been up to.'

Charlie turned to look at Jack. 'You've betrayed me?'

'No!' Jack cried. 'I've never seen them before in my life!'

Charlie raised his hand, and Jack knew what was coming next.

'You've let me down, Jack.' Charlie sighed. Charlie might have been broad-shouldered, balding and overweight, but you would certainly never bet against him in a fight, and Jack had learned over the years there was little he could say back to his boss when Charlie's bad temper was in town.

A bright ball of light built around Charlie's fist as he pointed it at Jack.

The light turned various shades of blue and purple before surging out in front of Charlie as bolts of bright, crackling lightning, forking at the edges and blowing dust particles into the air in a whirl of static energy.

Jack felt the lightning rip into him, the familiar pain as his muscles simultaneously paralysed and stretched to their limits. Numbness overcame him and he could smell the burning of the cells in his body. As the bolt faded away he collapsed to the ground, barely conscious, whimpering like a wounded animal.

'Leave this man alone,' urged the Doctor, horrified. 'He's nothing to do with us.' He stepped over to Jack and felt his pulse.

'He'll be fine,' Charlie said. 'The Lightning isn't fatal in small doses. He'll feel that for the next few hours, but he needed to be taught a lesson.' Charlie walked forward and grabbed the Doctor by the lapels of his jacket. 'Of course, I don't have to give small doses if I don't want to!'

He threw the Doctor to the ground and once again, fired a bolt of lightning from his glove. Only this time, the Lightning didn't seem able to reach its target. The Doctor held his hands to his face and the Lightning appeared to freeze, refusing to touch the man.

Through his singed and numbed face, Jack was amazed to see the Doctor moving his hands around as if trying to control the Lightning. After a few moments, the Doctor appeared to push the Lightning aside, letting out an animalistic exhalation as he did so.

The Doctor had resisted the Lightning. Charlie's weapon of choice when it came to torture and the source of all the terror and all the nightmares in Jack's life. He'd beaten it. Despite his pain, Jack had to laugh. Someone had beaten the Lightning!

The Doctor was breathing heavily, catching up with himself. He looked up at Charlie, smiled, then pointed towards Charlie's hand. 'Clever device you have there.'

Charlie looked worried. Charlie never looked worried.

'How did you do that?' His voice was quivering.

The Doctor moved closer to Charlie and grabbed his arm, twisting it up with surprising strength so that the gangster's hand was facing away from him, the Lightning glove between the two men's faces.

The Doctor stared at the Lightning glove. 'Very interesting. Very interesting indeed.' He backed away. 'I'd rather like to take a look at it, if you don't mind.'

'Barry!' Charlie called into the next room. An unshaven man of a wrestler's weight marched in. Charlie pointed to Peri and Erimem. 'Take these two away, will you. Don't let them out of your sight.'

Barry nodded and grabbed Peri and Erimem, one on each arm.

'Get off me you gorilla!' Peri yelled.

Jack was still in pain from the Lightning blast, but managed to struggle to his feet and stagger after them. He didn't need to be told when Charlie didn't want him around.

'Don't worry, Peri,' the Doctor called after his friends as Barry left the room, 'no cause for concern!'

'Now,' Charlie said, raising a gun to the Doctor's head. 'Where were we?'

Peri gave her best scowl to the large oaf as he threw her and Erimem onto a rug outside Charlie's office.

'Charming service,' she sniped, dusting herself off.

'Come on, Peri,' Erimem said, trying to calm her. 'The Doctor said it was important.'

Peri sighed. 'I know, but we've only just got here and already we're being treated like dirt.'

'Sorry about Barry,' said a voice. It was the man who had been hit by the lightning, who'd followed them out of the office. 'His methods are a bit rough, but he gets the job done.'

The man was in his late twenties with a face aged by years of stress. He held out his hand. 'Jack Green.'

Peri didn't return the gesture. 'I'm Peri. I've never met a gangster before.' She hoped Jack could detect the derision in her voice.

He turned away. 'It pays the bills. You wouldn't understand.'

Peri smiled. 'Oh I understand all right! You're just bullies, all of you. You think you're hot stuff, but at the end of the day...'

'Go on,' Jack said, reaching for his gun and raising it towards Peri.

'Making up for something, are you?'

'You saw that weapon he's got in there?' Jack held up his hand, and Peri saw the remains of the hairs on it scorched away by the Lightning. 'If I ever thought of leaving he'd kill me. If I so much as blink he attacks me. Besides, he looks after all his employees. He's a good boss.'

'Oh give me a break,' Peri said dismissively. 'It doesn't have to be like this.'

Jack said nothing, but simply kept his gun trained on the girls.

Charlie waited until Jack was safely out of earshot then took the glove off his hand and cautiously handed it to the Doctor. 'Try anything,' he warned, 'and you'll be dead before you've fired it.'

'It's the fabric in this glove that creates the Lightning, isn't it?'

Charlie nodded.

The Doctor pressed his hand lightly against the glove and a few tiny sparks of energy shot out of it, leaping onto the floor. 'How very interesting. It seems pressure from a human touch is causing some form of chemical reaction to take place, resulting in the release of electrical energy.'

'Yet the person pressing it never gets shocked.'

The Doctor nodded, and continued to examine the fabric. 'Where did you find it?'

Charlie wondered whether he should invent some story to deceive this Doctor character, whether he should tell him anything at all about the origins of the material, but the uncomfortable fact was Charlie needed the Doctor if the plan he was forming could be realised. For the first time since discovering the Lightning, here was a man who wasn't afraid of it, who could control it, even. The Doctor may well be a huge source of help to Charlie's ambitions, but as someone unfazed by the threat of the energy he was also a real threat, and for that reason alone Charlie had no choice but to keep the man on his side.

Charlie lit a cigarette. 'Almost a year ago, a guy named Bobby Caramel died. Now he owed me a few favours, did Bobby. A lot of favours in fact, and so with him out of the picture, I was able to take what was rightfully mine.'

'And who was this Bobby Caramel?'

Charlie shrugged. 'Antiques dealer of some kind. He had a whole house full of junk he'd collected over the years, festering away in his garage. I sold most of it, as you do, made a tidy sum too, but there was one thing I found in his stuff that I would never sell.'

The Doctor lifted the glove up and began flipping it around to examine it from all sides.

'A roll of fabric,' Charlie continued, 'it looked completely ordinary. Almost killed me when I picked it up. Knocked me out flat, it did. Now maybe it was the bump on the head or maybe there was more to it, but

I knew I hadn't imagined it, I remembered what I'd seen and I had to study the stuff further.'

'So you took it away, moulded it into a glove and found a way to keep yourself safe while using it to throw unrestrained balls of energy at your helpless victims.'

Charlie nodded. 'Everyone gets what they deserve, Doctor. You will too someday.' He took a drag from his cigarette. 'I soon realised that only one side of the stuff was dangerous. By making a glove, the safe side would touch me and it would only activate when I clench my fist. By padding the glove, I've reduced the sensitivity, and made a weapon which, if you don't mind me saying so, I'm bloody proud of.'

The Doctor stood up straight, stroking his chin. 'Indeed you should be, Mr Shutter, indeed you should be.'

'So what's your story then? How do you know so much about it?'

The Doctor let out a sigh. 'It was all so very long ago, but I was in India when I discovered the material, much as you did. I learned that it's not just electricity it emits, but concentrated heat and air currents polluted with a chemical mixture that can be resisted by the human body if one is in the right frame of mind. Unfortunately I lost the material and until today have never seen anything quite like it again. I heard reports of your little glove though, heard some rumours. It wasn't too hard to track you down.'

Charlie didn't like what he was hearing, but he believed everything the Doctor said. 'Who else knows where I am?' he asked.

'Nobody, probably.' The Doctor reached towards Charlie and put his hand on the man's gun.

'You're a big shot in this city, aren't you? But perhaps you're getting too big?' The Doctor looked into Charlie's eyes. 'Yes, that's exactly it, isn't it? You're worried the police will finally pin something on you. And even if they don't, you realise I've found a way to put a stop your little reign of terror.'

Charlie took a deep breath. 'Doctor, you have me at a slight advantage.' He took the glove from the Doctor and lovingly slipped it back onto his hand. 'I've grown rather attached to this particular garment, and if I'm honest I probably rely on it a little more than I should. I want you to teach me exactly how to overcome its power. If I can do that, perhaps I can find a way to stop people from defending themselves against it. I propose we work together.'

The Doctor's interest level seemed to perk up. 'Oh?'

'I'm a man on the up, Doctor. Business is booming, for me, and with this glove it's getting better by the day. I'm unstoppable, and pretty soon I'll have many, many business interests and resources at my disposal. I could pay you handsomely, ensure you never have to work again. In return, you teach me everything you know about the glove, and help me plan a few little jobs.'

'Robberies, you mean?'

Charlie nodded.

The Doctor seemed concerned. 'Have you any morals? Have you any scruples? Do you really think I'd get into bed with a murderer, a thief and an extortionist?'

Charlie smirked. Everyone started out a do-gooder, but they never stayed that way for long. 'Think of the money, Doctor!'

The Doctor paused, and looked skyward.

After several seconds, he smiled and reached out his hand towards Charlie. 'I've changed my mind, that money sounds rather tempting.' They shook hands. 'Something tells me this could be the start of a rather special friendship.'

Erimem and Jack were discussing the finer points of gangster life. Erimem seemed intrigued by the concept of power by fear, presumably finding it quite close to the fear of a deity that her own people had displayed so readily.

She very much seemed to be taking the moral stance in the argument. Jack wasn't letting much out, but it was clear he lived an unsavoury life he wasn't particularly proud of. The Doctor had told them to go along with what the gangsters said, to not antagonise them too much, and Peri had found it a struggle to steer Erimem away from preaching to the man, a conversation that could lead to them both getting a bullet in the chest.

She was relieved to see a friendly face emerge from Shutter's office. 'Doctor!' she said, running up to him. 'What's going on?'

'Mister Shutter and I have done a deal,' he announced, a hard edge to his voice. 'Come on, Erimem. We have robberies to plan!'

'Robberies?' Erimem was aghast.

Peri could tell immediately that the Doctor was speaking more for the benefit of the listening gangsters than his companions. She knew the Doctor better than Erimem did, and knew he wouldn't normally sanction criminal activity like this. She knew he'd be able to come across convincingly to those who didn't know him, but personally she found his act rather obviously false. Or perhaps that's just what she wanted to think.

The Doctor took Peri and Erimem to one side and whispered to them.

'Just trust me, please. Go along with what I say. If I'm right, we can use these people for good, but we have to pretend to play by their rules for a while.'

Peri had to believe the Doctor knew what he was doing, but that wouldn't be easy. She'd always tried to stay on the right side of the law, and she'd never been in any trouble with the cops. She suspected that turning a blind eye now wouldn't be as easy as her friend was implying.

* * *

The weeks following the Doctor's arrival had been the strangest Jack Green had ever experienced under the employ of Charlie Shutter. Every day Charlie and the Doctor would scan newspapers, maps and magazine articles to find the best source of money, saleable goods or blackmail material they could. Then Charlie would go to the place they picked, march straight in and would use the glove to send forks of lightning ahead of him to clear the way of any opposition. If anyone confronted him, a near-lethal blast from the glove would incapacitate them and leave Charlie free to take whatever he wanted. Jack would always be following close behind, blackmailed into loyalty to make sure all the loose ends were tidied up and the police had no reason to trace the robberies back to Charlie.

'Don't tell the Doctor,' Charlie would whisper conspiratorially every time he used the Lightning, but the disapproving lecture they would inevitably receive on their return made it clear the Doctor knew what they were up to.

The scheme worked like a dream, and across London, shops, businesses, the rich and the famous, began to live in fear that one day they might meet the mysterious attacker. They'd all heard the rumours, seen the medical reports of the damage the Lightning left. No one wanted to end up like that. The newspapers called them 'the Lightning Strikes': robberies that could occur at any time, in any place, and were over before the victims knew what had hit them.

It was always the Doctor who had the final say in where the robberies occurred. The vast wealth they were accumulating was testament to the man's skills as a strategist. He always insisted that no one was killed, that no one was permanently injured, and on more than one occasion threatened to pull out of the deal and tell the world how to overpower the Lightning if Charlie didn't agree not to hurt anyone.

If it had been anyone else, Charlie would have dismissed talk like that, probably with a shot from the glove; it was ridiculous to think that so much could be stolen in such a short time without serious injuries, but the Doctor's planning seemed to manage it. The Doctor made no secret that he wasn't happy breaking the law, but Jack could tell that as long as no one was seriously hurt, the promise of untold wealth was more than enough to keep the Doctor on-side.

Three weeks after he had first met the Doctor, Jack sat with Erimem at the kitchen table in Charlie's apartment sipping a coffee and reading that morning's paper. He turned a page and a sentence in an opinion article caught his eye.

Is Charlie Shutter Behind The Lightning Strikes?

He wondered whether he should mention it to his boss. The police may not have all the pieces yet, but it seemed somebody was starting to get an idea about who was behind the attacks.

107

Jack called his boss over, and Charlie marched into the room, ripped the paper from Jack's hands, scanned the article then laughed and threw the paper to the floor. 'They can't hurt me. No one can hurt me and my Lightning.' Charlie's voice had a slight quiver to it. Jack wasn't sure Charlie was being completely honest with himself.

The rattle of keys in the door interrupted the conversation. The door opened and the Doctor and Peri marched into the room.

'Good!' the Doctor said, glancing around the room. 'I'm glad you're all here. I have an announcement to make.'

'Go on,' Charlie said.

'"The Lightning Strikes" are at an end!'

'Finally!' said Erimem, who had complained about the robberies from day one. 'I was wondering when you'd all see sense.'

'Excuse me,' a visibly rattled Charlie interrupted. 'I'm the one in charge here Doctor, I think I'll tell you when it's time to call it a day.'

'No no, you don't understand.' The Doctor reached out an arm and placed it on Charlie's shoulder. 'It's time to end it all, after one more job. After this job, you won't have any need for the Strikes.'

Charlie's expression turned from incredulity to curiosity. 'One more job?'

The Doctor nodded. He reached into a pocket in his long cream coat and pulled out a tattered clump of newspaper that looked like it had once held a portion of chips. The Doctor smoothed out the paper and handed it to Charlie. 'Look what your friends in the Mickey Green gang have found.'

Mickey Green. Charlie's arch-rival, the real kingpin South of the river. A man Charlie had indulged in petty territorial disputes with for years. This would be interesting.

Jack scuttled over to the older men and began to read the article over Charlie's shoulder.

The piece told of a mysterious cabinet, recently dug up by archaeologists in Dorset that had been dated to come from Anglo-Saxon times. Despite that, the cabinet appeared to be made of a metal the Anglo-Saxons could never have created. Only once had scientists been able to get the cabinet open, and all but one were electrocuted in the process. No one had been able to open it since, and the article went on to speculate that whatever technology had been used to fake the carbon emissions that tricked science into believing the object was old, had also been used to electrify the box. The article concluded by saying that the box had been stolen, and police suspected Mickey Green was involved in the theft.

'Doctor,' Charlie said, looking up from the article. 'Is this what I think it is?'

The Doctor nodded. 'Don't you agree that cabinet sounds like it's lined with the same material your glove is made out of? My calculations have pinpointed the building where Mister Green is keeping the cabinet, so I suggest we pay them a visit and take it for ourselves.'

'Sorry if I'm not getting this, Doctor,' Jack interrupted, 'but are you implying if we steal another block of the lightning material we'll never need to pull any robberies again?'

'That's exactly what I'm implying.' The Doctor moved over to Jack and put an arm around his shoulder. 'I believe that inside that cabinet, lies the secret of this material's origin. If we unlock the secrets of the Lightning, discover how to turn any item of clothing into a power source for it, we'll have the greatest bargaining chip the world has ever seen.'

'And we'll shaft Mickey Green good and proper.' Charlie's eyes were wide with excitement. 'Yeah, I can see it now. Total control, total power. Hundreds of people to do my bidding, to give me whatever I want. Cars, houses... my own island, my own country! Ultimate freedom to do whatever I want with no one to stop me. Yeah Doctor, I can see it.'

Erimem snorted. 'Being all-powerful is not as good as you might imagine, you know!' She looked across at Jack. 'I was Pharaoh, you see...' She stopped when she noticed Peri shaking her head. 'Well,' Erimem muttered, more to herself now. 'I was...'

Charlie, of course, had ignored her and instead continued his train of thought. 'Yes... my little glove provides me with a great deal of power, and thanks to you, Doctor, I now know the secrets of how people can stop me, but complete control of the Lightning... the ability to make any object into such a weapon... no one would be able to defy me. No one would deny me my success.'

'Or mine,' Jack said, uncomfortable that Charlie seemed to be ignoring the people who put him where he was. The more powerful Charlie became, the more Jack came to terms with the fact that Charlie would always control his life. If that was the case, then at least he wanted a piece of the man's riches.

'Now, my terms,' the Doctor said. 'We'll help you get the cabinet, help you do this one job, but then it's over for you and the underworld. No more crime, no more intimidation... leave London, break off your contacts, sell your assets here. And let your staff go freely, without the risk of threats.'

The Doctor's extra demand floored Jack. If this worked out, he'd be a free man. He'd always convinced himself that Charlie was a reason to stay in the underworld, not the only reason, but now, faced with the prospect of being free to do what he wanted... was he brave enough to take that chance?

Charlie stared into the Doctor's eyes, his voice a low growl. 'You give me the true secrets of the Lightning, the ability to control it completely, to reproduce it.' He paused, working up courage to say something difficult. 'And I'll give all of this up. All of it.'

And so, two days later, the Doctor, Jack, Charlie, Erimem and Peri, found themselves creeping through an old storage building owned by the Mickey Green crime empire, in the middle of the night.

On their way in, Charlie had paralysed three of Mickey's goons with the Lightning, a necessary evil if they were to find their quarry. Erimem and Peri had protested bitterly at the action, but the Doctor silenced their objections. The man's expression was one of someone struggling with their conscience, but it was clear that at the end of the day he had more important concerns to worry about than knocking out a hired heavy.

It was surprisingly easy to find where in the building the cabinet was kept but, inside, the room where it was supposed to be appeared to be almost empty.

'I see nothing in here,' whispered Erimem, but she was silenced by the Doctor who pointed to a small crate tucked in the corner of the room. He carefully moved towards it, gesturing for the others to stay back. Charlie followed closely behind the Doctor, despite the man's protestations.

'There there,' the Doctor said, reaching out towards the crate. 'You're safe now.'

Erimem giggled. 'Anyone would think it was his child!' she whispered.

Jack looked up at her and smiled. 'If the Doctor's theories about this thing turn out to be true, it's certainly a more precious find than any kid, I'll tell you that much.'

The Doctor crouched down and laid his palms on the top of the crate. It glowed, and a slight crackling noise could be heard. Jack glanced at Peri, who returned the gesture. At that moment they knew they'd found what they came for.

The Doctor stood up and moved closer to Charlie, a broad grin on his face. 'You have to touch it. You have to feel the power. I can feel it inside this box... Charlie, we're going to be unstoppable.'

Jack watched Charlie intently for the nod, and when it came he raised his gun towards the Doctor. He and Charlie had prearranged this moment, to betray the Doctor at the last minute, but Jack was torn between two masters. He craved the freedom the Doctor promised, but he couldn't risk disobeying Charlie. If he did, and the Doctor turned out to be wrong, then Jack's chances of surviving the night were slim.

Jack froze, kept his gun trained on the Doctor, but stopped short of pulling the trigger. 'Get back, Doctor,' Jack warned, doing his best to stay on the fence. 'The cabinet belongs to us all, don't forget that. Don't try anything.'

The Doctor looked dismayed. 'Oh Jack, give it up,' the Doctor called. 'You don't need to be Charlie's hitman anymore. You're better than that. You're better than him.'

'Doctor!' Charlie said. 'It's time for you to leave, old chum. That cabinet is mine, and mine alone!'

The Doctor turned to Charlie. 'Oh no, not at all. I think you'll find I don't need you anymore.' The Doctor held up a small electronic device with a flashing red button on top of it. He grinned, then reached down and pushed the button. 'I'm afraid your life of crime is at an end.'

The moment the Doctor pressed the button, the building's intruder alarms sounded, a noise that would surely alert everyone to the intruders' presence.

'The police are on their way,' the Doctor said. 'They know everything about you, Charlie. You're going to be spending a very long time in prison.'

The colour had drained from Charlie's face. His eyes looked lost, confused.

Panicking at the Doctor's words, Charlie raised his fist and fired an incredible stream of lightning at the man. At first Jack thought the Doctor had been caught off guard, had been hit by the blast, as his body seemed to be enveloped in electricity and glowed like a fire in the dim lighting of the room, but then the lightning began to recede, and Jack realised the Doctor was fighting it off, as he had the day he had first walked into their lives.

No, the Lightning wasn't receding. It was moving. The Doctor was breathing heavily, his brow furrowed in furious concentration. The Lightning moved across the room, away from the motley crew of burglars and towards the cabinet.

'You're free to go!' the Doctor shouted, as if talking to the Lightning. 'There's nothing here for you now.'

The room shook as a blinding burst of light, accompanied by a loud crackle of electricity, shot out of Charlie's Lightning glove, flying across the room towards the cabinet and sending Charlie sprawling backwards on to the floor. The light got brighter and brighter as it rushed with greater intensity towards the cabinet. Finally, after over a minute where he could see nothing but bright, white light and could hear nothing but the hum and crackle of electricity, Jack opened his eyes to see the light fading. He looked to the centre of the room, where the cabinet had been, and in its place saw nothing but a patch of scorched flooring, still smouldering from its recent ordeal.

Peri was the first to break the silence. 'What happened? Where did it go?'

The Doctor brushed his hands together and walked over to where Charlie was cowering in a corner, shocked to his soul by what he'd seen.

'Your so called Lightning,' the Doctor explained, 'was an alien

111

intelligence trapped on this planet for hundreds of years. Like Charlie here, it was one of the bad guys. A cheap gangster on its homeworld. That cabinet was its lost spacecraft, its way home. Every time we used the Lightning, every time it reached out and felt a human touch, its sentience grew, it gained a greater awareness of where the location of the capsule might be.

'However, there were others looking for it. Other gangsters I believe. They swept through planets, destroying everything in their path in search of their enemy. I knew that the Earth would never survive their attacks on it, and I knew they would be here soon enough. I had to draw them all together, or millions of lives could be put at risk.'

Erimem nodded. 'I see. And where are they now?'

The Doctor smiled and tapped his nose. 'All safe and sound, don't you worry. I'll deal with them all later.'

Jack couldn't believe what he was hearing. 'But how did you know all this?'

'Well,' the Doctor continued, 'I simply made the connections, narrowed down the choices, and eventually worked out exactly where the cabinet was located.'

'But why, Doctor?' Peri asked. 'Why do all this? Why involve yourself in so many crimes?'

The Doctor shook his head. 'The creatures didn't belong here. It wasn't fair to do nothing when I had the power to act. Besides, the police have the details of all Charlie's accounts, all the things he's stolen, all the companies he's upset. His assets will pass to them and they'll all regain what they lost and more. Oh, and Mickey Green will have a few ideas of what's gone on too.' He crouched down beside Charlie's pathetic form. 'I'm sorry "old chum", but you really did have it coming.'

Jack realised the significance of the Doctor's words. The Lightning had left Earth for good. Whatever mad explanation the Doctor had spouted, it was clear to see there was no Lightning glove anymore. Charlie no longer held any power over Jack, and the gangster's world had collapsed around him. With Charlie out of the picture, Jack wouldn't need the safety net of crime any more. Perhaps the Doctor was right. Perhaps…

Jack cleared his throat. 'If you've dismantled Charlie's world, what the hell am I supposed to do?'

The Doctor reached into his pocket and handed Jack a bundle of papers. Jack flicked through them and was amazed to see that they were the deeds to several properties made out in his name.

'They're yours Jack, on one condition. You must turn over a new leaf. There will be no more suffering because of Charlie Shutter's influence. No more intimidation, no more blackmail. The gangster's life will be your life no longer.'

Jack nodded, scarcely believing what the Doctor had given him. He realised the man was absolutely right. There were better ways to get back at the world than petty thuggery. He eyed the deeds in his hand. Better ways, and smarter ways.

The Doctor and Jack shook hands, and as they did so, Jack saw a mischievous glint in the Doctor's eyes that he'd never noticed before. 'Thanks Doctor,' he said. 'Things will be different now.'

'Remember,' the Doctor reminded him, 'you can do great things if you put your mind to it. And no one needs to get hurt.'

For the first time in his life, Jack knew exactly what the Doctor meant by those words. True power didn't come from fear, or intimidation, but from the freedom to choose one's own path in life. A freedom Jack now had, thanks to his peculiar new friends.

The police had arrived within minutes and taken Charlie away, but not before the rest of the party had made their escape from the building. When they were far enough away to be unnoticed, the Doctor announced that he, Peri and Erimem were going to ensure the police were fed enough information to point their investigations away from themselves. Jack didn't want to be around Charlie a moment longer, so said goodbye to the Doctor and the girls, made his excuses then headed towards a phone box to call for a cab.

Jack reflected on the changes in his life. He'd promised the Doctor he'd turn his back on crime, and somehow he knew his future had taken a change for the better. For the first time in his life he felt confident that he had the ability to build the power and respect he'd always craved, but he'd do it his way, not Charlie's, not the Doctor's. He was his own man now, and his future had yet to be written. He imagined what tomorrow might bring, and smiled.

Charley stared at the cabinet.

'So it's not the people around it, it's the people inside?'

'They're not people,' the Steward corrected. Well, not as you or I might define people. But life nevertheless. Life that couldn't be allowed to roam free, I imagine.'

The Australian woman coughed. 'The Doctor seems quite content to decide what does and doesn't have rights.'

Charley, despite her earlier thoughts, still felt a bit of loyalty towards her absent mentor. At least, enough to give him the benefit of the doubt where the lightning creatures were concerned. 'I'm not sure that you are fully qualified to judge the Doctor's every action,' she said, trying to sound as imperious as she could. 'What has he done to you?'

'Not just me,' said the woman, 'but Erin as well.'

'Who's Erin?'

The woman pointed at the little girl to her left. And then to the dog-creature to the right. 'This is Erin.'

'Which one?' Charley frowned.

The woman finally caught Charley's eyeline and stared straight at her. 'I'll explain, and you tell me if you can justify what the Doctor's done, yeah?'

'Well, all right...' said Charley, cautiously.

'Name's Lillian Robinson. Born on Earth in 1850 before you ask. Everyone does. Helps place you.'

'Charlotte Pollard. Earth. 1912.'

Lillian smiled for the first time. 'English, yeah?'

Charley nodded. And smiled back.

The Bushranger's Story

Sarah Groenewegen

Patience, Lillian had learned as a child, was much more than a virtue. It was what brought you the good things in life. Like an extra portion of your favourite meal when it was your birthday, or praise from your father when you'd got something right first go after watching all five of your brothers get it wrong.

She sighed as she swatted at the bush flies swarming under the shade of her hat. She felt Ben's rump muscles twitch and his tail swish impatiently against the flies bothering him. Then he shifted the weight off one of his back legs and she squeezed hers to get him to move forward to stand properly on all four legs. The horse did so, throwing his head and chewing at his bit.

'I know you're bored, Ben,' she said. 'There's not long to wait now.' She leaned forward to pat his neck. He tossed his head again, and then she heard in the distance the sounds she'd been listening for: other horses approaching at speed and pulling something heavy behind them. 'Not long at all now, Ben,' she said as she checked the knot holding her handkerchief as a mask on her face. Then she took one of her Colt pistols from her belt and clicked her tongue and guided Ben forward through the sparse trees to the rise just over the track. She squinted as if it would improve her sight through the dust, and then only seconds later she could see the distinctive red livery of the Cobb & Co stagecoach as its four horses strained and pulled to get their burden up to the top of the ridge. There were no outriders she could see, which held true from her previous scouting trips. She allowed herself a smile as she counted a driver and a young-looking man in dusty black town clothes perched up on the seat. Behind them was enough baggage on the roof of the coach to suggest at least one lady was on board, and there was no doubt some money.

The coach neared the spot she'd calculated was best for her purposes and she cocked the pistol and kicked Ben forward. She made him stand square on the road to face down the stagecoach and its booty. She counted quietly to calm her thundering heart and she wished she could wipe the sweat from her brow before it trickled down to sting her eyes, but her hands were full with the gun in one and the reins in the other.

Then the stagecoach was upon them and she fired the first bullet into the air and Ben reared up just as they'd practised. He neighed his challenge to the four horses now straining to get out of harm's way. The reinsman was standing up in his seat, using every ounce of his skill and strength to keep them from bolting. Then she noted the boy begin to reach into his jacket and without thought she took aim and fired, the bullet finding its mark just above his left shoulder. The young man thrust both his hands high above his head and his already pale complexion faded further.

'Stand and deliver!' she yelled, remembering to deepen her voice so it would sound commanding over the noise of the horses and the carriage.

The driver had steadied his charges, but it was taking up all his physical capability to keep them steady. 'We're not a gold transport,' he shouted, and she smiled at his unmistakable colonial accent, glad he was not a Californian, like so many of the coach drivers. 'All I want is your passengers' money,' she said. 'Your chum's purse would do nicely for starters.' She nodded towards the young man who kept his arms straight up in the air. She watched him as he gulped, then glance quickly at the reinsman. She grinned as she saw him nod to the boy.

The boy looked steadily at her. 'I've heard of bandits like you. It's a disgrace.' His accent betrayed his Englishness.

She nudged Ben forward, never letting her pistol waver. 'Sir, it's a disgrace for me to hold up your journey any longer when Mr Cobb's horses plainly need refreshment and rest. So, hand over your purse and I can let you on your way with no further trouble.' She smiled again as she watched him reach into his jacket pocket and throw her his money pouch. It clinked with the sound of coins and felt heavy enough as she tossed it in the air and caught it again. 'Thank you, sir,' she said as she quickly placed it in her saddlebag. 'And welcome to the colonies,' she added.

She urged Ben forward a few more paces to look into the coach. There were only four people inside. An old man, two young women who looked like sisters and a child who looked about four or five years old. The three adults looked terrified, the boy enthralled by this adventure but held close by his mother. 'None of you will be hurt if you hand over your money,' she said calmly. She winked at the boy as the man tossed over a purse. Quickly, that joined the first and she wheeled Ben around as she bade them a good journey.

She drove Ben at a trot back up the rise off the road then heard a shot ping off a tree inches beside her. Turning to see where it had come from, she saw the blurred blue uniforms of troopers on horses galloping up on the road from where the stagecoach was heading. They must have heard her shots, she thought as she fired back once towards them then spurred Ben forward. Surefooted, he scrambled up the short embankment then into the trees. He needed little encouragement from her as he galloped, zigging and zagging through the gums. He leapt like a hunter across the gullies and over the small hillocks, and she let him have his head to negotiate through the brush while she kept her head down and out of the way of low-lying branches. The troopers behind them were loud, but had stopped shooting at her, then as Ben's legs stretched out she heard the noise of the police horses begin to fade into distance. Finally, she slowed Ben down as they reached the banks of the flowing river that meandered its way through the valleys. She listened and there was nothing, so she eased Ben into the shallow water and let him drink.

While the pony drank, she pulled the handkerchief mask from her face and used it to wipe off some of the sweat and dust, and thought about the troopers. It was obvious they had come from the station just down the road another mile or so, but she was sure from the glimpse she'd had they weren't native troopers, which gave her some breathing space. But, she knew they would use trackers and the trail she and Ben had made would be plain as a main road to them. She pulled Ben's head up from the water and urged him into a walk, sticking to the river for as far along as it was passable. Then, about a mile and a half along she guided him up the far embankment where there were more rocks than dirt. She was careful not to break any branches on the way up, and then she settled Ben onto the course back to where she was starting to think of as home.

Ben's comfortable gait relaxed her into a doze. She woke out of it when Ben suddenly stopped, throwing his head up with a surprised snicker. Then there was a noise like she imagined Hannibal's elephants would sound like from her oldest brother's history stories. Birds screeched in panic from the trees, and she had to pull on Ben's reins to stop him from bolting.

She stared as a shape began to form. It didn't take long for it to become solid, looking for all the world like a blue cabinet or wardrobe, but of a style Lillian had never seen before. It had a flashing blue light on its roof and a sign above its doors. She managed to spell out the first word: p-o-l-i-c-e – before one of the doors opened. She gathered the reins, preparing to bolt for her life but stopped at the sight of the woman who stepped from the cabinet. She was tall, with long brown hair worn loose and wild, which matched something in her expression, and matched her clothing. Animal skins, Lillian realised, but worn in a way completely different to the natives who still foraged in the hills near where she had set up camp. These skins were tanned dark and fitted the woman's torso snugly. Long boots covered her feet and legs up to her knees. 'Doctor,' the woman spoke as she lowered into a hunting crouch, a knife in her hand. 'There is a monster outside!'

'Monster?' exploded a man's voice from inside the cabinet. A head appeared in the doorway. 'Leela, are you sure?'

'Right in front of us, Doctor,' she said, sounding wary. The man emerged fully and doffed a floppy felt hat in Lillian's direction. 'You're not a monster, are you?'

117

'No,' she found herself saying.

'Indeed.' His face burst into the biggest grin she had ever seen. 'I'm the Doctor and this is Leela. I think you can put the knife away now, Leela.'

Lillian noticed Leela's stare never left her while she slid the large knife back into its sheath.

'And you are?'

'My name is Lillian Robinson, and my horse is Ben.'

'Hello, Ben,' he said to the horse, who tossed his head as though in greeting. 'The circus hasn't been through here has it?' he directed to Lillian.

'Circus? No,' she shook her head. She didn't know if she should laugh.

He looked the picture of disappointment. 'Ah. No P.T. Barnum?'

Lillian shook her head again, and he copied her movement. 'Pity,' he continued. 'I wanted to show Leela the Fiji Mermaid. Where are we?'

'New South Wales,' she said. 'Near the road to Bathurst Town.'

'Where the gold was found?'

'Yes.'

'But no circuses?'

'None that I have seen.'

'No mermaids, bearded ladies or griffins?'

'No.'

'No Fiji Mermaid or griffins here, Leela,' he said to his friend, sadly. Then he brightened again. 'New South Wales is in Australia,' he said. Lillian nodded, still trying to collect her wits against this torrent of nonsense following the appearance of the impossible. 'Kangaroos, platypus, wallabies and koalas! They exist, don't they?'

'Of course.'

'Superb,' he grinned his insane grin again. 'Do you know where some are so we can show Leela? She's never seen such creatures. I don't believe she even knows a horse if she mistook yours for a monster.'

'Where is she from if she doesn't know what a horse is?'

'I am a warrior of the Sevateem. I am not frightened of these horse creatures.'

'Oh, no one said you were frightened of them, Leela,' the Doctor said. 'I just thought you would like to see some animals. Perhaps I should have taken you to see the more unusual ones created by Barnum for his circus.'

'If it's unusual creatures you want to see, there are the Wolf-People,' Lillian said.

'Wolf-People?' His incredible blue eyes looked as though they were about to pop from his head as he returned his attention completely to her.

'Yes. There's a group of people who have camped in one of the valleys here. They have a pack of wolves with them. The Eora here call them White Dog-People, but they're more like wolves than dogs.'

'What year is this?'

His sudden seriousness surprised her more than the question did.
'1876.'

'There shouldn't be any wolves in Australia in 1876,' he said, his voice
low.'You've seen these people yourself?'

'Yes. Only in the distance, though. Billy, the Eora man who told me
about them, said they keep themselves to themselves but that they're not
like ordinary people.'

'I see. Can you take me to see them?'

'Of course.'

She led them through the scraggly white ghost gums to a small gully
where a trickle of water ran. She had stopped at one point to free Ben to
run in a place he knew, and had taken the time to hide the loot from the
bail up, and put the saddle and bridle in a small cave with other
provisions. She led her strange visitors on without any comment about
the place where they had stopped, and they had not seemed particularly
concerned about it.

The Doctor, she saw, was pointing out various types of trees and birds
to his companion as he strode, setting a pace suited more for the streets
of a town than the bush, his long woollen scarf and jacket trailing out
behind him. But he, and Leela, were as surefooted as she in this terrain,
and his knowledge of the bush was extraordinary, rivalling Billy and the
other Eora people she'd spoken with since moving to this part of the
bush.

Then they were at the place she had taken to calling Wolf Ridge. They
stopped when she did, and all of them looked through the trees and
down the gentle slope to the valley. 'They have chosen their camping
place well,' said Leela after a little while.

A fair comment, Lillian thought. There was water in the river that even
in the worst drought would still flow as a creek. There was shelter enough
with the trees that grew strong and green by the water's edge, and the
Eora people had told her the valley had always been a good place to hunt
kangaroo and wombat. One of the reasons why they didn't like these
Wolf-fellas, Billy had said. They'd killed off the 'roos.

It was Leela who had first seen where the pack was. Not too far from
the river, under the shade of the trees. The humans were stretched out
naked and pink in the yellowy-green grass, grey wolves at their side,
panting in the heat. The Doctor produced a small telescope and gazed at
them for a little while, not saying a word. He handed the telescope to
Lillian, who looked through it and was surprised to see how clear and
near the little thing made the Wolf-Men appear. 'Thank you,' she said, and
he beamed and told her to keep it.

'Stay here,' he commanded. 'Both of you,' he said, pointing to Leela. And he was gone, scarf trailing out behind him but somehow not snagging on the undergrowth.

Lillian watched his progress, and then heard Leela sigh angrily. She glanced at her. 'He always goes into danger and leaves me behind even though he knows I can protect him.' She blinked her dark eyes that were as brown as the skins she wore, and changed the subject. 'You have lived here a long time?'

'No, not really. I've travelled Bathurst Town to Ballarat Town in Victoria, following the gold but there was nothing but whoring as a prospect for me.' She smiled to hide the bitterness of the memories. 'I left my family because I did not want to be a wife, and my father did not believe I ought to go a-droving even though I'm more of a horseman than any of my brothers. So, I thought I would take up bushranging.'

'I do not understand what you are saying,' said Leela, her confusion shown on her face as plain as her words.

Lillian just smiled, rummaging about in her mind for words to ask the questions she had teeming about Leela and the Doctor, but a sudden crashing sound from the brush below wiped all those questions. Leela stood, Lillian too, and as Leela drew her knife Lillian had her Colt out and cocked. The Doctor appeared, striding forth, a flash of pink and silver-grey running behind him. Lillian straightened out the arm with the pistol, aimed at the wolf lowering to pounce, her finger squeezed the trigger as the blurry rush of silver-grey leapt and she fell back in a tangle of coarse fur and snapping teeth and the loud crack of the bullet as it exploded in its chamber.

'NO!' someone screamed.

Then silence for a long second of utter clarity. Lillian lay on her back, a wolf planted on her chest, paws on her shoulders and yellowed teeth bared ready to rip out her throat without any warning. She could smell rotting meat on the breath of the wolf as it breathed, and could see wisdom shine in its dark silver-blue eyes. In that long second she saw and knew this beast was no dumb animal.

'Lillian,' said the Doctor's deep voice. 'I would like you to meet the leader of the people with no name who you call wolf.'

The wolf licked her face, then moved to allow her to sit up. But she was content to lie on the stone-hard ground staring up at the eucalypt canopy and let her mind wander away from where she was.

'Doctor, she's hurt,' said Leela.

Hurt. Yes. Shot by Troopers and delirious with the pain, Lillian thought as she lay there. Only when she blinked her eyes clear of silent sudden tears she could see the Doctor, Leela and a small, wiry, naked man standing over her. She groaned the low and long groan of a hurt animal.

The Doctor knelt down on her right side, looking at her arm, then touching it. White hot pain stabbed from it through to her brain and she cried out. 'Your hand is hurt where your gun exploded, and it looks like you've broken your arm against a rock as you fell. I can help you. Make sure your arm and hand mend.' She couldn't watch what he was doing as the pain began to wash through her body and cloud everything. Only some things were clear enough for her to remember later.

The Doctor had given her something to drink, and that dulled her senses against the pain as surely as the laudanum doctors had given her mother before she died. Finally, she sank into a sleep deeper than any she could ever remember.

Hours later, when she woke she felt better than she had ever felt in her twenty-six years. Her head was clear, her muscles felt strong, when by all rights she ought to feel sore and sick. She sat in her shirt sleeves propped up against a gum tree, her right arm in a sling, booted feet stretched out in front. To her side was her jacket, neatly folded, and she could see both the telescope and a bottle of a type she had never seen before lying on top.

Voices attracted her attention and she could see people grouped together like drovers around a camp fire. Only there was no fire, and there were no sheep, and the only two people wearing clothes were the Doctor and Leela. She counted a dozen of the naked people, of whom more were women than men, each one with a wolf stretched out beside them. There were no children. Of the voices, she recognised the Doctor's baritone, and Leela's respectful, careful words. The third voice had an Irish burr, and the words were chosen in the same careful way as Leela spoke. That voice belonged to the older man who had stood over her after his wolf had attacked her. Leader, the Doctor had said.

She closed her eyes for a moment and when she opened them again she saw the Doctor, Leela and some of the wolf-people had stood up. Leela pointed in her direction, and the Doctor nodded to the leader. He strode over to her, then hunkered down, 'Hello,' he said.

'Hello.'

'Leela and I must go now. I have left you some medicine that will make you better. Use it sparingly. You won't be able to survive out here with a broken arm alone, but they have said they will look after you and keep you safe.'

'But…'

He smiled. 'They won't harm you. They are an ancient race belonging to a mythical time of faerie folk and unicorns. Their leader tells me they were brought here on ships for the amusement of families of the old country. Those families died and the pack escaped. They're dying, Lillian. A part of the world that will soon be no longer.'

Then he stood with a grin replacing the sadness she had seen in his extraordinary eyes. 'Goodbye, Lillian,' he said. 'Say goodbye, Leela.'

The warrior woman nodded, 'May your bushranging go well,' she said, and Lillian smiled in return. She watched as they retraced their steps, then closed her eyes to drift into sleep again. A sleep she knew she would wake from to find herself in a prison cell awaiting the noose, and not in a valley clearing with creatures that surely did not exist.

Months later she stood on the ridge where she had let Ben wander all that time ago. She'd been to the small cave where she'd kept the saddle and bridle and her small store of flour, tea and sugar. She'd stored them well, she had seen, with only minor spoilage of the tea. The leather was a little worse for the lack of wear, and the metal buckles and bit were now dusted with the red of rust. All of which was easy to clean and fix.

The saddlebag with the money was still where she'd hidden it so quickly from the Doctor and Leela. She used the time here and now to count the loot. Carefully, she poured the contents into her still damaged right hand and used her much stronger and surer left hand to sort the coins. There was not a fortune there, but enough for town or farm-bought provisions should the need arise. Perhaps for vegetables, she thought, which she'd missed in the diet the pack had been feeding her since the Doctor and Leela had left.

At first the pack had given her bloody meat warm from fresh hunts. She'd eaten it. Despite the Doctor's medicine she'd been still too weak to do much differently, and despite his words she'd been too wary of the pack to talk to them. After a few days she had spoken to them about fire. They knew fire, but had no idea about how to make or control it. She talked one of the women through it and they charred the meat they'd given her. Then she'd grown stronger and had helped, cursing her useless right arm. While the pack hunted, she took to gathering from the plant life she'd learned from Billy was safe and good to eat.

The pack only ever ate fresh kill, never the cooked meat and plants she needed to survive. She asked the leader once why that was so, and he had said it was just the way it was.

Just the way it was.

Like the fact they had no names. It was just the way it was, their leader had told her, which was what she remembered the Doctor had said. Only then she hadn't understood what he'd meant.

Now she stood on the ridge looking over the view that months ago had been so familiar to her and now wasn't. Now she was looking for Ben, and wondering if his loyalty would be more than fleeting. She whistled, long and low, then waited, cocking her head to listen better for the sound of his neigh. After a while she whistled again, but there was nothing. Perhaps he was too far away to hear. Perhaps he had been injured and couldn't return. Perhaps he was dead.

Finally, she turned to enter the cave to take her supplies down to Wolf Valley and her new home. Ben wasn't coming home, and she felt empty at the thought.

Years later she watched as the woman lay in the centre of a circle in a clearing under the light of a full moon. Lillian had mimicked what the pack women had done and they seemed to accept her. They let her be with them, watching the woman with the full belly shining with sweat despite the cooler night air blown down from the snow up on the mountain tops.

While they waited, her mind wandered to a memory she thought she had quashed. One from such a long time ago. Two days after she had arrived at the gold fields of Ballarat and one of the few other women there was in labour. Lillian had been expected to help, to know what to do. But she'd been the youngest of her brood, she'd said. She only knew of lambing and dogs whelping.

Dogs. That was one of the many things different about this birth and the Ballarat one. Lillian glanced over at the woman's bitch. Her great grey head lay in her paws. She panted as the woman did, whined when the woman gasped. Perfect synchronicity, perfect harmony, like everything in the pack's strange lives. The circle, now only five of the original eight, started to croon, the dogs' voices providing an unexpectedly beautiful counterpoint that Lillian couldn't join. It was haunting and Lillian recognised how alien it was in a land normally thrumming with crickets and cicadas or trilling with birdsong.

The woman screamed and the dog howled. The women seated by her shoulders leant forward as one to hold her down. The other two women leant in to stroke her glistening swollen stomach. Repetitive, calming rhythm. Lillian watched the muscles ripple with their contractions under their hands, the contractions pushing the new life down.

Lillian turned to look at the bitch. She had stood up, was walking in a comfort-seeking circle the way dogs do. The four other dogs helped her the same way as the women helped the mother-to-be, only by licking and crooning as she settled into a more comfortable position.

The births were quick and instinct drove both dogs and humans to do what they had to do. The smell of blood and sweat hung heavy in the night air. Lillian looked up to the moon, away from the squeaking of the pup and the squalling cries of the baby. Away from the cleaning and eating. Away from what made her different from them.

But they didn't let her escape. They included her even where they didn't include their own menfolk. Drew her into their circle. Gave her the baby – a girl – to hold with the pup, both little creatures still mucus-blind and slippery to hold. They expected her to lick them just as they had, but she couldn't bring herself to. A sudden memory of the Doctor made her smile as she quickly passed both babies to the next woman and reached into her pocket where she kept the precious bottle. Her wound no longer even had a scar. The bottle's contents had done her the world of good over the years, and it was time now to repay some of the debts she knew they didn't keep. She looked to the panting dam, who blinked her wolf-eyes and Lillian took that for permission. She poured the last remaining drops of the liquid into her hand, dipped a finger into it and gave it to the pup to suckle. With the same questioning look to the human mother, and the same permission granted, she gave the remainder to the baby. As the drops dripped into the mouth, the name Erin escaped from Lillian's lips. Erin for the land they'd come from. Maybe return to. One day.

She felt full of hope and life as she fed the human Erin the last liquid drops from the bottle the Doctor had given her. As she did so, she remembered his words about the pack dying and she smiled. Surely they would survive now they had proved they could still breed. Despite everything. Despite their dwindling numbers.

Decades later she felt as empty as she had when the Doctor and Leela had left her. Days before, she and Erin had burnt and buried the last of her people and the wolf-girl and cub had left on what Lillian knew was the same permanent walkabout as the Eora people before them. Alone in the world again, Lillian, too, began to wander with a swag of her belongings.

Lillian found the black snake highway cutting through her land. Huge loud monsters thundered along, bright colours marking each one differently but all plainly dangerous. There were lots of things left by the side of the road, Lillian had discovered, many of which were useful even though she had no idea what they were. Newspaper pages were left to disintegrate in the weather. She gathered one up to try to read about what was happening in the world that had moved on without her. She also wanted to know how Erin was faring in the days since she'd left.

She read, 'Unicorn stampedes through Palace', and other words describing one of the horned horses being seen at Buckingham Palace in England. It joined a Pegasus in Greece, and a Bunyip terrorising shoppers in a mall in Melbourne.

'But, that's not right,' she said softly to herself. Unless...

She cocked her head, listening for the whooshing and grinding sounds she had likened to the sounds of creatures she had never seen and never heard. Elephant creatures as mythical to her as the unicorns and griffins, centaurs and wolf-men. Wolf-men she had known and lived with.

'Well, why not?'

* * *

Charley sighed and nodded. 'I'm sorry.'

Lillian looked back at in apparant surprise. 'Yeah? Me too.'

'I mean,' continued Charley. 'I think I see why the Doctor had to take you all... both away.'

Lillian really was surprised now. 'Why? I mean, what did I do that was so wrong? I did the right thing by the Wolf People in giving them the last of the medicine the Doctor gave me. What's so wrong with that?'

Charley thought about this for a few seconds, glanced over to the Steward, trying to see if he would back her up. He was just smiling as usual, listening to them both. He gave no hint that he agreed or disagreed with either of them, just listened.

'Lillian, don't you see? The Doctor shouldn't have given you that medicine in the first place. Yes, that was his mistake and yes, you're paying for it, but it's the only option he could have taken.'

Lillian did not look like she was going to agree, so Charley carried on before the Australian could respond. 'I think he's given you some kind of... of future space medicine. Something that shouldn't exist on Earth by my time, let alone yours.'

'Nanotechnology,' offered the Steward. 'That's what it sounds like to me. Just my opinion.'

Charley nodded. 'Whatever it's called, it's affected your life hasn't it?'

'How?'

'How old are you? You look to me as if you are, oh, I don't know, forty-five? But you're not are you. You must be well over a hundred years old by now.'

Lillian thought about this. 'Yeah, probably.'

'Then this medicine, it's stopped illness, infection. Ageing even – or at least slowed it down. That's not right. Not natural for Earth, is it?'

'S'pose not.'

'And you gave it to Erin, to the Wolf-People. You thought that their becoming extinct was a bad thing. To be stopped, am I right?'

'Of course it was,' Lillian said, slightly angrily. 'Look at Erin. How could not letting her live be a bad thing?'

'Oh, this is so difficult,' said Charley, 'but please try to understand. This is nothing personal about you or Erin or any of her people. What the Doctor meant, I believe anyway, was that everything in existence faces a natural end. They were a race that should have died out.'

'Why?'

'Because... because they had a different role to play. As myths. As things for others to believe in and treasure. A legacy that was actually more important than their own actual survival. Erin's birth broke that aspect of the Web of Time, I think.' Charley took a quick swig of her drink. Dutch courage, she thought the Doctor would have said. 'Your

Wolf-People are mythical creatures that have stretched the epoch of mythical creatures actually existing in the "real world" without actually breaking it. Yet. The Doctor knew they would die out and no one else would be any the wiser. Except that Erin's birth did break it, because she is new life for a dead world plus she has some of the Doctor's space medicine, these…'

'Nanites,' added the ever-helpful Steward.

'Nanites,' she confirmed. 'They were… they are in her and who knows what repercussions that would have. The huge kindness you did has cost you – what you've done would bring mythical creatures back into the "real world".'

'So you're saying that because I did something good, something to save an entire race, I, and Erin, must be punished?'

Charley smiled sadly. 'Yes. Yes, I believe so. I'm sorry, but you and both aspects here of Erin cannot co-exist on Earth any longer. And that's so sad.'

Lillian looked hard at Charley, and then at the Steward, then at both aspects of Erin. 'Maybe,' she said finally. 'But I don't have to like it.'

And she walked away from the bar, slowly, across the room and to the huge windows. Charley watched her and the Erins, just staring into the blue nothingness for a moment or two.

'So sad,' she said quietly to the Steward.

He was polishing a couple of glasses. 'I can see why he wanted you here,' he said after a moment's silence. 'You're good.'

'Lillian would have done anything to keep Erin alive. And horrible as it sounds, one life can't always take precedence over many.'

'Good point,' said the Steward. 'I wonder if he thought about that as he snatched you from all that burning metal, cloth and petrol in France?'

Charley swung around on him. 'You know, Steward? I haven't a clue? But after listening to Lillian's story, I'm beginning to think he may have done. Maybe he rescued me because I have a purpose he knew about. Maybe he knew I wasn't supposed to die then.'

'Maybe' agreed the Steward. 'Time will tell.' He looked up as another customer approached. It was the American Charley had seen earlier with the Rag and Bone Man.

'Telling you his life story, is he?' he asked, nodding towards the Steward.

Before Charley could reply, the Steward leant over. 'No, Robert, but I think right now, she could do with knowing yours. After all, a little knowledge can't be a bad thing, can it?'

The Schoolboy's Story

Trey Korte

There was a monster howling in Bobby's closet. It wasn't a scary-sounding monster, Bobby thought, more like a sad or sick one, maybe one like an elephant. Bobby liked elephants, and remembered writing an animal report on them for a school project. He knew that there were both African and Asian elephants, and the African elephants' ears were larger. He knew that elephants' tusks were made of ivory and this made them endangered, which meant that they might go extinct. He also knew that elephants were herd animals, that they were herbivorous, and that there were over 100,000 muscles in an elephant's trunk.

He also knew that elephants weren't in the habit of hiding in kids' closets.

So, sheets clutched tightly, Bobby stared at the closet door and wondered what had made the howling noise. It obviously wasn't an elephant, but something had woken him up at this time of late night/early morning when the moonlight gave everything a glow. It probably wasn't a monster either, Bobby decided, but he wasn't sure what it was. And when the elephant noise had stopped, Bobby heard another noise, a gentle hum coming from inside the closet. And for a moment, Bobby thought he heard voices, normal voices, inside.

Bobby considered waking his snoring father sleeping in the bedroom down the hall. He didn't want to though. He'd probably yell. Daddy yelled a lot now that Mom was gone. And anyway, there was probably nothing in the closet. He remembered the time he had heard a monster outside his window and had run to his father screaming and crying. It had been a tree branch tapping against the wall of the house. Daddy had been upset, saying that it was only Bobby's imagination and that monsters don't exist.

Yet something was making that humming noise. And if it wasn't a monster, then what was it?

Bobby tried to ignore it, but in the silence of night, it only became louder. And the more he tried to ignore it, the more he found he couldn't. Ignoring things never did any good, Bobby thought. Daddy and his teachers always told him just to ignore the other kids. It never worked. The more he ignored the others, the more they'd tease him. And this humming from his closet teased him the same way, not actively bothering him, but humming, as if to say 'I'm watching you from this closet and I know you're there.' He had to investigate it. But he couldn't investigate it. The clown-faced night-light leered at him from the wall socket. 'Aren't you going to investigate the closet?' the clown seemed to ask. 'Or are you chicken? Bobby Zierath is a chicken! Bawk! Bawk! Bawk!' Bobby didn't want to be a chicken, so he reached a decision. He held Buster, his toy puppy, close to his chest, and, taking several slow steps – stopping for a full thirty seconds each time the floor creaked – Bobby ventured towards the closet door and the humming. And mustering as much courage as he could, Bobby opened the closet door and looked at what was inside.

It was another door, a blue door, with writing on it. Bobby sounded out the words, 'Po…lice Pub..lic Call Box….Pull To O…pen'. And he heard the voices again. It sounded like an old man and a young man having an argument. He pushed open the door and stepped inside.

Miss Colleen Griebel looked through the student file once again and sighed. Poor Bobby Zierath. She wished she could do more for him as he had been having such a tough time in school since his mother had died. His academic work had begun to slip, which of course was normal for bereaved children, but now these stories! While she valued creativity in children, she became concerned when the line between reality and imagination became blurred. And these stories and drawings of Bobby's convinced her that all was not right with the child.

That morning, Bobby had burst into the classroom, full of more enthusiasm than she had seen in a long time. When she asked him why he was so excited, he responded by telling her a story about having adventures with a strange old man and his two friends. When she questioned Bobby further about how he had met these three friends, he became silent and wouldn't talk about it. Instead he chose to elaborate about some adventure on a planet with giant talking mushrooms that he and someone named Vicki decided to call Mooshroos. Colleen then told Bobby not to make up stories to impress friends. At this Bobby grew red and insisted that this wasn't a story, it was true. When she told Bobby that it wasn't true, that mushrooms simply do not talk except in fairy tales, Bobby, tears streaming down his face, ran out of the classroom and hid in the boys' bathroom. Colleen had needed to ask Mr McCaskey to coax Bobby out again.

Recess hadn't been much better. Bobby, perched on the jungle gym, had been surrounded by a group of boys eagerly listening to his tales. As she had approached, she had overheard some of what Bobby had been saying.

'And then we went back and met some kings and queens and emperors and stuff and Steven had to fight a duel!' Bobby had said to his friends.

'And then what happened, Bobby?' asked Alex Ramm, a hyper boy with spiky blond hair and glasses, 'Did Steven kill the guy with his axe?'

'I don't believe your stupid story!' claimed Michael Usky, a rather angry chubby kid whose favourite activity was usually picking his nose and touching himself. Sometimes he did both at once.

'Well, it did happen, fat-ass! And if Steven were here, he'd kick your butt for saying that!' Bobby hopped down from the jungle gym, fists at the ready.

At this, Colleen intervened before a fight broke out. 'Bobby, Alex, and Michael!' she said in her best I-mean-business voice, 'We do not use language like that at Wilson Elementary, nor do we make inappropriate comments about each other's appearance. Furthermore, we do not make up stories in order to impress our friends.'

'But it really happened! It's not a story, Miss Griebel' insisted Bobby.

Colleen sighed, 'And where did this happen, Bobby?'

'Rome.' Bobby looked her straight in the eye.

'And when did you go to Rome, Bobby?'

'Last night.' Again, no evasion, no shiftiness.

'That is impossible, Bobby. And even if you did, they don't hold contests like that anymore, and even if they still did, they wouldn't be something an eight-year-old should see. So do not, I repeat, do *not* make up any more of these silly stories!'

Once again, Bobby turned red, tears welling up in his eyes. This time, however, he also screamed at her. He yelled that it wasn't a story, that it was true, and that he hated her for not believing him. Then he had stomped off and spent the rest of the recess pouting underneath the slide. Colleen had always liked Bobby, and it pained her to see him this upset. It appeared that Bobby believed every word of what he was saying. He had never lied before, nor did he usually use bad language or lose his temper.

And now she sat, staring at Bobby's file and a drawing Bobby had made in class. It featured stick figures of what she assumed were Bobby and his three imaginary friends: a young man, a young girl, and an elderly man. There was an odd piece of furniture, and there appeared to be circles drawn in the background, making some bizarre wallpaper. Above the picture was a caption Bobby had written: MY NEW HOME. There was, she decided, something clearly wrong with the child. Making a decision, she reached for her phone.

'Child protective services, please.'

Victor Zierath regarded his son carefully. Bobby sat at the kitchen table, staring listlessly at his tuna casserole. Victor hated to see the kid so depressed. It had only been about six months since Bobby's mother had died, and, God only knew, they both still struggled to adjust. Often Victor worried if Bobby blamed him for her death, although Bobby had never said or done anything to indicate that. The problem was he had generally left all the parenting to Nicole, and now he wasn't sure what to do.

'Aren't you hungry, sport?' he asked, a forced, hopeful smile on his face.

'No.'

'Well, you need to eat more than that, buddy.'

'I said I'm not hungry.' Bobby pushed a stray pea around his plate.

Victor sighed. 'Okay, son. Tell me what the problem is. Did something happen at school?' Bobby didn't answer, but continued moving his peas. 'Bobby, I'm talking to you.'

'I don't want to talk about it.'

Victor never knew how to handle this. Did Bobby want to talk about it? Or didn't he? On one hand, he didn't want to push the kid when he was obviously upset, but on the other hand, if some jerk kid had been bullying him, or if some jackass teacher had treated him unfairly, Victor wanted to know about it.

'Bobby, I promise you won't get in trouble. Just, tell me about it.'

Bobby looked at him closely. 'Promise you won't get mad at me?'

'I promise.'

'Okay, at school Miss Griebel didn't believe my stories that were true, and then Michael Usky tried to start a fight when he called me a liar.'

'Michael Usky? The smelly fat kid?'

'Yeah. And then on the school bus, you know that girl, Kayla Rizzo, who's in fifth grade? She started saying that I was a liar, and that no one liked me, and that she heard Mom would still be alive if you hadn't been a screwup.'

'Well, never mind what a girl like Kayla Rizzo says. There's something real screwy going on there if a girl is picking on kids three years younger than her. She's just saying crap that her tramp mother's been gossiping about. Don't listen to that talk, you hear?' God, Victor hated Nancy Rizzo and her stuck-up princess daughter. He remembered how Nancy would be the one who'd always tell Nicole what a mistake she had made marrying Victor. Like that rag should talk as her trophy husband left her as soon as something younger and sexier arrived in the picture. Victor actually felt a bit sorry for Kayla. Having a loser like Nancy for a mother and a disappearing act as a father, well, no wonder the girl had to prey upon other kids.

The phone interrupted Victor's thoughts. 'I'll just get that, Bobby. Finish your casserole.' He picked up the receiver. 'Hello?…Yes, this is he… Oh, yeah, I remember… Yes I figured something had happened today… Tomorrow?… Yeah… No he's fine, just won't eat… He what?… That's not like… Yes I'll speak to him… Thank you.' Putting the receiver down, Victor walked back into the kitchen. 'That was Miss Griebel. Now, why are you telling stories about going to see alien mushroom people and Rome?'

Bobby sat there, discovered a sudden appetite for tuna casserole, and quickly started to eat his dinner.

Victor lost his patience. 'Dammit Bobby! I have to go to your school tomorrow and meet with your teacher and some counsellor. They've called some protective services because of your stories and they probably think it's because I'm beating you or something. Now will you just tell me what the hell is going on?'

Bobby hesitated and then finally spoke up. 'Okay, don't get mad at me, but last night, a time machine landed in my closet and I went inside it and it was bigger on the inside than the outside and it was driven by this old man named the Doctor and his two friends Vicki and Steven and they took me on some adventures and then took me back home just after we had left and when I went to tell everyone, no one believed me so I got mad at them and called Michael a fat-ass.' And with this confession, Bobby returned to his tuna casserole, avoiding Victor's gaze.

Jeez, the kid has issues, Victor thought. Or maybe he had some sort of weird dream and, for whatever reason, was using it as a basis for telling stories. But he should know better. Oh, God, please let this be just a funny dream. I can't have a psycho kid. Yes, it was probably just some dream or story he made up. Why Bobby would go and tell stories about his dreams just to annoy the other kids was anybody's guess. And now Child Protective Services were involved. Heck with it. Tomorrow's meeting would straighten everything out, and maybe it could be a way to reach out to Bobby. Nicole had warned him that Bobby would get nightmares from watching all those science-fiction shows. Victor had thought she was full of it, but maybe she had been right.

'Okay, son. Well, maybe you shouldn't tell those stories. We'll talk about it with your teachers after school tomorrow, okay?' Victor smiled and patted Bobby's back to reassure him that everything would be all right.

'So I'm not in trouble then?' Bobby didn't look convinced.

'Of course not, kiddo.'

'Well, Doctor, where are we now?' The Ship had landed and Steven, pacing around the console room, was impatient to learn their new location. The Doctor, instead of checking the scanner, stood frowning at a series of console lights with Vicki at his side. 'Well, Doctor?' Steven insisted.

The Doctor barely responded, glaring at the readouts. 'Hmm? Oh, I'm so sorry, my boy. It appears we have a misreading here on the console.'

'Hardly unusual,' snorted Steven.

'What is the misreading?' asked Vicki, probably used to defusing tension between the Doctor and Steven by now. She wandered over to the Doctor as he started fiddling with an odd-looking contraption resembling something like a calculator and a bugle.

'Well, my dear, this light here indicates there's a disturbance with time, something that can threaten the whole of history. I installed it after our experience with that Monk fellow.' Apparently satisfied with the explanation, the Doctor once again turned his attention to the contraption.

'So?' insisted Vicki, 'Surely that simply means there is another time-traveller wherever we are. Shouldn't we investigate?'

'But the problem, child, is that according to my device here, there are no other time ships within the vicinity.' He held up and shook the device for emphasis.

'Well, if I may interject,' said Steven, annoyed at being ignored, 'just where is here? And when? I've only been asking three times now.'

'That's the other strange thing. We appear to be in early twenty-first-century America. An eventful period certainly, but not one that dealt with any time technology.' The Doctor consulted some more readings. 'Yes, it appears we are in the suburban Midwest, in a state called Indiana.'

'Ancient America!' gushed Vicki. 'Oh how I've always wanted to see more of it! Maybe we can see a shopping mall, or even one of those historic coffee shop franchises.' Steven smiled, remembering Vicki's stories of the time she had previously experienced a taste of Ancient America, when the Ship had briefly landed on the Empire State Building. Back then, her visit had been cut short, and so she had always asked to go back. When that didn't occur, she had immersed herself in the Ship's library, refreshing herself in the history and culture of Ancient America and believed herself to be something of an expert on the subject. Unfortunately for her, the Doctor's control of the Ship was erratic, and although she had pleaded with him to use the fast-return switch to get back to the Empire State Building, he had refused, claiming it was better not to tempt time. Or fate. Or something of that nature.

'Now wait a minute, Vicki,' interrupted Steven, determined to be as practical as ever. 'If the Doctor says there's some dodgy time business out there, maybe we should save the sightseeing tour for some other time.' In truth, Steven wasn't in the mood for one of Vicki's perky exploring expeditions.

'There's no reason why we can't do both, is there?' implored Vicki.

'Of course not, my child,' replied the Doctor. 'Shall we go and explore?' And, holding out his arm for Vicki, the two of them exited the ship, Steven following.

Stephanie Luck had finally returned to her desk and sat down, her show-and-tell presentation featuring the latest trading card fad involving pastel-coloured Japanese critters finished.

'Thank you, Stephanie,' Colleen said. 'Who wants to be the next volunteer for show-and-tell?' Colleen hated show-and-tell. She didn't really see much educational value in it other than to provide the rich kids with an excuse to show off all the plastic junk their parents had spoiled them with. Still, the kids enjoyed it, and it was a good way to start on those basic public speaking skills. And after last night's telephone conversation, she had neither the time nor the energy to create something more original.

Surveying the room, she was happy to see that Bobby had his hand raised high. Good, she thought. She had been worried that he'd be very shy today, but he seemed happy and eager to share his object with the class for show-and-tell. Wanting to encourage him, and also wanting him to forget yesterday's unpleasantness, she called him forward. She made a mental note to watch out for anything that might be pertinent to this afternoon's meeting.

Bobby was standing in front of the class, holding a stuffed panda. Colleen sighed, wishing he had brought something else. Yes, he was only eight, but stuffed toys weren't going to win him much respect from his peers. And, sure enough, a few boys near the front snickered. Pointedly clearing her throat, Colleen nodded at Bobby and indicated it was time for him to speak.

'This is Hi-Fi. I got him the other day when my friend Steven gave him to me.' He held the panda up for the class to see. A few girls made 'ooh' and 'aww' noises. Colleen had to admit that it was a cute toy. She told Bobby to pass it around the class. 'Hi-Fi was in lots of adventures with Steven. Steven said he's getting old and needs to retire and he thought Hi-Fi would have a good life living with me.'

'What sorts of adventures did Hi-Fi have?' asked Stephanie, twisting her ponytail.

'Well, Steven was a fighter pilot and he kept Hi-Fi with him. One time, during a battle, Steven was shot down and captured by some enemies. They let him keep Hi-Fi for company.' Colleen was impressed. Bobby had the class's attention and was enjoying telling the story of this high-adventuring panda. She wondered if this Steven guy was a veteran from Vietnam or Iraq. 'And then some new prisoners helped Steven and Hi-Fi escape, and they had many adventures before I joined them.'

Colleen felt her heart sink a bit.

'You went with them?' Ryan, a usually quiet boy, wanted to know.

'Yeah, and we had lots of adventures. We fought some robots that looked like drills and Vicki was kidnapped by the Most High after she called him a cuddly-wuddly, and Steven and I had to help the Doctor rescue her.' By now, Colleen noticed, Bobby was involved with the story, but once again she felt his grip on reality was slipping. Yes, his stories of Conidrons and the Zaksi were fascinating, but this was show-and-tell, not story-time. She noticed some of the other boys weren't quite believing it either.

'Man, your stories suck!' yelled out Michael Usky, scratching his armpit.

'Your panda's a sissy,' sneered Sophie Sugden, a mean-spirited little girl who always dressed in pink.

133

'Class be quiet!' admonished Colleen. The children ignored her. They were having too much fun. Michael, who had been sitting near the front, then took the opportunity to snatch Hi-Fi out of Bobby's hands. Ignoring her instructions to return it, Michael continued to play keep-away with it, taunting Bobby and saying that the only real friend Bobby had was this stupid panda. Before Colleen had a chance to retrieve the panda, Bobby jumped on Michael, pulled his hair, rescued the panda, and returned to his desk. Michael returned to his desk and exchanged a high-five with Alex. At the same time, Colleen blew the whistle, signalling that order would once again be restored. The students, realising the commotion was over, settled down and whispered excitedly amongst themselves.

'Bobby Zierath', Colleen admonished, 'you know that at Wilson Elementary we do not resolve our differences by fighting. Go to the Principal's office now.'

'But Miss Griebel, he took my...'

'No excuses! There is no excuse for fighting and you pulled his hair. Go now before you get into even bigger trouble.' Clutching Hi-Fi protectively, Bobby left the classroom. A few girls giggled as he walked past.

'Now children, after that, we won't be continuing show-and-tell today. Instead take out your math workbooks so we can practise our multiplication tables.' Dutifully, the children took out their math homework, the incident now forgotten by all apart from a very angry Mallory Hendricks whose turn was next for show-and-tell and who was anxious to show off her lilac 'Superstar!' feather boa she had been given during her recent trip to Universal Studios.

'Oh, Steven, you really ought to try this!' Vicki offered her drink, a tall brownish concoction buried under a bouffant of whipped cream and sprinkles.

'What is it?' Steven didn't feel too sure.

'It's a CaraMelocha Cha-Cha Chiller!'

'A what?'

'It's a coffee-based drink my boy,' the Doctor fluttered a dismissive hand, 'blended with caramel, ice, and more sugar and caffeine than either of you need.' The three friends had found a typical Ancient American coffee shop, and were sitting around a table, sipping their drinks, and reading some of the free newspapers. Vicki had been most confused by one until Steven had pointed out that it was a satire.

The day had been an enjoyable one. The three of them had made their way to the town centre – not difficult at all considering its size and had looked at various shops. A few passers-by stared at the Doctor's strange dress although, Steven considered, they might have been staring at Vicki, whose enthusiasm led her to run from window to window as if she were a seven-year-old in a toy shop. Of course, when she hadn't been scampering about, she had been lecturing Steven on more than he ever wanted to know about the history of commercial development in Ancient American suburbs. At around the time Vicki was engaged in recounting the wonders and perils of the fast-food industry, they had found the coffee shop. It seemed to be everything Vicki had been hoping for, and with the Doctor needing a rest, it was decided they should take a break.

Despite himself, Steven had been enjoying the visit immensely. While the Doctor had been continually on edge about the supposed time anomaly and Vicki had been darting to and fro eager to show off her knowledge, Steven had been happy to simply take in the surroundings. He enjoyed people-watching, and there were certainly many to enjoy: mothers with strollers, teenage couples on dates, elderly couples, and so on. As Steven scanned the people in the coffee shop, he became aware of a young man, about eighteen or nineteen, looking at him intently. Not sure of the proper etiquette in this time, Steven smiled at him. The man quickly looked away. Thinking nothing of it, Steven turned his attention back to Vicki and her enormous Caramelowhatever-it-was. However, sensing someone close, Steven looked up and noticed the young man now standing over their table.

The Doctor, nonchalant as ever, regarded the newcomer. 'Can we help you young man?'

'Just tell me,' the man asked, voice shaking, 'why did you try to ruin my life?'

Victor walked up the steps leading to Wilson Elementary School, hoping that the meeting with the principal, the teacher, and the others would go smoothly. Signing the visitors' book, he noticed a bulletin board dominating the lobby. It featured smiling children from various countries. One was wearing a sombrero, another a beret. A Japanese girl had a kimono. The board proudly proclaimed, 'Celebrating our rainbow of differences!' Victor was fairly certain that there weren't many children at Wilson who wore sombreros or kimonos.

'Mr Zierath?' Victor turned and saw a smiling, middle-aged woman wearing a navy blue blazer and skirt. 'I'm Arlene Santiago, the principal of Wilson Elementary. Please come into my office.'

Victor followed her into her office, an overly decorated affair with one too many ferns and motivational posters, like the one featuring a kitten barely hanging onto a tree branch advising him to 'Hang in There!'. Despite himself, Victor smiled. Maybe he ought to follow the kitten's advice. There were three other people in the room: a young woman whom Victor knew to be Bobby's teacher, a rather prissy man with a briefcase, and Bobby himself.

'You already know Miss Colleen Griebel,' said Ms Santiago, 'and this gentleman is Mr Brent Uden, from child protective services.'

'Does Bobby need protection?' asked Victor, perhaps a tad more sharply than he had intended. Without waiting to be asked, Victor sat down next to Bobby and placed a consoling hand on his back.

'Well, to be honest, we're not sure,' responded Ms Santiago.

'Bobby has been behaving oddly in the last few days, more so than usual,' interjected Miss Griebel. Glancing at Ms Santiago as if for permission, Colleen continued. 'He spent most of the afternoon today in the office because he got into a fight during show-and-tell.'

'Fighting?' Victor turned to Bobby. 'Is this true, sport?'

'Yes,' Bobby kept his eyes on the floor.

'Why? You know better than that!'

Colleen answered for him. 'Don't be too harsh on him, he was being egged on horribly and teased by the other students.'

'Well, they aren't in the office, are they?' Victor said sharply.

'*They*, Mr Zierath, were not pulling hair as your son was.'

'They took my toy and wouldn't give it back!' This was Bobby, now apparently anxious to give his side of the story.

'So let me get this straight,' Victor began, 'Bobby brings a toy to show-and-tell, kids tease him, take his toy, and you only discipline when he has to take action to get the toy back? What kind of school are you running here?'

At this, Ms Santiago stiffened in her chair. 'We at Wilson Elementary are very proud that we are a violence-free school zone, and we practise a zero-tolerance policy on any sort of physical violence. Why do you think your son should be exempt?'

'Okay, I getcha. It's just pretty pathetic that if his toy is taken away, the teacher,' – Victor glared at Colleen – 'can't get it back herself, thus forcing him to use his own methods.'

It was at this awkward point that Mr Uden politely coughed. 'It's actually the toy in question which is why I'm here. But first, I'd like Miss Griebel to take Bobby to the classroom.' He waited until the two had left, Victor reassuring Bobby he'd pick him up shortly. Mr Uden then held up a plush panda. 'Your son claims he was given this panda by a man named Steven. Do you know whom he might be referring to?'

Victor felt sick. No, he didn't know a Steven. He was sure he had never seen that panda before. Oh, god. Was some pervert messing with Bobby? Oh, god, oh, god, oh, god, oh, god, no not this! He fumbled for words to say. 'Um, no, I have no idea.'

Mr Uden continued, 'Bobby tells me he was given it by a pilot named Steven and that they are very good friends, along with two other strangers.'

'Well, Bobby has been telling stories lately… could these be some sort of imaginary friends?' It was possible, Victor thought, that it was just a toy that Nicole had bought for Bobby that Victor never knew about. There were certainly plenty of toys in that category.

'Mr Zierath, Bobby is a little old for imaginary friends, and you do understand our concern. If there's an older man giving him presents, especially one you are unaware of, it's a cause for serious concern. However, even if there isn't, and these are simply stories that Bobby is making up, it is also a cause for concern.' Mr Uden shuffled through his briefcase, before holding up a manila envelope. 'And, I've been reading his file…'

This was it, Victor thought. Everything about him, Nicole, the effects of her death on Bobby, everything. Yes, he had been driving. Yes, he could have been paying better attention to the road. Yes, Nicole was dead. Yes, he wasn't able to supervise Bobby as much. Yes, Bobby's behaviour had been affected. God knows, Bobby had been to enough counselling sessions.

'I must be honest, Mr Zierath, in light of these recent developments, Child Protective Services has severe doubts on your ability to adequately care for Bobby…'

'They put me in a foster home!' shouted the young man, attracting from the other coffee-shop customers the sort of furtive glances people use when they desperately wish they were someplace else. 'And it's all your fault!'

Steven really didn't know what to say. The young man, whose name they learned was Rob, had decided to tell them something of his life story. Evidently, Rob blamed them for his problems as a child. The Doctor had listened keenly, fingertips pressed against each other, sorting out the puzzle in his mind. Vicki hadn't said much, just sipped her CareMelocha-Cha-Cha Chiller as inconspicuously as possible. Steven wondered if this sort of informal emotion-spilling session was a common Ancient American tradition and whether Vicki would treasure forever her authentic experience. She didn't seem to be enjoying it. Steven, for his part, was a bit bewildered. As far as he could gather, this young man Rob had lived some traumatic experiences involving people having a passing resemblance to himself, the Doctor, and Vicki. As a result, he had found himself in trouble at school and at home, culminating in apparently living in this foster home that he was now complaining about.

'I couldn't see my dad for more than a brief visit for years, and he hadn't even done anything!'

'Well, my young sir,' said the Doctor. 'Much as I can sympathise with your plight and your estrangement, I must confess I really don't know what to say to you.'

'I just want to know why you set me up for this. Didn't you know what would happen, man? I was eight!' Rob was on the verge of tears.

'And as I keep telling you, young man, this has nothing to do with us. We've only just arrived in your town from... erm... abroad, and have never been here before. Now, you've clearly confused us with some other people from your past, and I would appreciate it if you would either leave us in peace or stop making such a nuisance of yourself.'

At this, Rob appeared a bit chastised and, in Steven's opinion, a little bit hurt. He mumbled an apology, and admitted he might have been mistaken. 'Maybe I shouldn't blame you, after all, you didn't intend to mess up my life, and things seem to be going better for me now.'

The Doctor dismissed the sentiment with a wave of his hand, 'Think nothing of it my boy, think nothing of it.' He leaned in closer to Rob. 'I do understand how you feel. I too have been separated from someone in my family I love very much.'

'Yes, I know, Doctor,' Rob said, looking the Doctor squarely in the eye, 'You've often told me how much you miss Susan.'

The Doctor's head snapped up, eyes alert. Steven straightened up in his chair. Vicki coughed Caramelocha-Cha-Cha Chiller sprinkles over the table.

For the third time that year, Bobby had to say goodbye to someone he loved. Daddy hadn't really explained why Bobby had to go live with those other people for awhile, but Bobby knew it had something to with what people like Kayla's mother said about Mom's death somehow being Daddy's fault. He also knew it had to do with him telling everyone about his adventures with Steven, Vicki, and the Doctor. He remembered that goodbye as well, and it had been tough.

The Doctor and Steven had had an argument. There had been some concern about how they were going to return Bobby home on time. Vicki had once told Bobby that the Doctor couldn't control the Ship that well. Bobby hadn't minded, as he liked the idea of staying with the Doctor, Vicki, and Steven. Eventually, the Doctor decided to cheat in order to return Bobby home.

'Now, Bobby,' he had said, 'There's a special button called the fast-return switch. If you keep pressing it, we'll go back to your room right after we left it. You won't have been gone for more than a minute.'

'But can't I stay with you?'

'No Bobby you can't,' the Doctor turned towards Steven, unable to look Bobby in the eye. Bobby thought that had been sort of strange. 'You see Bobby, if we don't return you now, well, it's hard to explain, but trust me, we won't know to meet you in the first place.'

'But you've already met me.'

'Yes, my boy, it's difficult to understand.' The Doctor smiled and tapped Bobby's nose, 'That's just why you'll have to trust me, hmm?'

Vicki then came over, 'Yes Bobby, you must trust us. And you'll always be able to remember the exciting adventures we had.' She hugged him tightly and smiled at him.

Finally, it was Steven's turn. He had come over to Bobby holding Hi-Fi, his toy panda. 'Uh, look Bobby, I'm not really good at saying goodbyes, and, well, you've been like a son I've never had. And, as you're going home now, well, I think the mascot needs someone brave to watch over him. Do you think you can do that for me, Bobby?' Bobby nodded. Steven hugged him,

'Now remember, do well in school, behave yourself, and make your father proud. That's your job, now.'

'Yes, yes, Bobby, you have a job to do. You do well in school and don't cause trouble now! Yes, goodbye. We'll always remember you,' said the Doctor. And, drawing Bobby out of Steven and Vicki's earshot, the Doctor whispered, 'You've seen the future. It's a secret that only a special boy like you can keep.' And with that, the Doctor opened the doors to the Ship and Bobby, with one last wave to Vicki and Steven, walked out of the ship and into his bedroom, Hi-Fi clutched in his arms. He thought he could hear arguing between the Doctor and Steven before that same elephant noise sounded in the bedroom. Looking once back in the now-empty closet, Bobby climbed into bed.

And now Bobby stood outside this new house where he'd now be living. Dad would still be close by, and they'd see each other once a week. That man Mr Uden had arranged it all. Bobby would try to be good. He knew the sooner he started behaving, the sooner he could move back with Dad.

Bobby thought about his adventures with the Doctor, Steven, and Vicki. All of the grown-ups thought he was making them up, but Bobby knew better. But the grown-ups wanted him to pretend that it was all a dream, and that Bobby was making up stories about visiting Rome or fighting the Conidrons. Well, he would pretend they were stories. Bobby couldn't understand why the grown-ups wanted him to lie when they had always before told him to tell the truth. Whenever Bobby told the truth, it seemed, he just got in trouble. So he'd lie about his adventures and pretend that the best friends he had in the universe never existed. Yes, better to lie and keep the grown-ups happy.

'Well, I don't like it. He's right, we will ruin his life!' Steven was angry, following the Doctor through the park where the TARDIS had landed, Vicki slightly behind him. After hearing his granddaughter's name, the Doctor had stormed out of the coffee shop, Vicki and Steven following

139

after having cleaned up. They had left Rob at the table, shouting at them for leaving him once again.

'And if we don't ruin his life, we ruin the timeline and perhaps the whole entirety of creation!' responded the Doctor. 'Don't you see?'

'No, I don't actually, he's hardly going to be someone important, he's just a kid! A poor, lonely, screwed up kid, who might have had a chance of a normal life if we hadn't – or don't – interfere with his life!'

'And how will we know not to interfere if we don't interfere, hmm?' snapped the Doctor.

'The Doctor's right, Steven,' interjected Vicki. Steven turned in disbelief. He couldn't believe that Vicki was willing to do this. 'I don't like it any more than you do, but think: if we don't interfere with Rob's childhood, then he won't be able to shout at us for interfering in his childhood, and then we won't know not to interfere, so we will interfere!' She frowned at Steven and then asked, as an afterthought, 'Didn't you study time paradoxes at school?'

'No, do you know, as a matter of fact, I didn't,' Steven retorted, voice full of sarcasm.

'The child is quite right, Steven my boy, in that our past is already affected by our future. We *must* take Rob with us. We have no choice.'

'Oh your precious Web of Time, again, eh Doctor?' Steven asked.

'Yes, as you put it, "my precious Web of Time" again,' replied the Doctor. 'Don't you see? We are the source of the time anomaly I detected on our arrival, and we must fix it. Now the Ship can hone in on the time anomaly, about ten years in the past.'

'Where Rob first met us,' added Vicki helpfully.

'Yes, and we won't need to worry about navigation since we'll be tracking the anomaly.'

'Oh, you make it sound so simple!' sneered Steven, 'Go back in time, kidnap a child, return him, and ruin his life. All in a day's work for the good crew TARDIS, I suppose.'

'Steven,' said Vicki, 'None of us want to hurt Rob, but the damage has already been done. It's an historical fact, surely you can see that?'

'Oh come on, it's not like he's a figure from history.'

The Doctor took Steven's arm. 'Neither are you, Steven, but you've made a difference in the world. Without your help, history would have been changed back in 1066, so while you yourself might be unimportant in your own time, you've become a pivotal figure in someone else's – even if the history books don't record your involvement.'

'I suppose that's true,' Steven conceded.

'And the same may be true with that young man Rob. He may be crucial on our adventures, ensuring things happen correctly. And, I might add, if he is to join us, we have a duty to make it the best trip he could possibly imagine, so I won't hear any further discussion of this matter.' The Doctor tutted, fumbled in his jacket for the TARDIS key, and ushered Steven and Vicki inside.

Rob, having followed the trio from the coffee shop, watched the TARDIS disappear with that same sick-elephant noise he remembered from a decade ago. So he wasn't crazy after all. Once again they had abandoned him. He wondered if the Doctor, Steven, and Vicki were directly on their way to meet his younger self, or if they would make a few stops on the way. The Doctor had been adamant they hadn't met, but Rob hadn't believed him. Of course, now he realised, that from the Doctor's point of view, he was telling the truth. He had watched enough of the Sci-Fi Channel to understand the basics of time travel – and how they often got it wrong. He wanted to go with them. God, his life was a mess. And just as soon as had begun to get himself together, those three showed up.

Rob thought back to the years with child psychotherapists. Had he been abused? Who was this Steven guy who gave him toy pandas? Were these three friends just figments of his imagination? He had been laughed at, treated as different, as some sort of freak. Eventually he had just decided to play along and tell the therapists he had been making it all up for attention. It had worked. Lies had set him free. And now that he had nothing, he wanted to escape. He wanted to travel with the Doctor again. But would the Doctor come for him? Unlikely. Unless…

He remembered his trips. He remembered that there would be an invasion by the Troxleks in three years. He remembered the political tensions that would rock Asia in thirty years. And there would also be that business with the Golden Gate Bridge. And he could write about these. Maybe he'd be the next Nostradamus. Yes, people would have to listen. At least, Rob felt, the Doctor would have to notice. And with that thought in mind, he went back to his apartment and started to write.

And ten years earlier, little Bobby Zierath lay in his bed, drifting to sleep with a toy panda nestled under his arm. He had a smile on his face because he couldn't wait to tell his friends at school about all the adventures he had experienced and the three wonderful new friends he had made.

Charley swallowed hard. 'So, you are telling me that the Doctor brought you here because of the knowledge you had? Knowledge he'd given you in the first place?'

Robert nodded. 'But he was right. I could have changed so much, none of it right.'

141

'Why?' asked Charley. 'Who's to say what would have been the "right" timeline?'

The Steward replaced her drink with another. 'That's the paradoxical nature of time travel, Charley. It's all about taking a leap of faith. You have to accept that the Doctor, as a Time Lord, does indeed know and understand time. Its flows and its ebbs.'

'Why? Because,' the Steward continued, 'it's what he does. What the Time Lords have done for millennia. They have watched, observed and record correct time. Every past, present and future is known to them. People like the Doctor are dangerous in fact because that knowledge, coupled with their curiosity can change so much.'

Robert Zierath agreed. 'The changes I could have made were huge. I mean, heck, there are others here who would have changed timelines on a small, local scale.' He pointed to a man in a check shirt and cream chinos. 'That's Thomas. He had the ability to change the fortunes of his own town but due to the Doctor's interference, he didn't. Nothing major happened as a result and, in the grand scheme of things, it made no real difference. But he's still the result of the Doctor's meddling. He should be dead.'

Charley looked at Thomas, and decided she'd ask him his story. If the Doctor had stopped him dying, why would that be such a bad thing?

The Steward continued Robert's story. 'You see, Thomas should've been killed by his neighbours in a dispute over oil. But he lived. And nothing changed. Big ripples or small ones, ultimately, they all matter to the Web of Time.'

Charley's view of Thomas was broken by a man she'd seen earlier, who pushed past Robert and sat at the bar, slamming an empty glass on the top of the bar.

'Same again, Mister Harris?'

'Doctor,' he snapped, and then nodded. 'A double.' He looked at Charley as if daring her to speak. Instead, he muttered, 'All the same. They're all the same. Never trust a doctor.'

With that, he took his drink and stomped away.

'What's his story?' Charley asked the Steward.

The Steward shrugged. 'He told me once but I'm not sure I recognised all the characters. Perhaps you can shed some light on this, Miss Pollard. It goes rather like this...'

The Juror's Story

Eddie Robson

Every day I've tried to read the old man's expression, and although it isn't exactly what I'd expect from a murderer, that doesn't mean he isn't one. On the contrary, I have been convinced for quite some time that he is. His demeanour throughout these proceedings has been confident – he is certainly not lacking in conviction – yet regretful. The issue is whether he regrets what he did, regrets that it was necessary, or regrets that he was caught.

'I had no choice,' he said. He has said it more than once, each time with a sigh, as if bored of being continually asked. How one can be bored when on trial for one's life is puzzling to me. Clearly he is not stupid, but he acts as though he doesn't quite appreciate what is happening. I do not think that this will end well for him.

The judge hands proceedings over to us, the jury, stating that he must insist upon a unanimous verdict – because he views the evidence as rather subjective, perhaps? If so, it strikes me that he is being unnecessarily equivocal. The accused glances at us one more time before he is led away, and his eyes momentarily settle on the fellow next to me – who in turn looks down to his lap, brushing off some dust that may or may not be there, in order to avoid making eye contact. Understandable.

The fellow jostles me slightly as we stand. 'Sorry,' he says gently, summoning up a pleasant smile.

I walk behind this fellow on our way out of the courtroom. I find him somewhat odd: his hair, ash blond, is rather long. Upon meeting him I wondered what employer would find this acceptable. He seems roughly my own age, perhaps a little younger: smooth-faced, slightly weak-chinned, but lean and sportsmanlike. His name, as I recall, is Smith, although when we met upon the first day of this trial he said his friends just call him Doctor.

'Why?' I asked. 'Are you one?'

'Yes,' he replied.

'Medical?'

He shook his head.

'Oh? What then?' I hoped it might be a subject of which I knew something, that there might be somebody here with whom I could intellectually engage.

'History,' he said, inadvertently dashing those hopes, and after that the conversation petered out. The 'sorry' that he just offered me may well be the first word we've exchanged since then, I don't remember.

We move through to a smaller room, simply decorated and disappointingly shabby. One might have expected these grand, life-or-death decisions to be taken in slightly more illustrious surroundings. But then again this is a room for thought, debate and deed, none of which demands luxury. There is a table in the centre, a long rectangular one. We all take seats around it, and as I take a place at the head of the table I note that Dr Smith has found his way to the opposite head. The door closes behind us and the talking starts.

Once we've introduced ourselves to each other, the foreman, Mr Sutcliffe (Mr Eastman suggests that we always refer to 'the defendant' so that the man on trial is not confused with Mr Sutcliffe), asks us to put forward an initial vote before we discuss the case. Even if we *are* unanimous, he says, it would naturally still be proper to talk over the issues before we return. Mr Sutcliffe fixes us each in turn with his one good eye and his rich voice asks: Is the defendant guilty, or not guilty?

Mr Sutcliffe casts his vote for guilty and prompts the man to his left, Mr Asher, to voice his opinion. Mr Asher also opts to condemn and passes the chair to his own left. Mrs Martin, Miss Mills, Mr Eastman, myself, Mr Hopkins, Miss Nichol, Mr McKee, Mrs Preston and Mrs Taylor all follow suit.

Dr Smith is on Mr Sutcliffe's right and is the last to speak. He takes a deep breath as he looks up from the middle distance and brightly declares, 'Not guilty.'

The effect of that tiny word, 'not', is like a pebble cast into the sea that somehow causes a tidal wave. At least three voices ask Dr Smith how he justifies this verdict: the voices range from curious to incredulous. He raises his eyebrows, leans forward with his arms folded onto the table. The grey suit he wears is not an ideal fit and seems borrowed or second-hand. He tugs at the cuffs before speaking. 'Because,' he says slowly, shaking his head, 'as I see it, there's more than enough evidence to support his plea.' He clears his throat and unnecessarily clarifies, 'The self-defence plea.'

'Evidence?' demands Mr Hopkins, his face caught between a good-natured chortle and a dismissive sneer. 'They didn't come up with *one* example of that poor lass ever having done a scrap of harm to anybody. What would she have suddenly attacked *him* for? For no reason?'

'A quiet one, they all said,' says Mrs Preston.

'Well, we *can* only take their word for that,' says Mr Asher, staring down at his fingers. 'We'll never know now, will we?'

'No, we won't,' says Mr McKee, 'and who do we have to blame for *that*?' He triumphantly taps a finger on the table. 'The only person who ever dreamed she was dangerous was that young girl's granddad. I mean, we *all* have to keep vigilant about who our children fall in with these days but he took matters into his own hands. And I reckon he was wrong.'

Mrs Taylor nods. 'You've got to let the law decide.'

'I must say I'm, er, surprised to hear you all so confident about this girl being so harmless,' says Dr Smith. 'The granddaughter supported his story.'

'She *would* though, wouldn't she?' says Miss Mills. 'She's probably afraid of him as well.'

Dr Smith shrugs. 'Isn't it possible Miss Sampson had a... *wild* side?'

Mr McKee laughs. 'Wild? Nice family, no problems. Her teacher, all her friends said she always kept her head down and worked hard. Sounds like *my* daughter, and the wildest *she* ever gets is when the Beatles are in town.'

Mrs Preston laughs and agrees that her daughter reacts in a similar way, and the discussion is briefly sidetracked onto the current appeal of the Beatles for our younger generation (personally I feel that nobody will remember them in a year's time) before Mr Hopkins drags us back to the matter in hand. 'I thought it was *disgusting* what they said about her in there,' he says with real feeling. 'They said she was on *drugs.*'

'They didn't *say* that,' says Dr Smith.

'As good as,' says Mr Hopkins. 'Talk about ill of the dead and all that. Why *would* she attack him? What reason could she have had? Tell me that.' Dr Smith is about to respond to this when Mr Hopkins simply carries on. 'I don't care how old he is, he looks pretty capable to me. Pretty capable, and he had the gun. And even then he didn't have to kill her.'

'The old man seems so *suspicious* of everybody, doesn't he?' says Mr McKee. 'I don't think he's got that much of a grip on things, to tell you the truth.'

'I suppose that means he might do it again,' says Miss Nichol.

'Exactly,' says Mr McKee. 'He might do it again.'

'I'm fairly certain he wouldn't,' offers Dr Smith. Mr Hopkins is about to speak again, but Dr Smith holds up his hand. 'Might I explain why?'

'Feel free,' says Mr Hopkins.

'Thank you,' says Dr Smith. 'There *is* a detail, an important detail which was presented in the courtroom but not actually discussed, for understandable reasons – it couldn't possibly enter into the records – but there's nothing to prevent us discussing it in *here.*' He glances around to see if we have caught his gist. 'Surely I wasn't the only one who noticed this? The murder weapon?'

'The gun?' asks Mrs Martin.

'Not so much the gun, more the bullets,' says Dr Smith. 'Why did he use bullets... that were made of *silver*?'

Oh good *lord.* He isn't seriously suggesting... I glance around the room and the same thought is written on ten other faces.

The ensuing silence is eventually broken by Mr Sutcliffe. 'What do you mean?'

Dr Smith gives him an infuriating half-smile. 'Tell me, Mr Sutcliffe – what do *you* think I mean?'

As I feared, Dr Smith has hypothesised that the victim, Roberta Sampson, was a werewolf. ('Is there a different word for *girl* werewolves?' asks Mrs Preston, which is scarcely the most pressing of questions.)

Mr Sutcliffe attempts to block this line of discussion before it gets out of hand. 'Dr Smith, it is outside the jury's remit to discuss new evidence at this stage.'

'This isn't new evidence,' counters Dr Smith. 'It's simply my own interpretation of the evidence that was presented in court. Are we to let the lawyers do our thinking for us, Mr Sutcliffe?'

Mr Sutcliffe backs down and what should have been a brief affirmation of the facts of the case degenerates into Smith's presentation of his childish theory, which runs thus: Miss Sampson had befriended the defendant's granddaughter and when he discovered that she was (I can barely form the thought without groaning out loud) a werewolf, he warned Sampson to stay away from her. Sampson was angered and upset, this triggered her 'lycanthropic transformation' (Dr Smith's phrase) and rendered her dangerous. The defendant, having anticipated this, was armed with the necessary equipment to vanquish the creature and regretfully did so. Smith further points out that Miss Sampson's wounds were located in places that would not usually be fatal to a human being – one bullet each in her shoulder and thigh – and concludes that death was probably caused by a reaction to the silver itself, rather than the physical damage done by the bullets. The pathologist had conceded in court that this could support the defendant's claim that he had not shot to kill, but the prosecution noted that since the defendant did not, by his own admission, hold much expertise with a firearm, the marks found by his bullets were scarcely indicative of his intentions.

'This being the case,' concludes Dr Smith as though it *is* the case even though any sane individual can clearly see that it is not, 'the defendant is no more guilty than if he had fought off a wild and dangerous animal, surely?'

There are a few seconds of silence, during which Dr Smith starts to grin hopefully.

'But...' starts Mr Eastman, then tails off uncertainly.

'Go on?' encourages Dr Smith.

'Werewolves don't exist,' finishes Mr Eastman. I think that he, like the rest of us, is so baffled by Dr Smith's rational manner that he isn't sure what to say – and each of us is taking the silence of the others as potential agrcement. He wonders whether he is the only person to have noticed the simple flaw in Smith's argument: the fact that there is no such thing as a werewolf and never has been. He looks around the room and I briefly nod my support, which seems to embolden him just enough to turn back to Smith. 'They're just from stories.'

Dr Smith has evidently anticipated this. He proceeds to reel off a list of documented cases – legal, medical, anecdotal – which point to the existence of werewolves. A spate of unsolved and brutal murders in Budapest, 1898. An apparent case of cannibalism in Tennessee, in which the culprit claimed to be unable to remember the crimes. A woman who lived in Stirling in the 1840s whose bones had thickened and teeth had lengthened for no accountable reason. An unidentifiable creature found dead in West Germany five years ago. Speculation and (mis)interpretation from around the world, all of it biased in Smith's direction. Again Mr Sutcliffe suggests that this has no direct bearing on the case but Dr Smith still spends more than an hour presenting his 'evidence', which he assures us can be backed up by reports filed in numerous newspapers, journals and studies. I try to distance myself from this debate as much as possible. Mr Hopkins puts it aptly when he asks, 'Are you available for children's parties, Dr Smith?'

Worryingly, others are starting to take his fairy stories seriously. 'These stories don't all seem to agree with each other,' Mrs Taylor says. 'Some of them have all that full moon stuff and getting infected by getting bitten, but others are… a bit more down-to-earth?'

'Yes, yes, you're right,' says Dr Smith. 'Much of the evidence is somewhat… subjective.' He ignores the half-suppressed snort of laughter from Mr McKee. 'Some of it may be completely unfounded, I won't deny it. But even if we take that into account there is still a compelling argument to be made here.'

'We're not *talking* about arguments,' asserts Mr Hopkins.

'No,' says Dr Smith gently. 'We're talking about a reasonable doubt.'

'I think he's right,' says Mrs Taylor suddenly. It's grossly unfair of Dr Smith to fill her head with this gibberish: she is an impressionable young woman and he is simply manipulating her for goodness knows what ends. I am starting to suspect that he is some kind of fanatic. He looks delighted as Mrs Taylor turns to us all and adds, 'Well, we don't *know* do we?'

Before we adjourn for the day – the evening is wearing on somewhat – we take a second vote. Mrs Taylor has altered her position and now casts a vote for innocence. I can't say I'm surprised, as she strikes me as the kind of fanciful young woman who entertains such fictions because she fails to see how much more intriguing *facts* are. I encounter such people regularly: my own wife Abigail, when we met, occasionally demonstrated such tendencies. I am more dismayed, however, by Mr Asher, who has also reconsidered and now chooses to abstain until he has heard more of what Dr Smith has to say. I, for one, do not wish to hear Dr Smith ever say anything again.

Mr Hopkins, sitting to my immediate left, closes the day by leaning out across the table and addressing Dr Smith, blocking my view of Smith as he does so. 'I can tell you now for nothing that you won't catch me voting your way no matter how long we sit here and no matter how long you reel off this claptrap.' I had hoped that this process wouldn't become confrontational, but at this stage it is perhaps the best way. We all have work to return to and I, for one, have already lost the tail-end of my summer research period as a result of this trial. Mr Hopkins continues: 'If they're after a unanimous whatsit they'll have to find another jury.'

We stand and disperse. Dr Smith is left behind, apparently lost in thought.

The next morning we all sit around the table in the same places as yesterday and Mr Sutcliffe again asks us to account for our present position on the case. Mr Asher, of course, changed his vote to not guilty the last time we did this. Mrs Martin, Miss Mills, Mr Eastman and myself all cast the vote for guilty but Dr Noble, sitting once more to my immediate left, has not changed his mind as I had hoped he would after the brief words we exchanged on the way out last night.

Dr Noble's call for a verdict of not guilty surprised me yesterday. Tall and white-haired, with a lined but lively face and a vaguely aristocratic air, he's a fellow of striking intelligence. He told me when we first met that his doctorate, like my own, is in physics, and we had a most fascinating conversation about my research (he explained that he couldn't talk about his own: he works on behalf of Her Majesty's Government, 'All somewhat hush-hush, old chap'). It pleased me greatly that there was somebody at the trial with whom I could intellectually engage.

'I'm writing a paper on K Mesons,' I told him. 'I have noticed what I think is a discrepancy between the decay pattern of the K Meson and that of its antiparticle. I'm in the process of gathering the data, or at least I *was*…'

Dr Noble's eyebrows shot upwards. 'Yes, of course!' he said. 'Wouldn't such a theory suggest why matter prevailed over antimatter during the Big Bang?'

I stepped back, somewhat surprised by the speed with which he had seized upon my conclusions. 'Indeed. As I say, the study is quite close to completion,' I said, which was rather defensive – I am often wary of speaking about my work in too much depth. I fear being 'beaten to it', perhaps irrationally.

'Good luck with it,' Dr Noble replied, placing a hand upon my shoulder. 'I *do* mean that. The very best of luck.' He then called over Dr Smith, to whom I had seen him speaking earlier on, and explained my study to him. Considering Dr Smith's own discipline he showed a remarkable understanding of the issues involved – giving an almost identical response, in fact, to that given by Dr Noble – but did not involve himself in the discussion. Whilst very different, the two men seemed to speak a great deal during spare moments, so I should perhaps have been less surprised that Dr Noble was sympathetic to Dr Smith's theories.

Following Dr Noble's confirmation of his standpoint, Mr Hopkins, Miss Nichol, Mr McKee and Mrs Preston declare the defendant guilty, whilst Mrs Taylor maintains a verdict of not guilty. Unbelievable as it may seem, the jury now stands at eight to four. Dr Noble, who was somewhat quiet yesterday, speaks up.

'I really must confess,' he says, 'that I was as flabbergasted as you all when Dr Smith here first put forward his ideas on this matter. I'm a man of science, not the supernatural.'

He seems about to say something else, but Mrs Martin interrupts him. 'You believe what you can see,' she says, rather haughtily.

Dr Noble, cut off in mid-flow, knits his fingers together and turns to her. 'Have you ever been to Peru, my dear?' he asks pleasantly.

Mrs Martin doesn't answer the question properly, but it is clear from her expression that she has not. 'Well, I –'

'But just because you haven't ever seen it doesn't mean it's not there.'

'That's a ridiculous comparison,' says Miss Mills. 'She hasn't been there, but plenty of other people have.'

'All right,' says Dr Noble, stroking his chin. 'Suppose Peru was a terribly dangerous place? What if few people who went there ever got out alive? You wouldn't hear much about it then, would you?'

Miss Mills starts to say 'Maybe,' but Dr Noble recommences his argument at the slightest noise.

'And what of the few who *did* get out? Might they be so shaken by their experiences that they never spoke of them?' He takes a deep breath, then speaks deliberately. 'Might the result of this not be that we would only hear... *rumours* of Peru?' He looks up and down the table. 'Myths?'

'Hmm,' says Miss Mills, and I do hope that her tone is supposed to be a sceptical one.

'To return to my original point,' says Dr Noble, 'I also subscribe to a process known in the scientific world as falsification. "A theory which is not refutable by any conceivable event is non-scientific," according to a chap named Karl Popper. "Irrefutability is not a virtue of a theory, but a vice." You see? The more times we *fail* to refute a theory, the more confidence we can take in it.' He stands, holding his tie as if he fears it

149

slipping out of place, and then plants a hand in each pocket of his black suit jacket. He walks slowly around the table, anti-clockwise. 'Now, when I look at the case made by Dr Smith, what I see is some evidence in favour. Admittedly circumstantial, but still *some*. Potentially refutable, but what do we have refute it *with*?' He stops behind Dr Smith and looks at us all. 'A supposition. Our supposition that it is simply ridiculous. And a supposition –' he removes a hand from a pocket and splays it upwards with a flick of his fingers – 'has no substance.'

At the next vote the jury is evenly split. Six to six. I despair.

Thankfully the rot appears to have stopped there, as Dr Smith's campaign to undermine this entire trial gains no further converts between then and lunch. Miss Mills and Mrs Martin have changed their verdicts to not guilty but Mr Sutcliffe, Miss Nichol, Mr Eastman, Mr McKee, Mrs Preston and myself are still holding firm. I am concerned about Miss Nichol, as I feel that the main reason she has not changed her vote is that she has not been paying a great deal of attention to what everybody else has been saying, but I still have confidence in the others and Mr Sutcliffe's presence as the foreman has been effective in countering Smith's adopted air of authority. The best we can hope for is a retrial, I suppose.

As we stand Dr Smith hurries away purposefully, presumably to work on further spurious arguments. Dr Noble approaches and invites me to join him for lunch. I politely decline.

The last to return to the room after lunch is Dr Bowman, who apologises for being late. To be frank we wouldn't have missed his input – in his capacity of foreman he has led the others somewhat and I am confident that the position would be more promising had he not succumbed to Dr Smith's argument so quickly.

Dr Bowman, although personable enough, has always struck me as somewhat unfocused. He has an air of agitation that I find unsettling and he speaks in short, rapid blurts. Like Dr Smith his hair is somewhat long and upon our initial meeting he, too, remarked that his friends tend to call him Doctor.

'Another?' I asked, and attempted to make a good-natured joke of the situation. 'There seems to be something of a surfeit of us on this panel!'

'Mmm?' he said, bowing his head slightly before turning to look at Smith and Noble, who were engrossed in conversation a few yards away. 'Oh! Indeed! I'm very sorry, I didn't catch your name?'

'Dr Harris,' I said patiently, having told Dr Bowman my name less than a minute earlier.

'Doctor of?'

'Physics.' I had already told him this, also. 'And yours?'

'Oh,' he said, and for a second or two I thought he couldn't remember. 'Philosophy,' he eventually said: then he looked around and excused himself. He has been only slightly less vague during the discussions in here and he often seems to be flirting with Miss Nichol: this is of course entirely inappropriate.

Dr Bowman pats his pockets and locates the notebook in which he has been supposedly keeping track of events (I would be interested to see just how extensive these notes actually are). 'Has anyone changed their mind since we last... um...' Bowman waves a hand in frustration at his apparent inability to form the sentence. 'Since we last counted up?' Prior to lunch we stood at five votes for guilty and seven for not guilty.

'Um...' says Miss Nichol, raising a hand. 'I've been thinking, and well...'

Dr Bowman grins and nods encouragingly. 'Go on.'

'I'm just not sure any more,' she says. 'I'm really not sure. And I've started to think that if I'm not sure...'

'Give him the benefit of the doubt,' says Mrs Taylor. 'We have to.'

'Yes,' says Miss Nichol, chewing on a fingernail. 'So I think I'm going to say he's not guilty.'

'Sure?' asks Dr Bowman, and Miss Nichol nods. 'Good,' says Bowman and turns to the rest of us. 'This is what I've been saying: how can we be sure? We can make a convincing argument in both directions and, this being the case –' Again that phrase Dr Smith used, *This being the case*, casually affirming his own argument in a way that makes me think he must believe in it completely – 'we must acknowledge the existence of *doubt*.'

The room has gone rather quiet, with the result that my impatient *tut* is heard by everybody. Dr Bowman turns to me and glares across the table.

'Dr Harris?' he says, prompting me to enter the debate.

Reluctantly, I do so. 'I'm sorry, Dr Bowman, I don't intend any disrespect, but this sounds like a first-term lecture.'

'Lecture?' asks Bowman.

'Philosophy,' I say.

'Oh, yes,' he says. 'That.'

'I simply don't feel it's applicable here. The doubt is not a *reasonable* one. It is predicated on the existence of a mythical creature. By *definition* that is not reasonable because it is not based on *reason*.'

'Are you telling me that you've never experienced anything you couldn't explain?' says Dr Noble.

'No,' I say. 'But I've always *looked* for an explanation and opted for the most likely.'

'All right,' says Dr Bowman. 'What's your most likely explanation for the silver bullets?'

Admittedly this aspect is puzzling, so I delay my response with a facile question. 'Were they *definitely* silver bullets?'

151

Dr Smith holds up a page from the court records. 'Says so here.'

'Well... Perhaps *he* thought she was a werewolf – that doesn't mean she was.'

Bowman takes a step in my direction. 'Surely his lawyer would have entered some kind of, of insanity plea.'

'Perhaps he wanted us to *think* she was one.'

He steps closer again. 'Something of a risk, surely. Most of us wouldn't even have *considered* that.'

'I don't know. Perhaps they were the only bullets he had.'

I instantly regret saying this because I know that he will seize upon it, which he does without hesitation. 'Who on *earth*,' he says with a chuckle in his throat as he steps towards me once more, 'keeps silver bullets in the house? Who can *afford* them when ordinary ones will do?' His face creases in perplexity and he turns to the others. 'What are bullets normally made of?'

'Originally brass, old fella,' says Dr Noble, 'but these days it's usually a lead alloy coated in some kind of copper alloy. And the tougher projectiles quite often incorporate a core of steel.' He punches a fist lightly against his palm by way of demonstration.

'Thank you,' says Dr Bowman, then does a slight double take. 'How come you know this sort of thing and I don't?'

Dr Noble waves a hand to dismiss any notion that the knowledge is desirable. 'Oh, it's all these military types ever talk about,' he says. 'You pick up a thing or two whether you want to or not.'

Dr Bowman turns back to me. 'Lead, then. Cheaper than silver.'

'More effective, too,' adds Dr Noble.

'Daft really, to have silver ones,' says Bowman. 'So why would you?' He falls silent, staring at me. 'Really, Dr Harris, I *am* very interested. Anybody. Can *any*body explain these bullets?'

'Ornamental?' suggests Miss Mills. 'Novelties?'

'Ornamental novelties that *work* when you fire them from a gun?' asks Bowman. 'Are you suggesting that he grabbed for a weapon and they were the only ones handy? And they *happened* to fit the gun he used?'

'Quite,' says Dr Smith. 'He must have known that he might need them. He bought them beforehand, he must have done. Nothing else makes *sense*.'

'So you're saying it was premeditated,' says Mr McKee. 'Murder.'

'No, I'm saying he knew he might have to defend himself,' says Dr Smith. 'He came prepared. He came very *specifically* prepared.'

Miss Mills is shaking her head. It's like watching a sawn-down tree sway before it collapses to the ground.

She sighs heavily. 'It really *is* the only way that it makes sense.'

Timber...

* * *

152

As the afternoon wears on, Mr McKee folds in the most deplorable manner imaginable, muttering limp phrases that add up to a position of believing that if so many of us find this theory convincing then there *must* be something in it and so he can no longer be sure of the defendant's guilt either. This actually makes me dislike him more than Smith or Bowman, who have at least displayed some fortitude in their arguments.

Dr Bowman suggests a break, which I oppose but the others agree to. As they stand and file out, I remain seated. I feel somewhat unwell. The only other member not to leave is Mr Eastman, now my only associate for returning a verdict of guilty. He takes a turn around the room, then arrives back at his seat, the one to my immediate right. There is a look of sympathy on his face. The least I owe him is to return it.

'Madness,' he says, shaking his head and folding his gangly frame back into his seat. 'Utter, utter madness.'

I concur.

'It's inexplicable. Totally inexplicable. Them, I mean, not the case. I mean, what do *I* care what kind of bullets he wanted to use? The girl's no less *dead*, is she?' Still shaking his head, Mr Eastman reaches into the pocket of his suit and retrieves a hip flask. 'I'm sorry, I wouldn't usually until after work or what have you, but under the circumstances...' He takes a quick sip, then offers the flask to me.

I refuse, although I am a little tempted.

It's only a brief recess and the others start to file back into the room within ten minutes. Even so, the chance to sit here and talk alone with Dr Mason has been most welcome, as I have now had time to absorb what he said last night. Whilst this trial has been nothing if not trying it has almost been worth it to make his acquaintance: the others affect to find him irritating, facile even, but I feel that there are deeper reasons for his lack of popularity, as he seems, to me, highly personable.

'Twelve people,' I noted when we met on the first day, 'and five PhDs between us. Extraordinary, isn't it?'

'Absurd,' he replied, casually. 'Statistically possible, I suppose, but still absurd. Personally, I think it's a covert Oxbridge plot to derail the research ratings of the London universities.'

This made me laugh.

His face lightened, taking a little pleasure from his own joke: his jowelled features creased in satisfaction, matching the shabbiness of his suit (which looked to have seen at least ten years of regular use) and his dark uncombed hair. 'Oh, not that they wouldn't do it, you know. Or that they couldn't do it. They're an insidious bunch.'

'Which were you?' I asked. 'Oxford or Cambridge?'

He glanced at me. 'Edinburgh,' he said simply.

'My mistake. Sorry, I took you for an old boy.'

'Oh, don't worry, don't worry,' he said warmly as though he had anticipated my complacent response. 'Oxford?' he asked.

I chuckled. 'Guilty. Although I'm at King's now. Yourself?'

'Oh, I'm not at an institution. I was referring to you and, er, Dr Smith and Dr Noble and Dr... Bow... Bowthingy,' he said, gesturing in Bowman's direction. 'I'm a psychiatrist.'

This is perhaps why the others deal with Dr Mason so badly: his semmingly innocent observations are often insightful to an unsettling degree and the others reject these because they are uncomfortable to take on board. Yet it is only the truth that he offers. I have found his company engaging, feeling that I learn a little something about myself from every conversation we have held – not least yesterday evening, shortly after he surprised me by changing his verdict. I was irritated at first, but he offered to explain over dinner at his club (he must be a member in excellent standing if they admit him dressed like this). I decided to give him the benefit of the doubt.

I was correct to do so. His own reasons for altering his position were complex but, on the whole, made sense. By the time the main course had arrived, we agreed to disagree and continued with normal conversation, which it seems, with Dr Mason, involves a great many questions from his side. 'I am sorry,' he apologised. 'I suppose it's force of habit.' But he didn't stop.

It was during dessert, when I mentioned my late sister who had died before I was born, that Dr Mason put down his fork and leaned forward. 'Oh that *is* very interesting,' he said. 'And I'll tell you why just as soon as I've finished my cheesecake. Are you sure you won't try some?'

I declined and asked him what he found so interesting about this aspect of my life. He held up a finger, finished eating his cheesecake and then told me.

'When did you become aware that there had been another child in the household?' he asked. 'If you don't mind me asking?'

'No, no,' I said. 'I can't really remember. Early. My parents talked about her. I don't think I remember a time when I *wasn't* aware of her.'

'Yes,' he said, nodding. 'And your parents spoke of her. In what way? What sort of things did they say?'

I shrugged. 'They'd talk about how old she would have been. Wondered what she'd be doing; what she would have looked like.'

'And did they imagine good things?'

'Usually.'

'Yes that's understandable,' he said, and then looked off to the side for a while, eyes screwed almost shut, fingers pressed to his lips. 'Have you

154

ever considered,' he said to me, 'that you might have developed some kind of resistance to the unquantifiable? That you perhaps value the tangible so highly above the hypothetical and the imaginary out of a sense of frustration with, er, with the pressure of living up to the postulated achievements of your sister?' He nodded, satisfied that he had expressed himself in full, then raised both eyebrows, curious about what I would make of his ideas.

I made a great deal of them. The conversation continued in a similar vein although in many ways he had said it all – there was no more compelling motivation for my opposition to Dr Smith's theory. Whilst I am still unconvinced by Smith – I shall not, indeed, be preparing to defend my home against a possible attack by werewolves! – I have started to see that I may not have been opposing him for the correct reasons, and plan to concede this when we resume.

'Are you busy next week?' I ask Dr Mason as the other jurors begin to take their seats.

'Oh, well, I hope so,' Dr Mason replies. 'I was supposed to be in America by now for some very lucrative and probably actually very easy consultancy work. They've said they'll wait for me but I don't want to risk them drafting in some *nincompoop* at short notice, for their sake as much as for mine.' He thinks for a second then shakes his head. 'Actually, mainly for my sake. I just want a paid holiday, really.'

'Please, then,' I say, pulling a pen and a small notebook from my pocket, 'take my number down and call me when you get back.' I write my telephone number on one of the notebook's leaves, tear it out and push it across the table to him.

'Yes,' he says, picking it up and squinting at it as though he might be able to divine some further knowledge from the digits – for all I know, he can. 'I certainly will.'

Dr Smith is the last to return. He catches Dr Mason's eye as he pulls out his chair. Dr Mason's expression betrays nothing: instead, he his attention to folding the piece of paper into quarters.

Dr Bowman stands. 'Are we all here?' he asks, looking for empty seats and finding none. 'Right. Now, I –'

'Before you start,' I say, 'I have been talking with Dr Mason and yes, I have decided to return a verdict of not guilty. We can go through the motions of the vote if you want, Dr Bowman, but…'

Dr Bowman nods his head, displaying that vaguely imbecilic grin again. 'I think it's best. Don't you?'

Back in the courtroom the defendant, Dr Foreman, awaits the judge's pronouncement with his chin raised, white hair tipping over his shoulders, hands grasping his lapels, braced against the worst. When he is told that he can leave the court a free man, he chuckles gently to himself. There is a degree of consternation around him. The victim's family look distraught, for which one can scarcely blame them.

Outside of that room, I wonder if we have done the right thing.

That impression is balanced, but not completely cancelled out, by the sight of Dr Foreman's granddaughter rushing to embrace him. She is on the verge of tears, whilst he now gives the impression that he was never in any doubt that the result would go his way.

As we rise and file out of the box for the last time, I notice Dr Foreman glance at Dr Smith again. This time Smith gives him an almost undetectable nod. Having detected it myself, I wonder if I should say something as Smith and the other doctors shuffle towards the exit, moving awkwardly around each other like magnets all turned to similar poles.

Behind them, I walk outside into the sunshine and abruptly feel utterly, utterly disorientated. My vision splits double. The world spins out of focus. I stop walking, dimly aware that I am at risk of stepping into the road, as without clear input I have become... unstable. After a few seconds I start to become aware of a hand on my shoulder: I turn and it belongs to Dr Bowman. His expression is difficult to make out, but its imbecilic aspect appears to have vanished.

'I'm sorry about this,' he says, a little reluctantly. 'This is the thing people just don't *get* about time travel – once you let yourself think "Oh, it's all right, if it goes wrong I'll just hop back and fix it" you never stop and before you know it you've overwritten the timelines so many times they're all sort of falling to bits before your eyes.'

I have no idea what he's talking about. But, lost in a sensory tangle, I let him lead me away.

Charley shrugged. 'So, he's met lots of versions of the Doctor. I'm beginning to realise that my Doctor isn't the definitive one, just the latest.'

The Steward smiled. 'Time in this airship, Miss Pollard, is confused. Past, present and even the possible futures of Time Lords are of as much importance to these people as their own stories are.'

They were interrupted as Robert Zierath came back over, bringing with him the man he'd called Thomas. Another American, Charley realised as Thomas spoke.

'Morning, Miss. Mister Zierath here reckons you want to know my story. Understand why us smaller fish are here with all of the bigger ones, right?'

Charley nodded. 'Yes, please...'

The Farmer's Story

Todd Green

The oil men had come to East Ridge, and there wasn't a damn thing Thomas Watson or anyone else could do to stop them. Thomas had better things to do with his morning than sit in the saloon. The horses' hay needed changing, the rusty fence hinges needed replacing, and he wanted to be with Bessie when she delivered her litter of piglets that were due any day. He'd ignored John Glassman's telegrams at first, but when he heard the oil man was coming to town, he figured he may as well look him in the eye and get it over with. So he'd dutifully ridden into town to meet him.

Glassman was from New York and wore an inefficient, brimless round hat that he didn't remove as he entered the saloon, looking with distaste at a few crumbs of Texas dirt that had had the misfortune to cling to his creased slacks and shiny shoes. City folk were rare, and ones from back East more so. There were plenty of farms between East Ridge and New York, and East Ridge didn't have much of anything else to warrant that long journey, three days by train to Houston and another day on the stage. A couple of stores, the saloon, and the church all lined Main Street, and that was about it.

There was hardly another soul in the saloon. Another party of out-of-towners sat at one table, two men and a girl. They hunched toward each other, sipping three glasses of water, talking quietly with accents he couldn't place.

Glassman talked loudly and quickly, as though Thomas were deaf or might interrupt before he could finish. He talked of progress, of modernisation, of the future – but mostly he talked about oil. Oil, he claimed, lay just below East Ridge, the Watson farm in particular, and it would make them rich. Them. Together. As if they'd already shaken hands, signed the papers, and started the drilling. Thomas barely listened. Nothing Glassman said made a bit of difference, he wasn't about to start digging for oil under the land that had fed three generations of Watsons.

'Well?' Glassman had stopped talking, fixing Thomas with a twenty-dollar smile. He pushed some papers across the table, holding a pen in his other hand. 'What do you say, partner?'

Thomas didn't stop to wonder whether Glassman meant 'business partner' or was trying to sound like a cowboy. 'Thank you, no, sir,' he said. 'My farm's not for sale.' He couldn't help but feel pleased to see Glassman's smile freeze a moment, dumb disbelief spilling through the crack.

'Of course it's for sale,' Glassman said. 'Were you listening, man? The oil on your property is worth a fortune.'

'We're doing just fine as a farm,' Thomas said. 'No need to fix what ain't broke.'

'Now see here, pardner,' said Glassman, this time making a point of pronouncing it with a 'd'. Thomas wondered where he'd gotten that impression. No one he knew ever said it. 'We've done the tests. There's oil under East Ridge, and your land has most of it. Texas needs oil – this country needs oil. Are you going to stand in the way of that? Five hundred an acre is a fair price for that dirt farm of yours.'

How did Glassman expect insults to help him make the sale? 'Your price was mighty generous,' he said. 'But a few thousand dollars doesn't make a difference. There are things more important than money.'

'There are?'

Thomas could still picture his daddy's grey face, lined not from age but from concentrating to speak before his body gave out. 'Make me proud, boy,' he'd said. 'I'll have my eye on you, come market day.'

'Yes sir,' Thomas had said, and said it again now. 'There are. The farm's not for sale.'

Glassman pushed his chair back and stood, gathering his papers back into his case. 'We'll speak again, Mr Watson,' he said. 'The law's on my side, you know. You can't hold back progress.' He stomped outside, muttering and brushing dust from his sleeves.

'Pardon me, do you mind if I ask a question?' The voice at his elbow was measured, the tones round and soft as musical notes. Thomas glanced down at a kind face, the man's smile matching the politeness of his words, though his mop of hair needed slicking back out of his eyes. The other out-of-towners from the next table – the younger man, and the girl – had equally pleasant smiles.

'What's that?' Thomas took a breath, trying not let Glassman make him rude to everyone he met.

'I'm sorry to have overheard your conversation, but I am curious,' said the man. 'What did he mean, "the law's on his side"?'

'Well…' Thomas stopped, looking from the men to the girl. All three looked out of place, the girl wearing a jacket like one his mother had turned into rags years before, the younger man in a skirt! The older man's suit was wrinkled and worn as though he'd walked a hundred miles on the trail.

'You're not from Texas, are you?' Thomas said.

'We're from England,' said the girl. 'I'm Victoria, this is Jamie, and the Doctor.'

Thomas remembered his manners. 'Miss,' he said, tipping his hat. 'I'm Thomas Watson, and I do apologise if our conversation disturbed you.'

158

'Ye dinna disturb us at all,' said the younger man – Jamie – his accent so thick it took a moment for Thomas to realise what he was saying. 'I'm no' English. I'm Scottish.'

'Scotland, eh?' Thomas said. 'That's a long way from East Ridge. What brings you this way?'

'We're travelling,' said the Doctor. 'Seeing the country.' He smiled. 'You were saying…?'

'Right,' said Thomas. 'Some fellows back East struck oil, and made a filthy lot of money. Word of that spread all over the country. Now the lawmakers in Texas, they figure if there's oil here, there's money to be had. So they made up laws letting the oil companies force folk to sell their land if they find enough oil there.'

'What a terrible law,' said Victoria. 'I hope they aren't planning something similar in England.'

'Things are different in America, at this time,' said the Doctor. 'Though it's not that different to the King imposing his will on his subjects, not so long ago.' He looked back to Thomas, encouraging him to continue.

'Mr Glassman's offering a fair price, and interest if he strikes oil,' Thomas said. '"For the greater good of Texas," he says, as though you're not loyal if you don't sell. I didn't work twenty years to build a farm only to tear it up.'

'And is there oil on your property, Mr Watson?' said the Doctor.

'A trickle,' he said. 'Mostly it's a pain in the neck. Got the stuff in a couple of my wells, so I have to carry water further to the horses, but that's about it.'

'Mr Glassman seemed very confident.'

'He's a fool,' said Thomas. 'Begging your pardon. His kind'll tear this country up looking for their dreams, and not spare a thought for the folk they leave behind. Make a few dollars and off they go. Can't eat their oil, or make a suit of clothes from it.'

'There are other benefits oil can offer,' said the Doctor.

'I know that,' Thomas said to the Doctor. 'I'm not against oil in general. But I want no part of it.'

'What sort of benefits, Doctor?' asked Jamie.

'Those motor cars in… ah, that we read about,' the Doctor said, raising an eyebrow. 'They run on processed oil, for a start.'

Behind him, the saloon doors swung aside to admit George Dayton and Martha Dibble – the heads of the 'East Ridge Planners', an association of the town's land and business owners. The moment the first sniff of oil reached their noses, they were repeating the oil men's words like the money was already in their pockets.

'There he is,' said George. 'Thomas Watson, we'd like a word with you.'

'We hear you're not selling!' said Martha.

'Good afternoon to you, Mr Dayton, Mrs Dibble,' said Thomas. 'And you're right. Let him dig for oil on someone else's farm.'

'It's his land,' said Victoria. 'He shouldn't have to sell if he doesn't want to.'

'Thomas, you can't be serious,' said George. 'Your farm has half the town's oil. Without you, there won't be a deal.'

'Is that what Glassman told you?' Thomas turned for the door, but George blocked his way.

'He's done the tests,' said Martha. 'Your land has the best chance for a strike. Think of the money oil would bring to East Ridge.'

'There's hardly enough oil on my farm to fill a tin can.' Thomas stepped forward and forced George out of the way.

'Glassman's a businessman,' said George. 'Like me. He knows what he's doing. If there wasn't oil there he wouldn't bother debating with you.'

'He'll find his oil somewhere else,' said Thomas. 'The rest of town's no different from my farm.'

'It's not worth his time if you're not in. Why would he say it if it wasn't true?'

The Doctor smiled, patting George Dayton's arm. 'Dayton… You own Dayton's General Store down the street?'

'That's right,' said George.

'You're a businessman too. So you think like Mr Glassman thinks. You understand him.'

'Surely it's the other way around, Doctor?' said Jamie.

'Oh, not at all, Jamie,' said the Doctor. 'Mr Dayton saw the benefits oil could bring. Even before Mr Glassman explained it to him. And why should he be anything but truthful?'

Thomas saw what the Doctor was thinking. 'I don't care if the whole town's against me. My grandpappy started our farm, my daddy ran it, I'll run it, and if I'm lucky enough to marry, my son will run it too.'

'Thomas, you work so hard, you may never have that chance,' Martha said. 'You've done right by your father, isn't it time for you to do something for you? And help the town grow.'

Thomas was done hearing what he should do for one day. 'I'll decide what's best for me.'

George backed toward the door alongside him. 'But we could become the centre of a Texas oil empire.'

Thomas pushed through the door. 'Don't you have a store to run?' he said. 'Think for a moment about today.' He'd lost half the day now. He'd have to work right through dinner and into the dark. The hands would have kept things up but any man works harder with his boss's shoulder next to his.

Thomas hopped onto Tawny's saddle and spurred the horse into

160

a reasonable trot out of town. The folks he passed on Main Street looked away, quickly, not even returning his nod. Had Glassman rallied the whole town against him, so soon? Was he the last man in East Ridge content to raise his crops and animals? The future could come rushing into East Ridge but as long as men had to eat, there'd be a Watson farm at the north end of town.

The sun had long since set before Thomas was ready to head in for supper. The sky was empty but for a giant full moon that lit the fence enough for him to see as he nailed the new hinge into the fencepost. He could have asked Bob or James to fix it, but the hands were exhausted by sunset and he'd sent them on home. His team had put in a solid day's work despite his absence in the morning; the least he could do was tend to the few remaining chores.

He didn't know what to make of the prank the oilmen had played while he'd been in town. He assumed it had been them, but no one had actually seen how the tall blue shed got behind the barn. It was a strange prank – he couldn't open the doors, and it wasn't in anyone's way, so he didn't understand how it was supposed to make him angry or convince him to sell his farm to Glassman. The word 'Police' was written at the top, so maybe the Sheriff knew something about it.

He drove the last nail home and swung the gate to test it, then snapped the latch closed. There, one less opportunity for animals to stray. Working late on a warm night didn't bother him. No family waiting on his arrival, no supper going cold on the table. He rode in, looking forward to a pleasant evening reading with a candle, or listening to the crickets chirping in the moonlight, the world to himself.

Suddenly Tawny's ears flattened, and she let out a nervous whinny. About twenty yards ahead there was a dark shape against the moonlight, too big to be a possum, ducking out of sight behind one of his wells. Then he heard muttered voices and a whispered 'Shush!'

Thomas reined Tawny in and drew his gun. Decent folk didn't skulk and hide after dark. 'I see you there,' he said, raising the gun skyward. 'You're on private property.' The dark shape shifted but there was no answer. He spurred Tawny to a trot and fired twice straight up in the air.

Two men jumped up and ran in the opposite direction, nearly breaking their necks climbing over the fence. Thomas pulled Tawny still, hearing them mount their horses behind a clump of trees and ride off at speed. 'That showed them, didn't it, girl?'

He waited until their hoof beats faded before dismounting alongside the well. He'd had to cap this well because of the oil bubbling up into the water. Couldn't drink or water the crops with it as it was, and couldn't boil the stuff out. He'd had a heifer take sick before he'd noticed and nailed a half-dozen boards across the top to keep the other animals from getting into it. One of the boards now lay askance, pried up on one end. Why would a couple of outlaws be digging into his useless well?

He followed the men's path from the well to the fence. In the moonlight he saw a strip of cloth from one of their trousers caught on a nail. The cloth felt soft – nicer than any working man would wear out in the fields, nicer than his best church suit. More like the suit a city fellow would wear – like Glassman, or perhaps his helpers. Was this what he'd meant by testing the land? Sniffing for oil from a useless well?

The following afternoon, after he'd helped sort the seeds for next week's planting, Thomas rode back up to town, the piece of cloth in his pocket. In the daylight he was certain it had torn from one of the oilmen's trousers, all the hands agreed it was nicer than anything they'd seen. He didn't know a thing about clothes but you couldn't make cloth shine like that without spending some money.

That rumpled Doctor and his friends were just coming out of Dayton's store as he reined Tawny in, and the Doctor clasped his hands as an old friend. 'Mr Watson, how nice to see you.'

'Did you miss your stagecoach?' Thomas said. 'I'm surprised to see you folks still in town. Most people pass right through East Ridge.'

'We're staying a couple of days,' the Doctor said. 'It's a lovely town. And we so rarely have the opportunity to relax without any worries.'

'And without getting yourself into trouble,' said Jamie. The Doctor frowned at him.

'Yesterday we took our dinner in a basket down to the river,' said Victoria. 'This morning we've been looking at the buildings on Main Street. The church is beautiful, so wonderfully modern.'

'It's a new building,' said Thomas. The church had been built two years ago, after the old one caught fire. 'But I didn't think it was that interesting.' Across the street, he saw Glassman striding into Sheriff Wilson's office, his round hat rolling with his head like a boulder.

'Everything in London is over a hundred years old,' said Victoria. 'Everything in America looks brand new. And so much space.'

'That's how we like it,' said Thomas. 'Though you'd think with this much space the oil men could find someplace else to do their digging.'

'I thought you told them off yesterday,' said Jamie.

'They're persistent. Last night I ran two of them off my land.'

Sheriff Wilson's door opened, and he and Glassman came out, each with half of a conniving smile. Glassman had probably just reminded the Sheriff how East Ridge would dry up and disappear if every farm didn't become an oil well.

'You'll have to pardon me.' Thomas crossed the street, dimly aware of

162

the Doctor, Victoria, and Jamie following at some distance behind him. 'I have a complaint against this man, Sheriff.'

Sheriff Wilson glanced from Thomas to Glassman. 'What's the problem?'

'I ran two of his men off my property last night,' said Thomas. 'They were rooting around in one of my wells.'

'I didn't send anyone to your property,' said Glassman.

Thomas pulled the scrap of cloth from his pocket. 'One of them caught his leg on my fence and left this behind,' he said, holding it near Glassman's own suit. 'A good match, I'd warrant.'

Victoria leaned forward. 'Oh, that's a nice suit,' she said. 'It looks expensive.' She smiled at Glassman, who seemed startled to see the three of them.

'You think Mr Glassman was there?' said the Sheriff. 'That's hardly evidence.'

Glassman brushed his trouser leg as though to emphasise that it wasn't torn. 'And I spent the evening in the saloon, entertaining your neighbours in the East Ridge Planners. Mr Watson, you should have joined us.'

'I wasted enough time with you yesterday,' said Thomas. 'I'm not saying you were there yourself. But no one from East Ridge wears clothes made from material like this.'

'I'd agree with you,' said the Sheriff. 'But that don't mean the man who wore this cloth works for Mr Glassman.'

'There ain't any other city folk around.'

Sheriff Wilson glanced toward the Doctor and his friends. 'Where are you three from again?'

'We are from out of town.' The Doctor smiled as he thrust the lapels of his worn coat toward the Sheriff. 'Though we don't go in for fancy dress.'

'There's another thing,' said Thomas, remembering. 'Sheriff, did you lose a blue shed about, oh, seven feet high and four across?'

He raised his hand over his head to demonstrate the height. All five of them blinked at him.

'Thomas, what are you talking about? I don't have any blue sheds,' said the Sheriff.

'A shed like that turned up behind my barn yesterday,' said Thomas. Victoria gasped. 'That's your...'

The Doctor coughed suddenly, perhaps from the dust. 'Behind your barn, really?'

'Only reason I asked if it was yours, Sheriff, it says "Police" at the top.' Thomas shrugged. 'I figured it was some sort of prank.' He glanced back to Glassman, who burst out with a roaring laugh that startled Tawny forty feet away across the street.

'You think I put a shed behind your barn, as a prank. Before I sent some men to check out your wells? And maybe I stopped your chickens laying, and your cows giving milk, while I was at it?' Glassman nudged the Sheriff, who smiled back.

Thomas could feel a band of sweat rising under his hair and travelling down his forehead. More time wasted due to Glassman. 'I didn't say you had a thing to do with it,' he said, keeping his voice level.

The Sheriff coughed. 'Thomas, I'm sorry you're having trespassers. And I'll come by and see this shed,' he said. 'But nothing you've said suggests that Mr Glassman's responsible.'

'Thank you, Sheriff,' said Glassman. 'And I assure you, I'll continue to stay away from Mr Watson's land.'

'You do that,' Thomas said. 'If I see any of your dressed-up oil folk on my property, I'll put a hole in him.'

Sheriff Wilson laid a hand onto Thomas's shoulder. 'If you go shooting people for looking at you funny, you'll have a heap of trouble. Mr Glassman's been mighty generous to our town. Don't let your opinion get in the way of progress. Some of us think East Ridge has a great future.'

Greedy, like the rest of them. He shook the Sheriff's arm away. 'My opinion ain't changed, the land's not for sale. He can buy off everyone in town and it won't make a difference.'

'We'll see,' said Glassman. 'The arbiter's coming the day after tomorrow. I'm sure he'll see things my way.'

'He'll show you for the fool you are.' The smugness of the man dug under Thomas's skin, making him itch.

The Sheriff turned back for his office. 'Leave Mr Glassman alone, Thomas,' he said.

'It does seem odd to call an arbiter,' the Doctor said. 'From what I understand you hardly have a claim to the land.'

'I thought America was a free country,' said Victoria.

'It's like this,' said Glassman. 'Mr Watson owns his land, I don't dispute that. But Texas agrees that if something better could be done with his land, that would benefit the town, the state – the whole country – then that's what we should do.'

'Whether or not I want you to,' said Thomas.

'I'm not going to steal it,' said Glassman. 'Here's an example. A few years back, the Atchison, Topeka, and Santa Fe Railroad was set to come into Houston. A hundred jobs in every town along the way, and thousands of dollars for Houston. And right in the middle of the route was a pack of Indians. Just sitting there farming the land, not building anything important on it. They wouldn't leave. The trains couldn't go around, the land wasn't suitable. The government had to step in. They worked out a deal – moved the Indians to better land, with money in their pockets besides. Everybody won.'

Thomas had read about the railroad deal. Better land meant a tiny scrap, packed in with other Indians from all over the country. Victoria and Jamie looked over to the Doctor, who shook his head.

'Everyone won except the Indians, as you call them,' he said. 'Banished, exiled, as far as the rest of the country is concerned. A tragedy.'

'No, no, you've got it all backwards,' said Glassman. 'They're happy. They're opening stores.'

'Not in East Ridge, I hope.' George Dayton trotted up to join them. 'Anything you need, Dayton's will supply it.' He shook Glassman's hand enthusiastically, like there was twenty dollars in it. Or a meaty bone.

George met Thomas's gaze and frowned. 'Mr Glassman, don't let a single dissenting voice worry you. The East Ridge Planners are looking forward to working with your company.'

'I appreciate that,' said Glassman. 'Most everyone has been very pleasant.'

'Yes sir! Just like you described it last night, we're looking forward to that first oil strike, to East Ridge becoming a… a…' George rubbed his chin. 'What was that word you used again, Mr Glassman? Met-something?'

'Metropolis?'

'That was it! A metropolis, right here in Texas.'

It was a pipe dream, all of it. And Glassman had sung the town to sleep. 'That's right,' said Thomas. 'A great empire, with ten horses for every man, woman, and child. Five-storey buildings lining the streets. And on every corner, a shiny new Dayton's store.'

George at least had the courtesy to pretend surprise. 'I suppose there could be,' he said.

Thomas turned his back on them. 'You people are full of your own grand ideas. Good luck keeping warm with ideas when winter comes and there's no oil.' He looked Glassman in the eye. 'You remember what I said.' He stormed off, not hearing Glassman's answer, which caused George to burst into high-pitched giggles.

Tawny bristled at him and reared her head away as he reached for the reins. She could sense the black anger in his gut as well as he could. Glassman was buying up East Ridge, one farm and one person at a time. They couldn't see that the town would end up nothing but machines from end to end, left behind when the oil didn't come and Glassman moved on to Shelbyville, or Pillfield, or some other town too greedy to see straight. Would no one stand with him? What could he do alone?

'I have a suggestion.' The Doctor's soft voice startled him as he swung his leg into Tawny's saddle, the little man appearing in front of the horse as if conjured from the dust. He reached out a hand to stroke Tawny's nose, cooing softly. Tawny rubbed her head against him.

'What's that?' said Thomas.

'If you can prove that the trespassers work for Mr Glassman, it would hurt his chances with the arbiter,' the Doctor said.

'It sure would,' said Thomas.

'Exactly,' said the Doctor. 'There are ways to gather proof without shooting people.'

The Doctor had refused to wear a pistol, but Thomas insisted on bringing his, just in case. They crouched in the tall grass a few yards beyond the well. The Doctor's two friends were back at Thomas's house, where Victoria promised to have a sumptuous meal ready when they returned.

'What makes you think those men will be back tonight?' Thomas said.

'Mr Glassman needs to have evidence of oil before the arbiter comes, doesn't he?' said the Doctor. 'Assuming the trespassers work for him, he'll have to send them back. He won't risk being empty handed before the arbiter.'

'Why doesn't he find another town to pester?'

'He must believe your town has oil,' said the Doctor. 'He's convinced everyone else to sell, and he doesn't want to leave anything to chance.' He lifted his head, looking like he was sniffing the air. 'When they come, see if you can sneak around the side and over the fence without being seen.'

The fence in question was two boards going across, nailed to posts every six feet along. The top board was about three feet high, so getting over it wouldn't be a problem, but still… The fence was also close to the well. 'That'll depend on where they are,' Thomas said.

'Of course. But I anticipate they will be focused on the well.' He held up a hand before Thomas could reply, and seemed to shrink smaller into the shadows.

Thomas strained to hear the approaching hoof beats. He leaned onto his elbows but the Doctor pushed him back to the ground.

'Not yet.' His voice was quiet in Thomas's ear.

The two men reined in their horses just outside the fence and climbed over.

'Careful of that fence tonight,' said one voice, chuckling.

'That Watson fellow cost me a ten-dollar suit,' said the other. 'Waving his gun, shooting the air.'

'We'll be ready for that tonight.' The first man patted his holster.

Thomas's hand dropped to his gun. He didn't have to shoot the air tonight.

But the Doctor already had his hand on the weapon, holding it firmly in the holster. 'No guns. Only if you must defend yourself.'

The two men set to work, struggling with the boards Thomas had resealed across the well. The Doctor nudged him. 'Go now. Don't let them see you. When you get past the fence, lead their horses away. Just a few yards should suffice in the dark.'

Thomas looked at the men and the fence just behind them. 'I don't see how they can possibly miss me, Doctor.'

'They are involved with their task.' As if to agree, both men bent to examine the boards, their faces half into the well.

Thomas rolled over and shuffled along the ground on his belly, holding his breath. Finally he reached the fence and lay flat, the two men still intent on the boards and the well. He rose slowly, keeping his body close to the fence, then lay across the top board, raising one leg over. The men continued their work by the well. Thomas brought his leg down on the outside of the fence, his other leg followed, and he dropped to the grass.

'What was that?' One of the men was looking toward the fence.

Both men squinted toward him, but didn't move. 'Probably just the horses.' They turned back to the well.

Thomas crawled along the ground until he was behind the horses, who didn't take any notice of him as they munched on the grass. Standing behind them, Thomas turned back but the men were still facing the well. He led the horses behind some trees, tied them, and peered back.

Beyond the well, the Doctor stood up.

'Lovely night for a walk.' The Doctor approached the well like he was strolling down Main Street. The two men dropped their tools and turned to him.

'What do you want?' The larger of the two took a step toward the Doctor.

'You gentlemen work for Mr Glassman, don't you?'

'What of it?' said one. The other slapped his arm.

'Just making sure my information was correct,' said the Doctor, his voice as pleasant as a preacher with a collection plate. 'For the Sheriff. When he arrives in a few minutes.'

'The Sheriff's coming?' The men drew their guns, took a step toward him.

'I sent word that he should come see the trespassers,' the Doctor said. 'If you could be so kind as to wait right there...'

'Or we could leave before he gets here.'

'We need the oil...' The second man stopped, cocking his gun. 'Nobody seen us but him.'

'You don't want to do that.' The Doctor's voice remained even, pleasant. Thomas drew his gun. 'Trespass is a minor thing. But murder?' He took a step toward the men, holding his hand out. 'You're not murderers.'

The men's aim faltered a moment. 'Let's just go,' said one. They turned toward the fence, and stopped. 'Where are the horses?'

The Doctor took another step forward. 'I think I hear horses coming. Maybe the Sheriff's here already.'

Thomas patted one horse's flank and it stepped away, grunting.

'I hear them!' The two men were looking straight at him but clearly their eyes weren't used to the empty dark of a Texas night. Thomas could see them reaching out blindly before them.

'You sure?'

'Might be.' The Doctor had come closer, now he had them against the fence. 'It'll look better for you without those weapons.' His tone hadn't changed but his voice filled the air around them.

The two men glanced at their guns. The Doctor reached out.

'No need to complicate matters. Just hand me the guns, and we'll forget you even had them.'

Thomas realised he had his own gun turned around as though he was about to give it away.

The men placed their guns into the Doctor's waiting hands. 'Thank you, that was very wise,' he said. 'Mr Watson, you can come out now.'

Thomas blinked, holstering his gun as the Doctor calmly tied the men's hands behind their backs.

'See, I told you there'd be no need for weapons,' he said.

'How'd you do that?' Thomas said.

'Just a matter of suggestion.'

'Where's the Sheriff?'

'Oh, back in town I expect.' The Doctor smiled. The men struggled, but their bonds held. 'I suppose we'll have to take them into town ourselves.'

It was late to ride back to town, so Thomas fixed up rooms for the Doctor and his friends, and the prisoners spent the night tied in the barn. In the morning they loaded the oilmen into the wagon and Tawny pulled them to the Sheriff's front door. Thomas found the Sheriff and Glassman sitting over a pot of coffee like old hands on a cattle drive.

'Sheriff, I've got those men who were trespassing on my land,' said Thomas. 'I'm pressing charges.'

Sheriff Wilson and Glassman followed them out and Thomas saw the flash of anger behind Glassman's eyes as the Doctor and Jamie helped the two bound men off the wagon.

'Sorry, Mr Glassman,' blurted one.

'There you go, Sheriff, they admit it,' said Thomas. The Sheriff frowned at Glassman.

'I had nothing to do with this,' Glassman said, watching the men carefully. 'Whatever reason you men had for visiting Mr Watson, I'm sure it'll come out in court.'

'No need for that,' said the Sheriff. 'The county penalty for trespass is three nights in jail and five dollars apiece.'

Glassman tossed his coffee on the ground and handed the empty cup to the Sheriff. 'That's it? No trial, no attorneys?'

'They admit it,' said the Sheriff, leading the two men into the office, the lone jail cell standing open behind. 'That's all I need.'

'That's a shame.' Glassman hoisted his belt, taking a deep breath. 'Two men come to visit Mr Watson and he calls them trespassers.'

'They came over the fence,' said the Doctor.

'After dark,' said Jamie.

'Whatever their reasons,' said Glassman, raising his voice. Across the street, Thomas saw Martha Dibble of the East Ridge Planners hurrying over. 'It's a shame that the law in East Ridge doesn't stop to consider their story, but simply puts them away.'

'The Sheriff's just doing his job,' said Victoria.

'It's only three nights,' said the Sheriff.

'I appreciate the hospitality I've enjoyed from most of the citizens of East Ridge.' Two men ran into Dayton's store and a moment later, George Dayton joined Martha. 'But if this is how the people of East Ridge settle their disagreements, I don't know whether we can continue our development here.'

'Good riddance, too,' said Thomas.

By now a dozen people had gathered around Glassman. Thomas pushed away from the group.

'It's not enough that Mr Watson rejects my generous offer.' Glassman was warming to his audience. 'But then he deliberately detains my assistants, disrupting my operations. That makes things very difficult for us here. Perhaps in another town...'

Several people in the crowd shouted 'No!'

'They were trespassing!' said Jamie.

Thomas turned away. 'I caught them on my land, and that's all there is to it.' He mounted his wagon seat and flicked Tawny forward.

'One man,' Glassman said, 'can undermine the hard work and dedication of so many fine people. Come over to the saloon, I want all of you to see the future that I'm asking you to support. Let me show you how I hope we'll handle the oil we find in East Ridge.' Thomas shook the reins to speed up the wagon and drown him out. Would Glassman leave over a couple arrests? Thomas could dream, too, couldn't he?

Behind his barn, Thomas pulled and pushed the door of the blue shed but it wouldn't open. As he turned away, he heard hoof beats and men's voices carrying over the snorts of the horses arriving out front. One of the hands called out, 'He's behind the barn,' and a group of footsteps trod closer. What now? Thomas turned to see George Dayton lead a party of a dozen men from the association around the corner of the barn. Some had their shotguns. Thomas laid one hand on his pistol, checking to be sure he had six bullets. Lord hope he didn't need them.

George looked for a moment at Thomas's hand on his gun. 'We don't want any trouble, Thomas,' he said.

'I've never known a dozen armed men to want anything but trouble,' Thomas said.

'You've got to understand,' said George.

'No, I don't,' said Thomas. 'I won't stop you buying into Glassman's plan. But I've made my decision, and you won't change my mind, no matter how many guns you bring.'

'I did tell them to leave the guns behind.' Two men stood aside as the Doctor pushed to the front, coming slowly to stand next to Thomas, facing the others. 'You men should return to your homes,' he said pleasantly. 'Mr Watson has no quarrel with you.'

George stepped forward. 'Thomas, he showed us the whole plan,' he said. 'Your farm's right at the heart of the operation. Without it, he'll need to run lines around for a mile. He'll spend all his time carting equipment around you. You have to sell!'

'No, I do not!' So this was Glassman's angle, gain the sympathies of the whole town. 'I don't need to solve Glassman's problems.'

'They're all our problems,' said George. 'The cost of all that piping and hauling is too much. He can't run his operation that way, he'll go to another town.'

Thomas shrugged. 'Sounds like that solves everything.'

Several of the men moved forward, one shouted 'You're ruining everything!'

'Listen!' the Doctor said. Everyone turned – Thomas was surprised that he could bring such a commanding tone to his soft voice. 'I've travelled to many places and I've seen other town invest their futures as Mr Glassman asks you to. In oil, or gold, or rare minerals. And I've seen what happened.'

'They all became rich!' said George.

'Some did.' The Doctor nodded. 'But usually just the owners of the drilling business. The towns they mined were often left behind.'

'Left behind?' George asked.

'Mined out … and abandoned,' said the Doctor.

'That's not the case here,' said George.

'There's only a certain amount of oil in East Ridge,' said the Doctor. 'When that oil is gone, the company has to move on, doesn't it? Leaving the land wrecked by digging, the shops full of merchandise with no one to buy it. New hotels and saloons built and standing empty, no one to visit them.'

'Is that what you want?' Thomas said.

'You're just trying to scare us,' said a man in the group. 'This ain't another gold rush.'

'That's right,' said George. 'Mr Glassman explained to us how the land, once it has oil, it keeps right on making more even if you take some away.'

'Oh, quite,' said the Doctor. 'But you may have to wait some time before drilling again.' The men shrugged. 'Thousands – perhaps millions of years!'

'That's not what he said,' said George.

'But that's how long it took the oil to get there in the first place,' said the Doctor. 'And it's quite a fascinating process, I'd be happy to explain…'

'Don't listen to him,' said George. 'I'm thinking about next week, not what might happen years from now.'

'That's exactly the problem,' said Thomas.

'Mr Glassman's ready to start work and make this town into something big. A place people will come and build up. You've got to sell.'

'And I'm not going to,' said Thomas. 'I'm tired of telling you. Now go away and let me get back to work.'

George turned to the others, shaking his head. 'It's like Glassman said. He'll hold us all up just to have his way.'

'If he doesn't sell we'll never have a chance,' said one of them.

The men moved forward as a group, Thomas and the Doctor backing up against the shed. 'We'll make him sell,' said one.

'He ain't going to keep us from being something big!' said another.

'He'll sell or we'll run him out of town,' said a third.

George frowned. 'Now hold on,' he said.

But the men pressed past him. 'We'll take his land and sell it ourselves!'

Thomas raised his gun. 'Not while I have a thing to say about it!'

'Look out!' A shotgun went up in the group, there was a crack, and a bullet flew past Thomas's head and skimmed off the barn.

'Damn you!' he said, taking aim as half the men ducked.

'No!' The Doctor grabbed his arm and his shot went wide. No one was hit but more guns were raised. 'We're outnumbered, get inside quickly.'

Suddenly the blue door on the shed swung open. Thomas fell inside, the Doctor pushing the door closed before the first bullets hit outside.

'How did you open that door?' Thomas could still hear the men shouting outside and another bullet ricocheted off the shed. 'No matter, they'll be inside in a minute.'

'They won't get in,' said the Doctor calmly.

Thomas stood up, blinking, and took his first real look at the inside of the shed. They were in some sort of white room that seemed bigger than half his barn, the walls panelled with circles, a strange table standing in the centre, with newfangled electric lights blinking on all sides. How could this be inside the shed?

'I'm sure you have many questions,' the Doctor said. 'I'm afraid I won't be able to answer them. But don't worry, we're quite secure in here.' A window in the wall showed George and the others pointing and shouting. Someone aimed a shot directly at the window. Thomas ducked, the gun fired, and… nothing happened. 'See? Quite safe. We'll watch from here, and come out when Jamie and Victoria bring the Sheriff.'

Thomas turned all the way around. Besides the door they'd come through, another door led away. He couldn't imagine where. Was this real?

171

He'd heard that some men shot during the war with the North had had deliriums when the pain got too great. Maybe he was dreaming. Maybe the first bullet had struck him and this was his mind's way of coping.

'At last.' The Doctor pointed at the window as Sheriff Wilson came around the barn with his deputies, firing his pistol in the air to get the men's attention. Before Sheriff Wilson had dismounted, the men had dropped their guns and held their hands high. 'Let's get outside before the Sheriff wonders if we're all right.'

They left the white room, the Doctor closing the door of the blue shed behind them as Jamie and Victoria ran to meet them. Thomas stared back at the door. 'All that… was inside this shed?' he said.

The Doctor nodded. 'Let's not worry about that, shall we? Too many questions, not enough answers, you understand.'

'Doctor!' Victoria hugged the little man. 'You're all right.'

Jamie smiled, patting the shed. 'You knew they would be safe inside.'

The Sheriff stood before George and the others, looking like a disappointed schoolmaster. 'No amount of money is worth shooting at our neighbours,' he said. 'Does East Ridge need oil, if this is what it'll do to us?' His men herded George and the others away. 'You're all right, Thomas? I understand Mr Glassman riled everyone up to come after you.'

'Fine, thank you Sheriff,' Thomas said. It was about time another man saw reason.

The Sheriff looked at the blue shed and shook his head. 'So this is the shed?' He pulled and pushed the door but it didn't budge. 'You're lucky it was here. How'd you get the door open?'

Thomas looked at the Doctor, who smiled, though his friends both looked anxiously up at him. 'Not sure, Sheriff,' he said. 'We must have hit them just right.'

'Well, I'll send a team to clear it away for you,' said the Sheriff. He turned to follow the others. 'Thomas, I'll need you to come along and make a full statement. I'll have to send this case to the county. You three, too, I'll want your side of it.'

'Certainly, Sheriff.' The Doctor cocked an eyebrow at Thomas and lowered his voice. 'Good luck to you,' he said, holding up a key and turning toward the shed.

'Aren't you coming?' Thomas pointed as the Sheriff went around the corner.

'Too many questions, not enough answers…' He smiled.

'Oh, must we go?' said Victoria. 'Just when we were enjoying the town.'

'He had to get involved,' said Jamie, raising a knowing eyebrow.

The Doctor frowned at them. 'I think Mr Watson would agree we were helpful. Time we were moving on in any case. I do hope everything goes well for you.'

'I'm sure I'll be fine,' said Thomas. 'Glassman won't dare try anything else now. Hopefully the arbiter will see my side.'

The Doctor opened the door and they disappeared inside. As the blue door closed, a sudden wind rushed up, howling from the dirt to the sky, swirling the dust and blinding him. Then the shed vanished, the dust settling back to the ground as though covering its tracks.

Thomas stepped into the empty space where the shed had stood. Where had it gone? He'd read about newfangled inventions but nothing that could travel without wheels, that disappeared. Was this the progress Glassman hoped to bring to East Ridge?

Thomas wondered if Glassman would really leave town if he couldn't buy Thomas's farm. Would he try another town? There were hundreds more farming towns like East Ridge in Texas. As long as the state laws favoured oilmen, Glassman could keep pushing other folk to sell. Laws could be changed, but it took men who could think about the future in the face of easy money today. And there weren't many of those in towns like East Ridge.

'So you see, Miss, if I'd have died like Glassman hoped, he'd have got my land, and East Ridge would have had its own oil boom.'

'But, then, the Doctor did the right thing. Found a way for you to live and made Glassman go elsewhere for his oil.'

'Ah,' said the Steward, 'but was that the right thing? Did the Web of Time require East Ridge to find oil? Might it, by the time of your departure from Earth, Miss Pollard, have become the new oil capital of the United States? Maybe been the capital itself?'

Thomas shrugged. 'Who knows? All I do know is that I'm here.'

'But I know I've never heard of East Ridge. And that Washington is the capital city of the Americas!' Charley shook her head. 'How can you be so calm, Mister Watson?'

'Because I trust the Doctor. And I trust he knows what he's doing. And besides, Miss, I'm still alive. Sure as eggs is eggs, I wouldn't have been if the Doctor hadn't turned up. This way, I get to travel.'

'Yes,' said Charley, more to the Steward than the two Americans. 'Yes, where are we actually going?'

'Somewhere better,' said Thomas Watson.

'Somewhere safe,' said Robert Zierath.

'Somewhere where my daughter can grow up alive and well,' said a third man's voice. Very English and rather rich and dark.

Charley realised they had been joined by the man she had seen earlier by the gaming tables, wearing seventeenth-century dress. The young girl was at his side, still holding on to the small tube of multicoloured confectionery. She rolled it from side to side, watching transfixed as the contents rolled around.

'William Rokeby at your service, dear lady,' he said, offering his hand.

Charley took it and then smiled as Rokeby leant forward, turned her hand and kissed the back of it.

'It has been a while since I have kissed such fair flesh,' he said, and Charley immediately felt comfortable in the presence of a man she could tell was a true gentleman. 'This,' he added proudly, 'is Polly-Anne, my daughter.'

'And do you know the Doctor as well?' asked Charley, already aware that the answer would certainly be in the affirmative.

She wasn't disappointed. 'And this,' he continued grandly, running a hand delicately through his daughter's hair, 'is our story.'

The Republican's Story

Andy Russell

It was the smell, Sarah decided, that most eloquently defined the latest world in which she found herself deposited. The cloying stench of putrefaction and decay, carried on what would otherwise be a pleasantly warm summer's breeze, crawled into her nostrils, clawing at her throat and choking every breath to an involuntary gagging splutter. Not that there was much else to go on, she thought, covering her mouth with a handkerchief; the impenetrable mist saw to that.

Straining her senses for any clue as to where she was, Sarah could just discern faint sounds on the edge of hearing. The tolling of a church bell, perhaps? The raised voices of men at work? The general hubbub of a busy city? Sarah had almost begun to believe that the Doctor had at last made good his promise to return her to London in her own time, albeit landing her in the middle of a rubbish tip, when the alien creature loomed out of the murky twilight.

It advanced though the wreathing fog, humanoid yet curiously bird-like, a long beak protruding from its face where the nose and mouth should have been, huge eyes staring blankly from beneath a wide-brimmed hat. It was clad in heavy robes that reached down to its feet and as it stalked towards her, Sarah could see that it was brandishing a long stick in one gloved hand.

Terror cramping her stomach, Sarah retreated, fighting the urge to turn and run for fear that she would lose herself in the murk and never find her way back to the safety of the TARDIS. The creature came on, neither increasing its relentless pace nor making any move to attack, but forcing Sarah back all the same. Suddenly, the ground disappeared from beneath her feet and Sarah felt herself pitching backwards into the darkness, a startled shriek escaping her lips.

And then strong hands were gripping her arms, hauling her back from the brink and away from the birdman. A familiar voice spoke softly close to her ear: 'I thought I told you not to wander off.'

'Doctor!' exclaimed Sarah, relief flooding through her at the miraculous appearance of her friend. 'Where have you been?'

'In the TARDIS,' replied the Doctor. 'I wanted to confirm our coordinates.'

'So where are we?'

'Earth,' the Doctor told her. 'London, actually.'

'Home?' asked Sarah hopefully.

'Well,' the Doctor looked shamefaced, unable to meet Sarah's eyes. 'Not exactly. We're a bit early.'

'How early?' sighed Sarah, sensing imminent disappointment.

'Oh about 310 years.' Sarah had the distinct impression that the Doctor felt that if he said it quickly enough it would sound less. 'Not bad after a journey of over thirty thousand, eh?' he grinned.

'If this is London in,' Sarah did a quick mental calculation. '1666, what is that thing?' She indicated the menacing birdman.

'That?' The Doctor squinted through the mist. 'That's the local quack.'

'A doctor, Doctor?'

'Precisely. The strange apparel is designed to protect the wearer from plague. The robes are made from linen coated with wax paste to prevent the infected atoms of air from sticking to it and the beak is packed with perfumed materials to counteract the smell. It doesn't work, of course. They haven't made the connection between the black rat and its flea and the spread of the Black Death yet.'

As the Doctor spoke the wind, increasing in strength, lifted the fog aside like a curtain revealing a scene of horror illuminated by the yellow glow of a lantern hanging from a pole embedded atop a pile of earth. The birdman was leading a pathetic little group of emaciated and ragged creatures. First came a gaunt man who looked to be in his late forties but who, Sarah guessed, was probably much younger. He was pushing a handcart upon which was a small bundle wrapped in grimy rags. A thin pale woman in a simple, much-repaired dress followed, tears flowing freely down her sunken cheeks. Two malnourished children were clutched tightly to her sides: a tousle-haired teenaged boy and a very small angelic looking girl with big green eyes.

As the procession came to a halt beside the pit that Sarah had almost fallen into, the birdman gestured with his stick and the man tipped the handcart over the edge. Sarah gasped in horror as a tiny, stick-thin arm flopped out from the bundle as it slid off the cart. Despite the Doctor's attempts to hold her back, Sarah ran across and peered down into the pit, fighting down the rising bile that revulsion brought to her throat at the sight of the mass grave below. Tangled human remains filled the excavation, most reduced to bones and empty skulls but some fresher cadavers still in the process of decomposition, their flesh rotting and crawling with bloodied maggots. The infant's corpse was on the top of the plague pit, the tiny body a mass of jet-black bruises, the face contorted in agony and swollen beyond recognition.

A wiry man, face swathed in a thick muffler, shovelled something over the child's corpse. Sarah dug deep into her memories, of school lessons about the Black Death. Of course! He was covering the body with lime, to aid its decay. Sarah turned towards the distraught mother but, unable to find adequate words of comfort, she simply folded the woman's head into her shoulder, waiting for the tears to run dry. As she listened to the woman's sobbing, Sarah became aware of the Doctor standing beside her, long coloured scarf wrapped around his face, gently disentangling her from the grieving family. The woman broke into a series of wracking coughs which, Sarah noticed, left her lips flecked with blood.

'Come on, Sarah Jane,' the Doctor encouraged her gently.

'There must be something we can do,' she pleaded. 'You've got antibiotics in the TARDIS...'

'These things must be allowed to take their course,' insisted the Doctor as he led her away. 'If it's any comfort, the plague has all but died out in London. Soon it'll be a thing of the past.'

'No,' said Sarah bleakly. 'It isn't any comfort.'

The back room of the White Hart was unusually full even for a Saturday night. On the face of it, the clientele standing in shadowy recesses or seated at rough wooden tables seemed to have little in common. Here, the rich rubbed shoulders with the poor, the city's dignitaries with vagabonds, landed gentry with common beggars.

At the far end of the room was a raised stage upon which was a long mahogany table surrounded by ornately carved high-backed chairs. On one of these sat a straight-backed man dressed in a severe black suit of simple design, a large white shirt-collar showing over the neck of the jacket. His medium-length black hair was streaked with premature silver and his face was serious, almost grim, his brow furrowed as he regarded the hands of a gold pocket watch. As they reached midnight he snapped shut the cover, standing to tower over the assembly, regarding them with intense grey eyes.

'Friends,' he began, his powerful voice carrying easily to every ear in the room. 'Friends, I beg your indulgence.'

The room gradually fell silent and, satisfied that he had the full attention of his audience, the man took a deep breath, closing his eyes for a moment before embarking on his carefully prepared speech.

'I call you my friends and am proud so to do though, in truth, I know few of you well, many but slenderly and most not at all.' A murmur went around the room, those present trying to work out if they had just been insulted or complimented. 'I address you as friends for the very reason that we stand united in the common fear, misery and persecution we suffer under the tyrannical reign of Charles Stuart.'

A serving wench moved between the applauding men, carrying a tray of tankards brimming with frothy ale. As she passed a large fireplace, empty of flames in the summer heat, a bony hand reached out and stopped her, drawing her close to its owner, a beggar swamped in a vast cloak that had long since seen better days. His one good eye watered in the smoky atmosphere produced by the clay pipes favoured by most of the men whilst his other was covered by a weather-beaten leather patch. He helped himself to a jar without even offering coin and scratched absently at the lice infesting his matted yellow beard and long greasy hair.

'That man,' he nodded towards the stage. 'What's 'is name?'

'Why, sir, surely you must know,' replied the wench, recoiling from the beggar's rank breath. ''Tis Master William Rokeby.' She looked up at the man on the stage admiringly. 'You see that scar on his cheek? They say he won that fighting beside Oliver Cromwell himself.'

The beggar smiled knowingly, propelling the wench on her way with a slap to her ample rump and leering at her departing back. Then he returned his attention to the stage where Rokeby was continuing his speech-making.

'We all know that since his restoration to the throne six years ago, Charles II has lived a life of debauchery and indolence. We have all heard the rumours of His Majesty's dalliance with that so-called actress, Nell Gwyn.'

He put up an appreciative hand to quieten the cries of 'Harlot!' before continuing. 'Yes, whilst the King should be producing legal heirs with his wife Catharine, a fine Catholic Queen, he wastes his seed elsewhere. And like the Queen, his Catholic subjects suffer also. Unless we act now, we will find ourselves hung, drawn and quartered.'

The crowd again growled, now demanding the head of their monarch and the return of the Republic. Again Rokeby quietened them.

'When he came to the throne, Charles II was given every chance to prove himself worthy. I myself was willing to serve him loyally. The son, I reasoned, should not be held guilty for the sins of the father. I was wrong. The son is the equal of his father and must suffer the same fate.'

The beggar, having seen and heard enough, stood and elbowed his way through the chanting crowd and through the door to the street.

Outside, the air, although still close, was nowhere near as hot and sticky as that in the crowded room. Grasping the edges of his cloak and flapping the garment around his body for ventilation, the beggar set off along the street. As he moved further from the White Hart his limp became less pronounced, his gait settling into a purposeful loping stride. Likewise, his bent frame straightened with every step revealing the powerful build of a tall, athletic man.

Turning into a narrow alley, the man was stunned to find himself flat on his back amongst the stinking contents of the neighbourhood's chamber pots, staring up at buildings that seemed to lean closer together the taller they grew. A veritable mountain of a man leaned into view and it occurred to the beggar that he might have come off better had he run full tilt into one of the alley's walls. Dressed in the uniform of an infantry sergeant, the man peered down at him with small bloodshot eyes.

'Wot we got 'ere, then?' rumbled the sergeant through his thick black beard. Chuckling, he reached down with huge hands and hauled the beggar to his feet. And then something unexpected happened. The beggar twisted and writhed, leaving the sergeant grasping thin air. The officer found the cloak of his uniform pulled over his head, which then cracked against the wall of the nearest building, leaving him seeing stars. As he recovered his wits, he reached for a sword that was no longer at his side, and instead found himself on the sharp end of it – with the beggar at the other.

The eyepatch was gone; two eyes as sharp as the sword's point appraised the sergeant with steely intelligence. The straggly beard hung limply from the man's left hand leaving behind it a carefully trimmed moustache nestling below an aquiline nose.

'Too much ale, Sergeant George Mullens, dulls one's reflexes,' chided the man in a cultured voice. 'Allow me to introduce myself. I am Sir Richard Stoneman-Merritt of His Majesty's Intelligence Service.'

Dropping the false beard, Stoneman-Merritt produced a scroll unrolling it with a single-handed flourish. Although the words were an unintelligible blur to Mullens's uneducated eyes, the royal seal at the bottom of the document told him all he needed to know.

'Sir Richard,' he fawned, 'my captain ordered that I meet you 'ere, sir. Didn't say what for though. Secret I shouldn't wonder.'

'No longer, Mullens.' Sir Richard spun the sword around handing it back to its owner. 'A gaggle of papist conspirators meet presently in the White Hart tavern and I have all the proof I need to effect their arrests. Your men are nearby?'

'Aye, sir,' barked Mullens proudly.

'In another local hostelry to judge by the taint of your breath and the rosy bloom of your nose. Pray fetch them and meet me in one hour in Chandler's Lane. And, good sergeant,' added Sir Richard as Mullens turned to go, 'no more ale.'

A disgruntled sneer on his face, Mullens shambled off into the darkness.

'We've been wandering for hours,' complained Sarah.

'Two and a half,' retorted the Doctor looking around the medieval street with interest.

'That means it's past midnight. I've got a headache and my feet hurt.' The Doctor merely grunted and Sarah pulled a face at his back. 'Oh, let's go back to the TARDIS.'

'Go back? But, Sarah, there's so much to see. Nell Gwyn, for one. I wonder where she's performing?'

'The theatres are probably closed by now.'

'Nonsense. The night is still young,' insisted the Doctor. 'We might get in to see a private performance for Charles II. I met him once, you know.'

179

'The Merry Monarch?'

'Yes. He wasn't king back then, of course. He was on the run from the Roundheads. I met him under an oak tree. Gave him a leg-up as it were...' The Doctor stood in the middle of the road, hands in his pockets turning in a slow circle as if hoping to catch a glimpse of the elusive theatre.

Sarah rubbed at her throbbing forehead and was mildly concerned to find her fingers coated with a sheen of cold sweat. Perhaps she was going down with a cold or, knowing her luck, flu. Wiping her hands on her trousers, Sarah wandered off across the street. She noticed a faded chalk cross beside the door of one of the houses and remembered some research she'd done into the plague of 1665. The crosses were to mark dwellings infected by the Black Death, all members of the household shut in and guarded by watchmen. The poor unfortunates would remain incarcerated until the infection had run its course. The phrase 'kill or cure' entered Sarah's head unbidden and she backed away from the grisly images it conjured up. She was oblivious to the low rumble of cartwheels and the clatter of hooves until something heavy hit her in the back, smashing her breathless into the gutter.

'Are you all right?' asked the Doctor, concern evident in his rich tones.

'I will be when you get off me,' gasped Sarah.

'Sorry.' The Doctor clambered to his feet. 'I saw the cart and you in its path and I just reacted.'

He helped Sarah up and she looked along the street after the receding cart. It was loaded with heavy-looking sacks of flour and, just visible at the reins, was the unnaturally hunched shape of the driver, covered from head to toe in a voluminous hooded cloak.

'He didn't even stop,' fumed Sarah.

'No. He seemed a bit odd, the little I saw of him.' The Doctor's eyes opened wide, his mouth performing the facial equivalent of a shrug. 'Perhaps he was foreign. Or ill.'

Sarah shivered involuntarily.

Concealed behind a tower of wooden barrels, Sir Richard Stoneman-Merritt silently observed the White Hart tavern. Few people had come or gone since he had been watching and he was certain that the meeting was still in progress. He was beginning to worry that that dumb ox Mullens was not going to find his way here when, with a splintering crash, the barrels came tumbling down to reveal the giant sergeant.

'All's ready, sir,' growled Mullens apologetically.

Sir Richard grimaced; it seemed Mullens had heeded his words about ale and moved on to cheap gin. 'Very well. Prepare...' Biting off his words, Sir Richard hauled Mullens back into the shadows as he espied two oddly-dressed strangers strolling towards the tavern.

The man was dressed in loose-fitting trousers unusual in that they reached to his battered shoes rather than ending below the knee as was the fashion. A long muffler wound around his neck and trailed along the floor as he walked. A shapeless felt hat was crammed atop a mop of unfashionably curled hair.

His companion looked to Sir Richard's practised eye to be a pretty young girl. She was dressed, however, in an approximation of boys' clothing: blue breeches and waistcoat with puffed sleeves.

'We could drop in on Sam Pepys,' the man was saying in a loud voice. 'Take his mind off the trouble he's having with the Dutch fleet.'

'We should arrest 'im,' rumbled Mullens. 'Spoutin' off 'bout the war.'

'Everybody knows of our quarrel with the Dutch,' said Sir Richard. 'We have matters of greater import which command our attention. Stir your men and remember I would have our quarry taken alive. Each man's testimony shall condemn his fellows.'

Sarah sneezed. She really was feeling unwell; her head was pounding and she felt hot and clammy. Not that the Doctor seemed to notice, he was too busy showing off his connections to the great and the good in this time period. She sneezed again. And again, the Doctor sauntering over and handing her a creased handkerchief with a knot tied in one corner. Sarah blew her nose loudly.

There was the sudden commotion of booted feet and a troop of about thirty soldiers clattered past. They were clad in leather jerkins, shiny steel helmets on their heads and long wickedly pointed pikestaffs clutched in gauntleted hands. As the Doctor and Sarah watched, the soldiers spread out to surround the White Hart.

'Works outing?' queried Sarah as the soldiers filed in through the doors of the tavern.

'Perhaps they know where Nell Gwyn is performing,' pondered the Doctor. 'You know what you need?' he asked rhetorically as Sarah succumbed to more violent sneezes. 'Vitamin C.'

Taking Sarah by the arm, he led her across the street to where a shape huddled in a doorway. As she looked closer Sarah could see that it was a woman in a rough linen dress, a shawl pulled tight over her head and shoulders. A basket of oranges sat beside her bare feet and the Doctor selected the best fruit from a very poor crop.

'Excuse me,' he smiled as the woman stirred from her slumber. 'My friend isn't feeling too well. I wonder if I might purchase one of your oranges?'

He held out some coins to the orange seller whose bleary-eyed gaze fixed on Sarah's jacket or, more specifically, the spots of blood on it. Her face contorting in horror, the orange seller struggled painfully to her feet and hobbled off with a whimper. Sarah looked down at the blood, the product, she assumed, of the consumptive woman at the plague pit. She coughed, unable to shift the lump in her throat.

'I think you need more than an orange, young lady,' the Doctor told her, his gaze focusing on the end of the street where the orange seller had just disappeared. 'Orange...' he mused, his eyes growing wide. Sarah followed his gaze to the east where the horizon was aglow with burnt orange.

'The sky,' she began.

'London's burning,' intoned the Doctor ominously. 'We should inform the authorities and they went this way.'

Gathering her strength, Sarah jogged after the Doctor as he galloped towards the White Hart.

William Rokeby gripped the back of the chair beside him in an effort to steady himself. He closed red-rimmed eyes, listening to the chorus of approval from his audience and waiting for this latest bout of giddiness to pass. Finally able to face the quieting crowd, Rokeby continued his speech. He had won their confidence and now he must spur them to action.

'I believe that now is our time. The omens are against the King. You all remember the falling star of April last and you all know what that dreadful harbinger presaged. We all lost loved ones to the Black Death. The plague pits claimed my own wife and eldest daughter. By this sign alone does our God show his displeasure.'

The crowd erupted into a seething mass of men, clenched fists punching the air, cheers of support for Rokeby mingling with an ever-growing refrain: 'Death to the King! Death to the King!' Rokeby raised his voice to cry out the final sentence.

'Charles Stuart must be brought down and I vow, before all present, that I shall not rest until that man's evil reign be undone!'

A new voice cut through the clamour of the mob: 'What you speak, Master Rokeby, is treason. Your words hasten you to the gallows.'

Rokeby turned to see a tall, blond-haired man in beggar's rags striding across the stage towards him. Heavily armed troops were storming into the room from every door, quickly encircling the conspirators and curtailing any chance of escape by levelling their sharpened pikes at them.

'Might I know your name, sir?' enquired Rokeby politely.

'I am Sir Richard Stoneman-Merritt.'

'Well, Sir Richard,' said Rokeby, 'I may be a traitor to your King but I do God's work. I and my fellows shall be judged by Him and Him alone.' Then, with a cry of 'For God and the Republic!' Rokeby drew his sword and threw himself at Sir Richard.

Their leader's actions reawakened the courage of the corralled prisoners, who surged outward as one, grasping the pikestaffs of their captors. Battle was joined, the confines of the room reducing it to a jostling scuffle, neither side able to seize the advantage.

Sergeant Mullens was aiming his musket at Rokeby, trying to get a clear shot, as the republican and Sir Richard fenced back and forth across the stage. Suddenly, strange hands wrested the weapon from Mullens's shaking hands and discharged it. The deafening explosion and resultant cascade of plaster dislodged from the ceiling brought all conflict to an abrupt halt.

'Gentlemen,' called a tall stranger cheerfully. 'Now that I have your attention, there's something terribly important you ought to be aware of.'

As he ran through the streets of London, Sir Richard marvelled at the skill with which the stranger calling himself 'the Doctor' had encouraged both sides in the White Hart to set aside their differences. He had pointed through the window to a point where flames could clearly be seen leaping into the night sky. The fire, he told them, had started in Pudding Lane and before long would engulf the entire city. Such was the authority in his rich voice that no one questioned his doom-laden prediction. Indeed many, Sergeant Mullens included, proclaimed their homes and families to be in the area of the city already threatened by the flames. Rokeby and Sir Richard, lowering their swords, ordered their respective factions to settle into an uneasy alliance and the unlikely union of republicans and monarchists had set off.

Now Sir Richard noted with satisfaction that though it moved with one purpose, Mullens had taken care to position his infantrymen on the outside of the group lest any of Rokeby's papists should take it into their heads to abscond into the side-streets.

As for the Doctor himself, Sir Richard eyed the man trotting along at the head of the column with some suspicion. Could he too be an agent of Rome? He certainly hadn't taken issue with Rokeby's assertion that the conflagration was yet another ill omen for His Majesty. Judging by their outlandish mode of dress it was entirely reasonable to assume that both he and the sickly-looking young woman with him were foreign. As a precaution Sir Richard had charged Mullens with the task of watching the Doctor and his companion closely.

Sarah had read many accounts of the Great Fire of London but none of them prepared her for the sight and sound of the disaster experienced at close range.

As she and the Doctor rounded the corner into Pudding Lane, the wall of heat almost knocked her flat. She felt the Doctor take her elbow, steadying her, whilst the huge form of Sergeant Mullens appeared at her other shoulder gazing in awe at the scene of destruction.

'The fire started in the bakery of one Thomas Farryner,' shouted the Doctor above the roar of the flames.

Mullens's piggy little eyes narrowed suspiciously. 'And 'ow would thee be knowin' that?'

'Never mind how I know, Sergeant,' the Doctor raged, 'just get your men organised.'

'What do you propose, Doctor?' enquired Sir Richard before the sergeant took matters into his own hands.

'The Thames isn't too far away,' explained the Doctor. 'Find buckets. Lots of buckets.'

'A human chain,' clarified Sarah. 'Carrying water from the river to the fire.'

At last Sir Richard caught on and soon had Mullens barking orders at both soldiers and republicans alike, bullying and cajoling them into position. The men picked up whatever buckets they could find and soon the fire-fighting action was in full swing. As Sarah searched for more containers to add to the effort, she saw the Doctor helping to heave the contents of a huge barrel into the blaze. The torrent of water had little effect and, far from being brought under control, the inferno was spreading through the tightly packed wooden dwellings, fanned by the fierce easterly breeze and aided by the dryness of a summer bedevilled by drought.

'It's futile, isn't it?' she asked as the Doctor appeared through the smoke wiping sweat from his soot-streaked brow. He didn't answer.

Sir Richard Stoneman-Merritt and William Rokeby staggered up side-by-side, all enmity forgotten in the struggle against a common foe.

'Pudding Lane is all but consumed,' gasped Rokeby. 'They say the fire has spread to the Star Inn on Fish Street Hill and gained hold in Thames Street.' He collapsed to his haunches coughing uncontrollably.

'I fear we fight a losing battle,' commented Sir Richard. 'I have sent for the parish constable and the watchmen but they will, I think, arrive too late.'

'Don't give up,' encouraged the Doctor. 'Time bought here will save lives elsewhere.' So saying, he rushed off along the human chain haranguing them to greater endeavour and acts of heroism.

Sarah heard a scream of pure anguish from somewhere above and behind her. She looked up to see a woman leaning from an upstairs window of a house and noticed that the flames had crept around and caught in the thatched roof. As she looked on helplessly, part of the thatch collapsed into the house taking the flame with it. The woman screamed again and, from the corner of her eye, Sarah saw William Rokeby levering himself upright and plunging into the burning building.

Without thinking, Sarah followed, the heat and smoke triggering another coughing fit and making her head swim. She tried to penetrate the billowing grey wall illuminated by dancing orange light but tears welled up in her eyes. And then she saw indistinct movement as two people staggered towards her from the back of the house.

William Rokeby guided the woman, hugging her baby to her breast, through the incandescent pillars that sprang from the fallen debris of the roof. Sarah glanced up at the sound of an almighty crack and saw a supporting beam crash down trailing flaming splinters behind it. Rokeby reacted in an instant, hurling the woman ahead of him into Sarah's arms. As she dragged woman and child to safety, Sarah registered a snapshot of William Rokeby obscured by blazing wreckage.

Looking around desperately, Sarah spotted the Doctor as he organised men into teams and set them to running battles with the flames. He turned at her cry for help and ran across to join her at the door of the burning house.

'Rokeby's in there,' Sarah yelled. 'He saved that woman and her baby. We've got to get him out.'

The Doctor knew better than to argue with Sarah under such circumstances and so he simply nodded and led the way inside.

They found Rokeby pinned to the floor by the remains of the thatched roof. He had been lucky in that one end of the heavy oak beam had come to rest against the stone fireplace at one side of the room preventing it from crushing him. He was, however, semi-conscious and the flames were creeping closer. Acting quickly, the Doctor and Sarah grabbed hold of Rokeby's legs and tugged him free. As they spilled into the street, the building finally succumbed to the fire and collapsed in on itself.

Sir Richard was there to help them to their feet and away from the smouldering remains. 'Rokeby risked his life to save them,' he told Sarah indicating the woman who was embracing Rokeby and thanking him in fluent French. 'She is Huguenot. French protestant,' he confirmed. 'It seems there are no differences between us save the lines we draw for ourselves.'

Sarah was about to comment on the profundity of this observation when she was bent double by a crippling pain in her stomach. It felt as if she had been kicked by a horse, the initial agony replaced with a searing ache that brought her crashing to the ground. Before she was granted the mercy of oblivion, Sarah was aware of the Doctor and Sir Richard's worried faces looming over her.

'I fear 'tis plague, Doctor,' was the last thing she heard for quite a while.

'Plague?' asked the Doctor. 'Are you sure?'

'I am no physician,' admitted Sir Richard, 'yet the symptoms are unmistakable.' He indicated the red marks on Sarah's neck and arms, dark bruises forming beneath the skin.

'Ring 'o roses,' whispered the Doctor.

'Get away from 'em, sir. If thee know what be good fer thee!'

Sir Richard looked up to see that a ring of soldiers had assembled around them though, he noted grimly, at a respectful distance. Mullens stood just inside the circle, musket at the ready.

'They be infected,' he thundered, waving his gun from Sarah's prone form to Rokeby, and back again. 'And atop that, they be papists.'

'My friend is ill,' pleaded the Doctor. 'I think she's contracted the pneumonic strain of the plague. Unless she receives treatment very soon, she'll die.'

'Then,' pronounced the sergeant, 'by God's will, she will die.'

'Sergeant Mullens,' stormed Sir Richard, 'you shall attend to your duty with the fire!'

'Oh I intend to, Sir Richard.' Mullens smirked viciously. 'See, I think that Doctor there, 'e did start the fire.'

'Don't be ridiculous, man,' protested the Doctor. 'I'd never allow myself to commit such an act of arson.'

'Then how'd thee know it started in Master Farryner's bakery?' The Doctor was at a loss to answer the accusation and Mullens's smile widened expectantly, his tongue flicking out to moisten his cracked lips. 'And since thee started it, it can finish thee. Drive 'em into the fire, lads,' he cried. 'Let the flames purify 'em!'

'No.' The soldiers had only taken one step before being brought up short as William Rokeby strode towards them sword in hand. 'You speak the truth, stout Sergeant, when you say I have the Death. Yet these good people have striven to deliver London from the very Devil and have saved my life into the bargain. Do what you will with me but you shall not harm them.'

He advanced on Mullens who back-pedalled furiously, a look of abject terror on his podgy red face. Rokeby swept his sword around the circle of soldiers all of whom fell back, a channel appearing between their ranks.

'They're frightened of catching the plague,' cried the Doctor. He hefted Sarah into his arms and carried her through the gap, the remaining crowd parting as they passed.

Sir Richard watched as the Doctor, Sarah and Rokeby disappeared beyond the throng and were lost to view in the smoke-filled streets. He turned to Mullens, favouring the sergeant with an icy glare.

''Tis our duty to get Rokeby,' said Mullens defensively. 'His Majesty shouldn't'a let 'im live after the way 'is lot cut off 'is father's 'ead.'

'Really?' said Sir Richard angrily. 'William Rokeby is a man of honour and conviction. He is not someone who has risen to his present station through dubious practice and shifting allegiance. Or do you deny that you once stood with Cromwell's New Model Army, Sergeant?' The last word was spat out with such disgust that Mullens found himself rendered speechless. 'Now,' continued Sir Richard, regaining his composure with great effort, 'it is my duty to report to the parish constable over there. It is your duty to fight the flames. Attend to it, Sergeant Mullens.'

'I'll thank thee not to lecture I about duty,' Mullens muttered darkly at Sir Richard's departing back. 'Griffin, get some of the lads,' he barked. 'We're goin' on a papist hunt.'

Sarah had only the vaguest recollection of the journey back to the TARDIS. Drifting in and out of consciousness, her main impressions were of smoke and flame, feverish nightmares of death and childhood images of Hell and the excruciating pain, the core of her being, tearing strangled screams from her.

Her eyes flickered open as the Doctor let them into the TARDIS. The comforting background hum and the soothing light of the interior seemed to cocoon her in a warm blanket of safety.

'Pull that big red lever,' she heard the Doctor instruct Rokeby, his voice drifting to her from an infinite distance. 'It'll lock the doors in case the mob comes calling.'

She smiled inwardly as she caught sight of the disbelieving expression on the republican's face as he struggled to accept the impossibility of his surroundings. Then, as the Doctor carried her through the interior door and into the corridor beyond, the pain returned with a vengeance. She grasped at a recent memory and the pain turned to stone in her stomach. She had the plague. She was going to die.

Rokeby trailed behind as the Doctor carried Sarah along another passage that could not possibly exist within the confines of such a small crate. Perhaps the Black Death had addled his wits and was preparing to carry him off as it had his wife and daughter. He felt a pang of regret that he would never again see his youngest child, Polly-Anne, herself dying of plague in a home that may have already burned to the ground.

He returned to his senses as the Doctor crashed through another door and followed to find himself in a large white room filled with beds and countless cupboards. Rokeby could only watch as the Doctor dropped Sarah onto one of the beds and began searching desperately through the cupboards. Boxes and bottles were pulled out and discarded unceremoniously when they proved unsatisfactory. Finally, with a triumphant 'Aha!' the Doctor held up a bottle.

'An advanced form of tetracycline antibiotic,' he announced. 'Just one of these will have Sarah up and about in no time.'

He opened the bottle, tipping out a tablet and carefully replacing the lid before throwing it onto an adjacent bed. Administering the pill to Sarah the Doctor perched himself on the edge of her bed waiting expectantly for the drug to take effect.

'Doctor,' ventured Rokeby, eyeing the discarded bottle, 'you appear a man of reason. Do you believe the fire to be an ill omen for the King?'

'No I don't,' said the Doctor as he smiled down at Sarah's opening eyes. 'Charles knew the dangers. Two years ago he tried to get the Lord Mayor to enforce new building regulations to guard against fire. I'm afraid it was an accident waiting to happen.'

'I fear I will not be swayed,' announced Rokeby. The Doctor looked round to see that he had retrieved the tetracycline and was slipping a tablet between his lips. 'Whilst I still draw breath I will oppose this tyrant King.' He swallowed, slipping the bottle into his pocket.

'Rokeby,' the Doctor stood up his face grave, 'I can't allow you to leave with those drugs.'

'I'm sorry, Doctor.' Rokeby drew his sword as he retreated from the room.

'You've already taken one of those tablets,' reasoned the Doctor. 'You're cured of the plague. Leave the rest.'

Tears welled in the republican's eyes. 'I have a daughter. I would spare her suffering also.' Rokeby turned and fled from the sickbay.

'What was all that about?' came a thick voice from the bed.

'Feeling better, Sarah Jane? Good,' said the Doctor, 'because we've got a well-intentioned fool to stop.'

Rokeby left the blue box feeling his strength returning, the aches and pains of the last days receding, his head clearing. He had but one purpose now; to give the Doctor's miracle concoction to his daughter.

The inferno had spread, the blazing skyline laid out before him like some monstrous vision of Hell. Deliverance, he knew, was in his hands and, strengthening his resolve, Rokeby strode on through the smoke until stopped in his tracks by a figure that stepped out of the gloom and into his path.

'William Rokeby,' stated Sir Richard wearily, 'In the name of His Majesty Charles II, I have no choice but to arrest you on a charge of high treason.'

'Stoneman-Merritt,' replied Rokeby bitterly, 'I have no choice but to execute you as a traitor before God.' He raised his sword and charged at the secret serviceman.

'See what your King has done,' screamed Rokeby as his blade met Sir Richard's in the fiery street. 'You close your eyes to the evil he has brought upon us.'

'My eyes have been opened, William,' yelled Sir Richard as he parried blow after blow. 'Evils like the Black Death and the fire care not whom they destroy. Catholic or protestant, republican or monarchist; each is equal before fate. We should stand together against such fate and build a world of tolerance.'

'You speak with honey on your tongue,' accused Rokeby, 'just like your master. And I shall despatch you both to the Hell you deserve.'

He resumed his attack with renewed vigour and Sir Richard, despite his strength and skill, found himself driven back towards the heat of a blazing building.

As she and the Doctor ran past a junction in their search for Rokeby, Sarah heard the clash of steel and glanced down the street to see two men silhouetted against the flames. One was slashing maniacally at the other with his sword, forcing his opponent back towards the raging fireball that had possessed the buildings.

'Doctor!' she yelled. 'Rokeby and Sir Richard!'

The Doctor was soon beside her and together they watched in horror as the upper storey of the building overhanging the street began to fall towards the duelling couple. Sarah buried her head in the Doctor's shoulder as the building collapsed into the street obliterating Sir Richard Stoneman-Merritt.

'Rokeby!' called the Doctor and Sarah looked to see the tall frame of the republican as it rose from the flames. For a moment he stood staring straight at them then, with a smile, he turned and walked into the flames.

'He's gone,' said Sarah sadly.

'We have to find him, Sarah,' stressed the Doctor. 'He's in possession of a drug that won't be discovered for hundreds of years. Its very presence here could change history, allowing your species to discover antibiotics centuries too early. The effect on the Web of Time could be catastrophic.'

'Oh come on, Doctor. We know history didn't change. Poor old Rokeby's probably ended up barbecued by now. He certainly didn't get rid of Charles II, did he?'

'I really must have a chat with you about the intricacies of effect and cause some time.'

'All right, Doctor, but not now, eh?' Sarah pointed down the other street where an angry horde of people was pointing and entreating them to stay put. 'The Mullens mob,' she said.

'And they still think we're responsible for the fire,' pointed out the Doctor. 'Time to leave, I think.'

As they pelted back to the TARDIS, the Doctor looked worriedly over at Sarah. 'I blame myself for this,' he admitted. 'I should have taken more notice of your illness. My negligence could have put the whole of creation at risk. Not to mention my best friend's life.'

And as he slammed the TARDIS doors in Mullens's face and

dematerialised leaving the sergeant haunted for the rest of his life by his experience of papist black magic, the Doctor grinned at his companion.

'I must learn not to be so cavalier in future,' he said, eliciting a groan from Sarah Jane Smith.

Battered and blackened, William Rokeby burst through the door of his home and stumbled inside. He was greeted by the red face of Florrie Dawson, his daughter's ample nursemaid.

'Master Rokeby,' she fretted, 'I didn't know what to do. What with the fire and all. I was so afraid. For you and the child, of course.'

Rokeby, breathing heavily, was only able to articulate one thing: 'Polly-Anne...'

'She's terribly sick, sir,' said Florrie as she followed Rokeby through to the child's bedroom, wringing her hands. ''Tis the Black Death to be sure. Dead by morning, I'd wager.'

Ignoring her, Rokeby lifted his daughter's head from her pillow and slipped one of the Doctor's pills into her mouth. He snatched a cup of water from the bedside table holding it to the child's lips and forcing her to swallow.

As Florrie watched, her face clearing of worry and filling with wonder, the child's eyes opened and she smiled up at her father.

'Papa,' said Polly-Anne simply. 'I feel quite well.'

''Tis a miracle,' babbled Florrie. 'Bessie Welton's brother works at the palace. They've been looking for a cure for ever such a long time. Wait 'til he hears about this...'

Rokeby was quite unaware of her as he held his daughter tightly. He was convinced that God smiled upon him and his cause. The future was assured...

'I just don't understand,' said Charley. 'Some of you have such sad tales, others such nice ones. Yet whatever the outcome, apart from poor Lillian, no one seems sad or angry about having to leave their lives behind. And yet, he's changed everything so for you all.'

'Maybe, my dear, some of us,' called a new voice from the far end of the bar, 'deserve all we get.' He stood. 'Heathcliffe Bower, dear child. Thespian, wit, raconteur and murderer. How d'you do?'

The Assassin's Story

Andrew Collins

One bullet was all it took.

One shot, and she was falling. One bullet slapped into her chest and immediately her blouse was marked by the stain of her blood, which spread black like oil on a powder-blue rag. No longer was she the unassailable lady of iron, but a fragile creature of flesh and blood. Not impervious inflexible metal, but merely weak and feeble flesh. And so much blood. Her true-blue blood was bleeding red as she crumpled to the pavement beside the open car door.

She was human after all. The bullet destroyed her heart: what a revelation to discover she actually had one. Just one bullet had revealed the truth of her humanity. Just one bullet had snuffed out that human life.

Of course, I emptied the rest of the revolver into her. Blasted her carcass with every bullet I had until the hammer fell on the empty chambers with a hollow *click, click, click!* Just to be certain, you understand.

But it only took the one bullet to kill her.

'Doctor!'

'Hmmm?'

'Look at this.' Tegan had stopped in front of a busy newsvendor's stand and was pointing at the board where, beneath the *Evening Standard* banner, two words screamed out their message in the falling dusk. The loaded shopping bag in her hand swayed fatly as she pointed. Joining her, the Doctor read the headline and frowned.

'Ah,' he said. 'Oh dear.' A woman in a pastel leather jacket jostled past him and bought a paper.

Tegan looked at her companion, looked back at the headline. 'Can that be right?' she said. 'I mean, is it true?'

The Doctor didn't answer. He gazed at the words as if trying to divine some secret meaning hidden in them, and then he reached forward and plucked a newspaper from the pile. Worriedly, he examined the front page.

The elderly newsvendor cleared his throat. 'You gotta pay for that,' he said, turning – as though to make the point – to sell another paper to a man in a suit. Tegan and the Doctor ignored him as they read. The Doctor flipped the pages.

Turlough sauntered over to them through the crowd; jacket slung over one shoulder and sleeves rolled to the elbows. 'Is there a problem?' he asked.

191

Looking up, the Doctor fixed him with a serious stare. 'It's 1984,' he said. 'Yes?'

'This didn't happen.' He thrust the newspaper at Turlough, who took it and studied the lead story. Between clamouring customers, the newsvendor scowled at them from under his bushy white eyebrows, and gave a loud eloquent cough.

'Hold on a minute,' Tegan said. 'What do you mean, it didn't happen? It's in the paper. It must be true.'

The Doctor raised his eyebrows, looked dubious for a moment, and then seemed to reach a decision. 'Back to the TARDIS,' he said.

'What –'

'Something's wrong with history. Time's gone awry.' He clutched the protesting Tegan's arm, and guided her through the throng of Oxford Street commuters, past the busy entrance to the tube, and towards the side street where the TARDIS was parked. Turlough closed and folded the newspaper, put it under his arm, and made to follow.

'Oi!' The exclamation stopped the young man in his tracks. He turned to see the newsvendor glaring at him, one hand extended in a universal gesture. With rheumy eyes, the man looked meaningfully at the paper tucked under Turlough's arm.

Turlough sighed and dug in his pocket. 'Thank *you*,' he said as he dropped change into the man's outstretched palm.

In many ways it was, I suppose, very much a crime of its time. In 1980, John Lennon was murdered outside his apartment building in New York City. Someone tried, in 1981, to take the life of Ronald Reagan. Two months later, someone even took a pop at the Pope in St Peters Square. It was therefore scarcely surprising that a person – and why not myself? – should step forward and perpetrate the act for which I gained such notoriety.

Of course, I was already no stranger to celebrity. As a young actor in the fifties, my reputation for strikingly individualistic interpretations of classic roles had rapidly spread throughout the world of repertory theatre. I was honoured to be given a supporting role in John Delaney's groundbreaking kitchen-sink drama *An Angry Taste of Chips* (the critic from *The Times* called my Danny 'stunning') and my stint at the Royal Court saw me showered with plaudits. During the sixties, I swiftly gained a name for myself in the televisual medium, making countless appearances in many well-loved series which, thanks to foreign sales and the frequency of repeats (not to mention these newfangled home video releases) would probably have seen me very comfortably through my twilight years, if only my then agent – a dear man in many respects – had been a better negotiator. In the seventies, the Great British viewing public welcomed me into their homes every week as Bill, the cantankerous publican, in the Nedwell/O'Sullivan sitcom *Are We Nearly There Yet?* And I won widespread acclaim as the secret service man in the celebrated BBC2 play *The Lubricious Popinjay* with Melvyn Hayes. I must say, with all due humility, that among my peers, the name of Heathcliffe Bower was synonymous with style, integrity, and the guarantee of a solid performance. To the great unwashed, I was a modest staple of their viewing pleasure.

No stranger to celebrity, then. But my new fame was of an altogether uglier, unsavoury and – yes – intoxicating nature. From being moderately familiar and somewhat famous, I made the grand leap to infamy.

It was 1984, the miners' strike was at its peak, and I shot Margaret Thatcher. I killed the Prime Minister. Shot her. Bang. Stone dead.

The control room hummed.

The Doctor watched the glowing central column of the control console as it repeatedly rose and fell like a piston. On top of it lay the folded newspaper with its sensational headline, 'Thatcher Assassinated'. The Doctor looked preoccupied, his youthful brow creased. Tegan and Turlough glanced at each other in resignation.

'That's the plan?' Tegan said.

'Not much of a plan,' muttered Turlough.

The Doctor rounded on them in irritation. 'Do you have a better idea?' he snapped. Then he sighed apologetically and shook his head. 'Time is out of joint,' he said. 'If we don't act there might be disastrous consequences for the space/time continuum.'

'I understand the ramifications, Doctor,' said Turlough. 'I'm just not sure that putting yourself directly in harm's way is the best solution.'

Tegan nodded. 'And I'm still not convinced you can steer this crate accurately enough to get us where we need to go.'

The Doctor looked hurt.

With an electronic chime, the central column glided to a halt. 'Come on,' said the Doctor, opening the doors.

They stepped out of the TARDIS, and into the bright afternoon of the past.

On 30 March 1981, Ronald Reagan lay bleeding outside the Hilton Hotel in Washington, DC. The gunman, John Hinckley Jr, had fired six disruptor bullets – designed to explode – hitting three people, one of them the President. The sixth bullet ricocheted off the presidential limousine and entered Reagan's body through the armpit, lodging in his lung, an inch from the heart. It did not explode. Just hours later in hospital, Reagan is reputed to have quipped to his wife: 'Honey, I forgot to duck.'

Margaret also forgot to duck. I, however, was a better shot than Mr Hinckley. He apparently did what he did to impress the movie actress Jodie Foster, whom he was stalking at the time. I, an ex-actor turned Conservative backbencher, did what I did because Thatcher had to die.

Shortly before her death, she contested that the Argentinian threat we faced during the Falklands War was the enemy without, while the currently striking miners were the enemy within. A very tough line to take. And she was terribly wrong, of course. As it turned out, I was the true enemy within. Out of her own ranks, I rose to destroy her. I was the party unfaithful.

Do I regret what I did? Let me put it to you this way: yes. My life was completely destroyed as a result of my actions.

At first, of course, the cathartic rush left me dazed and euphoric for days. To have succeeded in my intention – to have actually slaughtered the evil one – put me at the very pinnacle of fulfilment. It was a pinnacle from which, I'm afraid to say, the only way was down.

What a fall from grace! My successful career in the business of show had assured me a modicum of comfort in my private life which ill prepared me for the trials to come. In custody, I was spat at, threatened, mocked and brutalised. The cell I occupied was cramped and smelled bad. I was used to enduring bad theatrical digs while on tour, but this was discomfort on a whole new level. I suppose in a way that I was lucky; despite the problem of overcrowding, my exalted status ensured that I did not have to share. Apparently my accommodation was maximum security. Apparently I was high risk. The food in 'the slammer' was absolutely abysmal.

My court appearances further depressed me, degenerating into a circus of low farce, complete with demonstrating mobs pushing and chanting, and rocks and bottles sailing through the air. Some people even waved Bill the Barman placards courtesy of one of the gaudier tabloids; it was excruciating. My old catchphrase, 'Shall I pump you another round?' became a morbid punch line.

The press, of course, went berserk. I was no stranger to unfavourable reviews, but nothing could have prepared me for the unending viciousness and sensationalism to which I was subjected. They called me a monster. I was used to being adored, but now I was pilloried, lampooned and despised.

If I had thought at all beyond the moment – that single, glorious moment – then somehow, somewhere in the back of my mind, I might have expected to be honoured as a folk hero. The reality was terrifyingly different. Honestly, you'd think people would be a bit more grateful. Of course, there were many who admired, even envied, what I did; people whose hatred and indignation burned as brightly as my own. Many people, while feigning outrage, secretly applauded my stand. But prevailing morality taught that the taking of a life was not the solution. Not even the taking of hers.

My good name was demolished by the media. I was tried day after day in gossip columns and talk shows. My guilt was not in doubt: the nation saw me do it. The clip was repeated ad nausem. No, the media debate focused on whether I was 'evil' or 'insane'. Conspiracy theorists spun webs of intrigue, and the search was on for my accomplices or paymasters. Some idiot claimed I was Scargill's puppet, another that I was a pawn of the Kremlin: how ridiculous. Some woman came forward and claimed to have had my lovechild (maybe she did, I've led a colourful life).

The hyenas of the press gnawed unflaggingly at the bones of the story. I was news. I sold papers. As was my habit with theatrical reviews, I cut out all my press coverage and pasted it into a scrapbook, which I was allowed to keep.

My marriage of twenty-two years ended on a brightly cold summer day, a Tuesday.

Daphne was waiting for me in a small room furnished with a table, two chairs, and two unsmiling guards. She was standing, and turned as I was shown in, her hands fluttering in that familiar nervous dance. She was wearing her favourite blue dress yet somehow contrived to look small and defeated in it. Her face was drawn and tired, showing the strain of the past couple of weeks. She tried to smile, but it didn't reach her eyes.

'Daphne,' I began, 'my dear –'

'Oh Heathcliffe,' she said. 'My God, you look ghastly.'

I felt an overwhelming pity for this woman, who had supported and loved me all these years. Through lean times, disappointments, the wobbly years of alcoholic excess, she had always been there for me. She was like a rock, the foundation of our successful marriage. We had met as young party activists and never looked back: her father was something of a legend in local politics and before his untimely death he and I used to go shooting and fishing together when I was home from tour. He died in a hunting accident: not my fault.

Unbidden, I felt tears spring to my eyes. 'My dear, I'm so sorry.' The tears fell down my cheeks. 'Forgive me.'

She gave me a look then which was as miserable as it was pitiless. That look haunts my dreams. 'I cannot condone what you have done,' she told me. 'I cannot support you. You'll never see the dogs again.' And that was that. It was the last time I cried.

When word got out, the press lapped it up. I cut out the stories and glued them into my scrapbook.

And through it all, I watched in horror as my aspirations and expectations for the country were dashed, and the world around me failed to grasp the opportunity I had given it. Shock gave way within the party to power games and back-biting. The shaken and newly reshuffled government which emerged stomped mechanically on; unmindful of the little lives they crushed beneath their hobnailed boots. The early days of the Tebbit premiership saw an escalation in violence on the picket lines, with miners and police taunting and intimidating each other. Everything seemed to be locked into an endless downward spiral, apart from inflation, which soared.

With a sense of bitter regret, I saw the empty meaningless days stretching out ahead of me. I had infinite time to reflect upon what I had done.

They walked along a winding country lane. Flat sunlight filtered through thick layers of dirty clouds. A dry stone wall marked the boundary of a field where cagey sheep bleated and chewed.

'I knew it,' said Tegan as she trudged, 'we missed the mark. We could be anywhere.'

The Doctor pulled out his hat from an inside pocket and unrolled it, sniffing the country air.

'Over there.' Turlough pointed into the distance.

Tegan and the Doctor squinted back the way they had come and saw the small line of dots slowly growing as they approached. Two of the cars were police cars, and the one in the middle was gleaming black and important-looking. 'That's it!' the Doctor said, placing the hat on his head. 'We're not too late.'

'Yes,' Tegan pointed out belligerently, 'but we're not actually there yet. And the speed they're going, they'll be there long before us!'

'Ah.' The Doctor gave her a look. It was a look she knew well – not the 'Brave heart, Tegan' look, but the one that said 'Please don't mock, I'm really doing the best I can'. She relented.

Stepping hurriedly onto the grass verge, they watched the cars swish past. They all saw the familiar profile in the back of the middle car – there was no confusing that memorable stare, and the hair was unmistakable. At the last moment, the Doctor stuck out his thumb hopefully, but the cars kept going.

'Plan B?' Turlough asked ruefully.

'Not at all,' said the Doctor, breaking into a jog. 'While there's life, there's hope. Come on.'

They chased after the receding convoy.

I acquired the gun in a seedy pub in Bethnal Green. The deal had been set up by an old acquaintance, Fred. We had met many years before when he was the deputy stage door keeper at the Hackney Empire, and I was giving my Mercutio to nightly acclaim. Fred's links to the criminal underworld ran generations deep. One meets all kinds in the theatre.

My contact was to meet me at eight. I arrived a quarter of an hour early and sat in the corner nursing half a pint and using my beer mat to blot a lurking puddle at my elbow. The false moustache tickled my nose. A scattering of lonely patrons huddled over their drinks. The atmosphere in the pub seemed devoid of hope, and as I glanced around me, I saw Thatcher's Britain in all its glory.

At eight o'clock the door opened and a man walked in; after the briefest of pauses in which he impassively scanned the room, he crossed to my table and sat facing me. He was a squat, oily man with wiry black hair, appalling BO and a sinus problem.

'Pint of cider and some cheese and onion crisps,' he said. I dutifully trotted to the bar, mentally noting that bad breath was about to join the list of the man's manifold charms.

When I returned, an oilcloth package was perched on the table in front of him. I nearly spilled his drink with nervousness as I put it down. My mouth was suddenly dry and when I managed to shift my gaze from the parcel, I saw that he was watching me appraisingly. Hurriedly I sat and gulped down the rest of my drink, getting foam on the moustache, which started to unglue.

This sort of thing was always so much easier when I was performing for the cameras.

'Know how to use this, do ya?' He squinted at me curiously and opened his crisps. I nodded. After a moment, so did he. Then he popped a crisp into his mouth and crunched.

I pulled the envelope of money from the inside pocket of my raincoat and, feeling slightly foolish, passed it to him under the table. He took it and slid the wrapped gun towards me. I hurriedly tucked it away.

'Cheers,' he said, and swigged a mouthful of cider, washing down the crisps. The deal was done. Then he pushed a beer mat towards me. 'I don't suppose I could have your autograph, could I?' He grinned, producing a pen. 'It's not for me, it's for the missus. She's a big fan.'

The local party considered themselves to have scored quite a coup when, with my help, they secured Mrs Thatcher's presence at the summer fete. Little did they realise that I intended to provide the *coup de grace*.

I had come up from London that morning. I hadn't slept. Daphne met me at the station in the Land Rover, the dogs welcoming me with slobbering enthusiasm, and we drove directly to the high school grounds, where stalls and marquees were already assembled. Colourful bunting hung from street lamps and telegraph poles.

Before long, a herd of locals had assembled outside the school grounds, excitedly anticipating the arrival of the guest of honour. A news crew from the local television station loitered around their van, shooting footage of the eager crowd. Organisers and local dignitaries anxiously prepared for their big day.

When the police escort was sighted, a cheer went up, and by the time the official procession of cars drew to a halt, the street was a mass of waving flags and joyful faces.

The driver of the government car leapt out and opened the back door, and Mrs Thatcher emerged.

The sun peeped from behind a cloud, casting shadows on the ground and on the future. The cheering and flag waving intensified. I drew the gun and aimed.

A voice I recognised from the past yelled 'Heathcliffe! No!'

I turned for a brief moment to see a familiar figure in cricket gear and a long beige coat running in my direction. His hat flew off.

Margaret turned in acknowledgement of the crowd, and I squeezed the trigger and ended her life. A sudden eruption of blood blossomed on her chest and she staggered backwards against the glinting car. I heard screams at the same moment my brain registered the gunshot.

The running figure was almost upon me, his hands reaching out to snatch the gun. A policeman tackled him and they crashed to the floor. I returned my attention to the falling Prime Minister and fired again. Her body jerked backwards and hit the pavement, blood staining her clothes and frothing from her mouth. There were more screams. I walked unimpeded towards her crumpled form and fired again. And again. And again, and again.

The television camera from the local news team rolled, recording the event for posterity.

After my rage was spent, I allowed myself to be dragged away without a fuss. I was absolutely docile as I threw down my gun and offered my wrists for cuffing. Millions watched the footage on the evening news. Even as I was roughly dragged to the police van, a dazed little smile could be seen on my lips.

Though I say so myself, I was riveting.

Tegan looked glum. 'Well, that didn't work.'

The Doctor had been arrested. His headlong sprint towards the Prime Minister had been regarded as a threat, and security men and police had swarmed over him like ants on a jam sandwich.

Turlough paced in restless impatience, occasionally pausing to re-read a community information poster on the station's institutional-green painted wall. They had been here for hours, waiting for word of their friend and drinking unpleasant tea from a vending machine.

Suddenly the inner doors burst open and the Doctor breezed out followed by a couple of brisk and contrite policemen. 'Come on,' he said as he brushed past his companions.

'What's going on?' Tegan leapt up from the bench.

The Doctor turned, his training shoes squeaking on the tiled floor. 'Oh, they let me go,' he smiled. Then he turned to glower at the policemen, who paled. 'Eventually. Amazing what a well-placed phone call can do when you've friends in high places.' He pushed open the front doors and called back over his shoulder, 'Thank you gentlemen.'

'What a cunning escape,' said Tegan acidly.

'So now what?' Turlough asked, hurrying after the Doctor.

'Back to the TARDIS.' He bounded down the stone steps of the station three at a time. His friends followed, Tegan's high heels clicking as she struggled to catch up. 'I was a fool. I tried to stop a murder, but history doesn't even remember the attempt. We need to go further back and nip it in the bud. Time for Plan B.'

I must admit, it was quite a surprise to see the Doctor again in such a context.

Prior to that day, I had met him and his friends twice before. The most recent meeting had been on the occasion of election night, 1979. The returning officer for Beamish Northrop had just announced the result, and the losing Labour incumbent, while not the most accomplished of public speakers, had given a very generous – and mercifully short – concession speech. I stepped up to the microphone, taking centre stage.

'Tonight,' I declaimed in my famous measured, dark brown tones, 'dawns the start of the foundation of a new beginning.' I wrote the speech myself; I was very proud of it. My eyes flicked over the rapt audience, and were momentarily arrested by a vaguely familiar threesome watching me keenly from the side of the room. Though I couldn't quite place them immediately, their presence nagged at my memory throughout my oration and my attention kept drifting their way.

Later, at the celebration party, I had the opportunity to speak with them and it all came back to me.

As I remembered, the Doctor was articulate and engaging, though given to cryptic asides and oblique allusions of doom. The Australian girl was attractive, emotional and sharp, and the boy aloof and disparaging. They were exactly as I remembered them, though over twenty years had passed.

The Doctor made one comment which, in retrospect, was astonishingly prescient. At the time, of course, it merely made him appear something of a buffoon. We were discussing ambition, action, and the consequences thereof, when in reference to my past career, he made a comment about the American President having once been an actor.

'I think you'll find, Doctor,' I said, 'that Jimmy Carter was a peanut farmer.'

The Doctor seemed to catch himself, pondered for a moment, and then smiled disarmingly. 'Ah yes, of course. Silly me. The election isn't until next year. Forget I mentioned it.'

I chuckled, to make him think I appreciated his wit, though I felt somehow that I had missed something. Tegan, I noticed, was rolling her eyes.

An actor ascending to the presidency of the United States! The very thought both amused and appalled me, pretty much in equal measure. I had a vague memory of an old actor almost wresting the Republican nomination from Gerald Ford when he was up for re-election. That man had at one time been president of his union, and later the Governor of California. Frankly, though, just the thought of an actor governing California seemed ludicrously far-fetched. Whatever the case, I dismissed the notion as silly and unlikely in the extreme.

Just before they left that night, the Doctor's chatter became even more portentous. He warned me never to allow dissatisfaction to cloud my judgement, and I indulgently nodded and told him I'd bear that in mind. Tegan tugged at his sleeve, looking fretful.

The boy raised an eyebrow. 'Don't go shooting anyone,' he said inexplicably.

'Turlough!' The Doctor whisked him away.

As I turned away to greet more well-wishers, I could hear them bickering behind me. I caught a snatch of their conversation, but it made no sense to me.

'Well, I must say that Plan B appears to be a roaring success.' The boy, Turlough, sounded sarcastic.

'Back to the TARDIS?' Tegan.

'Yes. Come on.' The Doctor. 'Time, I think, for Plan C.'

'Oh good.' Turlough; facetious.

'Rabbits.' Tegan again.

A few short months into my incarceration, the hatred I had felt burning so brightly had ebbed away to be replaced by an empty nothingness of despair. I was almost ready to die when three inmates made an attempt on my life.

I was ambushed in the shower block, a place of clanking pipes and soulless stone and tile.

They pounced on me like wild animals. I didn't even see them coming. A great weight hit me and I slammed into the floor, my head cracking hard against the concrete. Before I could recover, my arms were pinned uselessly behind my back, while blows and curses rained down upon me. Suddenly a wire was cutting into my throat, choking the life from me.

An unearthly howling rent the air, joining the pounding in my head. My vision was clouding and darkness was setting in, so I was sure that the flashing blue light was a further symptom of my failing faculties.

More shouting voices seemed to join the confusion.

There was a *thunk!* And what I can only describe as a couple of *whumps!*

The bruiser behind me went slack. Suddenly I could breathe again, and I whooped in great lungfuls of air, coughing like a demon in the process.

'Are you okay?' The voice was familiar, accented and somehow out of place.

I was bent double, hands on knees, trying to bring my breathing back under control. Black splotches were still blossoming behind my watering eyes. A shapely pair of female legs hove into view. I followed the legs all the way up.

'Good grief!'

'Hello again,' said the girl.

Beside her, the two chaps were bending over my erstwhile attackers, who were all out cold. The younger of the pair was rubbing his fist. The taller man turned to me.

'Doctor,' I gasped, 'what the devil are you doing here?'

'Hello Heathcliffe,' smiled the Doctor. 'Welcome to your jailbreak.'

Tegan gave a twisted little smile. 'Otherwise known as Plan C.'

That was the third time I met the Doctor, and that time I went with him. Of course, he was there when I murdered the Prime Minister too – nearly stopped me in fact – but we hardly had time to chat on that particular occasion. Now he had saved my life.

He hadn't aged a bit; neither had his companions. They led me to a blue box which hadn't been there before, and I stepped into another world.

When I asked why they had saved me, the Doctor muttered something about putting history back on the rails. The girl – the pretty auburn-haired Australian – showed me a newspaper with my mug plastered on the front and above it, the one-word headline 'Evil'. I remembered that one; not a flattering portrait.

The lad in the school tie – he still looked so young! – gave me another newspaper. This was dated six years ahead and depicted Margaret Thatcher crying and getting into a car outside Number 10. 'That's how she ends,' said the Doctor. 'Not your way. Not now…'

'We have a proposal for you,' said Turlough

The first time I ever met these people, who would so drastically alter the course of my life, was following a show.

The theatre snug bar was a favourite retreat after a performance. Its low

201

lighting and comfortable seats were very conducive to happy hours of gossip on the road to oblivion. And I did enjoy a good post-show drink. I remember, the bar was moderately busy, with groups of people clumped around tables and standing, chatting in a low buzz. I was ensconced at my usual table sharing an anecdote with a couple of fellow cast members when I felt a presence hovering at my shoulder.

'Ahem,' said the presence.

My first impression was of a young good-looking blonde chap, probably about my own age, sporting cricket gear and a long beige coat. He was flanked by two more youngsters, a red-haired boy in a school uniform and a very pretty young woman whose dress was colourful and scandalously short. I liked her immediately.

'We just wanted to congratulate you on your performance. I'm the Doctor; this is Tegan, and Turlough.' He extended his hand. I took it, shook it and thanked him graciously. Then I turned back to my friends.

'Um,' said the Doctor.

I turned back.

'Very good work with the gun,' he said. 'Convincingly menacing.'

'Yeah, where did you learn to hold it that steady?' The striking young woman had an endearing accent.

'RADA,' I told her, and gave her a devilish smile. 'What was your name again?'

I was distracted by the sudden realisation that the man had a stick of celery on his lapel. I wondered how on earth the thing had got there and whether the fellow was aware of its presence. Attempting to spare his embarrassment, I plucked it from his jacket and used it to stir my Bloody Mary.

A fleeting look of mortification crossed the man's face, during which time the boy sniggered and the pretty young woman – Tegan – looked pained. Quickly regaining his composure, the Doctor pointed at my drink. 'Would you like another?' he asked.

'Thank you,' I said. 'Now you have my full attention.'

While we chatted, I became aware that there seemed to be a fourth member of the party. A doddering, crazy-eyed man was hanging back and watching me intently. There was something strangely familiar about him which I couldn't quite put my finger on. His salt-and-pepper hair was sparse and dishevelled; his skin unhealthily pasty, highlighting a couple of livid bruises at cheek and jaw. He was somewhat overweight, and his jowls flapped like canvas in the wind. In a way, he slightly resembled my father, but my father gone to seed. I decided to ignore him; he probably wasn't important.

That man, of course, was me – freshly sprung from prison in late 1984. I think my young self may be forgiven for not anticipating that eventuality.

I had persuaded the Doctor to allow me a small self-indulgence before performing my final act. He had granted me the chance to go back and see myself treading the boards. *The Mousetrap* was an early success, but in retrospect, probably my crowning achievement.

My young self was trying hard to keep up with the flow of the conversation which was confusingly full of portents, moralising, and oblique observations about guns. 'It's always a good thing to stay true to the text...' The Doctor was in mid flow when he glanced over my shoulder and stopped abruptly, mouth open. He blinked. 'Good grief,' he said, and suddenly guided me across the room to where a young woman was talking with friends. 'Heathcliffe Bower,' he said, 'allow me to introduce Margaret Roberts, a young politician with a bright future.' He smiled.

'Do I know you?' she asked him, but he had already rejoined his friends.

The woman and I appraised each other with bemusement. Of course, at the time, I had no idea how intricately entwined our fates were one day to become. I wondered fleetingly if the Doctor was trying to set us up on a date. My first impression was of a striking woman with, I noticed, delicate ankles, and a noticeable accent.

Years later, from just across the room, I watched my younger self as he spoke for the first time to the future Mrs Thatcher. Naughty thoughts of Tegan had clearly flown from my mind as I became entranced by this creature from Grantham. She looked so young and hopeful – not at all twisted, ravening and batty. It was a revelation. My younger self was clearly smitten – I'd forgotten what a crush I had on her in those days. It's what drove me in the end to politics.

Beside me, Turlough turned to the Doctor with a quizzical expression. 'Was that really such a good idea?' he asked. 'Unless I'm very much mistaken, you might just have started the whole thing.'

The Doctor looked faintly troubled. 'Hmmm...' was his only comment.

In the end, the final execution of Plan C was astonishingly easy.

We judged it best to call on me at the height of my fixation and feverish preparation. My mania was at its zenith. I remembered those anxious, solitary days now with no pride and an appalled sense of regret. I had, I knew, thus far spent much of today alternately practicing my aim in the mirror, and putting the gun to my own head in an agony of indecision.

My cumulative disappointments – both personal and political – had proved too much for me. I never made it to the cabinet of course, but I never even made junior minister. I watched helpless as riots erupted in the inner cities, and as our glorious leader dragged the country into a war, on the back of which she won another term. In the huge majority, I was a nobody on the backbenches; a bitter pill to swallow for someone so used to the limelight.

All my frustrations had become focused on what I saw as the arrogant manoeuvrings of a once-delightful woman. The Iron Lady had become, in my mind, a real automaton. I could no longer view her as a feeling being; merely as a harsh emotionless principle, an attitude embodied. She was a function, a symbol – one which had to be destroyed. Such was the extent of my obsession that I truly expected, when I shot her, for the bullets to ricochet from her body in small bursts of sparks, or for a smoking hole to open in her chest revealing cogs, wheels and little blinking LEDs clustered among nests of multicoloured wires. Perhaps I had been reading too much Ray Bradbury or Philip K Dick, but my delusional horror was perfectly in proportion, I felt, with the delusional horror that was our Prime Minister. The woman believed herself impregnable, unassailable, and somehow people let her believe it, let themselves believe it too.

I could hardly trust the Opposition to bring her down. You couldn't trust that lot with anything. If you wanted a job doing, I reasoned, you had to do it yourself.

The same thought crossed my mind as I trotted up the steps to the front door and rang the bell. I knew I would be in, as I had rarely left in the days leading up to the assassination, venturing out only to buy the occasional necessary provisions.

The flat was in a charming little square in south London: I used it when I was down on parliamentary business. It also had the benefit of being away from Daphne's prying eyes. The TARDIS was parked, incongruous and blue, in the middle of the square. I rang the bell again.

After a moment I heard the chain rattling and the bolts being drawn back. The door opened.

I always prided myself on being quick to detect the subtleties and nuances of any given script. The man who opened the door, however, had completely lost the plot.

There I stood, looking tattered and vexed in an old cardy and a two day old shirt. My red-rimmed eyes were puffy and shone with suspicion and fear. Tension radiated from me in waves. The remains of spirit gum clung to my upper lip where the false moustache had been attached the day before.

'Hello,' I said to my earlier self. 'I know what you're planning, and we really need to talk.'

I saw my eyes flicker to where the Doctor and friends were pretending to feed pigeons and trying to look unobtrusive. A frown creased my brow. Then I looked back at my future self. 'You'd better come in,' I said.

I led me into the familiar flat and offered myself a cup of tea, which I gratefully accepted. While I waited I looked around the place nostalgically, smiling at the old theatrical posters on the walls and the little Labrador figurines.

When the tea was made I sat down and had a long hard look at myself. Then I gave myself a damn good talking-to.

The TARDIS was in flight.

'Well, that's that,' said Turlough.

'We saved a life,' asserted Tegan. 'And we saved Heathcliffe from himself.'

The Doctor looked pensive. 'Later in the year,' he murmured, 'someone else will make an attempt on Mrs Thatcher's life, and that of her government. Five people will die in the Brighton bomb and many others will be injured, some critically. Mrs Thatcher will survive; the Iron Lady will go on.'

Tegan looked uneasy. 'We did the right thing though, right?'

Turlough grunted.

After a moment, the Doctor replied, a slow poignant smile playing about his lips. 'I think it's safe to say that the universe won't be unravelling today. That's a good thing. We did what we had to do.' He caught his friend's look. 'Yes, Tegan,' he said, 'we did the right thing.'

How true is the truth, and how real reality? That's a potent question for an actor, who deals professionally in false truths, and the presentation of alternative worlds. Decisions can render some truths false and pave the way for new realities. Given the chance, I opted to revise my choice and reinvent the course of my life. That Thatcher lived was ultimately, to me, incidental. The thing is that I'm out there somewhere, leading a better, perhaps more truthful life. As I understand it. As I believe. As I choose to believe.

We talked it through, me and I, and the decision was taken not to do the bloody deed. Instead, I settled on a bit of a break in the Algarve to get my head on straight again.

Apparently he – I – he chose not to attend the fete that day. I avoided fate – ha! He had a minor breakdown from which he recovered well. He retired quietly from politics shortly after I didn't kill the PM, and spends his days gardening with my wife, walking the dogs, and reliving past glories. He still does the occasional appearance on *Wogan*, telling all my best anecdotes… *his* best anecdotes, sorry.

Please forgive my confusion of identity; you see, he's me now and I never existed. The Doctor told me that I was a paradox and would fade away. But there's life in the old dog yet.

There's a phrase; 'Old actors never die'… or is it murderers who never die? I forget.

Memory's going.

I'm not the man I was…

* * *

205

Bower raised his glass in a toast to Charley, knocked his drink back in one and stood, turned and became just one of the crowd again as everyone was milling around.

Charley realised she could sense a change of mood in the air. The two Americans, plus Rokeby and his poor daughter had also moved away from the bar and she was alone. The Steward was busying himself collecting glasses.

The only person who didn't seem caught up in the new mood was the little tramp, who was slumped in an armchair, the same one in fact that Charley had awoken in. But Charley ignored him, opting instead to head back to the big windows, where the majority of the crowds were gathering. The Centaur had given up on his game (although a big bag, presumably of winnings, was slung over his shoulder). The Inquisitor and a small, hamster-like creature carrying a reporter's notepad were chatting away. The young man with the 'Agora' shirt was there, an arm draped cautiously around the shoulder of a small, blonde human girl wearing a similarly styled shirt, although hers declared 'I went to Hyspero and all I got was this lousy shirt'.

Charley made her way over and stared outside. The expanse of blue had given way now to a range of mountains, either side of the airship which was expertly flying between them.

'Nearly there,' said a woman beside her. Charley smiled at her – she was probably in her mid-fifties and reminded Charley of one of her teachers back at school. One of the nicer ones.

'Charley Pollard,' she said, shaking her hand. She noticed the woman had a gold wedding ring on her finger. It felt hard and cold pressed against Charley's hand.

The woman nodded. 'I know. Ives, Ormsin Ives. I gather everyone's been telling you their stories of woe.'

Charley nodded.

'Time for another?' asked Mrs Ives. 'Because I fear I may be what you're looking for. The one who begrudges all this. The one who doesn't feel like shaking the Doctor's hand and thanking him for saving the universe at the cost of my existence.'

Charley didn't know what to say, although she felt she ought to have. After all, Mrs Ives was exactly what she had been expecting all day.

'I did nothing wrong,' Mrs Ives continued. 'It was all his fault. At least the likes of young Jake Morgan or poor, fractured Doctor Harris can understand why it happened to them. But no, not me.'

The Diplomat's Story

Kathryn Sullivan

Ormsin slowly stirred her *tom yum* soup. Des would have complained that it was much blander than his, as it was made from her mother's recipe. 'Ha! They call *this* Thai?' he would have said. 'Needs more green curry.' But Des was gone.

Des is dead.

She was aware of other conversations swirling about her in the makeshift cafeteria. Formerly the Assembly Hall, its acoustics could enhance even the softest murmur. The decibel level of conversations after the aliens' missiles had hit the outer settlements needed no such enhancement. The current topic, however, had shifted from the attacks to speculations on the two newcomers. But Ormsin wasn't interested in gossip at the moment, even if the gossip concerned the two who had stopped the aliens before more missiles destroyed the colony. Nor was she interested in the discussions of the possible terms of the peace treaty. Once she would have been, and she would have used those discussions later in her classes. But now she could hear only the polite words the Marine had spoken an hour (*was it only an hour?*) ago. 'I'm sorry, Ormsin. Des is dead.' *Des is dead.*

They had had so many plans for this stage of their lives. She had retired from teaching only a month ago, Des was set to retire in another three, and they'd move back permanently to their allotment back in the hills and really begin to explore their new home. And perhaps one of their children might leave Earth to join them. Des had been hopeful of that. 'It's getting too restrictive on Earth. This is their home, and it's a good place to raise our grandkids,' he'd said. But Des was dead.

Hunger reminded her to take a spoonful of soup. It was cold. How long had she been sitting here?

She slowly grew conscious that the conversations around her had shifted again.

'So the aliens claim they attacked because we killed their people? There were no signs of a colony there when this system was surveyed.'

'We have every right to explore other planets in this system.'

'... bunch of primitive animals. How were we supposed to know that they were intelligent?'

'And how would humans in a nudist camp demonstrate intelligence if aliens suddenly landed and started killing people? Would you stick around and try to talk to them?'

'Not me. I'd run like hell.'

'They just swatted us out of the sky. We lost several good people.'

'They must have called for help. There were no signs of the technology that could have produced those ships on that planet.'

'A planet with that many resources and they put a back-to-nature colony on it? There must be some way that we can claim prior rights to it.'

'Excuse me, but we're having a *private* conversation.'

Ormsin slowly looked up from her soup. Other snippets had passed unheard as so much noise, but not this. She knew *that* voice.

'And a hard time you're probably having of it, too, with all these people sitting around you.' Down the table, the grey-haired woman seated next to Delegate Wolfe's associate shook her head. 'Never mind, dear, you go right ahead. I'll find someone else to pass me the sugar. Or whatever sweetener that is.'

Wolfe flushed, then straightened with the meaningful look Ormsin had often seen directed at members of the opposition. In her last class one of her students had started a betting pool as to how many times in a session 'The Look' would be used. 'Do you know who I am?' Delegate Wolfe asked, raising his voice.

Heads turned along the table in the sudden stillness.

Well, he *would* be familiar with the room's acoustics, Ormsin thought wearily. A bowl of sweeteners was within reach. She pushed it down towards the woman.

'Thank you.' The woman sipped her sweetened drink, blinked and looked down into her cup. 'That's not coffee,' she remarked.

'She's one of the newcomers,' someone near Ormsin whispered in a shocked voice.

That explained the reaction to the *fee* root beverage, Ormsin realised. It had taken Ormsin a few years to adjust to the colony's substitute for coffee. The bitter drink smelled much better than it tasted. Des thought *fee* was better than Marine-issue coffee, but not by much. *Des is dead.* Her eyes filled with tears, and Ormsin looked down at her soup.

'Are you all right?'

Startled, Ormsin looked up. The woman was standing next to her, looking at Ormsin with concern. Past her, Ormsin could see Wolfe and his associate watching them, Wolfe obviously angry at being ignored.

'Are you all right?' the woman repeated.

'No, my husband…' Ormsin took a deep breath and brushed at her eyes. 'Thank you; I'll be all right. I'm Ormsin Ives. You're new here?'

'Evelyn Smythe. Yes, I'm still finding my way about. This is rather elaborate for a dining hall.'

Ormsin smiled. 'This was our Assembly Hall before the bombardment.' She looked about at the carved panels and statues, remembering the colony's excitement and pride in its construction. 'We decided to be functional with most of the buildings, but here we decided to celebrate our new government. Grandiose, but as Emerson said, "When I have seen fine statues, and afterwards enter a public assembly, I understand well what he meant who said, 'When I have been reading Homer, all men look like giants'".'

'Dr Smythe, there you are.' A tall, dark woman appeared behind Evelyn, and Ormsin, with a faint shock, recognised the Vice President. 'The Doctor says he's ready for the next round of talks.' She turned to Ormsin. 'Mrs Ives, I'm so sorry for your loss.'

Ormsin looked down, struggling to maintain her composure. Audreau Skemp had long ago been one of her students. Although it was pleasant to know Audreau remembered her teacher, the unexpected sympathy overwhelmed her. 'Thank you.'

Evelyn Smythe glanced at the suddenly worried Vice President Skemp, then back at the obviously grief-stricken woman. Where were her friends? They couldn't leave her here like this. Yet, at the same time, they couldn't stay; the Doctor needed to hear what Evelyn had learned so far.

Deciding quickly – the Doctor probably wouldn't notice an additional person – Evelyn asked, 'Mrs Ives, would you care to join us?'

She glanced quickly at the Vice President for support and was pleased to see the younger woman agree. 'Yes, do come, Mrs Ives. We could use your insight.' Skemp met Evelyn's eyes and nodded firmly.

Insight, Evelyn thought. There's a history there. Wonder what the Doctor will make of this?

The Doctor seemed relieved when Evelyn and her party arrived in the chamber. 'Evelyn, there you are. The Defence Leader was asking about you.'

'Really?' Evelyn turned toward the communications screen. The large brown eyes of the antelope-like being – if said antelope was allowed two arms as well as four legs and antlers – pictured within studied her. Light glinted off a wide collar of metallic interlinking plates. The wide ears flicked forward and the head bobbed, showing the four sharpened points on the antlers.

'Of course,' the Defence Leader said calmly. 'Negotiations cannot begin without the presence of a matriarch.'

Oh dear, Evelyn thought. She noticed the sudden interest of those about her as the being spoke. So the Doctor did get a translator working. Pity there wasn't one earlier. During their previous session she had spent most of the time translating for the President and the military.

'Of course,' the Doctor agreed. 'Defence Leader, may I introduce Vice President Skemp and…' He glanced at Mrs Ives and raised an eyebrow.

Both women were staring at the screen. The shorter woman started at the Doctor's introduction. 'Ormsin Ives,' she said, putting her hands together and nodding over them to the being on the screen.

Evelyn was relieved that the woman was not immediately berating the aliens for her loss. In fact, her face seemed suddenly alive with interest.

'A great teacher,' Skemp whispered proudly behind Evelyn. 'It's thanks to her that I got into politics.'

Not a bad idea to bring her along after all, Evelyn decided. She recognised the intent look in those dark slanted eyes now: that of any teacher facing a new challenge. And if she understands politics well enough to interest others, so much the better that she's here.

The Defence Leader bobbed her head and gestured another being into view. 'I introduce our matriarch, Mehit.' The second alien nodded, and Evelyn noticed that, although her fur was streaked with patches of silver, the six antler prongs were still sharp. Jewels sparkled in the harness about her shoulders, which appeared to hold several knives as well. 'She will speak for our colony on Teuba as well the Hufko people.'

The Doctor looked around. 'Right, then. Now that we have the introductions done...'

Evelyn glanced aside at President Henry, but he was conferring with one of his assistants. Skemp motioned her to a seat right beside Ormsin. 'That's...' Evelyn whispered to Ormsin, starting to point towards the President.

Ormsin smiled. 'Ted Henry. I know; I taught him, too.' She turned an indulgent look on him. 'Always a charmer, that one.' She tucked some of her black hair behind an ear and looked back at the screen.

'Defence Leader, would you care to repeat the conditions you told Evelyn and myself earlier?' the Doctor asked.

The Defence Leader lifted her head, her nostrils flaring. 'First, that the humans return the heads of our colonists that they stole.'

Evelyn mentally winced, remembering how the Defence Leader had first described the murders of their colonists. Judging from the conversations she had overhead among the human colonists, those involved had thought the aliens to be game animals and had taken trophies.

Appearances can definitely be deceiving.

'Second, we have three missing colonists. We demand their return or the return of their bodies. Third, that humans will turn over those responsible for punishment.'

'We will deal with that,' President Henry said. 'Let me say again, Defence Leader, how sorry we are about this tragic misunderstanding.'

'Misunderstanding?' the Doctor repeated.

Henry frowned at him. 'But we will conduct our own investigation first, to prove to you, Defence Leader, as well as ourselves that the persons involved did not deliberately set out to murder intelligent beings.'

'Predators,' Mehit snorted. 'There's no dealing with them. They kill for sport as well as for food. Best kill them now, before they harm us further.' She lowered her head, showing the sharp points of her antlers, then turned away.

'Hold on a moment,' Evelyn replied. 'You can't punish the entire colony for the actions of a few. You said you'd listen.' She appealed to the younger alien. 'Defence Leader, you promised the Doctor that you would hear what the President had to say. I'm sure he wasn't finished.' She turned expectantly towards the President.

President Henry nodded quickly. 'The corporation involved will also be heavily fined and will make some form of restitution to the families of your colonists.' His assistant keyed the addition into her pad.

'And?' Evelyn prodded.

The President spread his hands and spoke to the screen. 'Beyond that, I can't make any promises. We have laws we must follow. All we ask is that you give us time for our investigation. Those involved won't escape – you already destroyed most of our ships.'

Mehit leaned forward and conferred briefly with the Defence Leader. The Defence Leader looked back at the screen. 'What form of… restitution?' she asked. 'Do you think lives can be replaced?'

'Lives were lost here, too, because of your attacks,' Ormsin broke in. 'My husband…' she faltered, then took a deep breath and continued: 'My husband was killed today, protecting this colony. Will you turn those responsible for his death over to me for punishment? Should I demand restitution from you?'

The two aliens studied her. 'You are matriarch as well?' the Defence Leader asked. 'Do you speak for your colony?'

Ormsin glanced at the president, who nodded. 'Yes,' she said.

The Defence Leader turned toward Mehit.

The Doctor whispered to Evelyn, 'I think you've been upstaged.'

Then Mehit blew out a breath. 'I respect your death.' She turned to the Defence Leader. 'You may continue.'

The negotiations went on for while longer, and in the end Evelyn thought both sides benefited. The Hufko military would continue to maintain a presence in the system, looking after its otherwise defenceless colony. The humans would still be allowed ships, and there would be no interference with its trade with Earth and other planets. And both colonies would open diplomatic relations. Evelyn thought the Doctor was most persuasive on that, pointing out that it would prevent future misunderstandings between Hufko and humans.

Finally the screen was disengaged.

'Well, it's a start,' President Henry sighed, as he leaned back from the table. 'We're not out of trouble yet, but at least we're not under fire. And we have you two to thank for that.' He nodded towards the Doctor and Evelyn.

'Only too glad to help,' the Doctor replied airily.

'We'll let the diplomats work out the smaller details. I don't envy them that.' Henry sighed, staring at the screen.

'Do you have someone in mind?' Skemp asked.

The president gestured at his assistant. 'Delegate Wolfe, for one. He is the more experienced of the delegates, and he's been sending a constant stream of "requests" to remind me of that ever since the meeting started.'

'Fifteen so far,' his assistant confirmed, glancing at her pad.

Henry sighed. 'Although how he ever found out we were in negotiations…'

'That was probably my fault,' Skemp acknowledged. 'He was at Mrs Ives's table when I found Dr Smythe.'

'Was he?' Evelyn asked. 'Not the white-haired gentleman with a certain manner of looking down his nose?'

Ormsin nodded. 'The one who thought you should know him. Don't take it personally; he directs "The Look" at many delegates.'

'I don't know,' Skemp said worriedly. 'Will the Hufko accept him? Mrs Ives?'

Ormsin looked up from gathering her notes. 'Oh, they'll probably accept a male for a representative. They had no problem with the Doctor or you, Mr President, after all. Still, it was apparent that they paid more attention to the Vice President, and Evelyn. They don't seem to be purely a matriarchal society and although I gathered from some things they said that only a female can be a defence leader to speak for them, that could just be their military.' Ormsin smiled. 'What an interesting society. Studying the structure of that would be…' She searched for a word.

'Challenging?' Evelyn suggested.

'The chance of a lifetime,' Ormsin agreed. She looked down at her notes again. 'And then, of course, dealing with their military should be different from their colony leaders. It all depends on how "back to nature" their leaders are. If they're nomadic rather than territorial, for example…'

Evelyn had a sudden mental picture of the haughty Delegate Wolfe trotting across the plains in pursuit of the Hufko colony leaders and had to stifle a smile. And then mentally frowned. If the Hufko ask for a translation of his name, there'd be that 'predator' bias again. That reminded her of the person seated next to Wolfe in the cafeteria, the one who had seemed a bit more knowledgeable about the deaths at the Hufko colony. Who, if she remembered correctly, had seemed very intent on rights to the planet.

212

'Well, we've got them talking,' the Doctor said softly, coming alongside her. 'Time to –' he waggled two fingers in an imitation of walking legs – 'slip away, don't you think?'

'You're leaving?' Skemp asked, overhearing. 'Now? But…'

'Our ship is undamaged,' the Doctor said, 'and we seem to have helped stop a potentially devastating war. But now I think you need to make your own decisions.'

'But before you do,' Evelyn said, 'could I make one suggestion about your choice of diplomat?'

Skemp and Henry looked at each other. 'Please do,' President Henry said.

Evelyn gestured to Ormsin. 'Her.'

Ormsin looked up to see them considering her. 'Me? Oh, no, I couldn't. I – I wouldn't know where to begin.'

'You saw how the Hufko listened to her,' Evelyn continued. 'And it was a well-known practice on Earth for teachers to become diplomats. They're better trained to see several points of view.'

'You'd be wonderful,' Skemp assured Ormsin.

'That she would be,' Henry said thoughtfully. 'No ties to any lobbies or special interest groups… And I know I can trust you to work with the Hufko, not try to control them. Please, Mrs Ives. You wouldn't let your students down, would you?'

Ted Henry always was a charmer, Ormsin reminded herself. She looked around the small office, then back at the view through the large window. The vast plain stretched from the border of the small spaceport for Teuba to the foothills of the mountains. Long grasses rippled in the wind. And she considered that if *she* had four legs she was sure she'd be tempted to just go out there and run. She sighed at a twinge in her right knee and reached below the desktop to rub it. Of course these days, she'd settle for two healthy legs. 'Don't let yourself grow old, Tabitha,' she told her assistant.

'I'll be fighting it all the way, ma'am,' Tabitha replied, not looking up from her pad. 'How do you want me to respond to this interview request?'

Ormsin turned her chair away from the view. 'Who's it from? Not Daginate Mining again?' She still felt suspicious of the company's management, even though the investigation had decided that only one of the surveyors who had killed the Hufko colonists had realised the colonists were intelligent beings.

'Oh, they've got a request in, too, but I'll just give them the usual "The Hufko are not interested" reply. No, this one is from someone who wants to develop a ski resort in the mountains.' Tabitha tapped a few keys on her pad. 'Obsidian Reaches. They're already got a successful resort back home. On Mount Ahadi.'

'And now they want to have one here on Teuba?' Ormsin paused. She heard hoofbeats pounding toward their door.

The door flew open and in skidded Rheoli, her Hufko legal assistant. 'Mrs Ives! Ma'am!' He caught himself on the edge of Tabitha's desk and looked wide-eyed at them. 'The colony leaders are coming in!'

'So soon?' Ormsin looked at the calendar and the map of herd territories beside it. 'They're not due in for another week.'

'I know! And they look angry!'

'Tabitha? Have there been any problems recently?' Ormsin tried to remember the last reports from the Hufko military and human patrol ships. Even after the treaty of good will had been signed, both agencies had been on the lookout for unscheduled landings on either planet.

The younger human shook her head. 'Nothing that I've heard.'

Ormsin turned back to Rheoli, who looked as if he was trying to find some place to hide in the small office. 'Rheoli, male or female leaders?'

Rheoli gulped and closed his eyes. 'I – I think, I think just the male leaders.'

'Not an emergency, then,' Ormsin said with relief. She started for the door. 'Come along, then. Let's see what the problem is.'

She led her small parade out to the plaza between her office and the port. The Hufko colony leaders were gathering on the side close to the port, some obviously waiting for several of their members to stop gawking at the ships.

She decided to wait as well, to see which way they were planning to go, towards her office or towards the base headquarters. Rheoli still seemed very uneasy, so she approached the young colonist.

'You seem to know a bit more about this than you're saying.'

Rheoli started. 'No! That is… I heard some things, but nothing definite.'

'But enough to make you jumpy.' As usual, whenever she was surrounded by her staff, she felt very tiny. Tabitha was tall for a human, but Rheoli was taller still. And, even with the shorter single-pronged antlers of a young adult, he was average-sized for a Hufko. Ormsin thought she probably looked like a mouse comforting an elephant, but she did her best to project what she was starting to call her 'matriarchness'.

'Out with it. Let me be the judge.'

Rheoli expelled a noisy breath. 'What I heard was that a detachment of troops decided to spend some recreation time on the plains. I didn't hear whose territory. They had some races, grazed, taunted some of the locals, then left.'

'That's it?' Tabitha asked. 'And the leaders are upset about that?'

Not all, Ormsin thought. Otherwise the female leaders would be here as well.

'Well…' Rheoli shuffled his hooves. 'They did look rather impressive.'

214

Tabitha smothered a laugh.

He turned toward Ormsin. 'The leaders are still unhappy about me dealing with technology.' The young colonist sighed. 'They think I'm being corrupted. And if they feel the troops don't respect their ways...'

'They can't think they'd be better off without them?' Ormsin asked.

'We've signed a treaty,' Tabitha bristled.

'Yes, but we don't have enough ships yet to protect both planets against pirates and smugglers.'

'Oh,' Tabitha relaxed. 'I thought you meant...'

'And I wouldn't put it past anyone... well, anyone greedy enough to think the Hufko colonists wouldn't notice mines in unexplored parts of this planet, to try something.' Ormsin paused, thinking. She noticed that the leaders were finally regrouping. 'You two wait here. I'll be right back.'

'But – don't you need us?' Tabitha asked.

Ormsin had already started on her way toward the colony leaders. 'Greetings!' she called. 'You've returned at the right time.'

'Honoured Diplomat,' Neekhm replied, in what Ormsin was beginning to suspect was a faintly mocking tone. His twelve-pronged antlers creaked faintly as he nodded. Some behind him flicked their ears in a friendly manner while late-comers opted for more formal bows or even the *wai*. She *wai*ed back, her hands at colleague-to-colleague level. 'We cannot stay,' Neekhm continued, 'we have urgent business elsewhere.'

'And if you have time later, could you stop by my office? I have some trade items I wish you to consider.' She spread her arms in the encompassing gesture. 'All of you.'

One leader brightened. 'More *fee*? I will be there.'

'And other items. It will not take much of your time.'

The colonists glanced among themselves. Several nodded. 'We will consider it,' Neekhm replied.

'Thank you.'

The leaders and Ormsin *wai*ed to each other. The group slowly started toward the base headquarters.

Ormsin returned to her staff. 'Back to the office. They'll be stopping by later. Rheoli, I need you to find maps of the entire planet. Tabitha, I'm going to need you to do a little research. And I need to do some cooking.'

Des would be laughing at me about now, Ormsin thought as she arranged the platters and pots about the low table in the plaza before her office. Worrying about cooking for people who prefer vegetables raw. But there was no help for that. She wanted the others who would be joining them later to try the full range of flavours. So that meant hot foods as well as cold. She adjusted another pot of what would normally be considered decorations on a human table but here probably would be an appetiser.

'Can't I have just one?' Rheoli pleaded as he followed Tabitha and her tray.

'Didn't you eat enough of them when you were taste-testing for us?' Tabitha scolded.

'But they're so good!'

'You can finish up the leftovers later,' Ormsin said, standing back and studying the patterns of colour in the arrangement. She moved one last pot.

'I doubt there'll be any left over,' Rheoli said mournfully. His ears lifted and he turned toward the base. His frown deepened. 'Oh no, here they come.'

'Rheoli, you can serve the *fee*,' Ormsin directed.

The young colonist moved to obey, but Ormsin heard his muttered, 'I hate that stuff.'

'That's why you get to serve it,' Tabitha whispered back smugly.

Ormsin had grown accustomed enough to Hufko body language and facial expression to be able to tell that the colony leaders were still angry. The meeting at the base had apparently not gone well. Which could mean they may be more amenable to *her* proposal, now. She stepped forward to greet them, Rheoli and his tray beside her.

'Welcome, Leader Neekhm. Would you care for some *fee*?'

Neekhm refused a cup. 'Too bitter for my taste, thank you.' He saw the table beyond her, and his head and ears went up. 'What do you have for us, Honoured Diplomat?'

'Just a small selection of foods my colony is interested in offering in trade.' She gestured the leaders toward the table. 'We had to wait for confirmation that all these were safe for Hufko consumption. The final reports came in just the other day.'

Tabitha appeared with her tray at that point. 'Rose, sir? We have with thorns and thornless.'

'Oh, thorns for me, please.' Neekhm took a rose stem and chewed thoughtfully on its blossom, whilst he followed Ormsin to the table. She pointed out the platters. 'Over here are the grains. And here is a selection of grasses.'

Neekhm finished the rose and picked up a pot. 'And this?'

'That's called an *impatiens*.'

He chewed slowly on the flowers. 'This is very good. Your people are willing to trade for these?' He wandered slowly down the table, nibbling as he went.

Other leaders were less restrained. 'That looks tasty', said one. 'What is it?'

'That's an azalea,' Tabitha replied.

Ormsin stepped back and watched the leaders sample the various grains and flowers. Her staff helpfully supplied names and details of each plant.

'That's a pansy.'

'Over there, that's maize. We have fields of that at home.'

Ormsin smiled at the pride in Tabitha's voice. She had been right to refuse the President's offer of a larger staff. The Hufko had been more accepting of a small group. Establishing trust between the two colonies was far too important at this point to risk on games of political favouritism. Delegate Wolfe's pointed snubs seemed rather childish in view of that.

She looked towards the base and saw her second group of invitees approaching. It was time to see how much trust the colony leaders were willing to extend her.

Antlered heads lifted and turned to face the newcomers. Moving in unison, the leaders trotted forward to stand before the table. Almost as if they're blocking the view, Ormsin thought, wondering whether to be amused or honoured.

Either way, she couldn't let this stand-off continue. She hurried to welcome her other guests. 'Defence Leader, welcome. Do come and see what foods we have for trade.'

The Defence Leader was extremely wary, although the two armoured soldiers with her seemed cheered at the mention of food. 'We have prepared meals on our ships.'

'Yes, I understand. Space is at a premium on ships. The same is true for our ships.' Ormsin steered the tall Hufko to the far end of the table where the hot foods waited. 'That's why we have items like these oat and honey cakes, oatmeal and dried fruits and these bran bars. Here, try one.'

Ormsin could see the colony leaders resuming their sampling, with occasional glances toward her and her guests. While the three military Hufko chewed, she signalled Rheoli to bring more *fee*. 'And over here we have cooked samples of grain – oat mash, corn, rice. These small bowls have spices you can add for extra flavour.'

As she had expected, the spacers preferred to spice their foods. Des had always said that space travel tended to dull the taste buds.

A female trooper sampled Ormsin's special dish. She choked, sputtered, and grabbed the nearest flask of water. After a quick gulp, she gasped, 'That's wonderful! What is it?' Without waiting for an answer, she slung her rifle further back in its harness to free both hands. Holding the flask in one hand she took another spoonful with the other. The second soldier dug in as well, while the nearest colonist eyed them both with alarm.

'My family calls it *Kaeng Phak*,' Ormsin said, almost hearing Des's laughter. 'Vegetable curry.'

Both groups soon dropped their wariness to concentrate on the food.

217

Ormsin was pleased to notice colonists directing the troopers to the hotter dishes, although she wasn't sure if the reason was friendliness or just a desire to watch the troopers' reactions. Before too long, the flower pots contained only dirt and roots, and all the platters were empty.

'Thank you, Honoured Diplomat,' Neekhm said. 'We will definitely be interested in trade agreements. May I meet with you within a day or two?'

Ormsin spread her hands. 'My door will be open.'

'I, too, see the benefits of trade with your people,' the Defence Leader said. 'I will meet with you as well.'

'Thank you. I have one other proposal to offer both of you.' Ormsin nodded to the waiting Tabitha and Rheoli, and they quickly set up their prepared maps and charts.

Ormsin turned to Neekhm. 'I understand there was a problem recently with trespass into colony territories.'

Ears flattened among the colony leaders. 'More than once,' Neekhm agreed.

'My people need room to stretch our gait, just as yours do,' the Defence Leader said stiffly.

Ormsin nodded. 'My people have encountered the same problems. We have special areas, called resorts, where we can relax and exercise. In our colony we have a resort in our mountains, where we –' she tried, then gave up on a translation for 'ski' – 'can play in the snow. This company would like to make such a play area here in your mountains. And in return they would make a resort for Hufko.'

'Not in our plains,' a colony leader said.

'No,' Ormsin agreed. She turned to Rheoli, waiting beside his maps. 'There is an island outside the established herd area, with plains and beaches. There.' Rheoli pointed as she continued. 'This could be prepared as a resort for *all* Hufko.' The owner of Obsidian Reaches had seemed dubious about the plan when Ormsin had first talked to him, but had grown more excited about the possibilities the longer they talked. By the end of the call, his research team was going to look into the challenge of designing a snowboard for Hufko. 'It is far enough away from the territories that transport to it will be needed. But that way none of the territories will be encroached upon. And your protectors can sample the simple life without having to join your herds. They would appreciate what you enjoy and be more willing to protect it.'

'They could run and not disturb us,' Neekhm mused. He glanced at the other leaders. There were several answering nods. 'I like this idea. And you, Defence Leader?'

'It… has possibilities.'

'Good.' Neekhm nodded briskly. 'We will discuss this further among ourselves before deciding. My thanks for these proposals. We will talk with you later on this as well, then, Honoured Diplomat.' The mocking tone was noticeably absent.

The colony leaders began to trot away, some checking the table for leftovers before they departed.

Ormsin turned to the Defence Leader and her group. 'So that you can see what they can provide, Obsidian Reaches has offered to conduct a tour for you and other interested parties at a human resort, Mount Ahadi.'

'Where your people play. In the snow.' The Defence Leader seemed puzzled by the idea.

'I've seen vids,' Rheoli said excitedly. 'They balance on thin planks of wood and slide on snow.'

The Defence Leader still seemed puzzled, but something about the expressions of the other two told Ormsin that a Hufko snowboard might be very popular. And, glancing at Rheoli, Ormsin had a feeling she knew who would be the first volunteer to test one.

'There're also water activities,' Tabitha added. 'And spas.'

'Hot tubs. Just the thing for sore muscles,' Ormsin agreed.

The Defence Leader looked thoughtful. 'This all sounds… intriguing. We will be interested to see what this Obsidian Reaches could do.'

The military Hufko glanced at the table littered with empty platters, bowls, flasks and pots, and then away at the now distant colonists. 'I never thought I would see the colony leaders agree on anything. And now they have, not just once, but twice.' She shook her head, then flicked her ears. 'The Doctor was right. I am very glad we did not destroy you humans.'

'So am I, Defence Leader,' Ormsin agreed. 'So am I.'

The Defence Leader glanced at her troopers and Rheoli, still examining the tables for any overlooked remains, then studied Ormsin. 'I don't think you understand. Without you, my people would have destroyed your colony. And followed your people back to the human homeworld.'

Ormsin remembered what Mehit had said at the meeting with the Doctor and Evelyn. 'Best kill them now, before they harm us further.'

The Defence Leader looked again at the departing Hufko colonists. 'You think those colonists still need my forces here to protect them from your people.'

Ormsin had to reply honestly. 'Yes, I do.'

The Defence Leader nodded. 'Then we will go to your colony and look at this Mount Ahadi.'

A week later she was still looking thoughtful, which Ormsin took as a good sign. At least the Defence Leader hadn't totally rejected the possibilities. 'But those "swimming pools" are so deep,' the Hufko leader was complaining.

219

'Because our people like to dive, unlike yours, distinguished Leader,' the designer said. 'Since your people do prefer immersion, the relaxation pools for your resort will have the same depth as the hot tubs. You do like the depth for the hot tubs, correct?'

The Defence Leader looked at her staff, who all nodded, Ormsin was pleased to see. They did seem to have enjoyed the hot tubs.

'Good.' The owner of Obsidian Reaches displayed another design. 'Now, we thought to separate the race area from the spas with gardens.'

Ormsin's pad beeped softly, and she excused herself from the meeting to take the call. The Hufko soldiers closed the doors behind her as Ormsin entered the hall. 'What is it, Tabitha?'

'I thought you'd want to know that Delegate Wolfe is demanding a meeting with the Hufko.'

'Is he now?'

'I told him the Hufko's schedule was full, but he wasn't having any of it. I think he might be on the way there.'

'Sir, you can't go in there!' a voice said down the hall.

Ormsin turned and saw the white-haired delegate enter the hallway, followed by another man who seemed vaguely familiar. 'He's here. Please alert Security we might have a problem.' She nodded to the Hufko soldiers on guard at the meeting room door and went to meet Delegate Wolfe.

'Delegate Wolfe,' she greeted him.

'Mrs Ives,' the delegate nodded, looking past her to the guarded door. 'I've made exceptions for your inexperience in this position, but enough is enough.'

'You've been refusing my applications,' the second man said. 'I demand to talk to the Hufko directly.'

'And you are?' Ormsin asked.

'Surely you recognise Sander Daginate, owner of Daginate Mining,' Wolfe said.

'No, we've never been introduced,' Ormsin replied, although she was certain she had seen the balding man somewhere before. 'Mr Daginate, the people you wish to talk to are not here.'

'I see several Hufko right there,' Daginate said.

'The Hufko military are here about a project. The colony leaders are back on Teuba, and they are the only ones who can decide what is done on *their* planet.'

The meeting-room door opened, and the Defence Leader stepped through. She looked down the hallway. 'Honoured Diplomat,' she called, 'we are invited to lunch at this time.'

'If you will excuse me, gentlemen,' Ormsin said.

'Not this time,' Wolfe persisted, pushing past her. 'We'll just see about this.' Daginate scowled at her and followed.

Ormsin lifted her pad, and spoke to her assistant. 'Tabitha?'

'Security is almost there.'

'Excuse me,' Delegate Wolfe called as he neared the Defence Leader. 'I would like a word with you.'

'Yes?' the Defence Leader asked politely.

As the two men came closer, however, Hufko heads snapped back, nostrils flaring. The Defence Leader backed away, one hand lifting to cover her nose.

The two soldiers stepped before her, their antlers lowered to block the men. 'You stink of death,' one guard said.

'What?' Delegate Wolfe said.

Ormsin mentally sighed as she approached the group. Didn't the man think? Ormsin had asked that any of the resort staff who planned to meet with the Hufko have the courtesy to refrain from eating meat at least a day in advance of the meeting. She and Tabitha kept to a vegetarian diet while on Teuba.

'My apologies, Defence Leader,' she said. 'Delegate Wolfe wished to ask if you could speak with the colony leaders on...'

'On mining rights,' Daginate interrupted. 'My company can handle mines for your colony, and in return –'

'I do not speak for what the colonists wish for their planet,' the Defence Leader said behind her sheltering hand. She looked past her guards at Delegate Wolfe. 'Wolf? You are named for a predator?'

'My name means "courage",' Wolfe said, clearly irritated. He glared at Ormsin. 'Is this some kind of joke?'

'My company will pay very well for those rights,' Daginate persisted.

'Please go,' the Defence Leader said, 'both of you.'

Wolfe's brows lowered, preparatory to "The Look".

The guards advanced, antler points at the ready. 'You will not look at the Defence Leader in that manner,' one said.

'What?' Delegate Wolfe said.

'That's a predatory stare,' Ormsin explained. Delegate Wolfe turned his glare on her, but Ormsin wasn't afraid of his theatrics. 'The Defence Leader has asked you to leave. Your audience is over.' She was pleased to see human security guards coming down the hallway towards them. 'Please escort Delegate Wolfe and his... guest from the resort grounds.' She would have to talk to President Henry about these two. Assuming this confrontation hadn't damaged her relationship with the Hufko.

The Hufko guards permitted her to pass, and she joined the Defence Leader at the door just as it opened. The owner of the resort stood in the doorway. 'Lunch?' he asked brightly.

The Defence Leader was quiet as they followed their guide to the prepared luncheon and Ormsin wondered how she was going to salvage the situation. 'Have you heard any further word from the colony leaders?' Ormsin tried. Rheoli would have relayed anything he heard as well, but the question was a safe start.

The Defence Leader blew out a breath as she surveyed the hot dish choices. 'They are still undecided whether to grant us land for this,' she said, picking up a bowl and adding her choices.

'Well, if you think the project has merit, I can talk to President Henry and see if we could build the resort for your troops on this world. I can't make any promises, though,' she added quickly.

The Defence Leader looked at her. 'You would do that for us?'

'Of course. This resort would benefit both our worlds.'

The Defence Leader nodded. 'And you always think of that.' She flicked her ears. 'I find it interesting that your names have meaning, just as ours do. My personal name cannot be used until I step down as Defence Leader, but it means "Dances with Starlight." What does "Ormsin" mean?'

Ormsin mentally sighed in relief that the Defence Leader trusted her still. She wondered how to best explain her family's naming practice. Thai females were usually named for flowers or sweets, but her great-grandmother had been named for a bank. 'It means financial stability and reliability,' she tried.

Hoping to change the subject, Ormsin picked up what looked to be a vegetable curry and sampled it. 'Needs more curry,' she decided.

Mrs Ives looked at Charley. 'He took me away because I enabled peace and co-existence between two races that, he later learned after he and Evelyn set me up there, were never meant to be friends. Many future colonies and species would band together to overthrow the Hufko, but my skills and foresight apparently changed that.'

'So, if the Doctor hadn't interfered in the first place, time would have continued on its right course?'

'Yes, and thousands would have died in wars against the Hufko but ultimately a galactic peace would have existed.'

Charley shook her head. 'I'm sorry for you but as with the woman I met earlier who tried to keep the Wolf-People alive, I can see the bigger picture and understand why he did it.'

Ormsin shrugged. 'I'm glad you do, because no matter how rational I try to be, I can't. I did good. A lot of good. I showed that the Hufko and humans could coexist and yet he made sure they never did.' Mrs Ormsin turned away from Charley. 'I preferred my version of events.' And with that, she was gone. One of the crowd.

The Steward was at Charley's side. 'We're landing in a few minutes.'

Charley looked at him. 'And are you here because of the Doctor, too?'

The Steward's Story

Mark Michalowski

Once upon a time in the east, many centuries ago, there lived a wise and powerful maharaja. He ruled over his subjects with strength and benevolence, and was a great patron of the arts and sciences. So when a magician from a distant land arrived in his palace, the maharaja welcomed him. The magician – who called himself 'the Doctor' – spent many nights discussing the universe with the maharaja and they became good friends.

However, the maharaja had his own magician, Nehra, who was less happy about the arrival of the Doctor, especially when Nehra discovered that he had left a strange, wooden box in the basement of the palace. Nehra had the box brought to his own quarters, and whilst the Doctor talked with the maharaja into the small hours, Nehra examined it.

It was constructed from wood, painted blue, with mysterious characters on its surface. But despite Nehra's best efforts, the Doctor's box resisted all efforts to open it.

'No matter how powerful this Doctor thinks he is,' Nehra said to himself, 'his cabinet is no match for my magicks.'

And so Nehra wove a spell about the box and consulted all manner of prognosticatory devices to ascertain the true nature of the mysterious object. But Nehra was unable to penetrate it, and whatever it contained remained irritatingly, stubbornly, out of Nehra's reach. So the magician tried a different approach, and conjured a magic that would reveal to him the box's history – and he was shocked at what it revealed to him.

'This cannot be,' Nehra said to himself, as he peered into a bronze basin of water, muttering the words of power that his ancient books contained. In the light of his oil lamps, the surface of the water shimmered and rippled, and an image swam into view.

Nehra saw the disc of the Earth, as if viewed from above, wound about with luminous threads. They formed a net about the world, and spread out into space, even to the sun and the moon and the planets. And as he watched, new threads formed, tangling and constricting the world. Many of the luminous threads, he could see, traced back to the Doctor's box – as though it were a spider, wrapping the world in a silken cocoon, smothering it. Peering closer, Nehra saw, to his horror, that there were other cabinets, other boxes, of all shapes and sizes – all of them weaving more and more of the glowing threads. Nehra felt his own chest tighten, as if the threads were winding around his heart, squeezing the breath from his lungs and the life from his body. With a cry, he banished the

223

image and stomped angrily across his room to the box. He placed his hand on it, feeling it sing and vibrate under his palm.

'This is indeed a dark power,' he whispered, clasping his hand to his chest where his own heart thumped anxiously. 'And one that I shall not allow to destroy the world.'

This Doctor had managed to fool the maharaja, Nehra realised. Whilst they sat in the maharaja's private quarters and talked of the stars and the planets, the Doctor's cabinet was quietly smothering them with its threads of fire. Nehra could not allow that to happen as long as it was in his power to prevent it. He crossed to his bookshelves and took down a large volume, smiling quietly to himself. He knew that there was only one way to counter the Doctor's magic – and that was with a more powerful magic. And so, chalking symbols onto the stone flags of his chamber, incanting words of power and burning herbs and incense as directed in the book, Nehra summoned up a demon, an *asura*.

And the demon appeared in a mighty cloud of yellow smoke. Standing over ten feet tall, with the body of an ape and the head of a tiger, the demon stretched out its arms and bellowed. The fingers of its mighty hands were snakes, coiling and hissing, their tongues tasting the air as their black eyes watched the magician.

'I am Vishathra!' the *asura* said, and the room trembled. 'Who has summoned me?'

'I have, demon,' said the magician. 'You must do my bidding.'

Nehra stood before the demon and commanded it to bow down before him which it did, its eyes burning fire and its limbs writhing.

The magician instructed the *asura* to examine the Doctor's cabinet, and the demon rose and crossed to the box, its eyes roving over its surface and the strange markings upon it. One hand reached out, and the serpents' tongues licked over the box's surface. As if burned, the demon pulled back its hand with a roar and turned upon the magician.

'You seek to harm me, magician?' boomed the demon, and the room shook. 'For that I will inflict a thousand times a thousand the pain you have inflicted on me!'

But the magician was not cowed; he stood his ground and stared up at the demon, waiting for its fury to abate.

'You may be an *asura*,' said the magician, 'one of the mightiest of the demons. But you are also one of the most stupid! Why should I summon you here only to hurt you? The pain you felt was from the box – do you need me to tell you what flavour of pain that was?'

The demon was confused and puzzled. 'I do not understand,' it said, narrowing its eyes suspiciously at Nehra.

'Then taste the box again,' commanded the magician. 'But this time be more careful.'

Vishathra tipped back its head, suspecting some kind of trick. Perhaps it was curious about this little man, and the box that burned it so. It turned back to it and approached it cautiously, letting the tongues of the snakes of its fingers play in the air around the box.

'Ahhhh,' said Vishathra eventually, letting out a hiss. 'I see! This is a magic cabinet. A cabinet that is both here and not here. A cabinet that is present at all times and yet at none.' Vishathra rounded on Nehra. 'This is indeed a powerful magic. Is it yours, magician?'

Nehra shook his head. 'It belongs to another magician, one who would call himself "the Doctor". He seeks to gain influence and power here at the palace. Even now he is with the maharaja, spinning him tall tales of the world to come and the world that has been.'

'And what would you have me do with this cabinet?'

The magician walked past the demon and laid his hand upon the box's surface. Vishathra seemed surprised, as the magician did not appear to be burned by the box's magic as it had been.

'I have woven powerful spells,' said the magician quietly, 'and I know this box's secret. It is a cabinet of time, a mechanism for moving from the past to the present to the future – and back again! And I have seen more: more cabinets like this, in shapes both strange and terrible. They weave a net about the world like a cat's cradle, pulling tighter and tighter.'

'And this is… bad?' said Vishathra.

'Of course it's bad, you fool!' snapped the magician. 'Each new thread that these cabinets of time weave weakens the fabric of the universe. I did not see it before because I did not think to look, but now I see those threads everywhere, binding the universe ever tighter, strangling it.'

'Ahhh…,' said Vishathra as though it understood – although it did not, since the magician had been right, and Vishathra wasn't the brightest of *asuras*.

'I foresee a time,' went on the magician, 'that this Doctor and his kind, those who travel through the past and the future in cabinets such as this, shall bind the world so tightly in these threads that reality will be threatened. As a limb bound too tightly with a cloth will eventually die and wither, so will the world.' The magician turned and stared up at Vishathra. 'I must prevent this!'

'And so you summoned me.'

'Yes – I command you to sever those threads, Vishathra. You are eternal, you have existence in the past, the present and the future. You can follow those threads, take them in your hands and snap them like cotton.'

Vishathra narrowed its eyes and nodded.

'Oh dear,' came a small, worried voice from the corridor. '"Snap them like cotton"? I don't like the sound of that at all.'

'Doctor!' exclaimed the magician.

225

Out of the shadows stepped the Doctor, his hands clasped together nervously. He looked up at Vishathra and gave a polite little nod.

'How long have you been listening?' asked Nehra.

'Quite long enough, thank you,' said the Doctor, keeping his eye on the *asura*.

'My demon,' explained the magician. 'Vishathra. One of the most powerful *asuras* I could conjure.'

'Is he?' The Doctor caught sight of the snake heads, hissing at Vishathra's fingertips. 'Very impressive. I'm sorry if I came in halfway through your little rant, though – please carry on. It sounded most interesting.'

'Hah!' snorted the magician. 'You think you're so clever – currying favour with the maharaja, travelling through time in this!' He slapped the side of the blue box, and for a moment, the Doctor looked almost apologetic. 'But not for much longer…'

'That would be the bit about snapping threads like cotton, then, would it?'

'You and your kind will condemn the world to slow strangulation,' the magician hissed. 'Tying it ever tighter in those threads you weave.'

'Really?' said the Doctor. 'I rather thought I was doing quite the opposite – liberating the world, making sure that it's safe from people like you: petty-minded individuals who can't see any further than the ends of their noses.' His tone had hardened and he stalked towards the magician, seemingly oblivious of Vishathra who stood watching with an amused smile. 'You have no idea what you're meddling with, do you? These threads that you keep rattling on about: you don't even know what they are, do you?'

The magician sneered contemptuously. 'Of course I do: they are the guidelines that we follow through eternity, laid down for us by the gods. I have done my research, Doctor. They describe our past and prescribe our future.'

'And you wish this…' The Doctor glanced up at Vishathra and raised an eyebrow. '…this demon, this *asura*, to sever them? All of them?'

The magician shook his head slowly. 'Not all of them, Doctor: only the threads that belong to those such as you – travellers in time. Through my magicks, I have seen what is to come; I have seen how your kind run and race through history like a child with a kite, tangling and ensnaring everything with its line. Like a dog on a leash that knows not what it does, you dart here and there, wrapping the leash around everything. Sooner or later, Doctor, one tug on that leash will bring everything tumbling down.'

'Oh poppycock!' exclaimed the Doctor. 'And I'd stick to one simile if I were you. Makes you look awfully amateurish!'

At this, the magician drew himself up and jabbed a finger at Vishathra.

'Now, demon! I command you! Seek out those who travel in time! Gather up their threads and tear them asunder!'

'Now?' asked Vishathra, suddenly thrown.

'Yes!' chimed in the Doctor. 'Now! Only make sure you do a proper job – there are enough amateurs in this field already, you know.'

Vishathra looked from its master to the Doctor and back to the magician again.

'You're sure?'

And for a moment, the magician wasn't. Perhaps he'd expected the Doctor to fight against him, not agree. Perhaps he hadn't expected this at all.

'This could be a trick,' said the demon. 'You know the kind: caught in my own trap etcetera etcetera.' It looked doubtful.

'Oh I'm sure a great big demon like yourself – one who can slip through time like a fish through water – couldn't be caught out by someone as stupid as me,' said the Doctor with a coy expression.

'Ahhhh….,' hissed Vishathra. 'I see it now, Doctor. You seek to tie me up in my own net. You think that as a demon I must have travelled in time, and thus, when I sever the threads, I shall cut my own.'

The Doctor stared at his shoes. Vishathra gave a low chuckle and the Doctor felt the flagstones beneath his feet tremble.

'Well, let me tell you,' said Vishathra, 'I have never travelled in time, so that one just won't work.'

'Oh,' said the Doctor quietly. 'Well.'

'Get on with it!' shouted the magician.

And Vishathra nodded, raised its serpent hands to the ceiling, closed its eyes –

– and vanished.

'Oh dear,' said the Doctor with just a hint of smugness. 'We weren't expecting that, were we?'

'What happened?' The magician stalked over to the spot that the demon had been occupying, as if expecting to find the creature still there, perhaps wrapped in a cloak of invisibility. But there was nothing. He rounded on the Doctor.

'What did you do?'

'Me?' The Doctor clasped his hands to his chest. 'Me? Oh, you're too generous. I didn't do anything – it was your demon, after all.'

'Then where is it?'

The Doctor looked around as if he'd only now realised that the demon were gone.

'Oh my,' he said, 'it looks like it's gone and cut itself off, doesn't it?'

'But Vishathra said… it said that that wouldn't happen,' moaned the magician. 'That it *couldn't* happen! It hasn't travelled in time. How could it cut its own threads if it hasn't travelled in time?'

'Ahh…,' said the Doctor, a slightly guilty look crossing his face. 'Perhaps I ought to tell you about a friend of mine.'

227

'A friend? Another magician, I expect.' Nehra was feeling not only angry but also stupid, for allowing the Doctor to trick him – even though he didn't quite understand *how* the Doctor had tricked him.

'Well....' The Doctor looked a little awkward. 'Perhaps work colleague would be a better term. Name of Einstein. Albert Einstein.'

The magician scowled.

'What are you babbling about? Who is this Einstein? And where is my demon?'

The Doctor strolled insouciantly over to his blue box and made a show of rubbing a smudge from its blue surface.

'You probably won't have heard of him,' he said. 'Seeing as he hasn't been born.'

'Another time traveller!' spat the magician.

The Doctor spun on his heel.

'Well, I suppose you could say that, although I'm sure dear old Albert would have argued with you about such a possibility. But, as with so many things, Albert would have been quite, quite wrong.

'You see, he came up with a rather astounding piece of scientific theory: the Theory of Relativity. Or rather, he *will* come up with it in a few hundred years.' The Doctor waved his hand dismissively. 'Lots of very good things in there. A couple that were a little wide of the mark, but you can't knock his basic principles. What it boiled down to was that, in this universe of ours, there are no privileged observers.'

'What?'

The Doctor's mouth tightened in irritation at the interruption. 'No privileged observers: as far as the universe is concerned, no one's viewpoint is any more special than anyone else's.'

'Your words have no meaning,' snapped Nehra irritably.

'Well, if you'd let me finish, I was about to *explain* their meaning: that there is no fixed frame of reference that the whole universe uses to measure things. Apart from when acceleration's involved, if two people are moving apart you might as well consider one of them at rest and the other one moving away from them.'

'Nonsense!' sneered the magician. 'Sophisticated nonsense.'

'It does seem that way, doesn't it? But from the point of view of the laws of the universe, I'm rather afraid that it's true: if you took away the world and any fixed landmarks, there would be no way to tell which of the two was "moving" and which one was "at rest".' The Doctor wiggled two fingers of each hand in the air as he spoke, which baffled the magician even more.

'But what's this got to do with my demon? How did you trick him?'

'I'm coming to that. Have a little patience. This story is going to take some time.'

'It feels like it's been going on forever,' sighed the magician. The Doctor took no notice.

'Well, you see, another aspect of Albert's work involved time.'

'Did he find a way to make it pass faster?' asked the magician quietly, but the Doctor seemed to be ignoring him.

'Albert discovered that time doesn't pass the same for all of us. In fact, if you had the tools to measure it, you'd find that time doesn't pass the same for *any* of us. Gravity affects the passage of time: a hermit living at the top of a mountain experiences time at an infinitesimally faster rate than does a washerwoman on the banks of the river down below. Movement – specifically acceleration – does the same: a bird that launches itself into the sky every morning lives an immeasurably tiny bit longer than a priest who sits in his temple all day long. Gravity, acceleration, time – they're all tied up with each other.' The Doctor folded his arms and stared long and hard at the magician. 'In a very real sense, we're *all* time travellers. None of us has the enviable position of being stationary in time: indeed, we all travel forwards in time at – *roughly* – the rate of 60 seconds per minute. But some people move a little faster, some a little slower. Even Vishathra – who, quite genuinely I imagine, believed that it'd never travelled in time – wasn't immune. It moved around this room, I take it? Accelerated from standing still to a casual sauntering pace? And even when it was standing still, it wasn't, you know: this planet is accelerating around the sun; the sun is accelerating around the centre of the galaxy; the galaxy is – oh, you get the picture, I'm sure. You're a bright man.'

The magician slumped into his chair and rubbed his eyes. His head had been sent spinning with all these words and ideas that the Doctor had thrown at him. Surely it made no sense, no sense at all. And yet… Nehra had to face the fact that, somehow, the Doctor had made Vishathra destroy itself. Could there be truth in this pale magician's words?

'So you're saying that Vishathra didn't know any of this? That it grabbed at the first thread it could see and snapped it – and that it was its own?'

'You did say it wasn't the brightest demon around.'

The magician shook his head disconsolately as a thought suddenly occurred to him. 'It could have been *my* thread it found first. I could have been destroyed just as surely as it was.'

'You were lucky,' said the Doctor, but there was no amusement in his voice. 'If you'd told Vishathra to ignore its own thread, it could have wiped out everyone and everything that had ever existed. That ever *would* exist.'

The magician shook his head, not willing to believe that he could have been so wrong.

'But the threads,' he protested. 'I saw them in the water: they were strangling everything – the world, the moon, the stars. *Everything!* All of existence was bound up in them as they drew ever tighter. Are you telling me that, knowing what I knew, I should just allow you and your type to destroy everything? How could I let that happen when it's within my power to stop it?'

The Doctor crossed to the magician and perched himself on the edge of the desk.

'You weren't to know,' he said softly. 'The threads you saw – they aren't strangling everything. They're what make up the Web of Time.'

The magician looked up, frowning.

'It's what binds everything together,' continued the Doctor. 'The network of pasts and presents and futures that we weave: they define causality, they make a framework that keeps the mechanism of the universe ticking like a clock.'

'Like a what?'

'Oh, sorry. Like a, erm, like a sundial.' The Doctor pulled a pained face. 'Forget that one. The universe is bound together by the timelines of everyone in it. And part of what I do – what many of us time travellers do – is to make sure that the fabric they form stays intact.'

The magician frowned, not sure whether to believe this Doctor. After all, he had tricked Vishathra. Perhaps he was an avatar of one of the gods – and now that the magician had thought it, he thought that, perhaps, he could see something of the Lord Shiva in this pale little man. Shiva was known to descend to Earth in the guise of beggars, to trick humans, to spread enlightenment. That might explain how he had been able to dispose of the *asura* so easily. It all made a horrible sort of sense, and the magician suddenly felt humbled and bowed his head and clasped his hands together, fearful that the Doctor might decide to end his life. After all, if the Doctor was right and Nehra was wrong, what more did he deserve?

'Oh stop all that,' said the Doctor, jumping to his feet. 'I'm sure you thought you were doing the right thing. I don't suppose I can fault you for trying, can I? Just as long as you don't try it again: it's a very dangerous thing, fiddling with the Web of Time. Especially when you're trying to destroy it. Even snipping one or two threads could unravel the whole of causality, you know. Leave the fiddling to those who know what they're doing.'

Nehra nodded, beginning to realise what the Doctor was talking about, 'The web of Indra,' he murmured. 'You use words that I do not understand, but their meaning is clear: the web of Indra – the ultimate connectedness of all things, all times, all places.'

'Yes,' said the Doctor thoughtfully. 'I suppose that's one way of looking at it. And it's a web I have to protect. Along with the freedom that my, erm, time cabinet gives me comes a great responsibility: the responsibility to ensure that the Web of Time, the web of Indra, remains intact. D'you see?'

The magician nodded, his eyes wide, for he now saw what before he had been blind to. He begged forgiveness of the Doctor for his foolishness, his hubris.

'Not at all,' said the Doctor magnanimously, clearly embarrassed by Nehra's show of humility and abasement. 'We all make mistakes – well, most of us.'

Nehra nodded seriously, not sure whether the Doctor was making a joke at his expense. He looked up at him, his hands still clasped before him. 'How can I help?'

'Help?'

The magician nodded. 'To maintain the web of Indra. In my stupidity, I was almost the architect of its destruction. It is only fitting that I should make amends. Tell me what I can do. Tell me how I can appease the Lord Shiva.' Nehra looked around his desk, his eyes alighting on a large, brass knife. 'I shall take my life if it is what the Lord Shiva demands.'

The Doctor seemed awkward, almost embarrassed.

'Oh no no no,' he said. 'No need for anything like that. I'm sure the Lord Shiva has already forgiven you. Probably busy elsewhere, knowing him.'

Nehra was almost shocked at the casual way in which the Doctor talked about the Lord Shiva. But, then, perhaps that was the way that the Gods and their emissaries discussed each other. 'But there must be something I can do,' he said. 'Some way to make amends, to serve the Lord Shiva and his emissary.'

The Doctor pursed his lips. 'Let me think about that for a while,' he said, rubbing his hands together thoughtfully. 'I'm sure I can come up with something.' He leaned forwards and the magician cowered back. 'But in the meantime, no conjuring up demons!' His voice was stern, but Nehra could see something of a mischievous twinkle in the man's eyes.

'Never again,' agreed the Nehra, hurriedly. 'I shall burn my books, destroy my equipment. I shall join a monastery and leave the palace.'

The Doctor rolled his eyes. 'No need to be too hasty, Nehra,' he said. 'Just cut back on the prognostication. Invent the telescope or something.'

'The...?'

'Never mind, never mind.'

The Doctor drew himself up.

'About time I was off, I think,' he said, suddenly brisk. He nodded at Nehra and crossed the chamber to his cabinet, taking a key from his pocket. 'I shall be back,' he said, almost as a warning. 'Now remember what I said – no demons, no magic.'

And with that, the Doctor unlocked and entered the cabinet, closing the door behind him.

The magician sat and waited, not sure what to expect. Suddenly, there came a vast grinding and crushing sound, like the groaning of the timbers of a ship. And before the Nehra's eyes, the cabinet began to fade as though it were nothing but mist.

And then it was gone, and he was left, shaking, alone in his chamber.

Scant seconds later, the air was rent by the same sound, and the cabinet reappeared, growing more solid with every moment until it was as it had been before. The door opened, and-

'Ah! You're there!' said the man who stepped out. Like the Doctor, he was pale, a westerner. But he was taller, his hair curlier, and his clothes were different. Whereas the Doctor had looked impish and almost scruffy, this man wore an aristocratic face and an elegant jacket in dark velvet.

'Who are you?' demanded the magician. 'Where is the Doctor?'

The man frowned, looked down at himself.

'That,' he said with a smile, 'is a very long story. Now come on, Nehra! We have work to do!'

'And I've been working for him ever since. By the way, we've landed.' The Steward pointed towards the vast room. It was empty.

'I didn't feel us land! Didn't see them go.' Charley looked around her. 'Where are they?'

'Safe,' said the Steward. 'In so many ways.' He started clearing up glasses. 'Goodbye, Miss Pollard,' he said quietly. 'It's been fun helping you understand. You'll find the Doctor outside, too. Near the cockpit.'

And before Charley's eyes, he seemed to just melt into the air, although for a few seconds, Charley could still hear the chink of glasses being moved around until that too faded.

'Your name is Charlotte Elspeth Pollard,' said a voice at her shoulder. 'You're eighteen. You were born on the day the RMS *Titanic* sunk. You hold the fate of the universe in your heart.'

The speaker was the Tramp. He and Charley were alone.

'I was like you,' he said. 'But I chose to stay here. Time after time.'

'Why?'

'Because it's easier. Easier than carrying on. Easier than carrying the burdens he provides us with.' The Tramp reached out and tried to touch Charley's shoulder but instinctively she pulled away.

The Tramp shrugged. 'Not ready yet, are you? Open your mind, Charley. Your mind as well as your heart. Yes, I can see why he brought you here. More potential. Good luck. I think you should leave.'

As if following a command, the door of the room swung open, revealing a lush green field visible outside.

'I'm staying in here. I always do. I made my choice.'

'But... but who are you?'

The Tramp's Story

Joseph Lidster

If you stand on top of the hill, you can see the entire city. You can't see any people; you're too far away for that. But, look at the thousands of yellow street-lights. For each one of those lights there must be at least twenty people. Now, look over to your right at those tower blocks. Each lit window represents another three or four people. There are thousands of them. Living their lives. Interacting with each other. Each individual's actions causing ripples across the other lives. In that window, yes, that one there, a mother is hitting her son with a belt because she missed her favourite soap opera. You see, he wasn't at the bus stop when she went to collect him. Tomorrow, the son will be angry. He'll mug a younger boy for a few coins. The younger boy will tell his father who will call the police. A policeman will be late home because he has to type up that extra report. This will be the final straw for the policeman's wife, who will decide to move back in with her parents. Her mother will buy steaks as a special treat. That means the supermarket will run out. Which means that they'll increase the order next week. And so it will continue, all the way down to a farmer who lives miles away. He'll have to kill an extra cow and all because a tired, young woman missed her favourite TV show. Such a minor incident, but try telling that to Daisy. One minute she's happily chewing the cud, the next she's shrink-wrapped and on her way to Sainsbury's.

Thousands of people. And tonight, they're all moving. In cars, buses, on foot, they move. They meet in train stations, in pubs, in each other's houses. They hug, clap each other on the back, and shake hands. As the year draws to a close, they huddle in groups with the ones they love, like or can tolerate.

All except for the tramp.

They say he had a name once. They say he even had a postcode. Now he lives on the street, next to the shop you pass every day on the way to work. You remember him? You gave him cigarettes one night when you were drunk. You're about to pass him again, as you go to meet your friends in the Rose and Crown. You're in your new clothes and you're running late. It's cold and nearly half-eight, so don't stop. There he is. Quicken your step. That's it. Bury your face in your scarf. And move to the right of the pavement. Safe, straight ahead. Quicker. He's spotted you. Ignore him. Ignore the outstretched hand. You can't help them all and, besides, you gave money to that *Big Issue* seller in September and you've got to meet your friends and you can't be late and he's probably on drugs anyway and, goodness, it's cold and thank God, someone's coming in the other direction. And they're giving him money. That's nice to see.

And you've passed him. Well done. Now you can have that pint and possibly another one after. You must remember to phone your mum though. Check your mobile. Good stuff. Now, go and celebrate. You've worked hard this year and you deserve it.

Your name is Chris. You're twenty-eight. You remember *Challenger* exploding, John Lennon dying and Scott and Charlene getting married. Merry Christmas, Chris.

The tramp mutters a thanks to the person who gave him a handful of coppers. His face lights up as he counts them with his cold fingers. Fifty-seven pence. He now has exactly fifteen pounds and two pence. He only needs fourteen pounds and ninety-nine pence. He's rich! His knees crack as he stands up. He starts to walk along the pavement, and then stops to stare, open-mouthed at the exploding fireworks in the dark blue sky. Pure beautiful colours lighting up the ugly grey buildings and then immediately reflected in the murky blackness of the river. He can't stop though. He needs to light up his own darkness. He needs to celebrate the birth of Jesus Christ and the death of another year like everyone else.

He shuffles further down the street and approaches the off licence. He pauses, then crosses the threshold into the warmth. Immediately, the pissed-off security guard moves oh-so-subtly towards him. The tramp flashes him a toothless smile then continues on his journey. He passes the Doritos, passes the Smirnoff Ice and he passes the Strongbow as he shuffles onwards towards the counter.

You're working on Christmas Eve. You're not down the pub. You're not even down the Social Club. You've switched off the black-and-white telly. You've switched off the smug bastards out celebrating. You've drawn the short straw and life can't get any worse. Then you see the tramp. Correction, then you smell the tramp. Piss and chips. He shuffles towards you, grinning like a mentalist. You look over at the security guard, your eyes pleading for him to come over and 'kindly escort the gentleman off the premises'. He ignores you because you didn't get off with him earlier. You start to...

'Champagne, please.' The tramp interrupts your mundane thoughts.

'What?' you grunt.

'A bottle of champagne, please, young lady.'

You try to stifle a laugh and grunt once more.

'Got any cash?'

You regret asking the question as the tramp begins to empty his pockets. Coins cascade across the counter.

'That's exactly fourteen pounds and ninety-nine pence there,' he smiles.

You wonder whether to count the money but then think better of it. You reach behind you and grab a bottle of cheap champagne.

'You want it wrapped?' you ask, placing it on the counter.

'No. No, young lady. That's fine as it is.'

He picks up the bottle, turns and begins to shuffle towards the door. You look over at the security guard as he watches the tramp leave. You decide that maybe you will let him stick his tongue down your throat tonight. It is Christmas, after all.

Your name is Karina (Kazza to your friends). You're nineteen. You remember the Oklahoma bombing, Jill Dando dying and Grant marrying Tiffany. Festive Greetings, Kazza.

The tramp leaves the off-licence and begins his slow, purposeful shuffle once more. He's heading towards the old railway bridge. You know, the one you always shoot over every day on the 20:26 to Central Station. When you're working on your laptop so you can spend more time with Jack and Chloe. Your name is Richard. You're forty-five. You remember the moon landing, JFK dying and Princess Anne marrying Mark Phillips. You don't even notice that you cross a bridge twice a day so you certainly don't give a damn what happens underneath it. Happy Holidays, Richard.

The tramp continues his shuffle. He smiles as he hears the tuneless singing from underneath the bridge. He smiles as he...

You're in a hurry. You're always in a hurry. Tonight, though, you're in even more of a hurry. You've got to get back to the flat or Steven's going to leave. He warned you. He said that if you didn't get home by nine then not to bother getting home at all. Sod the job. If you want to keep your boyfriend, you'll be home in time to celebrate Christmas. You flinch as you barge into the tramp. You mutter an apology as you keep on walking. You must remember to... your name is Jonas. You're thirty-two. You remember the Gulf War, Jamie Bulger dying, Andrew marrying Fergie and when it used to snow at Christmas. Have a good one, Jonas.

The tramp collapses to the pavement, scrabbling at the shards of broken bottle. His fingers are sliced open as he tries to gather up the one thing, the one thing that he's been saving for. The blood bubbles and froths with the champagne like an unholy bucks fizz. Giving up, he crawls away. That's it. He's had enough. The fireworks explode once more but this time he knows, he knows that they're taunting him. The flashes of light, so brief and fulfiled. No endless struggle. Not cold or tired or pitied or ignored. The tramp knows what he must do.

* * *

You watch as the tramp crawls into the road. You watch as he curls up into the foetal position and closes his eyes. You know as well as he does that the number seven bus will soon be turning the corner. You know he's going to be crushed as the wheels on the bus go round and round. You've seen it. You've heard it. The screech of the brakes. The look of horror on the driver's face as she crushes and splinters and shatters the tramp's body. You know she'll blame herself. You know that Rita, thirty-eight, won't be opening her presents this year. You know that she'll feel so guilty, that she'll throw herself off the bridge you're now leaning against.

You know all this because you're the Doctor and, let's face it, you know everything. You remember that first discovery of fire and the end of the Universe itself. You look across the street and you see Her. You see Her hateful little smirk as She gives you a little wave. You raise your hand as if to wave back. Then you turn your palm towards you and stick two fingers up at Death. She adjusts her tinsel crown, laughs and skips off into the night.

You're changing gears as you approach the corner. Momentarily distracted by a young woman, lit up by the headlights as she dances along the pavement, you stall the engine. 'Oops! Nearly there!' you trill to the passengers. 'Driving home for Christmas'. You sing along to the radio. You know that next year's going to be good. You think of Patrick at home. He'll have the rum open and two shots carefully poured. But he won't touch a drop until you get there. You love this time of year. Framed in your fairy lights, cheerily greeting your passengers. Most just grunt as they struggle with their shopping but occasionally, maybe once, twice a day, a face will light up as someone realises that you'll be the one to take them on the last leg of their journey home. You love that you can make people happy. You're just obviously the nicest person alive, aren't you? Still, can't have kids though, can you? Not with your tubes all messed up the way they are. You turn the steering wheel as you drive around the corner.

Your name is Rita. You are thirty-eight. And you are going to die.

Except that you're not.

The tramp that should be there, isn't. The accident you should have, you don't. You're going to live a few more years so keep on singing and remember to tell Patrick how much you love him.

Oh, and maybe think about adopting, you stupid cow.

So many lives. So many people. All this happening, in one city, in such a short space of time. And we haven't even mentioned the passengers on the bus. Or the other tramps under the railway bridge. Did you notice something though? Did you notice how quickly they all forgot about him?

He wakes to the feel of cold steel against his throat.

'Just take whatever you want,' he mutters.

'Ssh.'

He opens his eyes, sees where he is and swears. Actually, he doesn't just swear. He unleashes such a stream of profanities that the man holding the blade to his throat is forced to step back.

'Where am I?' asks the tramp, his voice echoing around the huge cathedral of a room. It's impossible to comprehend. Wooden walls, books, chairs, a piano, some kind of wooden table with a column of blue light connecting to the impossibly high ceiling.

'Keep still,' says the stranger. 'I'm trying to…'

His voice cuts off as the tramp grabs him by the throat.

Then the tramp notices something. He no longer smells. He's been washed. His hands have been bandaged and he's… and he's wearing clean clothes. The stranger is halfway through shaving him. He releases his grip.

'Now, just sit back and relax.'

The stranger reaches towards the tramp and gently scrapes the razor up the tramp's skin. He feels a sudden rush of cold air against his neck as the strands of beard fall into the bowl of cloudy water. The stranger speaks again.

'I'm the Doctor. You have to let me help you.'

The emotion in his voice suggests that this is as important for him as it is for the tramp.

'Why are you doing this?'

'It's what I do. It's what I am.'

And, that night the tramp sleeps in a proper bed. For the first time in eight hundred and forty-two days he sleeps under a quilt instead of under his coat. For the first time in eight hundred and forty-two days, he sleeps inside instead of on the street. For the first time in eight hundred and forty-two days he sleeps a full night's sleep.

That Doctor, eh? What a great bloke. Top man, what! But the tramp knows. He knows that nobody does anything for nothing. What does the Doctor want?

Whistling a happy tune, you spread the butter across the slightly undercooked toast. Suddenly, you notice the water boiling over the edge of the pan. You jump across the kitchen shouting 'Ha!' in a way that you hope is amusing and then you remember that there's no one there to entertain. You are alone. You take a spoon and scoop the egg out of the water. You plop it into the eggcup and pick up the tray.

You are the Doctor and you remember… you remember everyone. You remember all those you couldn't save. A boy and his parents dying on a burning world. A young soldier pushing you to safety as a building explodes. Your oldest friend trapped in a thousand lifetimes of darkness.

And then you think about the life you have just saved. And, smiling grimly, you leave the kitchen.

And life goes on…

Balancing the breakfast tray in one hand, you enter his room. Will today be the same? Will he throw the lovingly-buttered toast across the room? Will he scream again? Will he demand to know why you've saved him? Today, won't he understand that you just want to be his friend?

You run into your TARDIS, laser blasts singeing your hair. You shut the doors, set the coordinates and collapse into a chair as the Ship leaves.

'Well, they weren't exactly a friendly bunch!'

The tramp ignores you.

'I managed to stop their dangerous experiments with time.'

The tramp ignores you.

'I wish… I wish you'd have been there. It's not healthy being in here all day.'

The tramp just asks the same question. 'Why did you save me?'

And life goes on… Karina (Kazza to her friends) is now pregnant with the security guard's baby which suits her as it means that she'll get child benefit and won't need to work. Tomas loses his job because he left early on Christmas Eve. His money runs out so Steven leaves him anyway. The Doctor keeps on saving the Universe and keeps on making breakfast for the tramp.

Oh, and Chris forgot to phone his mum.

Then, one day, the tramp gives in. He eats the egg and toast. And then, one day, he helps the Doctor save the Universe. And the wheels go round and round…

You sit in the cell, counting the bricks in the wall. You wish you'd never attacked the Emperor's weapons factory. You look over at the other prisoners and silently apologise to them. Ever since the death of your father (or was it your brother?) all you've done is lead them into danger time and time again. You've started to suspect that the Emperor will never be overthrown and that perhaps… perhaps you should just give up. It would be easier just to slice open your own throat and end it quickly. You hear the metal handle of the door being pulled back and wait to see which of your men will now be taken for 'questioning'. Slowly, the door opens and a face appears. It's not one of the guards! It's the Doctor! Amazed, you stare at him as he winks and doffs an imaginary hat. It's meant to be cheerfully inspiring but in reality it's just irritating.

'Well? Are you just going to sit there? This is a jailbreak!'

238

You and your men jump to your feet and begin to pile through the door, past the Doctor and his companion.

Your name is Hanse and you're twenty-one years old. You remember the Emperor's soldiers burning down your village and you remember the Doctor arriving to save the day. Tonight, he's going to do something very clever that will end the Emperor's tyranny once and for all. Tonight, you will lead your people to freedom with the Doctor's help! Oh, yeah, and he's got some old bloke with him.

He asks you why he can't go home. You tell him that you wanted to save just one person from Death and that you chose him. For the very first time, he thanks you as for the very first time in his life he feels that he is someone.

Your fingers are starting to turn blue in the cold Salzburg wind. But, you don't care. In your hands, the disgusting baby, the disgusting Creature of God Himself, squirms and squeals. You hold it over the edge of the bridge, ready to smash it into the overflowing river.

'Antonio! Wait!'

It's the Doctor's companion. The old man. You ignore him, for like so many, he is talentless. He's unworthy of being your foe. Unlike…

'God!' You scream up at the sky. 'Take back your Creature!' You raise the infant higher and…

'Salieri! No!' It's the Doctor. This one isn't as unworthy as his companion. He has great intelligence and you remember how he had been able to manipulate the various members of Joseph's court. Not too unlike yourself, then. You turn to the Doctor, still holding the child over the water.

'Salieri!' he pleads. 'Antonio, listen to me. I understand why you want to do this.'

Understand? He thinks he understands! To have devoted your entire life to God and to music and to then see everything destroyed by an infantile, pathetic genius. God had given His skill to Mozart. Well, he won't be able to now. You have finally beaten Him.

'Doctor! Mortimus brought me back in time to fulfil my destiny. I shall destroy God's protégé before he has spoken a word, let alone composed an opera!'

The Doctor takes a step towards you.

'Mortimus has gone, Antonio. He's left you.'

'No! You lie, Doctor. He's going to take me back so that, untroubled by the God-given skill of a slovenly and lustful child, I shall be recognised.'

The Doctor takes another step forward.

'Antonio, Mortimus has left you. You're trapped. There's no way home.'

Again, he takes another step.

239

'And if you kill that child, there will be no home for you to return to.'

'Mortimus told me that…'

He interrupts you. 'Mortimus says a lot of things. They're mostly untrue. If you kill Amadeus as a baby, then you'll be destroying your own past.'

'I know, bu…'

He begins to shout at you.

'But nothing, Antonio! Did our friend explain about the Web of Time? Well? Did he?'

You shiver as the wind begins to pick up. Why is he so angry?

'Think of it… think of it as a concerto. A melody. You, of all people, understand these things, don't you?'

Slowly, you nod.

'Now, what happens if you take away just one of a melody's notes?'

You stare at him. You start to wonder…

'What happens, Salieri?' he shouts.

'The melody is… well, it would be destroyed.'

The Doctor takes another step forward and speaks, quieter this time.

'Exactly. Mozart is one of the notes. The Web of Time is the melody. It's that simple. Trust me. You've travelled in time and you are an intelligent man. If you destroy Mozart you could very well end up destroying everything.'

You know he's right.

You bring the baby to safety and hold it out for the Doctor's companion to take. You want it – him – out of your hands.

'Here, fool,' you say to the Doctor's companion. 'Take the infant.'

But he's staring at the Doctor with a look in his eyes that chills your heart.

You are Antonio Salieri. You are seventy-three. You remember a lifetime of hard work destroyed by a vengeful God and his despicable child composer. You remember a promise made to you by the time traveller, Mortimus. Mortimus, a Man of God. How delightfully suitable to use one of His own against Him. You remember… you can hardly remember your life from before it was ruled by hatred and jealousy.

Don't worry, Antonio, the Doctor's going to take you back to your time. Then he's going to lock you in a mental asylum where you will die and be forgotten.

'Doctor…'

'Hmm?' He doesn't look up from his book.

'I was thinking about what you were saying to Salieri.'

'Hmm?' He turns a page of his book and chuckles.

'About Mozart! About the Web of Time!'

The Doctor looks up.

'Oh, I wouldn't worry about thaaaarrghh….'

240

The Doctor falls out of his chair as the TARDIS begins to violently shake. 'Doctor! What's happening?' shouts his companion.

And the tramp enters the diamond-studded cave. His reflection is distorted in jewelled walls causing a thousand of his own eyes to follow his every movement. He tries to ignore them as he shuffles cautiously on towards the great glass jar that dominates the room. Inside the jar, floating in the silvery-clear liquid, he can see what looks like a giant foetus. A giant foetus made of glass.

'So, you're the great Auctor.'

Indeed, I am.

The voice chimes in the tramp's mind.

'Why did you drag us down here?'

I was bored. I needed a distraction. The people on this world can be so... limited.

'The Doctor says that you've been controlling them for years now.'

Yes, I have.

'Well, he's going to stop you. He's on his way, you know.'

Why would he stop me?

'People aren't meant to live like this! All controlled and... well, like sheep! I fought in wars to stop monsters like you!'

And you won?

The tramp starts to speak then stops again. Then he starts again.

'Yes. Where I'm from, we're all different. We all live our own lives.'

I would like to know of this place.

'Well... I can...'

There's no need to tell. Let me experience.

Before the tramp can move, a blue light explodes down from the roof and holds him still.

Let us experience it together. Let me feel the minds of those who you have met. I am... we are... can you see it?

'No!' screams the tramp.

I will tell you then. We're walking. No... climbing. We're on a hill. If you stand on top of the hill, you can see the entire city. You can't see any people; you're too far away for that. But look...

And, finally, the tramp understands. He knows why the Doctor saved him. But, life has to go on...

The fiery explosion is reflected throughout the jewel-encrusted caves and the planet's inhabitants cheer as their minds are freed from the Auctor's control. The Doctor and his companion leave the jubilant crowds and head back to the TARDIS. A few drops of rain start to fall as they walk across the muddy field.

'You're very quiet,' says the Doctor. 'I mean, we did do good there. The people on this world…'

He notices that the tramp has stopped walking. He turns back to him. 'What's wrong?'

Slowly, the tramp speaks. 'The Auctor showed me.'

The Doctor, concerned, walks back to his companion.

'Well, you shouldn't believe everything that it…'

'It showed me. It told me.'

The Doctor, the saviour of the world, suddenly looks very small as the rain begins to fall harder.

'Doctor. I know why you saved me.'

And the tramp reveals what the Auctor told him. The rain lashes down on the two men as

you give him cigarettes instead of money one night when you are drunk and move to the right of the pavement safe, straight ahead, quicker he's spotted you, ignore him and you've passed him, correction, then you smell the tramp, piss and chips, you certainly don't give a damn what happens and you flinch as you barge past the tramp and you're just obviously the nicest person alive, aren't you? oh, yeah, and he's got some old bloke with him… and life goes on, and then you think about the life you have just saved, and life goes on as the wheels on the bus go round and round… 'why are you doing this?' will he demand to know why you've saved him? 'why did you save me?'

'Why did you save me?' he shrieks.

The Doctor quietly, 'I've told you. I didn't want to see you die.'

'Didn't want to see me die? Or…'

'nearly there!' you trill framed in your fairy lights and a face will light up as someone realises that you'll be the one to take them on the last leg of their journey home and you love that you can make people happy because you're just obviously the nicest person alive, aren't you? and you are going to die. except that you're not

'Rita?' The Doctor is stunned.

'The bus driver. My death would have meant her death. She was meant to kill herself because of me.'

'Oh…'

The Doctor looks down at the puddle forming at his feet. The raindrops fall, violently splashing into each other. He crouches down and looks up at his companion.

'Imagine. Imagine that this puddle is your city.'

The tramp looks down at the puddle. He watches as the drops of water fall and splash and live. He leans further forward, over the puddle and it becomes still as the rain bounces off his back. He sees his face reflected in the now-still water.

The Doctor continues, quietly. 'Now, imagine that these raindrops are the people. As they fall, they create ripples that reflect and bounce off each other. Do you understand now?'

A tear rolls down the man's face, holds onto his chin, then falls...

Almost unnoticeably, it splashes into the puddle. It creates one lone ripple of water that slowly moves, unhindered to the edge of the pool. The water becomes still once more.

'I wanted to save at least one person. No, I needed to! Death has stalked me recently and I needed to remind myself of the difference that I can make. I'm the Doctor. I can change things. I can make things better!'

He pauses. 'Rita was meant to die but she was a good person. She can live a good life. But it wasn't that simple. Her life touched too many others. If I had acted directly, *they* would have noticed. She created ripples that danced and played with the other ripples. You didn't. You had no name, no postcode, no friends and no family. In your entire life, you created one ripple. You caused Rita's death. You were one drop. No one will notice that you've gone for as far as they're concerned, you were never there. A drop that wasn't meant to fall...'

And the Doctor reaches out his hand and catches a raindrop

And the tramp that should be there, isn't.

'Take me back.'

The Doctor asks if he really wants to be responsible for her death.

'No... no, but I don't want to be... I want someone to notice that I've gone. I want to do something so that they'll notice that I've gone.'

'I can't. If I do, then *they'll* know that I've disrupted the Web of Time. Rita's non-death will be ignored because there's no trace of you ever existing. Nobody has noticed you. It will be seen as a glitch in the Web. Don't you see? She was meant to die but there's no trace of the man who would have caused it.'

'So, what now? Where do I go? Where can I go? If I go back, she dies. So where can I hide myself away? Where can I go and quietly die so that everything's nice and neat and tidy? Well?' He screams out the final word.

The Doctor, drowning in the rain, pleads with the tramp to stay with him. 'Don't you understand? You are somebody now. You are my friend. *My* somebody... I need you.'

'It's not enough, Doctor.' The tramp spits out the words. 'I'm nobody. Nobody has missed me. Nobody even knows my name. You don't know my name!'

Purple lightning crashes across an alien sky.

The Doctor, quiet once more, says, 'I didn't want to have to ask. I wanted you to choose to tell me. I wanted you to reclaim your name... but I have always known it.'

'So, you know the name of the man whose life you've destroyed.'

'What?'

'If you hadn't saved me, I'd have... I'd have existed. I'd have been somebody important.'

'You are important.'

The man stomps on, towards the TARDIS, his voice shouting upwards to the pouring heavens. 'Just not important enough for any of them to know who I am. Not even important enough for your bloody Web of Time.'

The Doctor shuffles after him. He knows that this is the end, as another one leaves him. But this one... this one he can't just take back.

... and it's his sister's wedding and she's never been more beautiful as the sun shines bright, reflected off her white dress and he's proud because he's the usher, and he's ushering in his mum and dad and they are so utterly happy but his mum is dying of cancer and there goes his dad in a car crash but he can't cry because he's in the army and fighting for queen and country and he's got his mates back at the barracks and, oh, they've all gone now and he's got a job but he's no good at it and his family have left him, mum and dad have died and his sister's moved away and his friends have left him and he's nowhere to go so when he can no longer afford his rent on the pathetic pension he's been given, he has no choice but to live on the street and be alone on those cold, dark nights and what else can he do and he knows that they all see him as just shit on the street outside the shop that they pass every day and he watches as the wheels on the bus go round and round and round and the fireworks explode and life, life goes on...

'And so the Doctor brought me here. He's forgotten about me already. As will you. You've listened to my story and you either feel sorry for me or you're just cross that I've gone on and on and whinged for so long. You think "the bitter old sod just wants some human attention" and so you've given me some. You've smiled politely and you've made a mental note to try and help someone worse off than yourself. Possibly not today, though, because you're a bit busy. You've listened to this... to my story but you'll have forgotten it by the time you've moved on and got back out there. Met one of the important people. One of those who will create ripples. One of those people who actually matter. Your name is... your name is Charlotte Elspeth Pollard – Charley to your friends – and you remember your friends aboard the *R101* dying and the life you've lead since then. You're so full of life. You create ripples. You are somebody. Wait... don't go, I want to tell you my name...'

Charley woke with a start. Golly, how comfortable the TARDIS floor could be... wait a minute!

This wasn't a floor, a carpet. This was grass.

And that's an airship!

'Doctor?'

'Yes, Charley?' The Doctor was sitting slightly closer to the vast dirigible, nestled as it was on the grassy ground, distant mountains topped by low clouds in the blue sky.

'Where are we, Doctor?'

The Doctor didn't turn to look at her. 'Penance,' he just said simply. Quietly.

And it came back to Charley. 'Those people! Jake and Robert and the Professor! And poor Ormsin and Lillian and those children! And... and...'

'Yes, I know.' The Doctor finally turned to face her. A tear was rolling slowly down his cheek. Very slowly. Too slowly, as if it really needed to make a point that it was there. 'I'm sorry. For all of them.'

'Did you have any choice?'

'To interfere? Or to bring them here?'

'Both.' Charley got up and sat beside him, instinctivly wiping the tear from his face. He didn't flinch, but just stared back at the airship.

'Penance,' he said again. 'Every time I make a decision, who knows what damage I cause?'

'You do, it seems,' said Charley. 'We're... out of time? Would that describe it?'

The Doctor nodded. 'At the very heart of the space/time vortex. The calm eye at the centre of the mayhem. I can leave them here, to exist. They can't be anywhere else where time might touch them because of the damage they might do. Damage I created in the first place.'

Charley remembered how one minute they had been there, in that vast room. The next, they were gone. 'Where exactly are they?'

'Here. Standing around, chatting, talking. Caught in the last few seconds of the journey, as they will be forever. Anticipating an arrival they'll never have in case I make another mistake and time touches them. Sending the ripples back out there.'

'Penance indeed,' Charley said.

The Doctor stood up. 'No, Charley, my penance. I know what I've done and how trapped they are. I'll always know. My guilt, my meddling. My penance.'

'And Nehra?'

The Doctor nodded. 'Still aboard with them and also in other times and places. Gathering. Collecting. Keeping the next batch happy. And the most recent batch. And the first batch. And will still be here with the last batch. One day.'

'Will there be a last batch?'

The Doctor nodded. 'Of course. I'm not immortal. One day, I'll stop creating ripples. But until then, Nehra's loyalty, his sacrifice, continues.' The Time Lord began walking towards the airship. 'Still want to travel with me, Charley? Still want to explore?'

She jumped up and caught up with him, linking her arm through his. 'Of course. But I'm glad you showed me all this. Let me learn their stories first hand. Remember them when others won't.'

He looked at her and smiled. For the first time, she guessed, in ages.

'I know I do good, Charley. That's been proven time and time again. But it's good to have balance. A perspective. To know that I'm not infallible and sometimes I make bad decisions. With costs that I can never repay.'

Charley stared at the airship. Next to it stood the TARDIS. The familiar blue box-shaped Police Box TARDIS. 'Home,' she breathed.

'Our home,' the Doctor added.

As the TARDIS wheezed and groaned out of existence, two figures watched from a small knoll. Nehra raised a glass in toast to the departing craft. 'See you next time, Doctor.' Beside him, a smaller, scruffy tramp shrugged his shoulders.

'Where next?' he said and walked back to the airship.

The Steward shrugged. 'Have to see what the future brings, won't we?'

Dalek Empire

Dalek Empire – The Scripts
by Nicholas Briggs (ISBN 1-84435-106-8)

Professor Bernice Summerfield

Professor Bernice Summerfield and The Dead Men Diaries
edited by Paul Cornell (ISBN 1-903654-00-9)
Professor Bernice Summerfield and The Doomsday Manuscript
by Justin Richards (ISBN 1-903654-04-1)
Professor Bernice Summerfield and The Gods of the Underworld
by Stephen Cole (ISBN 1-903654-23-8)
Professor Bernice Summerfield and The Squire's Crystal
by Jacqueline Rayner (ISBN 1-903654-13-0)
Professor Bernice Summerfield and The Infernal Nexus
by Dave Stone (ISBN 1-903654-16-5)
Professor Bernice Summerfield and The Glass Prison
by Jacqueline Rayner (ISBN 1-903654-41-6)
Professor Bernice Summerfield: A Life of Surprises
edited by Paul Cornell (ISBN 1-903654-44-0)
Professor Bernice Summerfield: Life During Wartime
edited by Paul Cornell (ISBN 1-84435-062-2)

COMING SOON...

Professor Bernice Summerfield and The Big Hunt,
a novel by Lance Parkin (ISBN 1-84435-107-6)

Professor Bernice Summerfield: A Life Worth Living,
a short-story collection edited by Simon Guerrier (ISBN 1-84435-109-2)

A novella collection edited by Gary Russell, featuring stories by
Joseph Lidster, Dave Stone and Paul Sutton (ISBN 1-84435-108-4)

Professor Bernice Summerfield: The Inside Story,
a behind-the-scenes book by Ian Farrington

Star Quest

Star Quest by Terrance Dicks
(ISBN 1-84435-066-5)

www.bigfinish.com